TWISTED OBSESSION

The second in the Daniel Kendrick series

RUTH SEARLE

The Book Guild Ltd

First published in Great Britain in 2024 by
The Book Guild Ltd
Unit E2 Airfield Business Park,
Harrison Road, Market Harborough,
Leicestershire. LE16 7UL
Tel: 0116 2792299
www.bookguild.co.uk
Email: info@bookguild.co.uk
Twitter: @bookguild

Typeset in 11pt Minion Pro

Printed and bound in the UK by TJ Books Limited, Padstow, Cornwall

ISBN 978 1916668 584

British Library Cataloguing in Publication Data.
A catalogue record for this book is available from the British Library.

To all my lovely readers

PROLOGUE

It was the day Ava Hildegard had to die.

Her killer stalked the wards of Riverbeke General Hospital but took little pleasure from watching the life drain from their victims. There were no voices demanding they take a life, no urge to exert control or power over others, no psychopathic personality disorder, no insane bloodlust.

The killer's callous, pitiless urge to kill was far more sinister.

Ava Hildegard smiled trustingly as the killer approached her bed. She was recovering from surgery – a bowel resection for a tumour that had been blocking her large intestine. A malignant mass that had been eating away at her body, unnoticed, for the past six months. Her husband had insisted she see her family doctor when the pain had become unbearable; he had been by her side during the round of investigations and had held her hand as the specialist delivered the devastating cancer diagnosis.

But now there was hope. With a good prognosis and no signs of metastases, she was expected to make a full recovery after a short course of chemotherapy. She longed to get home to her husband and their two teenage children. They had so much more living to do.

The killer coolly returned Ava's smile, retrieved a syringe from a pocket and connected it to a venous canula in the back of her hand. Slowly, the killer pushed the plunger, delivering three times the lethal dose of pancuronium bromide, a rapid-acting non-polarising muscle relaxant often used in euthanasia. In less than three minutes, the drug would reach its full lethal effect.

Within seconds, Ava's skeletal muscles weakened as they became incapacitated by the toxic drug. Her arm trembled before she lost the ability to move. She stared, terrified, into her killer's eyes; unable to grasp what was happening to her. Or why. She tried to speak but the words were trapped in her throat as paralysis crept into her face and neck. She felt her heart beat urgently against her ribs as hot flashes ravaged her body. The pressure in her arteries was plummeting dangerously. She felt her heart flutter and begin to fail as it lacked the blood pressure needed to keep it pumping.

Ava was fully aware of everything going on around her, the pancuronium having no effect on her level of consciousness. She watched the killer's face contort into a self-satisfied sneer as paralysis seeped into her diaphragm and respiratory muscles. A terrorising panic overwhelmed her when her breathing slowed and stopped as the pancuronium did its deadly work.

Ava Hildegard was being buried alive in her own body.

She looked into her killer's eyes, pleading for her life, but the last thing she saw was the frigid darkness of a narcissistic soul that cared nothing for her. A malevolent, reptilian creature that could take a life with neither shame nor regret.

The killer alone saw the final violent body spasm that Ava Hildegard suffered just before she gasped, desperately trying to take her final breath.

ONE

"What are you in for?" the inmate asked. He was a gorilla of a man with a bashed-up face only a mother could love.

"Remand for murder but – like everyone else in here – I'm innocent." Daniel Kendrick had made it a rule to keep conversations with other inmates to a minimum. *Keep to yourself, do your time, mind your own business.* He had learned, in the few weeks he'd been at HMP Ravenwood, that it was not wise to show weakness with the other inmates. His cellmate had taught him that before he'd been ghosted away that morning, presumably to another prison.

"Come on, ladies, get a move on." A prison officer, with yellowing teeth and a shirt-busting paunch, was herding the line of inmates toward the holding room next to the visiting hall. They were searched, each handed a bright red bib to wear and given a table number.

Daniel shuffled into the visiting hall with the rest of them. The room was starkly lit with overhead florescent tube lighting and there were several vending machines lined up against the far wall offering coffee, tea, chocolate bars and crisps. The visitors' café was temporarily closed, and grey metal shutters covered the serving hatch, due to a shortage of volunteers, apparently.

He found his table and sat – the room smelled of sweaty feet and stale tobacco. Echoing around him was the sound of chair legs scraping the painted concrete floor and a spate of throat-clearing. A prison officer with a shaven head and a bullish demeanour was cracking his knuckles as he strode around the room impatiently. When the inmates were finally settled, the visitors were let in.

Daniel searched past the stream of people until he saw his wife, Fay Kendrick. She seemed small and vulnerable in a loosely fitting navy print dress that swamped her tiny frame. She dodged a sprightly old chap with a walking stick and sat at the table opposite Daniel. He took her hands in his, leaned toward her and kissed her. Her soft lips warm, comforting and familiar.

"Fay, I'm so glad to see you."

"How has it been this week? Are you coping?" she asked.

"Alright but I'll be glad to see my barrister and get the court case out of the way." He stroked her wrist with his thumb. She was wearing the silver bracelet he'd bought her last Christmas.

"Yes, how long has it been now?"

"Ten weeks, three days, six hours and..." – he glanced at the clock on the wall – "thirty-five minutes," Daniel said with a wry smile.

"I'm so sorry." Fay's gaze fell to a small chip in the Formica tabletop.

Her skin felt warm as he squeezed her tiny hand in his. He knew she would never have coped in prison. He had to be strong, if only for her. He hoped they had done the right thing.

Fay seemed so innocent, so vulnerable, yet she carried a deadly secret that only they knew. A secret that would lock them together for the rest of their lives. He felt a fusion of love, protectiveness, pity, sympathy, along with a touch of fear at the all-consuming hatred he'd realised she was capable of.

Fay glanced at the supervising prison officer. He was speaking to a visitor on the other side of the room and out of earshot. She leaned toward Daniel and lowered her voice to barely a whisper. "We should have hidden Wixx's body in the lake and left him to rot. You'd be free now."

Daniel shook his head slightly. He knew he would never have been able to live with his conscience. He might have killed Damon Wixx in self-defence and, he admitted, with a torrent of anger when he realised that Wixx had murdered their little Sophie, but he'd taken a life, nonetheless. How could he be a doctor – a surgeon – knowing that he had deliberately killed someone? Justice had to be done.

Daniel leaned in toward her, glancing at the prison officer who was now scrutinising everyone from the far corner of the visiting hall. He whispered back. "He's taken your secret with him to the grave. It's better this way." He gave her hand a reassuring squeeze.

Fay smiled at the irony and whispered back. "At least he finally got what he wanted."

Daniel leaned further across the table toward his wife, the hubbub of conversations almost drowning his whispers. "Have you disposed of your journal yet? You really must get rid of the evidence."

She shook her head slightly. "Not yet. I can't face it. Going into Sophie's nursery, I mean."

"You must, Fay. Burn it. Get rid of it. Nobody must find out what really happened." Daniel held her hand tightly as he sensed her pulling away from him.

"I will," she said. "I will… I promise."

Daniel nodded and released her hands. After Wixx's death, he'd been arrested and sent to Ravenwood on remand so quickly that they hadn't had time to talk things through apart from snatched conversations during her weekly visits. They needed to talk, to clear the air, to look to the future and whatever that might hold for them. He desperately wanted to be free, to be out of prison, to carry on with his life, but dared not put all his hopes on an acquittal. He had to manage both his own and Fay's expectations. It would be too much to bear if he was handed a long custodial sentence.

A drugs sniffer dog, a lively brown and white English springer spaniel that seemed to be on duty every week, patrolled the room with his handler.

Daniel tried to lighten the mood. "How are the dogs and Maisie?"

Fay smiled as she recalled their antics. "Chester and Ella are missing you on our walks and all Maisie seems to do is meow for food. I think she's fattening up for the winter."

Inside the prison, Daniel hadn't even noticed the weather and time seemed irrelevant apart from the unescapable daily routines. He missed their pets and their life together, the normal everyday things that they had always taken for granted. Cooking dinner together, walks in the woodland near their home, goofing around with the dogs, a lazy Sunday morning with the newspapers. Would things ever be normal again?

"I think I've gained a few pounds too with the stodge they give us in here."

Fay smiled and looked at his face, his hair. "You could do with a haircut before the trial. You look more like an old English sheepdog than the Bradley Cooper lookalike I know and love."

Daniel laughed. "Yeah, I'll find the prison barber." Fay had always said he looked like a rugged version of the actor Bradley Cooper – he couldn't see it himself.

"You'll scrub up just fine." She gave him the sweetest smile that sparkled from the depths of her eyes.

Daniel squeezed her hands again. Her skin felt so warm and soft. "Will you go back to the clinic? I hope you'll consider a change of direction after all that's happened. I know you are dedicated to forensic psychiatry but I can't bear to think of you working with those bloody maniacs a minute longer."

"I'm still thinking about it. I don't feel ready to go back to it yet, so we'll see. A break from it would be good, though. You know, put things into perspective."

"You could sell the clinic to Oliver. He'd buy it from you in a heartbeat for his cosmetic surgery business." Daniel wanted Fay to give up work, to be free of the drama, the mental anguish it brought to their lives.

Fay nodded pensively. "I might but I have to think about it. It's a lot to give up. I might not get another position and we need my salary, especially if..."

Daniel knew what she was about to say. *Especially if you end up in prison for the rest of your life.* It didn't bear thinking about. All he wanted was his life back. Before Sophie's murder, before that bloody psychopath, Wixx, had barrelled into their lives. "Well, we'll know more next week at the trial."

Fay nodded, her eyes unable to meet his. "I really am so sorry."

"I know, sweetheart." He didn't know what else to say.

Behind them a scuffle broke out. Everyone turned to look. A woman was flapping spindly arms in the air and shouting obscenities at one of the inmates. He was retaliating. They were both on their feet, leaning in to one another over the table, the woman now jabbing a long, skinny finger into the man's face. The prison officer was on them immediately and another two appeared out of nowhere. The officers pulled them apart and pushed the man into his seat. The woman was marched out of the visiting hall by two officers.

Daniel turned back to Fay. "Never a dull moment in this place." He rolled his eyes. "That bloke is in for armed robbery and manslaughter." He twisted his head toward the man, still being stood over by a burly prison officer.

Fay managed to get a surreptitious look.

They chatted about home, Fay's mother, Daniel's grandson. Then pondered what they might do over Christmas if he was acquitted. They decided to spend it alone, stuffing themselves stupid, watching TV and dressing the dogs in reindeer antlers and flashing collars.

Then, all too soon, their allotted ninety minutes was over, and the visitors were asked to leave.

Daniel's heart sank. It would be another endless week before he saw Fay, yet they had so much more to say. They needed one another now. Would she cope without him? Would he ever be able to go home again? Be allowed to practise as a doctor? Would his life be over – just waiting to die behind bars? He felt a familiar visceral panic beginning to heave at his gut and tried to breathe through it as he'd done during so many long, wretched nights in prison.

They both stood and held on to one another. Daniel could barely bring himself to let her go. He clung to the warmth of her body, the familiar scent of her hair, her unique aura. He buried his face in her hair and fought the wrenching tide of sorrow that threatened to overwhelm him. He pulled her closer and felt her arms tighten around his back.

"Come on, that's enough." A prison officer was barking orders – a patronising and self-important old bastard, Daniel had decided.

"Just a minute." Daniel glanced at the officer, shot him a warning and pulled Fay closer.

"I love you, sweetheart," he whispered into her ear.

"I love you too, Daniel."

He could feel her trembling and sobbing, then, reluctantly, he released her from his embrace. Daniel tasted her salty tears as they kissed their farewell.

She looked up at him, her eyes deep, wet pools of sadness. "I'll be in court next week."

He nodded and watched as she walked out of the visiting hall. He wiped his palms over his face. He had to stay strong. Had to get through this thing. For Fay. For himself. For the memory of their dead baby.

Once the visitors had left, Daniel was led away to be searched again and taken back to B wing and the hollow loneliness of his cell. It felt as if he was alone and floating away into space, looking back at the Earth and longing to go home.

TWO

Fay Kendrick drove home, barely able to see the road through her tears after the visit with Daniel. He didn't deserve this, she thought. She was the one who should be in prison. Murderers and paedophiles they might have been, but she *had* killed them. She should be the one being punished. She wiped her face with a wad of kitchen roll she kept in the car to clean the windscreen. Instead, Daniel had told the police that Damon Wixx, her psychopathic patient, had confessed and the police seemed to believe him – that Wixx was the serial killer that had been at large around Riverbeke for the past few months. Daniel was protecting her, even after all she had done. The anger, the recriminations. She didn't deserve him, she knew that. All he had ever done was love her – he was a good husband. He was a decent, caring man and she had betrayed him and their marriage. Would they ever be the loving couple they once were? Could they live with the deadly secret that tied them together?

Fay dabbed at her eyes again as she eased her Mercedes into the driveway behind Daniel's abandoned BMW.

Fay let herself into the house and was greeted by Maisie, their Maine Coon cat. She threw her bag and keys onto the oak chest of drawers in the hallway and picked her up. She hugged her tightly and stroked her long, fluffy fur, drawing comfort from her.

"Oh, Maisie… what the hell have I done?" She kissed her beloved cat, burrowing her face into her soft fur.

Maisie purred loudly as Fay carried her into the kitchen. All around them were Daniel's things. His daft novelty gadgets, a snap of him pulling a silly expression with the dogs, his novelty mugs and notes with jokes written on them stuck to the fridge door, a photograph of Chester, their Great Dane, wearing sunglasses. He was everywhere in this house. It was both comforting and lonely, being in their home without him. This is where he had looked after her through her pregnancy with Sophie. Where they had made their plans for the future. She still found it unbearable to recall the anguish they had been through over their daughter's murder.

Fay put Maisie on the floor and poured some dried food into her bowl. She unlocked the back door and let the dogs into the garden from their room – Daniel had converted the double garage into what he called the "Dog House". Chester, their harlequin Great Dane and Ella, their Dobermann, greeted Fay with frenzied tail-wagging, then bounded off into the lush greenery of the garden.

Fay wandered back into the house. Daniel's words were echoing in her mind. *Burn it. Get rid of it. Nobody must find out what really happened.* She knew she must dispose of her journal. It was essentially a handwritten confession with the names of her psychiatric patients and the dates that she'd killed them. There were enough details to convict her of multiple murders – the journal had to go but she couldn't face it alone. Daniel was never meant to see it but, now he had, they would have to face it together.

Fay knew she should prepare something for dinner, to eat and keep herself healthy, but she couldn't face food. All she could think of was Sophie and the destructive grief and anger that had almost torn her apart. Now Daniel was in prison because of her.

Fay knew she owed it to Daniel to destroy her journal. She mentally pushed herself to climb the stairs to Sophie's nursery, as she had so many times before. She hesitated before slowly opening the door. Sophie's room was just as she'd left it two years before. Her wardrobe and chest of drawers still held her baby clothes; her lamps were ready to softly illuminate the room; her cot was made up with snuggly flannelette sheets and a colourful patchwork quilt. A large teddy bear, the one Daniel had bought her just after she was born, lay in the cot, its black, beady eyes staring sightlessly at the ceiling. Fay could hear in her mind the sound of Sophie's laughter and the cute gurgling noises she made when she was being snuggled into bed after her bath.

Fay noticed the journal under Sophie's pillow, where she had hidden it. She knew she must destroy it. Obliterate every damning word she had written in the days after their little girl's death. The utterly devastating feelings of desolation she had poured onto the paper. She had to burn every angry word, every incriminating piece of evidence to the murders she had committed.

Fay sat heavily on the rocking chair beside the cot. She could still feel Sophie's presence in that room. She could remember the fragrance of her precious baby and the comfort she took from holding her in her arms. Sophie. The baby they had tried so hard for – had wanted so much. Her baby was gone, and she could never touch her or hear her beautiful voice again. Fay's journal had been part of the process of confronting her grief, the expression of love for her daughter. It was part of her – of them. She couldn't face parting with it. Not yet.

She closed her eyes and reached for Sophie in her mind as she had so many times before. Was her little girl's soul still out there somewhere? Could it be possible that she could communicate with her somehow? The thought had been eating away at her for weeks.

Perhaps she could find a psychic that could close the wrenching chasm of death that lay between them. Someone that would seek out a spiritual connection and act as a conduit between her and Sophie. Fay wasn't sure if a person's soul lived on after death or whether the end came with the blackness of eternal sleep, but she realised it was time to do something before Daniel came home. If he was acquitted next week, he would try to stop her.

Fay left Sophie's nursery, the journal still under the pillow where she kept it. She went downstairs and fired up her laptop, searched for local psychics and found one that came highly recommended. She took a deep breath, grabbed her phone and tapped out the number.

"Hello, Grainger Psychic Consulting. Felicia Grainger speaking."

"Ms Grainger, I would like to make an appointment please." Fay suddenly felt nervous.

"Yes, of course. For a psychic reading?"

"I want to try and communicate with my baby daughter. She was murdered nearly two years ago."

THREE

The sound of cell doors being kicked and banged after lights out finally abated but the shouting and swearing along with the stench of cannabis lingered long into the night. Finally, Daniel heard the thundering snores of around eighty sleeping men on B wing at Ravenwood prison. He finally had a cell to himself, but it was impossible to sleep. His mind churned constantly with thoughts of Fay, of Sophie and the events of the past ten weeks. The image of Wixx's face and the terror in his eyes as he was about to die haunted him constantly. In a heartbeat, his life had changed irrevocably. Three months ago, he was a respected consultant surgeon performing complex operations and procedures that saved lives. Now he was on remand for murder. He felt like a stranger in his own life. Being on remand had been a living hell and he wasn't sure he could go through much more without losing his mind. Prison, he'd discovered, was a cold and brutal place.

He glanced at the luminous hands of the cheap watch that Fay had brought in for him. It was 04.40 and sleep was eluding him. He looked at the photographs of Fay that he'd sellotaped to the wall next to his bed and lingered on his favourite one of her cuddled up with the dogs. He wanted to write a letter to her.

To tell her how much he loved her, to give her his commitment to working things out together and reassure her that her secret was safe and that Wixx really had taken Fay's deadly secret to his grave. But he knew that whatever he wrote would be read by the prison staff. Even if he was able to slip a sealed letter to his barrister to avoid scrutiny, it would be too risky. Their phone calls were limited to ten minutes during association time – that was when he was able to access a phone on the wing. Even when they did manage a conversation, there was precious little privacy to say the things that needed to be said. More than anything else in prison, that lack of discretion was the most frustrating. Paranoia was starting to gnaw through his brain. Would he cope if he was handed a custodial sentence? Would he find the strength and resilience needed to do the time? Would his marriage survive years of separation? Questions rattled around his head as they did most nights. Maybe, he mused, he *should* have hidden Wixx's body in the lake, as Fay had urged him to do, but he knew he could never square that with his conscience. Perhaps he needed this time in prison for his own personal retribution. To face the judgement of society. He wondered how Fay was reconciling her own morality.

It was still dark outside with clouds obscuring a waxing gibbous moon. A sliver of light from the landing illuminated the cramped double cell. There was a narrow bed along each of the long walls with a desktop between, on which stood a small TV. There was a tiny window above the desk behind metal bars. It didn't open but afforded a glimpse of the drab grey buildings of the prison and the thirty-foot-high stone walls that separated them from the freedom of the outside world. A small wardrobe stood at the bottom of each bed and a stainless-steel toilet and sink unit was barely hidden behind a manky plastic curtain. Not exactly five-star accommodation. He craved the release of sleep. Needed to clear the persistent brain fog. His resilience was dangerously low but at least the nightly darkness of his cell afforded him a brief respite. A cocoon, of sorts, within the surreal nightmare that his life had become.

Endless scenarios reverberated through his mind until he finally felt himself drifting into a dreamless sleep. Then, abruptly, he was jolted awake by bright lights and the rattling of keys and cell doors being unlocked. Daniel glanced at his watch again: 08.00. His breakfast pack lay untouched on the desk beside him, and he knew he would have to dress quickly before he was escorted to work. The core daily timetable was rigid and there was no escaping from it – 08.00 unlock for work or education; lunch in your cell at midday; afternoon activities start at 13.15; evening meal at 17.00 prompt; association and free time between 18.00 and 19.15, providing there were enough prison officers on duty to supervise.

Daniel leaped out of bed, grabbed his clothes and put them on over the boxers he'd worn to bed. Since he was on remand, he was allowed to wear his own clothes and Fay had brought in some old jeans and T-shirts along with a few sets of underwear and the tatty trainers the dogs had chewed. His messy hair and three-day stubble were a stark contrast to his usual work wear of surgical scrubs or a smart suit.

A prison officer appeared outside his cell and unlocked the door. He was a basic-grade officer with dark, gelled hair and a protruding nose. He wore black trousers and a white shirt with a single silver stripe along each epaulette. Daniel hadn't seen him before.

"Morning, boss," Daniel said. Most of the inmates addressed the prison officers as "boss" or "miss" and it was easier for him to conform. He was greeted with a grim expression and stony silence.

Daniel went out onto the landing and followed another officer as he escorted the men to their areas of work. Some worked in the kitchen or laundry; others cleaned around the wing or worked in the packaging areas where offenders were employed by various local manufacturers. Daniel had been given the task of painting the landings on his wing, a tedious job that paid £10 per week for a six-hour day. Daniel was less restless if he kept busy, whatever work he was given. Sitting in his cell all day watching mind-numbing daytime TV, as many inmates did, would have driven him bananas. An empty mind is the Devil's workshop, his mother used to say, but, if things went well, he would be out of there in less than a week. He had to cling to some shred of hope.

Daniel was taken to one of the workshops, where he picked up a tin of pale, apple-green paint, a paintbrush and some old rags. He'd spent the previous week sanding down the railings on the far side of the landing on B wing and was ready to start the painting. He was escorted back to the landing by a petite female prison officer who looked like she would be blown over by a slight breeze. He opened the tin and began to paint, his stomach now rumbling with hunger. He could have murdered a cup of tea.

Each wing of HMP Ravenwood was split into separate spurs and landings with a central office where the prison staff were based. Each wing had an open-plan shower room, usually jam-packed with naked, sweaty blokes along with the intimidating posturing he'd come to expect in prison.

Daniel worked until midday, when the inmates ate lunch. With no communal dining area at Ravenwood, inmates ate in their cells. It was the usual cheese sandwich with a packet of crisps. There was not even an apple to be had. Daniel made a cup of tea with his weekly rations and used the tepid milk that had been standing in his cell all night.

Lunch over, he was escorted back to continue painting the railings but, just before 14.45, Daniel and the other inmates on the wing were ordered back into their cells.

It was black eye Friday and the canteen the prisoners had ordered was being delivered. Every Monday, the inmates filled in their canteen forms and, every Friday, DHL delivered the thousands of items that had been ordered – mostly packets of biscuits, chocolate bars, snacks, bottles of decent shampoo and toothpaste. The list of items to choose from was limited but those who worked and earned money or had money sent in by relatives and friends had a "spend" balance added to their account. It was the one day of the week the inmates looked forward to – and the prison officers dreaded. It was called black eye Friday because it was the day inmates settled their debts with one another. If they didn't pay their dues, they literally got a black eye. Everything in prison was a commodity but there was no actual money changing hands. You could have a million pounds parked somewhere but it would be worthless behind the prison walls.

Back in his cell, Daniel could hear the commotion outside as inmates squared up to one another and excitement grew. There were often scuffles among the usual suspects and sometimes violent attacks when debts were not paid or if canteen bags went missing or were short of the items ordered.

By 15.00, delivery men began distributing more than two thousand canteen bags. They left them outside cell doors for the prison officers to hand in to the men. It was the busiest afternoon of the week and the tension between officers was palpable as they sensed the heightened aggression among the inmates. Many of the officers wore body cams and CCTV was recording constantly in the communal areas.

Daniel heard a bag being dropped outside his cell door. His canteen had arrived and, shortly after, a stocky male prison officer, with jowls like an ageing bulldog, unlocked Daniel's cell and handed him a clear plastic bag filled with chocolate, biscuits, salted peanuts and snack pots of noodles. There was also a large bottle of shampoo and a stick of deodorant and the balance on his canteen sheet showed the phone credit he'd ordered.

"Thanks," Daniel said as he took the bag.

Just then a high-pitched shriek echoed around the wing and a scuffle broke out in the adjacent cell. The prison officer ran out to see what had happened, leaving the cell door ajar. Prison officers began sprinting to the scene, slamming metal gates behind them to contain the landing. Officers were shouting orders and gathering around the open cell doorway. The sounds of men shouting "get down, get down on the floor" were heard above scrambling feet. Daniel watched from the doorway, aghast, as several prison officers barged into the tiny cell, mobbing one of the inmates.

Daniel saw a female prison officer crawl out onto the landing. Her white shirt was soaked with blood and the red sticky fluid dripped and pooled on the floor. He rushed to help her. She managed to crawl free of the commotion and collapsed, on her side, outside his cell door. He saw a prison shiv protruding from her upper abdomen. Before he could stop her, she cried out in pain and pulled it out, throwing it across the landing. It looked like a chicken bone sharpened to a point at one end, the other wrapped in thick fabric and bound with string to fashion a handle. Daniel guessed who was responsible – Dean Tyler, from the neighbouring cell – a lifer in for murder, who worked in the kitchens and had once bitten off his cellmate's ear in an altercation over a drug score. He was bellowing like a territorial walrus at the prison officers as they tried to subdue him.

Daniel knew the shiv should have been left in place as it was likely stemming the flow of blood, but it was too late, blood was seeping freely from the wound. He rolled the prison officer on to her back and ripped her shirt to expose the wound. She was groaning, trying to clutch at her abdomen.

"It's alright. Keep still, I can help you."

He called to the prison officers, but they were engaged in a brawl with the now-out-of-control Tyler, as they tried to wrestle him to the ground.

Daniel could see the wound was deep and had probably punctured her stomach or liver. She was doubled over in pain and bleeding profusely. She would have to go to hospital.

"OK, try to relax," Daniel shouted to her above the noise.

He knew a stab wound to the abdomen could be potentially deadly, requiring quick action and a level head to control the bleeding. He tried to focus on the woman, trying to tune out the pandemonium from inside the neighbouring cell.

Daniel pulled off his T-shirt, rolled it up into a ball and used it to apply pressure to the wound to slow the bleeding and allow a clot to form. Again, he called out to the prison officers, but they were still embroiled in a scrum with Tyler and oblivious to what had happened.

The woman was going into shock. Her skin was pale and clammy, her breathing was rapid and she seemed agitated. Daniel called out again. To his right, he could see two prison officers running down the landing toward him, one a scrawny young man in his twenties, the other an older man with a bald head and a white goatee beard.

"Call an ambulance," Daniel shouted to them. "She's been stabbed."

The older officer radioed for someone to call the emergency services. The other officer called a "code red" on his radio to signify that blood had been spilled before he crouched next to the woman, ready to push Daniel away.

"Wait," Daniel said. "I'm a doctor; a surgeon. I need to stop the bleeding."

The officer seemed to believe him. He glanced at the shiv, then grabbed it by the handle. "Let's get this out of harm's way," he said.

"The ambulance is on its way," the bald officer said, as he too crouched to help his colleague.

"I *am* a doctor, honestly." Daniel reiterated, concerned they would make matters worse.

"I know you are. I remember your case," the older man said. "Can you help her?"

"If I can slow the bleeding until the paramedics get here, she might stand a chance but she's going into shock."

The commotion in the cell next door reached a crescendo and a loud thud told them that they had Dean Tyler on the floor. It took four men and a pair of handcuffs to restrain him.

Daniel could see the woman was slipping in and out of consciousness. He pressed down on the wound, desperately trying to slow the bleeding.

Then he sensed she had stopped breathing.

He lowered his head toward her face. There was no sign of breath or movement in her chest. He placed the fingers of his free hand at the side of her throat. There was no pulse from her carotid artery.

"She's arrested," he said. He glanced at the older prison officer. "Here, press down on the wound and don't remove the T-shirt."

The officer did as he was asked, and Daniel started cardiopulmonary resuscitation – CPR. He counted breathlessly – fifteen compressions, then two breaths, fifteen compressions, two breaths. The bald officer continued to apply pressure to the wound, but blood had soaked the T-shirt and was still pooling onto the metal floor of the landing.

The commotion inside the neighbouring cell had finally abated and Tyler had been restrained and dealt with. Several more prison officers had arrived on the scene and gathered around Daniel as he tried desperately to save the woman's life. One had fetched a portable defibrillator and was opening the pack in readiness.

Fifteen minutes later, Daniel stopped CPR and checked for a pulse. There was a weak, thready heartbeat and the woman spluttered and began to breathe unaided.

The clanging of metal gates brought two paramedics rushing to the scene with bags of equipment.

"OK, we'll take it from here," one of the paramedics said.

"Sorry, I'll have to ask you to go back into your cell, Mr Kendrick," the bald officer said. "We might have lost her if it hadn't been for your quick action." He gave Daniel a pensive smile.

Daniel took one last look at the injured woman before he was locked into his cell.

FOUR

Daniel cleaned up the female prison officer's blood from his hands as best he could with the paltry dribble of water that seeped from the tap on the stainless-steel sink in his cell.

He listened as paramedics stretchered the woman away to the ambulance and presumably, on to Riverbeke General. Dean Tyler was marched to the "Block": a segregated section of the prison where the punishment cells were located. He was laughing like a demented hyena, but the officers would have the last laugh. He would lose all his privileges for at least a week and have plenty of time to reflect on his behaviour.

The canteen delivery was resumed and one of the inmates was tasked with cleaning up the blood on the landing. The usual hubbub of the wing continued as if nothing had happened, although the antagonism among the prisoners had crept up a notch.

Daniel was glad of some time alone in his cell. He felt safer there. Prison was fraught with tension with the potential for fights and violent attacks constant. Like packs of wolves, prisoners were constantly vying for dominance. Status, apparently, was everything.

The adrenaline rush that had fuelled his quick, life-saving

action had ebbed away, leaving behind a warm glow and a familiar peace within himself that he hadn't known for some time. It felt good to save a life again. It was what he'd trained for and what he'd done throughout his career as a doctor. It was what he was meant to do – his purpose in life. With an unpleasant spasm of realisation, Daniel knew what was at stake if he was handed a custodial sentence.

More than ten days before, Daniel had written a letter to his registrar and colleague, Matthew Clarke, at Riverbeke General. Prison bureaucracy took its time, but he was becoming impatient. He had asked Matt to find out what he could about his position at the hospital and if he might be able to continue with his job in the event he was acquitted. He was desperate for news, to have some shred of hope in this desolate, unforgiving place.

Locked in his cell, Daniel fell into a fitful sleep but was woken for the second time that day by the sound of keys rattling as his cell door was unlocked. It was 17.00. Time for the evening meal, or tea as it was called in prison.

He walked along the landing to the hatchway. Today it was vegetarian stew and lumpy mashed potatoes.

As he waited in the queue, a runt of a man with an attitude and badass hair barged into him. He grabbed Daniel roughly by the arm and through gritted teeth he snarled, "We don't do nufink for effin screws in here – got it?"

Daniel assumed he was referring to the incident with the female prison officer earlier. He turned, glared at the man and pulled his arm away. He wasn't going to be intimidated for what he'd done to help her – especially by a lowlife scrote like him.

The man glared back, his fetid breath on Daniel's face, then shoved into him again before swaggering off down the landing.

Another inmate had clocked it and gestured that he'd help Daniel go after him, but Daniel shook his head. It wasn't worth getting into trouble. Not now, so close to his trial. *Mind your own business, keep your head down and do your time.* He knew that toxic, nasty people like him are only projecting their own inner misery. He didn't take it to heart.

Daniel's meal looked bland and unappetising, but it would keep the worms quiet, for a while at least. He was also given a breakfast pack for the following morning, which consisted of a portion of cereal, a small carton of milk and a bread roll. He went back to his cell, passing a line of dour-looking inmates in grey prison-issue tracksuits, some of them heckling one another and hurling insults. One of them he recognised as a premier league villain who had led a robbery at a jewellery shop, injuring the owner with a shot from a 9 mm Smith & Wesson revolver.

Even after ten weeks of living behind bars, Daniel felt nervous when mixing with the other inmates and dreaded association time. HMP Ravenwood was a category A prison – not for the petty criminals and street-level crack dealers, along with the sados that were their clients, having stolen to fund their habit. Here were hardened criminals: murderers, armed robbers, rapists and paedophiles – those abhorrent creatures despised even by their fellow inmates. Small skirmishes could quickly escalate into a near riot. He tried to keep his head down and mind his own business without appearing to be a pushover – but, like wild animals at a watering hole, it was a fight for survival.

Daniel sat on his bed and ate his stew, trying to obliterate the constant noise of prison life. He longed for a decent home-cooked meal and remembered the times that he and Fay had cooked together at the weekends, quaffing wine and chatting about family and friends or their week at work. They were happy times – before Sophie had been murdered. If he was brutally honest, Daniel was glad Wixx was dead – that he had killed him at the lake that day. But he also felt torn. The psychopathic bastard would have suffered in prison – taking the punishment for his crimes. Now, *he* was the one doing bird. He wondered if he might end up hardened by prison. If the experience would change him as a person. It had certainly given him an insight into a totally alien world. He didn't belong there, and he wasn't sure he'd cope for much longer, but he knew that to overcome the pain he had to live through it. Without an acquittal, his career, his marriage and his life as he'd known it would be over.

He checked the time, 18.25. The association period was supposed to have begun at 18.00, when inmates were unlocked and able to have some freedom to move around. He badly wanted to get to the exercise yard, have a run and take a shower. He wasn't the only one to be disappointed. The banging and noise level on the wing had ramped up considerably and the prisoners were making their feelings known. Unhappy hour was about to begin.

Daniel tried to ignore it. He picked up a book he'd been reading, a thriller he'd borrowed from the prison library, but was distracted by the constant commotion on the wing with shouting from the prison officers to "cool it down". Then the sound of keys jangling in the locks of the cell doors. They would have some association time after all.

Daniel grabbed his towel and the bottle of shampoo from his canteen bag. At least, there was time for a shower – to wash away the stench of prison that clung to him, for a while, at least.

He waited behind the cell door for his turn to be unlocked. He heard footsteps outside, then a prison officer peered through the small observation window, the so-called wicket, between his fingers – a routine precaution. The door was unlocked. Daniel stood back while the door was pushed open by a sweaty, overweight prison officer with a beer gut so immense it might cause gravimetric interference.

"You've got thirty-five minutes, Kendrick."

Daniel didn't answer but went out onto the landing and walked toward the shower block. The noise level among the inmates was intense, with groups of men haranguing one another. Daniel was surprised they'd been unlocked at all with the hostility he was witnessing with rival gangs vying with one another.

Daniel managed to get past a group of men who were pushing and heckling one of the inmates into a cell: a foul-mouthed career criminal with a reputation for robbing old ladies. He quickened his pace. With any luck, the shower would be quiet with so much activity on the landings.

Daniel heard a scuffle behind him and a group of agitated men in grey, prison-issue tracksuit bottoms pushed past him, shoving him forcefully against the wall. They were followed by another group of men, bellowing obscenities and threatening violence, some brandishing makeshift weapons and shivs. They filled down the narrow landing.

Ahead, a fight broke out between two gangs. He felt the reverberations from men thumping into one another, the sound of fists connecting with opponents and bodies crashing against the walls and railings. He felt the metal floor of the landing judder from the mass of so many brawling men.

Daniel tried to turn back the way he came but more inmates were running toward him, weighing into the fight. He was jostled backward and pinned against the railings. He sustained a painful blow to his back. Daniel realised he had to move away before he became embroiled in the fight, but he was trapped on the landing between the opposing gangs amid the heat of angry bodies and the stench of body odour and cannabis. He sensed the terrifying escalation of tension and rage.

Metal gates clanged at the end of the landing and several prison officers rushed to the scene. They moved in to grab the ringleaders but, like cowboys in a saloon brawl, more inmates were gleefully joining in the fight. A group of onlookers gathered on the opposite landing, jeering them on. Daniel tried to back away but he was pushed and jostled among the melee of angry men, shoulders crashing into him, elbows flailing into his chest and face, bodies knocking him off balance. He was trapped and winded from an elbow that had connected with his stomach. He'd dropped his towel and shampoo somewhere in the confusion.

More officers rushed to the scene and several of the main perpetrators were dragged off, kicking out and bellowing with hernia-busting rage. One of the inmates, who had been charging around like a hippo in a mud wallow, was pulled free of the melee by two of the officers. It took four of them to wrestle him to the floor and snap handcuffs on him, but there was still a mob of inmates engaged in a hostile gang fight – the ringleaders vying for supremacy.

A tall, hefty man jubilantly wielded a metal bar at the prison officers – the leg of a chair as far as Daniel could tell. He tried to push through the horde but was knocked back into the thick of it, surrounded by inmates bristling with anger, lashing out at one another; the prison officers battled to restore order.

Another inmate joined the brawl – a serial rapist who was despised by most of the prisoners and officers alike. Daniel saw him throw a prison napalm – a broiling mix of sugar and hot water that stuck to the skin, causing burns that could scar for life – at the face of one of the other inmates. The victim reeled in agony, clutching his face.

B wing was out of control.

The violent clashes escalated, with drugs likely fuelling the aggression. In an understaffed, overcrowded Victorian prison like Ravenwood, a conflict could spiral out of control in seconds. Prison officers struggled to regain control, many of them inexperienced rookie officers taken on to stem the rising tide of disgruntled staff leaving the service.

A female prison officer clobbered one of the inmates with her baton, a glancing blow to the head. Three male officers pounced on him, bending him forward and pulling his arms behind his back. The woman fumbled for handcuffs and managed to cuff him. He was dragged, kicking and shouting, to the Segregation Block by four officers.

More prison officers ran along the landing as Daniel was jostled between the groups of brawling men. Five officers tried to down one of the main perpetrators, but he pulled away, spitting and bellowing obscenities. Daniel felt like he was trapped in an alternate reality – a malfunction on the holodeck of the star ship *Enterprise. Computer, end program…*

In a blur of bodies, kicking feet and flying fists, Daniel heard the smash of glass, then felt an arm grab around his neck from behind. He was propelled backward into an empty cell, feet crunching on shards of glass beneath him. He felt the heat of a man's body and his laboured breaths against his back; sensed the sharp edge of broken glass against his cheek.

The inmate was shouting to the prison officers. "I'll fucking glass him… I'll kill him, I swear… get back. Fucking get back."

Daniel could smell the man's putrid breath on the side of his face above the stench of the cell and his rank body odour. His darting eyes saw the filthy toilet beside them, rotting food left on the windowsill, graffiti sprawled over the walls and the clutter of stuff strewn everywhere. It was the Costa del Hellhole.

Daniel could barely breathe as the man's left forearm crushed his windpipe. In his peripheral vision, he could see the glass held to his cheek, the man's arm covered with crude tattoos, mostly acquired in prison by scratching the skin with razor blades and rubbing ink into the wounds.

Several prison officers crowded into the cell, trying to pacify the inmate; one of them was the bald officer with the goatee beard.

The squawk of an alarm signalled a prison-wide alert.

"Hostage situation," someone shouted.

FIVE

Daniel stood, terrified, as Glen Glover tightened his grip around his throat, the broken glass pressing into his right cheek. He couldn't feel if the skin was broken but he tried to stay as still as he could. One false move and the glass would penetrate.

"Come on, Glover, stop pissing about. What the hell are you doing?" The bald officer took the lead.

Another officer was shouting, "Put the weapon down… let him go."

Glover held his ground. Daniel felt him shift the weight on his legs as he contemplated the prison staff. Daniel could hear brawling gangs on the landing and the constant squawk of the alarm echoing around the wing. Daniel tried to speak but the pressure on his windpipe only allowed him a choked, rasping sound.

The bald prison officer stepped forward. Daniel could see his name badge now: "Frank Rivers". A supervisor, with two silver lines on his epaulettes, he had a seen-it-all-before air about him.

"Come on now, Mr Glover, what's this all about? What is it you want?" Rivers's voice was calm and low.

Daniel could sense the inmate hesitate behind him; his hand

trembled and the sharp edge of the glass pressed harder onto his cheek. Daniel felt a warm trickle of blood run down his jawbone and drip onto his shoulder.

Behind Frank Rivers, officers with riot gear – face shields, Kevlar vests and helmets – arrived on the scene. Handheld radios crackled with voices giving updates on the situation.

Daniel heard shouting on the landing as inmates were herded back into their cells for lockdown, one prisoner crowing to his cellmate about how he took down a female prison officer. The fighting abated as, one by one, the ringleaders were marched off to the Block.

Rivers tried again. "Come on, Mr Glover… Glen. What's this all about?"

Daniel felt Glover take a breath behind him, then his voice reverberated as his glacially slow brain kicked into action. "Smokes, chocolate, spice…"

"It's black eye Friday – you have debts to pay, am I right?"

Behind him, Daniel could feel Glover's belly fat wobble as he nodded.

Rivers continued. "Didn't you get your canteen this afternoon?"

"Sure, but the effin thing was short – no chocolate, no effin nicotine patches, no vape – no fucking nothing. All I had was fucking soap and toothpaste. Can't do fuck all with that."

Rivers considered his answer. The sharp edge of the broken glass was pressing hard into Daniel's cheek. He winced.

"Who do you owe this debt to?" Rivers asked.

"Fucking Cody McKee and Darren effin Gilmore."

"Ah yes." Rivers sighed. He was obviously aware of the troublemakers. "Right, well, you know very well that we can't let you have drugs in here, so no spice. But what if I lend you some chocolate until next canteen day and get some nicotine patches from stores. Will you let Mr Kendrick go?"

In the thriving black economy of prison, Daniel knew that

nicotine patches were a valuable commodity. It sounded like a good trade. His life for Mars bars and nicotine patches.

There was silence for some moments while Glover considered his options. "Yeah, alright, boss."

"Right. Let Mr Kendrick go, and you'll have your stuff. You know I'm good on my word. And you also know you will have to pay your debt to me in full, or there'll be consequences. Are we good?"

Glover nodded again, withdrew the broken glass from Daniel's cheek and released the pressure on his windpipe.

Just like that – the stand-off was over.

Daniel twisted away from Glover and lurched toward the door of the cell, clutching his throat, grateful his ordeal was over. The officers let him through and one of the rookies escorted him back to his cell. He had never wished more fervently that he could be standing on the transporter pad of the *Enterprise* about to have Scottie beam him away from this hellhole. Anywhere would do but the Bahamas would be rather nice right now.

The wing had finally been brought under control and the landing cleared as inmates were locked back into their cells for the night. A near riot had been averted, although the atmosphere was still tense with no outlet for latent aggression.

"I was hoping to get a shower," Daniel said pleadingly.

The officer began to shake his head then glanced at his colleague as if looking for permission. The senior officer nodded.

"OK but make it quick." He jerked his head in the direction of the shower block.

Daniel grabbed a bar of soap and a towel and practically ran down the landing to the shower block. It was deserted. Daniel stripped off his grimy clothes and stood in blissful appreciation as warm water flowed over his head and down his back, his nerve endings tingling with pleasure as he washed away the stench of prison and the stress of being held hostage by an inmate desperate to avoid a beating.

Back in his cell, he put on clean boxers and stuck a plaster over the small cut to his cheek. He lay on his bed, the sounds of banging, kicking of doors, jeering and hollering resounded around the wing. It was early evening, but the November sky was dark outside the tiny cell window. He longed for fresh air in his lungs, the winter sun on his face. He missed his family, his home, his car, his career, the freedom that most took for granted in the western world. He missed his life on the outside. Dear God – how had things come to this…

Daniel felt like a failure. Maybe he deserved to be in prison. He'd killed Wixx. Alright, it was in self-defence, but he'd taken a life. It was the wretched, corrupted life of the psychopathic murderer that had killed their daughter but a life, nonetheless. He knew that, if he was handed a custodial sentence next week, he would have to toughen up if he was to survive prison life. The incident that afternoon had shaken him more than he'd realised but he couldn't just shut himself away from the prison population as tempting as it was. Somehow, he would have to integrate and find a way to live some semblance of a life behind bars.

The near riot that afternoon, Daniel now realised, was due to a power vacuum that was left when Dean Tyler had been taken to the Block for assaulting the female prison officer. Prison had its own hierarchical society where the top dogs of criminal gangs gained and kept their position by violence and intimidation. The hostage incident was something else – a desperate man trying to find a way to pay his debts and avoid a beating. Only in prison could a life be exchanged for a chocolate bar.

Prison Officer Rivers appeared at the door, the glare of fluorescent light highlighting the sheen of sweat across his bald head.

"Everything alright?" Rivers asked.

"Fine, thanks."

"No cuts and bruises?"

"Just a small cut but nothing to worry about." Daniel touched the plaster that covered the shallow gash on his cheek. "How is the woman officer?"

"Louise Barlow. She's in hospital but stable. Recovering from surgery."

"Give her my best wishes," Daniel said.

"I will. By the way, this came for you." Rivers handed Daniel a folded piece of paper.

He took it. "Thanks."

"See you tomorrow." Rivers smiled and closed the door to the tiny four-by-three-metre cell. The keys rattled in the lock.

Daniel unfolded the paper. It was an email from the "Email a Prisoner Scheme". Dated two days ago, it was the long-awaited message from Daniel's registrar at Riverbeke General.

Hi Dan,

Hope you're coping in there. We're all rooting for you. I've spoken to Colin Mathias, and he said that as far as he's concerned you still have a job provided you are acquitted (obviously!). The board are discussing it and will make a decision after the trial and in agreement with the BMA.

Hold tight mate! I know you can't reply but I will be in court next week.

Hope things turn out well.

See you soon.

Matt

Daniel sighed with relief. It had seemingly taken forever to get that tiny shred of hope that he might still have a career to look forward to if he ever got out of this godforsaken hellhole.

However, he had to remind himself, his future still hung on a decision made by twelve members of a jury.

SIX

Fay pulled up outside Felicia Grainger's house, the other side of Riverbeke. She felt a tinge of guilt at sneaking behind Daniel's back, but he would never approve of her seeing a clairvoyant. A row of semi-detached houses glowed under the sodium street lighting, 1930s Tudorbethan style with half-timbered gables and rounded bay windows with diamond-shaped leaded window panes.

Fay took a breath to calm her nerves. She wasn't sure if she should have come here but knew it was driven by her growing obsession with Sophie. Could she somehow communicate with her dead daughter's spirit? Was that even possible?

Fay walked along a tiled path flanked by lawn, to a blue painted front door with a stained-glass sunburst in the top window panel. It had a shiny brass letter box and knocker. There was an outside light under which a discreet brass plate read *Grainger Psychic Consulting*. She rapped on the door and waited. Fay saw the fuzzy outline of a woman's head and shoulders approaching. The door opened and a teenager around fifteen ushered her in. She was whip thin, with long dark hair, a sullen expression and bright yellow nail varnish.

Fay followed the girl through the hallway and into a small sitting room.

"Have a seat. Mum won't be long." She gestured to an ageing leather chesterfield sofa and retreated into the kitchen.

A few minutes later, a tall woman with soft features and thick black eyeliner came to fetch her.

"Hello, I'm Felicia. You must be Fay. Please come with me." An attractive woman in her fifties, she was wearing a purple and black patterned kaftan over black leggings and several strings of brightly coloured glass beads.

Fay followed her into a small square room at the front of the house. She closed the door behind them and gestured for Fay to sit on an antique chair beside a table that was covered in what looked like an old woollen bedspread.

The woman sat adjacent to her, taking a moment to make herself comfortable. She closed her eyes briefly as if she were tuning in to her clairvoyance. The room was dimly lit and coven-like. Along one wall was a fireplace with a stepped art deco profile, the mantlepiece home to a mishmash of mystical-looking ornaments, stones and crystals. On the table stood a large crystal ball, which the woman constantly glanced into. It glowed eerily in the flickering candlelight and there was a strong smell of incense, which Fay didn't care for. In Felicia's hands, gnarled with arthritis, was a pack of well-worn tarot cards, which she was absently shuffling.

Felicia turned to Fay. Her eyes were dark and intense, her heavy eye make-up dramatically accentuated in the dimness of the room. Her hair was short, slightly wavy and black with a sheen of blue like a raven's wing.

She smiled at Fay and passed her the deck of tarot cards. "Now give these a good mix. Just put them face down on the table and jumble them up."

Fay took the cards and began mixing them, her hands swirling in circles across the table. Felicia glanced into the crystal ball.

"You've had a lot of sorrow lately. I sense anger too." She

frowned and stared more intensely into the crystal. "There's a man here. He could be your husband. Rather good-looking but hasn't been at his best lately." She closed her eyes. "Yes, he's going through some sort of trauma, I think. And I see a hospital."

Fay glanced at the woman as she continued to mix the cards. Then she felt nervous – what if Felicia could see or sense what she had done? What if the spirits of the people she'd killed were lurking in the ether waiting to tell Felicia that she had murdered them? She wondered if she should leave.

Felicia held her hand above the cards. "That should be enough. Now push them to one side and pick out a card and put it face down." She indicated where she wanted the card with a long fingernail, painted with glossy purple nail varnish.

Fay hesitated but was too intrigued to leave. She carefully picked the card she felt drawn to and placed it face down on the table.

Felicia turned it over. "Now, I know you wanted to make contact with your daughter since she passed but I'd like to do a short general reading to start with. It tells me how you are feeling, what you want, your fears and so on."

"Alright," Fay said, still a little nervous.

"Now this first card" – she placed her index finger on the tattered card – "this is the world card, but it's reversed. This tells me that you're feeling incomplete and that you can't get closure on something."

Fay nodded. That felt right. She couldn't get little Sophie out of her mind. How could she feel complete when all she wanted was her baby?

"Another card please."

Fay picked a card and placed it face down.

Felicia turned it over. "This, I'm afraid, is another reversed card. The moon, which means confusion, fear and misinterpretation. They are both major arcana in the tarot deck, which means they have some significance." She glanced at Fay. "Let's have another."

Fay, again, drew a card from the pile.

"The ten of cups: reversed. Another card telling me you have shattered dreams and domestic disharmony." Felicia glanced into the crystal ball and nodded as if she had seen something in there. She looked at Fay. "Your trouble is not over yet, I'm afraid. This man I see, he loves you very much, but I can't see you together in the future."

Fay felt the tiny hairs on the back of her neck prickle. She couldn't believe she was talking about Daniel. They had survived so much over the past few years. She refused to believe what Felicia was saying. They loved one another.

"Now a card here, please." The medium tapped the table.

Fay drew another card.

"The six of swords – transition, leaving things behind and moving on. This card tells me what you want. You want change and something more in life." She glanced into the crystal ball. "But I see great unhappiness for you if you act hastily. You must be careful."

Fay wondered when she would get some good news. Maybe the winning lotto numbers?

As the reading went on, none of the cards was giving Fay any hope. She was beginning to wonder why she'd come here to put herself through this when all she wanted was a message from Sophie.

Felicia stared into the crystal ball. "I see another man. A very charming man but death surrounds him. You must avoid him."

Wixx haunting her from beyond the grave? Fay wondered. Perhaps she shouldn't have come. What if Felicia would reveal her deadly secret. It suddenly seemed as if she was taking a big risk and regretted coming.

Felicia looked more deeply into the crystal ball. "Ah, yes, it's clear now. I see someone on the other side – a beautiful little girl with bright blue eyes and a huge brown teddy bear. Her passing was very sudden. She says she misses the cat – Mitzie… Daisy… Maisie. I'm not sure which."

Fay froze. Sophie. It had to be her, and the bear was the one Daniel had bought for her. She looked at Felicia. Her eyes dark with heavy make-up, she was looking toward the ceiling. Her lips were moving silently as if she were talking to an unseen spirit.

"She is a wise soul. A very old, evolved spirit. She is telling you to move on – you must move on. She also needs to be at peace. You both do." Felicia turned, her gaze locked into Fay's. Her eyes were soft and compassionate. "She is always there with you."

Fay looked up as if she were expecting Sophie to materialise out of the gloom. "Will I ever see her again?" Tears welled in her eyes as she thought about her beautiful daughter.

Felicia put her hand on Fay's. It felt soft, warm and comforting. "Yes, you will someday when the time is right, but you need to listen to her and start thinking about your future. Think of this reading as a warning. You need to change direction. Your little girl wants you to know she's happy and she wants you to be happy too. Follow your heart, my dear. Just follow your heart."

Fay felt elated. Here was the proof she needed that Sophie's spirit had survived death.

SEVEN

Daniel had finally managed to get a decent night's sleep. He'd blocked his ears with plugs of toilet paper and revelled in the hope that he might still have a career to go back to once this nightmare was over.

If it would ever be over.

It was 07.15. He was just spooning the last of his cornflakes into his mouth when his cell door was unlocked. Stood in the doorway was Prison Officer Rivers with a youth who looked barely fifteen, although he must have been over twenty-one to have been sent to prison. He was thin and pale and had the stooped posture of someone with the world on his shoulders.

"Mr Kendrick, I have a new cellmate for you. Jayden West – Jay, he likes to be called." Rivers stood aside to admit Jay into the cell.

The young man wore standard prison-issue tracksuit bottoms and a white baggy T-shirt that had turned grey in the wash. He shuffled into the cell carrying a small carrier bag containing his belongings. He sat on the bed opposite Daniel, clutching the bag as if its contents were all he had in the world. He seemed unable to look at Daniel but glanced around the cell.

"Jay, this is Daniel Kendrick. He's a doctor out in the real world, a surgeon. You can trust him." Rivers smiled benevolently at the man.

Daniel was hoping to have a cell to himself in the run-up to the court case. The man seemed as nervous as an impala at a watering hole. "Hello, Jay. Nice to meet you. I'm Daniel." The man glanced up briefly but turned away, drawing the bag closer.

"Take care of him. He's just been given a life sentence and has been intimidated pretty badly on C wing."

"I'll try my best," Daniel said.

Rivers left them alone and relocked the cell door.

Daniel reached for two mugs. "Tea?"

Jay nodded without looking up. He was still clutching his carrier bag as if his life depended on it.

Daniel made two mugs of prison-issue tea.

"Sugar?"

Jayden held up four grimy fingers.

Daniel stirred in the sugar and handed Jay the mug. He rummaged in his canteen bag and pulled out a block of Galaxy milk chocolate, breaking off three squares and offering them to Jay.

The man finally looked at Daniel beneath a long, unkempt fringe of dark blond hair. His eyes were dark and wary.

"It's OK," Daniel said, "no strings – call it a gift to welcome you to the cell. Honestly. I'm not going to swindle you." Daniel had been told never to give anything to an inmate – always trade – or you could be storing up trouble. But Daniel needed allies, especially if they were going to live in a tiny cell together. What harm could it possibly do to give someone a few squares of chocolate?

The youth looked harmless enough but, in prison, appearances could be very deceptive. Things could change in an instant, as Daniel knew from the hostage situation that had come out of nowhere just the day before. On the outside, Jay would pose no threat but here, behind bars, the rules of survival were different. He could be out of there a free man in the next week or so – or he could be back for a very long stretch. He had to hedge his bets.

The youth reached across cautiously and took the chocolate, nodding slightly as if to thank him. He sipped his tea, still clinging to the plastic carrier bag.

They drank their tea and ate chocolate in silence for some minutes. Perhaps he should try to make conversation.

"So, Jay, it didn't go too well for you on C wing?" Daniel ventured.

The man looked tense and uncomfortable. He simply shook his head.

"You know, I found it hard too when I first got here – still do, to be honest. Is it your first time in prison?"

The man nodded, wiped a tear with the back of his hand and sniffed loudly.

Daniel sympathised. Here was a young man with the prospect of a lifetime behind bars. No release date to look forward to. No goal in sight. It was a living death sentence. "Want to talk about it?"

The youth sat in silence for a few minutes, tears threatening to overwhelm him. Then he turned to Daniel, his eyes set into a heavy stare, as if he was trying to convince himself to trust him.

"I killed my stepfather." He seemed to be searching for signs of condemnation.

Daniel smiled pensively at the man. "You must have had a reason, Jay."

"I had a million reasons."

Daniel leaned forward. "Go on."

The man took a deep breath and clutched the bag protectively. "He abused me. Since I was eight years old, he abused me nearly every night."

"I'm so sorry you had to go through something like that.

God… it must have taken its toll. Did your mother know what was going on?"

The man shrugged.

"So, you felt you had to take matters into your own hands. To make it stop?"

"I guess." Jay looked away as if he was reliving the traumatic events in his mind.

"Yet you got a life sentence. That doesn't seem right." Daniel began to wonder about his own trial.

"It was complicated…"

They both turned toward the cell door as keys rattled in the lock. A female prison officer stood in the doorway. Her crumpled trousers were three inches too long and her pillar-box-red hair had been scraped into a scruffy bun.

"Mr Kendrick. Come with me. Your brief is here to see you."

There had been no notification of a visit from his barrister. "On my way," he said, as he gathered up a few papers and a leaky biro.

Daniel turned to Jay. "We'll talk when I get back…"

The man gave him a strained smile.

Daniel accompanied the prison officer along the landing to a small private meeting room. His barrister was sitting at a desk that, like everything else, was bolted to the floor. They shook hands.

Miles Parker was a sturdy sixty-something with wiry eyebrows over half-rimmed spectacles and coarse hair that was greying at the temples. He wore a William Fioravanti suit with a pale pink silk tie and had an air of professional authority about him that Daniel found reassuring. Parker was a silk, a colloquial term for a QC or Queen's Counsel. Fay had found him and had insisted the extra cost was worth it to get the expertise of a senior barrister. He'd been leading counsel in a number of high-profile murder trials and appeals, with an unrivalled reputation for securing an acquittal.

“Please, sit down,” Parker said. He turned to the prison officer. “It’s alright, you can leave us.”

The officer left, closing the door behind her. The men sat, metal chair legs scraping the painted concrete floor. Daniel detected a faint whiff of expensive aftershave.

The barrister cleared his throat and removed his spectacles, placing them carefully on a stack of papers before him. He had large, clean hands with immaculately manicured fingernails. He dispensed with the preliminary social pleasantries. “Now, firstly, the inquest has been postponed until after the trial, which, you might be pleased to know, has been brought forward to Monday. I haven’t been able to ascertain why. Bit of a cock-up, I suspect.”

Daniel wasn’t sure whether to feel elated or worried but the sooner the trial was over with, the better. “Won’t it cut our time to prepare?”

Parker shook his head slowly. “No, I think we’re ready, Dr Kendrick. All the legal papers are in order, and I have the witness statements in now. You are, of course, a defendant of absolute good character.” He looked directly at Daniel. “I assume you have no previous convictions or blemishes on your record that you have not disclosed?”

“No, nothing,” Daniel said.

“Then I suggest we call a single character witness to the stand and read out the testimonials from the others, if the prosecution agrees. Your senior colleague, consultant Colin Mathias, will be in court. I spoke to him yesterday.”

Daniel knew Mathias would support him.

“Now, Dr Kendrick, I have to ask you once more whether you still intend to plead not guilty.”

“Yes, I do.”

“You are aware that a guilty plea given at the first opportunity after you arrive at court will, in most circumstances, result in a discount of sentence. In other words, you would likely be given one-third off the sentence that would have been imposed if you are found guilty at trial." Parker waited for an answer.

"How long might I get if I was sent down for murder?" Daniel had to ask.

Parker took a deep breath and twiddled with his spectacles. "Life imprisonment is the only sentence that can be imposed for murder."

Daniel stiffened. The prospect of spending the rest of his life behind bars didn't bear thinking about.

Parker went on. "However, the judge must reach a starting point with a whole-life sentence of thirty years and then adjust according to the mitigating or aggravating features of the case. The sentencing guidelines in Schedule 21 suggest that, since you acted in self-defence through fear of violence, you would be handed a minimum term of fifteen years. Of course, the time you have already served on remand would be deducted as well."

Daniel shuddered. Fifteen years of his life in that hellhole. His life would be over. "But I could get out early for good behaviour…"

Parker raised his hands along with his wiry brows in a simple gesture that indicated *it might be a possibility but don't bank on it.* He seemed unwilling to give Daniel any false hope.

"I still intend to plead not guilty." Daniel had gone over and over it in his mind during the past few weeks but knew he had to plead not guilty to murder. He had killed Damon Wixx, that was without question, and that couldn't be blithely explained away, but he was adamant it was in self-defence, and he wanted a clear acquittal. His future career as a surgeon, not to mention his sanity, depended upon it.

"Alright, Dr Kendrick. I understand."

"Fay, my wife. Is she aware that the trial has been brought forward?"

"Indeed. I spoke to her this morning, and she will be called as a witness. Also, Ms Shelly Winters, your wife's colleague, has given a psychiatric assessment of the victim's mental state, although she may not be in court given her recent illness. I understand Mr Wixx was well known to the mental health services as a psychopath."

Daniel nodded. "Yes, he was. My wife treated him, and he was a particularly dangerous individual. Should have been sent to Broadmoor years ago."

Parker ignored the comment. "I've put in a bad character application to the judge. He will have to rule on whether the evidence can be used in the trial."

"Do you think he will approve it? It's pretty important to the case."

Parker glanced at his notes. "We have grounds for relying on the bad character of Mr Wixx under section 101 of the Criminal Justice Act 2003, which relates to the background and context of how you and Mr Wixx were acquainted. I think it will be admissible, even though Mr Wixx is now deceased. But don't rely on it."

Daniel nodded pensively, although he was not entirely reassured. Somehow, the jury had to hear about Wixx's despicable actions, especially the fact that he had murdered their baby daughter.

"Is there anything more you would like to add?" Parker tucked his spectacles into the top pocket of his suit and gathered his papers together, placing them into a battered brown leather briefcase, a gesture that indicated the meeting was over.

"I can't think of anything," Daniel said.

"Then I'll see you in court first thing Monday morning."

EIGHT

Daniel was escorted back to his cell. The prison officer didn't check the wicket in the door beforehand, as was the usual procedure. Daniel reasoned she wasn't aware that he had a new cellmate. The officer stood aside as Daniel went into the cell. The door was quickly slammed behind him.

Daniel gasped when he saw Jayden lying prone, his head and upper torso on the mattress, the lower half of his body hanging over the side of the bed, his skinny legs sprawled across the floor. Jay had tied one end of a bed sheet to the radiator pipe and looped the other around his neck. He'd twisted his whole body over and over until the loop was strangling him.

Daniel rushed to his side. He called out to the prison officer, but she had already gone.

"Jay… Jayden." Daniel heaved him further onto the bed, trying to release the tension in the sheet. He turned him over to see the man's bloodshot eyes were bulging and staring. His face was a blotchy purplish red. "Jayden, can you hear me?" Daniel frantically tried to loosen the tourniquet around the man's throat.

Jayden gave out a throttled, gasping sound but his body was limp and unresponsive.

Daniel reached out and hit the affray – an alarm bell on the wall of the cell – that was used strictly for emergencies, then tried to uncoil the bedsheet to ease the compression on the man's neck and allow him to breathe but the sheet was twisted too tightly.

Jayden rasped for air. His eyes, dark with terror, were locked onto Daniel's.

Daniel redoubled his efforts to release the tension in the bedsheet. He turned to the knot on the radiator pipe, trying to untie it and release the tourniquet before the man asphyxiated. The knot was tight but, as he worked on it, it began to give way. He could hear Jayden fighting for air – his body responding to its innate instinct to survive.

Jayden pulled at the thick coil of material that was crushing his windpipe, now panic-stricken and desperately trying to take a breath.

"Hold on, Jayden – I've nearly got it." Daniel fumbled desperately with the knot. Finally, it began to give way.

The sheet fell away from the radiator pipe just as the cell door was unlocked. Four prison officers piled into the cell.

"Bloody hell," one of them shouted as she reached for her radio. "Suicide attempt in cell three. Jayden West – just brought over from C wing."

Another officer helped Daniel to unwind the bedsheet and pull it free of Jayden's neck. The man lay gasping for air on his bed, his cavernous mouth gaping, chest heaving, urgently trying to suck in air, his bulging eyes darting between Daniel and the prison staff.

"What the hell happened?" A prison officer, six-foot-three, built like a rhino and sporting a part-shaven head with a man bun, turned to Daniel.

"I came back from seeing my brief and found him like this. I knew he was upset but I didn't think he was suicidal." Daniel began to blame himself.

"He should have been on suicide watch, given his recent sentencing and the violent bullying he took on C wing." The officer seemed sympathetic.

Jayden began to breathe more easily and Daniel helped him to sit up on the bed. "Are you alright?" he asked.

Jayden nodded, rubbing his throat.

"Let's get him to the medical centre." Officer Rivers had arrived on the scene and quickly assessed the situation.

Two prison officers helped Jayden to his feet and began to walk him slowly out of the cell. Daniel grabbed the man's carrier bag, slipped the rest of the chocolate bar inside and handed it to them.

Officer Rivers turned to Daniel. "We haven't had an incident like this for a while. A hanging the other week but this was quite inventive."

Daniel was astonished at what he had just witnessed. "What will happen to him now?"

"We'll keep him at the medical centre for a few days. Get him some psychiatric help. You know, we spend £150 million on mental health in prisons every year treating personality disorders, schizophrenia, psychopathy but we still can't get on top of self-harm and incidents like this." Rivers stroked his goatee beard.

"I shouldn't have left him alone," Daniel said.

Rivers shook his head slowly. "You know, you can't be responsible for others or for what they've done. People need to live their own lives, take the actions they see fit. You have to let them make their own decisions and learn their own lessons in life." He looked at Daniel pensively.

Daniel barely heard what the prison officer had said. He felt bad about leaving Jayden. Along with the violence and pent-up aggression in prison, there was desolation, despair and the utter waste of life. He couldn't help feeling at least partly responsible.

"I heard your trial is on Monday," Rivers said, changing the mood.

"Yes, I just saw my barrister." Daniel pulled himself out of his sombre reverie.

"Excellent. Well, we'll put a good word in for you. We have a record of your behaviour on your P-Nomis. It lists all your actions and your attitude while you've been on remand." Rivers smiled at Daniel. He seemed to have a genuine respect for him.

"Thanks." Daniel returned the gesture. He hadn't had much to smile about in recent weeks.

"Right – get some fresh bedding from the laundry and get this cell cleaned up." Rivers turned and left.

NINE

Daniel tidied his cell and put fresh sheets on his bed after the near-fatal incident with Jayden West. He couldn't get the image of the young man's suicide attempt out of his mind – his bloodshot, bulging eyes, the desperate struggle for breath as his body fought for survival. What wretchedness could have provoked him to want to kill himself in such a terrifying ordeal? He didn't want to contemplate it.

Daniel tried to block the images from his mind. He needed to call Fay.

He walked through the wing, past a group of inmates leaning over the railing, jeering at something on the landing below. They were openly smoking weed. One of them he knew slightly from a run-in during his first week on remand, a man in his early thirties who looked like his mother had married a blobfish; he had more fingers than teeth, a head full of ginger stubble and a hostile attitude.

He'd been arrested for aggravated burglary following a botched house robbery and was getting "clucky" as he came off his £1,000 a week heroin habit. His eyes were staring, he was yellowing with liver disease and he was clearly agitated. He constantly wiped his runny nose with the back of his hand.

Daniel hurried past to get to the phone in the communal area.

He waited thirty minutes in a queue to call Fay. Finally, he tapped in his PIN number and dialled the landline but there was no answer. He tried her mobile and she answered on the fourth ring.

"Daniel. Are you alright? I heard from Miles Parker that the trial has been brought forward to Monday. You must be getting nervous." She sounded concerned and slightly out of breath.

"I'm fine, sweetheart. Just glad to get it over with. How are you? Everything OK at home?"

"Yes, fine. I'm out walking the dogs. I just had to scold Ella for chasing a rabbit." She sounded distant and the wind was crackling into her phone.

Daniel pictured the scene, wishing he could be there with them. "What's the weather like?" He felt so cut off from the outside world, he didn't know if it was sunny, raining, cold or whether a meteorite had wiped out the rest of life on Earth.

"It's cold but sunny. A perfect autumn day. You should be here with us, Daniel." Her voice was beginning to break.

Daniel swallowed hard. It was difficult for both of them. "Don't worry; if things go well on Monday, we'll have plenty of time together." He had to stay positive.

"Hope so."

"Listen, I need my suit. Can you bring it in? I want to look respectable in court."

"How about your Marks & Spencer's charcoal one and I'll get you a new white shirt?"

"Perfect. And bring in a tie, maybe the plain blue one, some undies and my best black shoes. Actually, bring in a couple of changes of clothes to go with the suit in case the trial drags on."

"I'll bring them in this afternoon. Do you need anything else?" Daniel could hear Chester barking in the background.

"I think that's it. Look, I'd better go." He could see a long line of inmates glaring at him, impatient to use the phone.

"OK. Love you!"

"Love you too. See you on Monday."

They hung up and the next inmate in the queue snatched the handset from him. Daniel wandered back to his landing. It was almost midday. Time to eat. He called in at the serving hatch on the way back to his cell. Lunch was another cheese sandwich and a packet of crisps, this time with an optional apple, which he gladly accepted. He craved the generous portions of cod and chips from their local chippy.

Once lunch was out of the way, Daniel settled on his bed to read over his defence statement for the umpteenth time, indigestion burning his stomach. He'd made numerous annotations over the weeks and now he knew his defence statement by heart. It was an impassioned plea for leniency given the horrendous ordeal he and Fay had endured at the hands of a psychopathic killer. He hoped he would be given the chance to deliver it to the jury.

For once the wing was relatively quiet, with some of the pent-up frustration and boredom having been dissipated with a longer spell of free association time. Many of the inmates from the wing were in the exercise yard or watching movies in the recreation room. Daniel preferred to be alone. Yet time was passing inexorably slowly, and the court case couldn't come soon enough, even though he felt a mix of apprehension and impatience to know his fate.

He wandered down the landing toward the library. He had books to return and maybe he would take a look at the newspapers. He breathed in the constant stench of filth and drugs and as he passed a few of the cells; he could see inmates openly smoking cannabis and prison staff turning a blind eye. He hurried past a cell with four inmates crammed in together, all smoking mamba, a synthetic form of cannabis that can give an intense high and even a short hallucinatory trip. By all accounts it wasn't usually a pleasant experience and Daniel wondered why anyone would want to subject themselves to it.

Drugs were rife in prison and in the ten weeks alone that Daniel had been inside he had witnessed the persistent drug taking, dealing and smuggling that went on. Even class A drugs such as crack cocaine, ecstasy, heroin and methamphetamine were common and there seemed to be a constant supply of designer drugs such as spice, which was a major cause of violence. There seemed little the staff could do to prevent it. Despite X-ray machines and sniffer dogs, drugs still managed to find their way into prison. Sometimes they were thrown over the wall or dropped by drones and, contrary to the media reports, not all contraband was concealed up the backsides of visitors. Some was brought in by corrupt officers – "hooky screws" – around 1,000 out of a prison staff of 40,000, according to unofficial Prison Service estimates.

Then there was the frequent use of illicit alcohol, known as hooch, that was made by the inmates, often from alcohol hand gel, fruit and yeast. The staff were confiscating up to ten litres of the stuff every week.

Daniel reached the library and returned his books: two on legal procedures and a thriller he never really got into. The library was quiet apart from a group of older prisoners who were fairly well behaved. One of them, Reginald Hicks, a weathered-looking man with cauliflower ears and a shock of grey hair, was halfway through his sentence for manslaughter. He'd been kind to Daniel when he'd first arrived on remand. Reg had shown him the ropes and told him which inmates he could trust and who to stay well clear of. Daniel had heeded his advice.

"Hello, Reg." Daniel waved a hand in acknowledgement.

Reg raised his hand. "Doc."

Daniel found a few books and settled into a quiet corner to read for the afternoon but his mind kept returning to the trial. By tea time, he was starving and picked up a disgusting-looking pasta meal in a plastic container from the serving hatch.

Back in his cell, the pasta and the bland sauce it swam in were tepid, dried at the edges and looked like it had been cooked a week ago and warmed up in the microwave. It was tasteless but it would keep him alive until the trial.

Lock-up was at 17.15 but, as the prison officers tried to get the inmates back to their cells, two men refused to be banged up and had to be handcuffed and frogmarched into their cells. Daniel heard the commotion but switched off from it – he'd heard it too many times before.

TEN

Monday: the trial

Sunday had passed interminably slowly. It was one of those days when inmates were locked up for almost twenty-three hours. Apparently, according to one of the prison officers, several staff had gone off sick, one had been injured by an inmate while on duty and one had quit after being potted in the face for the third time in a month, by an inmate who liked to amuse himself by throwing his faeces at people. She seemed to have the knack of being in the firing line. They had been unlocked to retrieve their meals to eat in their cells and had managed forty-minutes of association time, which Daniel used to take a shower. He had managed to get some prison-issue shampoo – harsh but it was better than soap and he'd managed to get a crude haircut in exchange for snacks from his canteen. Fay had managed to get his suit and other clothing to him.

Apart from the constant jeering and banging from the inmates on the wing, the day had been quiet. A fight had broken out between two cellmates but had quickly resolved. Daniel was glad of some time alone to read, pass the time and keep his mind from constantly worrying about the trial and all it entailed. He had to stay positive and hope that it would be the last he would see of the inside of a prison. Without an acquittal, he couldn't bear to imagine what his life would become.

It was 05.30 and he had been told he would be collected at 07.00 and driven to the crown court. He would be detained in a cell at the court until the hearing started at 09.30. Daniel had spent thirty minutes watching a spider weaving a new web in the shaft of light that spilled in from the landing but was becoming restless and decided to get up. Better to be too early than late, he reasoned, and he wanted to look presentable. He washed, wetted down his newly trimmed hair, and put on his charcoal suit over a new white shirt. He pocketed the tie and left the first button at the collar undone. Fay had polished his shoes and put a note in his suit pocket:

See you tomorrow! Love you xxx

As ready as he could ever be, he sat on his bed and waited, his mind a jumble of thoughts. The whole experience in prison had seemed surreal, as if he'd been put into suspended animation and brought back to life in a scary parallel universe. He felt too nauseous to eat but made himself a strong mug of tea and managed a couple of squares of Dairy Milk chocolate. At 07.05, Officer Rivers unlocked his cell.

"Ready, Mr Kendrick?"

"I guess."

Daniel followed the officer down the landing and out of B wing, waiting as the metal gates opened to allow them through.

"How is Jayden?" Daniel asked.

"Still in the medical centre on suicide watch. He's pretty depressed by all accounts."

Daniel's heart went out to the man. They walked in pensive silence through the final metal gate and reached a side door that led to an underground car park. Daniel was handcuffed with his arms to the front and handed over to the prisoner escort and custody service – PECS – that would transport him to the court.

Rivers handed the staff Daniel's "person escort record" and they bundled him into the Serco van. He was told to sit inside the caged area, or sweat boxes as they were known, on account of how hot they became. Daniel felt like a dangerous animal being transported to a zoo.

"Good luck," Rivers said.

"Thanks."

The doors were slammed shut and Daniel could hear mumbled voices and jovial laughter as the prison officer chatted with the men outside. Then the rear van doors opened again and a plump, forty-something man with a sparse ginger combover and a ruddy complexion got in and sat at the back, on the opposite side of the van. He looked as if he'd had all his front teeth knocked out.

Daniel gave him a strained smile, which was not returned.

The driver jumped in, and they were driven through the prison gates. He nosed the Serco van out into the Monday morning traffic and Daniel strained to see the outside world through the blacked-out windows. The escort officer was glued to his mobile phone for the whole twenty-minute journey into Riverbeke town centre. The van was parked at the rear of the crown court, a traditional Grade II listed Victorian building. Daniel was led into the detention area in the basement. He was handed over and taken to the cells. They were damp, sparse, windowless and depressing but he would only be there for a short time, since there was no overnight accommodation at the court for prisoners. If the trial dragged into the next day, he would be taken back to HMP Ravenwood.

He hoped more than anything he'd never again see the inside of that hellish prison cell.

ELEVEN

Ricardo Estevez scanned the scene from the picture window of his slick second floor apartment – it was large, contemporary and open plan with expanses of minimalist clean white lines, groaning bookshelves packed with medical textbooks, and white leather sofas. The centrepiece of the apartment was the vast, south-facing windows off the living space and bedroom, which opened onto balconies and uninterrupted sea views. The kitchen window looked out over the bay to the side and the whole apartment seemed to welcome in the dynamic seascape. A rocky headland and a traditional, whitewashed lighthouse lay to the east with a sandy bay and open sea beyond to the west. The prevailing westerly wind was whipping up whitecaps on the water and surging waves were crashing onto the beach. A flock of gulls were squabbling over a dead fish on the shore and above them, the sky was overcast with an occasional glimpse of sun through grey November clouds. Rick had fallen in love with the place – he'd moved in just ten weeks previously, but he felt more at home, more relaxed, here than he had in all the years he'd lived in Spain and the suburbs of Barcelona. Maybe it was the connection he felt to the natural world and the raw power of the sea. Something he'd sorely missed.

Rick lingered in the shower, then dressed in casual black chinos and a faded denim-blue shirt, under a black leather jacket with brogues. He was well over six feet and a dead ringer for the actor Javier Bardem, with his ruggedly masculine good looks – intense brown eyes, collar-length dark hair that was persistently messy, and a short, heavy beard.

He was late, so he grabbed his briefcase and car keys and pulled the front door closed behind him. He made his way to the underground car park beneath the exclusive apartment building, his footsteps echoing around concrete walls. He found his car – a silver Lamborghini Huracan – the yellow leather interior unashamedly luxurious and equipped with all the extras. The left-hand drive reminded him of his Spanish origins, and he felt the swell of pride as the V10, 5.2-litre engine roared into life. Rick accelerated out into the traffic, headed along the coast, then turned inland for the forty-minute drive to Riverbeke. The CD player blasted out rock songs and soon Rick was feeling upbeat and ready to get down to work.

As he reached the outskirts of the town of Riverbeke, the traffic ground to a halt. A flurry of police cars and ambulances flew past him, blue lights flashing, ear-splitting sirens piercing the air. They were turning north toward Riverbeke General Hospital – where he was headed. The early-morning traffic was at a standstill and Rick revved the engine impatiently, attracting contemptuous stares from other motorists and pedestrians alike. He knew the Huracan looked pretentious to most people but to him it was a symbol of his success and a just reward for the hard work he'd put into his career as a surgeon. He had hoped to get a job in a big city hospital in cardiothoracic surgery, his preferred specialty and one for which he was well qualified, but the field was highly competitive, and openings were few and far between. His core surgical training and years of experience at Hospital Clínic de Barcelona had given him the skills he needed for the surgical consultant's role at Riverbeke General and they had needed a consultant general surgeon urgently. The rumours had been rife, but the story was that the previous post-holder, Daniel Kendrick, was on remand in prison for killing someone. He didn't know much about the details, but one man's demise was another's opportunity and he grabbed it. It was either that or go back to Barcelona, with all its reminders of the past and the painful memories he was trying to forget. He reached into the glove compartment and broke off a piece of dark chocolate from the stash he always kept there – he savoured the rich, bitter-smooth taste on his tongue as he tapped his fingers to the rhythm of Queen's "Tie Your Mother Down".

Soon the traffic began to inch forward, and Rick flicked the automatic transmission into "drive". The Huracan's engine growled satisfyingly as he slowly picked up speed and weaved his way through the ring road traffic then on into Riverbeke.

He turned the Huracan into his consultant's designated parking space and entered the hospital through the main doors. He'd taken up the post just six weeks ago but was already dating one of the scientists from a biotech company he'd met on the ward – Isobel Duncan – a blonde woman in her early thirties with supermodel looks, a PhD and a feisty attitude. It was never going to be a serious relationship, as far as he was concerned – none of the women in his life had been since his wife had died – but she was a bit of fun while she was around, supervising a phase two clinical trial for a new drug that was about to start on his ward.

Rick grabbed a coffee from the kiosk, took the lift to the surgical floor and swiped himself into the ward with his pass. He was treated to the smell of vomit as he walked the length of the corridor, past the nurses' station and into Daniel Kendrick's old office. Now his. He threw his jacket over the back of the chair, checked his bleep and went to look over his theatre list for the day. His heart sank – two minor hernia repairs, a laparoscopic cholecystectomy and a gastric band removal. The usual tedious procedures. He'd hoped for something more exciting as a consultant. Cardiothoracics, with someone's heart, and their life, in his hands had been far more stimulating.

Then, behind him, a nurse, cradling a phone handset, called out, "Mr Estevez, you're needed urgently in A&E – a penetrating trauma wound."

Now that was more like it…

TWELVE

Daniel was called to court and escorted to the dock. The dock officer, an attractive West Indian woman with warm brown eyes and a huge, gleaming smile, sat behind him. He looked for Fay in the public gallery but couldn't see her. He realised she must be in a witness room waiting to be called to give evidence. He could see representatives of the press, the court artist and several members of the public. He gave a small wave of recognition to his friend and colleague, Matthew Clarke, who had been his registrar at the hospital.

Amid the polished Victorian splendour, he could see his defence barrister, Miles Parker, sitting silently beneath his huge legal brain. Adjacent to him was the jury. Trial by jury – the magnificence of English law. No longer settled by a duel at dawn but decided by twelve men and women pulled randomly off the street. Daniel scanned their faces. One middle-aged woman was constantly glancing across at him as if she were trying to decide if he looked like a murderer. The jury seemed young, mostly thirty-something men and women, but there were two women with matching perms who looked much older. His future was in their hands. He wished the arrow of time could run backwards and undo all that had happened in the past couple of years.

The usher appeared next to the judge's bench. "All rise," she said.

Everyone in the courtroom stood; the sound of rustling clothes echoed around the room.

Her Honour Judge Charlotte Baron-Tomlinson, a respected circuit judge, appeared from a side door, wearing a black and violet robe with a red tippet and a short, greying bench wig. She was in her seventies; tall, willowy and elegant, she carried an air of authority. She walked across to the judge's bench and, with a slight stoop, turned and nodded fleetingly toward the jury before taking her seat in front of the royal coat of arms. Everyone in the courtroom sat.

The clerk was a baby-faced man who looked about twelve, with floppy dark hair and pimply skin. He stood and addressed Daniel. "Please stand."

Daniel stood. He felt the tingle of nervousness as a cold shiver crawled along the length of his spine. He repeated over and over in his mind that he was innocent until proven guilty. That was the way it worked, wasn't it? So why did he feel like his world and everything in it was about to implode? The trial, now a brutal reality, felt like a free-dive into the unknown, the verdict the toss of a coin – yet he himself had thrown down the gauntlet and demanded a trial by pleading not guilty.

"What is your name?"

"Daniel Kendrick."

"You are charged with murder, contrary to the Offences against the Person Act 1861 and the Homicide Act 1957. And that you, Daniel Kendrick on the twenty-fourth day of August 2019, murdered Damon Wixx. Do you understand?"

"Yes, Daniel said." The chilling words hung in the air.

"How do you plead – guilty or not guilty?"

"Not guilty," Daniel said decisively.

"You may be seated."

Daniel sat and scanned the room once more from behind

the reinforced glass partition of the dock. He recognised a few familiar faces in the public gallery. Mostly colleagues from the hospital. He looked ahead at the judge, her expression sombre. A stenographer was tapping at keys, recording everything that was said. He tried to quell the trembling fear that had taken hold of the pit of his stomach.

The clerk glanced toward the public gallery at a woman that could have been his mum, then turned to the jury. "Will the jury please rise?"

The twelve men and women of the jury stood and were sworn in. Then it was the turn of the prosecution to outline the case of the Queen against Kendrick in their opening statement.

Daniel took a deep breath.

Judge Baron-Tomlinson turned to the now-seated jury, regarding them over her black cat-eye reading spectacles. "Now, members of the jury, your role will be to assess the evidence, decide the relevant facts and in due course deliver your verdict. I'm now going to ask prosecuting council to open this case to you."

Ms Alicia Braithwaite, a barrister in her early forties, briefly spoke to the solicitor on the bench behind her, then rose to her feet. She was dressed in a black gown with white ribbons over a dark, pinstriped pinafore dress, black sheer tights and shiny-black kitten-heeled courts. She wore a white tie wig and scarlet-red lipstick. Her expression was akin to a flea-ridden Rottweiler baying for blood. "Your Honour, members of the jury, along with my learned friend, Mr Quentin Baily, I appear for the prosecution." She gestured to the older barrister sat next to her. "My learned friends Mr Miles Parker and Ms Bridget Hart appear for the defence." She gestured toward the defence bench.

Miles Parker QC nodded graciously in acknowledgement.

Daniel fiddled nervously with his wedding ring as he watched the proceedings. The court smelled of wood polish, the benches gleaming under the tungsten lights. His hands were starting to feel clammy. He glanced at the jury. One man seemed fascinated with his cuticles and the woman was still watching him, her eyes swivelling like a chameleon's between him, the barristers and the judge.

Alicia Braithwaite looked directly at the jury and began her opening speech for the prosecution, her scarlet lips mouthing the words that could ultimately have him banged up for life. "The defendant, Daniel Kendrick, is charged with murder. That he did attack and kill Damon Wixx. Now, there is no dispute that this attack actually happened. Indeed, Mr Kendrick himself called the police to the scene of the crime and has confessed to the killing." She paused for effect, sweeping her eyes along the jury benches. "On 24 August 2019, Mr Kendrick strangled Damon Wixx with a length of rope and held his head under the waters of Otterbrook Lake. The defendant's actions that day led to his victim's death. The first witness you will hear from is Detective Sergeant Harper, who was called to the scene of the murder. DS Harper will inform you that he saw the body of the deceased at the lake and heard Mr Kendrick's confession of the killing. You will also hear from the pathologist who conducted a post-mortem on the deceased. He will be giving evidence that the attack on Mr Wixx could only have been initiated from behind. The prosecution asserts that the murder of Mr Wixx was caused by a pre-emptive attack and not in self-defence, as defence counsel would have you believe. If indeed you accept as true that Daniel Kendrick unlawfully killed Damon Wixx, he may be guilty of murder. Remember, members of the jury, that you are the sole judges of the facts. You must take the law from the judge. Thank you." Braithwaite sat, giving a slight self-congratulatory nod to her colleague.

Daniel felt the knot twist tighter in his stomach. How the hell had his life come to this? He fiddled with the collar of his new shirt. The material was scratchy, and he was too warm in his M&S suit, but he resisted taking off his jacket at the risk of looking overly casual. His QC had warned him about the importance of demeanour. The jury would be making subconscious decisions from their impression of him. Was he nervous? Did he seem like a nice, innocent, honest person or a manipulative liar? A murderer? Everything counted – appearance, gestures, voice – everything.

The second barrister for the prosecution, Quentin Baily, stood and addressed the judge. A distinguished-looking man in his sixties, with thick, greying hair, he was also wearing legal attire over a dark suit. "If it pleases Your Honour, the Crown would like to call the first witness, Detective Sergeant Harper of Riverbeke Police."

The judge nodded her approval.

The usher called DS Harper and escorted him to the witness stand.

"Please say after me," the usher said, "I promise to tell the truth, the whole truth and nothing but the truth."

DS Harper repeated the oath.

Prosecution counsel, Alicia Braithwaite, now stood and faced the witness box. "For the benefit of the court, please state your name."

"Ian Harper."

"Now, I will be asking you questions but would you keep your voice loud and clear and direct your answers to the jury."

"Certainly." Harper twisted to face the jury benches.

"Can you recall what happened on 24 August 2019?"

"I received a call from Daniel Kendrick. He told me he had just killed Damon Wixx and asked me to attend the scene, which was at Otterbrook Lake, North of Riverbeke. I assembled a team of police officers and we drove to the location where we saw Mr Kendrick and his wife, Fay Kendrick, along with the deceased, Damon Wixx."

"And you were certain at that time that Mr Wixx was dead?"

"Yes, his face was underwater. He was most definitely dead."

"And what else did you find at the scene of the crime?"

"A length of rope and a knife. A dagger, I believe."

"Would the usher please show the evidence to DS Harper?"

The usher gathered up two clear plastic bags containing the items in question and placed them on the rail of the witness box.

"Are these the weapons you found at the scene of the murder?"

DS Harper looked at both bags and turned them over in his hands. "Yes, they are."

"If it pleases Your Honour to show exhibit A."

The judge nodded and the usher passed the exhibits to the jury to examine. They passed them along the benches. The chameleon flashed a glimpse toward Daniel as if she was imagining the deadly weapons in his hands.

The prosecution barrister, Alicia Braithwaite continued. "Now, DS Harper, how did Mr Kendrick seem to you when you arrived at the lake?"

"He was shaken, upset and comforting his wife when we arrived."

"But he confessed to the murder of Mr Wixx?"

"Yes, he reiterated what he had told me over the phone, that he had killed Mr Wixx following a fight between the two men."

"And what happened after that?"

"My officers and I examined the scene and the SOCOs began their investigation."

"Could you explain the term SOCO to the jury, please?"

DS Harper looked directly at the jury. "Scenes of crime officers. Their job is to investigate a crime scene and collect evidence such as blood or fingerprints."

Counsel for the prosecution continued. "What happened after you arrived, saw Mr Wixx's body and heard Dr Kendrick's confession?"

"I arrested him, and he was taken to Riverbeke Police Station, where he was charged with murder."

"Thank you. Now, I'm sure my learned friend would like

to cross-examine, so please stay in the witness box." Alicia Braithwaite sat and adjusted her wig.

Daniel's defence barrister, Miles Parker QC, rose to his feet to begin his cross-examination. His voice was calm and deliberate. "Now, Detective Sergeant, you told the court that Mr Kendrick was" – he glanced at his notes – "shaken and upset. How upset was he?"

"Very upset. He had obviously just been through a traumatic experience." Harper glanced briefly at Daniel in the dock.

"And you say he was comforting his wife, Fay Kendrick."

"Yes, she was crying."

Daniel felt a wave of emotion as he recalled the whole horrific episode. He wiped a tear from his face with the back of his hand. Would he ever be able to erase the awful images in his mind? The chameleon shot him another glance. She was absorbing information like a whale shark sucks in plankton.

"Were either of them physically hurt in the incident with Mr Wixx?" Parker was clearly laying the groundwork for his defence.

"Yes." DS Harper turned and looked at the jury. "Mr Kendrick was limping badly from a leg injury, which he asserts had been inflicted by Mr Wixx approximately an hour before the killing. His wife had ligature marks to her wrists, legs and torso, as well as a shallow stab wound to her abdomen, which Wixx had inflicted."

"If it pleases Your Honour, the defence would like to show exhibit B."

The judge nodded her approval.

The usher gathered up a few photographs and handed them to the jury to pass around. The images showed the injuries that Daniel and Fay had received at the hands of Wixx. One women juror winced and quickly passed the photographs on, another could barely look, and the chameleon studied them carefully before handing them to the next juror.

Daniel's QC continued. "And was there anything else at the scene that you should divulge to the court?"

"Yes, a wooden cabin at the lakeside had been burned to the ground. In fact, it was still smouldering when we arrived. Allegedly, Mr Wixx had set fire to it."

DS Harper once again glanced at Daniel in the dock. He gave a tight smile and nodded slightly as if to acknowledge him. Daniel wiped another tear from his face. He had to stay strong – get through this ordeal. He took a deep breath in an effort to compose himself.

"I see." Parker considered his notes once more. "Now, Detective, please tell the court how you and Mr Kendrick – *Dr Kendrick* – are acquainted." He emphasised the title as a reminder of the defendant's respected status.

Harper cleared his throat and turned once again to face the jury. "Dr Kendrick's wife was missing, and we were conducting a missing person's investigation."

"And how was that progressing?"

"Not very well, I'm afraid. We had no leads on the case." Harper glanced at the prosecution barrister as she rustled a sheaf of papers.

"And yet Dr Kendrick, desperate to find his wife, had been trying to help you with your enquiry, had he not?"

"*Umm—*"

Parker interjected. "Did he not suggest that Damon Wixx might be responsible for his wife's disappearance? Why was that not followed up?" Parker asked.

Harper fidgeted with his wristwatch. "Well, yes, Dr Kendrick did believe that Mr Wixx was involved in his wife's disappearance but, on questioning Mr Wixx, we were satisfied that he had an alibi."

"At what stage in the investigation did you question Mr Wixx?"

"At the beginning."

"But not again when Dr Kendrick told you he believed Mr Wixx was involved?"

"No. We were extremely busy trying to find a serial killer in the area."

"I put it to you, Detective Sergeant, that, had the police been doing their job, then Dr Kendrick would not have been forced to have dealings with a known and very dangerous psychopath."

Harper's face reddened. His mouth flapped like a dying fish on a slab.

Then, with the afterthought of a Columbo investigation, Parker delivered a final question to the policeman. "One more thing, Detective Sergeant Harper. Did you catch this serial killer?" A slight smirk played around the barrister's lips.

"Apparently, Mr Wixx confessed to the serial killings before he died."

THIRTEEN

"No further questions, Your Honour." Defence counsel Miles Parker turned to the usher. "You may release the witness from the stand." The QC sat.

DS Harper stood down and was escorted to the witness bench, where he sat. He briefly acknowledged Daniel with a strained smile. The chameleon had clocked the gesture.

Daniel's stomach churned as he relived in his mind the torment of the whole ordeal with Wixx. There was so much more to be said. He knew the dreadful truth about what had happened, and he wanted the jury to know too. Surely, they would acquit if they knew what Wixx had been like, the depravity of his actions, the depth of his psychopathic personality. Yet he was at the mercy of the barristers and the jury to decide his future. He felt as insignificant as a mote of dust adrift in the universe.

Judge Baron-Tomlinson turned to the prosecution bench. "Any further witnesses, Ms Braithwaite?"

Alicia Braithwaite stood, her red lipstick stark against the whiteness of her wig and ribbons. "If it pleases Your Honour, the prosecution would like to call a second witness to the stand. Forensic scientist Miss Emily Askwith."

"Very well," the judge said, peering over her spectacles.

The usher escorted the witness to the stand, and she was sworn in.

Braithwaite turned to the scientist. "You examined the weapons and the crime stain found at the scene?"

"Yes, I did."

"If it pleases Your Honour to show exhibit A?" Braithwaite was clearly taking pleasure in her props. It was all part of the theatre of the courtroom.

The judge nodded and the usher handed the bags containing the rope and the dagger to Miss Askwith.

"Are these the items you examined?"

"Yes."

"And what were your findings?"

The scientist turned to the jury. "I found the blood of Fay Kendrick and the DNA of Damon Wixx on the dagger and the DNA of Damon Wixx, Daniel Kendrick and Fay Kendrick on the rope."

"And what are your conclusions?"

"That there is a one in one billion chance that the blood or DNA could have come from anyone other than these individuals."

"Thank you. No further questions, Your Honour." Braithwaite shot Parker a triumphant sneer.

The judge turned to the defence bench. "Do you wish to cross-examine, Mr Parker?"

Miles Parker stood. "Yes, Your Honour." Conceit fleetingly crossed his face.

"If it pleases Your Honour, I would like to show exhibit C."

"As you wish," the judge said.

The usher carried a long plastic bag to the witness stand, balancing it on the rail.

"Now, Miss Askwith. Do you recognise exhibit C?"

"I do. It is the sword that was used by Mr Wixx to attack the defendant approximately an hour before the events at the lake."

"And what did your investigations conclude?"

"That Daniel Kendrick's blood and DNA were found on the blade and Mr Wixx's DNA was on the handle. Again, a one in one billion chance that the DNA could have come from any other individuals."

"Would you show the weapon to the jury, please?"

The scientist took the sword from the bag and, in one fluid movement, grabbed the handle and unsheathed a niike katana samurai sword. Its seventy-centimetre carved carbon steel blade glinted in the tungsten lights of the courtroom.

The jury gasped.

The judge startled and sat bolt upright. "Thank you, Miss Askwith. That will be all. You may step down." She scowled at Parker as if to say, *don't you ever pull a stunt like that again in my courtroom.*

The scientist meekly resheathed the sword, handed it to the usher and took her seat on the witness bench.

Parker gestured a sombre apology to the judge. He would never admit he had pre-arranged this little misunderstanding on the part of the scientist in a move that would emphasise for the jury, with a powerful image, the intimidation and attacks that Wixx had inflicted on his client. It had been pure alchemy – turning lead into gold right before the jury's eyes. He exchanged a subtle signal with Alicia Braithwaite that told her she'd been outdone. He was now indebted to Miss Askwith to the tune of a very large brandy.

"Do you have any further witnesses, Ms Braithwaite?" the judge asked.

Emily Braithwaite rose to her feet. "If it pleases Your Honour, the prosecution would like to call pathologist Dr Phillip Campbell." Braithwaite narrowed her eyes at Parker.

Daniel scanned the faces of the jury once more. They were settling down after the surprise demonstration. The chameleon continued to assess Daniel with fleeting glances, as if she were searching for signs of guilt – or, perhaps, innocence now. Daniel couldn't tell.

The pathologist was sworn in. He was a man of over six feet with snow-white hair and the sallow complexion of someone who rarely saw the sun.

"Now, Dr Campbell. Would you tell the court what you found on examination of the body of the deceased, Damon Wixx?" Alicia Braithwaite flicked through her notes briefly.

Campbell cleared his throat. "On external examination, Mr Wixx's face was markedly swollen and cyanosed and there were petechial haemorrhages around the eyes and conjunctivae, consistent with strangulation. The skin showed blunt force injury and constriction marks from a ligature. There were also bruises from fingers caused by manual throttling. Internally, the lungs were oedematous and congested. There were also froth lines in the trachea, bronchi and distal air passages due to the inhalation of water and the lungs were heavy and sodden, which is consistent with drowning."

Daniel winced as he realised he had caused those injuries. Ashamed that he was capable of such vehemence – even under extreme duress.

"So, did Mr Wixx die of strangulation or throttling or did he drown?"

"A positive diatom test confirms he died from drowning, although the mechanical damage inflicted by strangulation and throttling would have contributed. It's possible he may have died from strangulation had he not been submerged in water. It is difficult to draw a definitive conclusion." The pathologist shook his head as if to emphasise his last point.

Braithwaite quickly moved on. "Now, Dr Campbell. Your report states that ligature marks were found across Mr Wixx's throat. Does that prove that he was attacked from behind? In other words, that a rope was constricted against his throat from someone standing behind him?"

"The marks are consistent with that, yes."

"So then, Mr Campbell, would it be accurate to assume that the attacker, Dr Kendrick, by his own admission, was not, in fact, acting in self-defence but carried out a pre-emptive attack from behind Mr Wixx?"

The atmosphere in the courtroom bustled with steely focus. Several members of the jury glanced at Daniel. He shook his head, silently denying the accusation. If only they could have been there – known what had happened – experienced, it for themselves. If only they could understand the whole background of the case. His thoughts were interrupted by the pathologist's words.

"The ligature marks suggest that, yes, but it is not possible to draw firm conclusions given the other injuries."

"No further questions, Your Honour." Emily Braithwaite quickly sat and gave way to cross-examination by the defence.

Silk Miles Parker rose to his feet. "Dr Campbell. Would it be accurate to assume that the actual cause of death is somewhat ambiguous? That Mr Wixx could have died either from strangulation *or* drowning?"

"Yes, that would be accurate."

"Is it possible that Mr Wixx could have survived the strangulation had his face not been immersed in water?"

"Yes, it's possible."

"And were there other injuries to Mr Wixx's body that indicate a struggle or a fight took place between Mr Wixx and the defendant?"

"I found several bruises on Mr Wixx's body that are consistent with a fight, yes."

"So, considering your findings as a whole, would you say that it is impossible to conclude that Mr Wixx's death was solely due to a pre-emptive attack from behind."

"Yes, I would say that it is impossible to draw that conclusion."

"No further questions, Your Honour. You may release the witness."

FOURTEEN

Ricardo Estevez draped his stethoscope around his neck and practically ran to the accident and emergency department on the ground floor, taking the stairs two at a time with people stepping aside to let him through. He ran the length of the corridor, weaving around staff, patients and trolleys, knowing it must be a serious injury for them to have called him from the ward. He threw open the double plastic doors, dodged an incoming stretcher and went straight to the resuscitation area.

"Over here, Mr Estevez," a nurse in scrubs called to him from a large cubicle.

Rick was slightly out of breath as he approached the patent. A young man was lying supine on a trolley and groaning in agony. He squirted alcohol gel onto his hands and rubbed it in. A nurse had set up an intravenous infusion and was attaching it to a Venflon in the back of the man's hand. He could smell a mixture of disinfectant and the sickeningly sweet metallic pungency of blood. Then there was the pervasive background noise of heart monitors bonging and alarming – constantly demanding attention.

The senior house officer – SHO – on duty briefed him; a tall man in his late twenties with straw-like hair, pointy, rodent-like features and eyebags like suitcases from a weekend on call. "This is Lawrence Shaw, thirty-two. He fell from a ladder this morning and landed on a metal railing spike in his garden. He pulled himself free before collapsing but the paramedics said he's lost a lot of blood. Looks like it might be a visceral injury but I'm not sure. I thought I'd better call you down here."

Rick snapped on a pair of latex gloves that were offered to him and examined the wound, a two-inch-diameter hole in the man's exposed upper gastric area. There was a lot of dried blood around the edges. "Penetrating wounds are difficult to assess and it's hard to tell if it has breached the peritoneum. You were right to call me." Rick spoke perfect English with a heavy Spanish lilt.

He turned to an ashen-faced young woman sitting in the corner of the cubicle. "Are you with Mr Shaw?"

"Yes, I'm his wife."

"How high up the ladder was he when he fell?" Rick was trying to assess how deep the railing might have penetrated.

"Near the top – maybe eight feet up. He was clearing the guttering when the ladder slipped."

"OK, thank you. Sounds like a nasty fall." Rick turned back to his patient and addressed the SHO. "Circulation could be compromised if there is any concealed intra-abdominal bleeding." Rick placed the flat of his hand on the man's upper abdomen and palpated gently. It was rigid.

The man groaned in pain and a nurse rubbed his arm reassuringly. His wife slid to the edge of her seat, straining to see what was happening.

Rick listened to the man's abdomen through his stethoscope for a few seconds. "I can hear some bowel sounds but that doesn't exclude a major peritoneal injury."

The SHO nodded. "Do you think he will need surgery?"

Rick probed a gloved index finger gently into the wound. "His abdomen is rigid, and the wound seems to be tracking upwards. There could be a liver laceration. I could order a CT scan to check. How are his vitals?" Rick looked at the man's heart monitor screen. "BP is a bit low and heart rate is pretty rapid."

Everyone in the cubicle glanced at the monitor. The man's wife was pale and looked as if she was about to vomit.

Rick palpated the man's stomach again. "The abdomen starts at the level of the fifth rib, so it's possible the railing may have penetrated the chest cavity as well. How's his breathing been since admission?"

"Rapid and shallow but I can't detect any problems with his lungs," the SHO said.

"He's probably in a lot of pain," Rick said, trying to account for the rapid breathing. He turned to the nurse, who was standing on the opposite side of the patient. "Can you pass a nasogastric tube and let me know if you aspirate any blood? I want the stomach empty. We'll need a urinary catheter as well, please." He turned to the SHO. "We'll need four units of blood cross-matched and the usual FBC, U&Es, PCV, WBCs… and do a serum amylase as well."

The SHO nodded and reached for a trolley with drawers containing syringes, needle-holders, tourniquets, blood collection tubes and lab forms.

Rick was wondering whether to order a chest and abdominal X-ray when the heart monitor sounded a persistent alarm. Both he and the SHO looked up to see the man's vital signs were in bad shape.

"Blood pressure is crashing," Rick said. "Push fluids, fast bleep the anaesthetist and let's get him straight into theatre."

Rick felt the buzz of adrenaline and the pent-up energy of excitement. His day was about to get a bit more interesting…

FIFTEEN

Daniel wasn't sure whether he felt more confident after hearing the pathologist's evidence. The prosecution seemed to be relying on the post-mortem findings that Wixx was attacked from behind as proof of his guilt, but it was much more complicated than that. Had his absurdly expensive QC done enough to convince the jury that there was a reasonable doubt? He wasn't sure. He sat in the dock, nervously waiting for the next witness to be called. He glanced up at the public gallery to see reporters scribbling notes and the court artist studying him, memorising his features, so that she could later sketch the scene that would have his face plastered all over the evening news.

Judge Baron-Tomlinson turned to the prosecution. "Do you have any further witnesses?"

"Not at this time, Your Honour." Alicia Braithwaite stood briefly as she answered.

The judge looked at Miles Parker. "Case for the defence, then, please."

Parker stood. "If it pleases Your Honour, I would like to call upon the first witness, Dr Daniel Kendrick."

The judge nodded.

Daniel felt the pounding of his heart explode in his chest as a jolt of adrenaline surged through his veins. His whole body was trembling as he was escorted to the witness box. As Miles Parker had instructed him, he slightly exaggerated a limp from the injury to his thigh. As he walked past the jury, all eyes were upon him – like vultures waiting for something to die.

He repeated the oath after the usher and looked across at his barrister.

"Please state your name."

"Daniel Kendrick," he said, fighting to subdue the quiver in his voice and the bile rising in his throat.

"Occupation."

"Consultant general surgeon."

"Now, Dr Kendrick, please tell the court about your involvement with Mr Wixx."

Daniel took a deep breath in a futile attempt to steady his nerves and gripped the polished rail of the witness box. The stakes had never been so high. "When my wife, Fay, went missing, I suspected Damon Wixx was involved in her disappearance. He was a psychiatric patient of hers and was a known psychopath – a very dangerous man. When he told me he was holding my wife as a hostage, my suspicions were confirmed."

Parker interjected. "And did you inform the police?"

"Before I knew for certain that Wixx was holding my wife but not after."

"And why not?"

"Because Wixx was threatening to hurt Fay if I involved the police." Daniel caught a glimpse of DS Harper in his peripheral vision.

"And you believed him?"

"Yes, I did. He was an extremely dangerous psychopath." Daniel looked at the jury. "He murdered our daughter."

"He admitted this?"

Daniel turned back to the QC. "Yes, he did. At the lake."

"Why were you at the lake?"

"I had carried out my own investigation and realised it was where he was holding Fay. I went to rescue her."

"And you got into a fight with Mr Wixx?"

"Yes. He was viciously attacking both of us and set fire to the cabin when we were inside. We only just got out alive." Daniel shuddered at the recollection.

"Now, Dr Kendrick, bearing in mind that you are under oath in a court of law, did you make a pre-emptive attack on Mr Wixx?"

Daniel shook his head decisively. "No, I didn't. I was trying to protect my wife and myself from Damon Wixx." Daniel's voice faltered as surging emotions threatened to overwhelm him.

"No further questions, Your Honour. Please stay in the witness box for my learned friend to cross-examine." Parker took his seat on the bench.

Alicia Braithwaite rose to her feet. "Dr Kendrick, do you or the police have any evidence whatsoever that Mr Wixx killed your daughter?"

"No, but Mr Wixx confessed to the killing."

"That is your word against his. Of course, Mr Wixx is no longer here to defend himself." She paused and swept her eyes along the jury benches. "Would it be accurate to assume that Mr Wixx could have simply been taunting you and, in the absence of any evidence, he did not, in fact, kill your daughter?" Braithwaite pursed her scarlet lips together.

"It's possible, but I believe he did kill Sophie." How could this woman advocate for a psychopathic maniac like Wixx? Daniel could feel his nervousness morph into irritation. All he wanted to do was read out his ready-prepared and emotive statement to the jury.

Braithwaite left an uncomfortable silence as if she was waiting for him to gabble himself into a straitjacket of guilt.

"I put it to you, Dr Kendrick, that you attacked Mr Wixx in a wilful act of revenge for the alleged killing of your daughter. For which there is not a shred of proof. That you put a rope, exhibit A, around the victim's neck and strangled him before pushing his head under the water, causing him to drown." The Rottweiler with the scarlet lips was going in for the kill.

Parker QC exuded an air of supreme confidence as he watched the prosecution tear into his client.

Daniel felt his hackles rise. "No… Wixx was violently attacking me – both of us. I was defending myself and my wife. He is… was… an extremely dangerous man."

"Then how do you explain the fact that Wixx was attacked from behind as the pathologist has just told the court?" Alicia Braithwaite tiled her head in defiance.

Daniel felt infuriated at the vehemence coming at him from the barrister. He gripped the rail of the witness box. "Wixx had turned briefly to grab the dagger and I knew he was going to use it to stab me. I had to stop him. He would have killed us both – that was his intention." Daniel scanned the faces of the jury – his eyes pleading for some shred of compassion.

"No further questions, Your Honour." The prosecuting barrister sat; a smug sneer passed fleetingly across her face.

Judge Baron-Tomlinson turned to Daniel. "Thank you. You may step down."

Daniel was distraught. There was so much more to say. So much about Wixx they needed to hear, yet he wasn't being given a chance to tell them; for the jury to hear the whole truth – to know about the pain and torment they had gone through at the hands of that evil monster. Parker glared at him to back down and he reluctantly let go of the rail of the witness box and was escorted back to the dock by the usher. He sat, bewildered and shaking with emotion, trying to get his barrister's attention once again. To remind him there was more evidence that needed to be heard. Much more. Tears were welling up as the dock officer handed him a tissue.

Daniel struggled to control his feelings of disappointment, of frustration. His future depended on an acquittal by the jury, yet they didn't know the half of it. Would Parker do enough to sow reasonable doubt in their minds?

Miles Parker for the defence stood. "If it pleases Your Honour, I would like to call my second witness, Dr Fay Kendrick."

The judge nodded. "Very well."

There was a delay of some minutes while the usher fetched Fay from the witness room. She was escorted to the witness box and sworn in.

Daniel leaned forward, his elbows resting on his knees as he watched his wife through the glass partition of the dock. She looked vulnerable, so fragile, dressed in a floral dress, her long blonde hair flowing in glossy waves, her make-up minimal. She appeared as the type of girl-next-door that everyone loves. It was hard to reconcile the undercurrent of hatred that lay beneath her demure appearance. The chameleon watched her with the diligence of a grizzly bear waiting for the salmon run. The man had finally stopped admiring his fingernails and Fay had his full attention.

SIXTEEN

The QC turned and faced Fay. "For the benefit of the jury, please state your name."

"Fay Kendrick."

"Your occupation?"

"Forensic psychiatrist."

"Now, Dr Kendrick. You are the wife of the defendant, are you not?"

"Yes, I am." Fay looked up at Daniel and smiled.

"And you were with your husband when he killed Mr Wixx?"

"I was nearby, yes."

"Take us through the events of the afternoon of 24 August 2019."

Fay twisted slightly toward the jury. "Damon Wixx had been taunting me for hours about the fact that he had murdered our baby daughter, Sophie." She paused as if she was trying to control her emotions. "He had me tied to a chair and was threatening me with a dagger. He held me hostage and demanded money from Daniel."

Parker interjected. "If it pleases Your Honour to show exhibit A?"

The judge nodded.

The usher collected the dagger and the rope once more and handed them to Fay. She visibly shuddered as she turned them over in her hands.

"Are these the weapons used by Mr Wixx that afternoon?"

Fay nodded. "Yes, they are."

"Tell us what happened after he threatened you with the dagger."

"Daniel arrived at the cabin and tried to stop Wixx. He managed to knock him to the ground but before Daniel could untie me Wixx set fire to the cabin... Daniel managed to drag me out just in time and was able to untie the rope. We both would have been burned to death..."

Parker glanced at the counsel for the prosecution, then back to Fay. "Now, Dr Kendrick, you must be very clear about what happened next."

"Yes." She turned to look at the jury. "Wixx attacked my husband outside the cabin, and they got into a fight. Daniel was defending himself against a vicious attack."

"Did you feel that your life or that of your husband's – the defendant – was under threat from Wixx?"

She nodded vigorously. "Yes, I did. Absolutely. Wixx was a very dangerous psychopath. I have no doubt that he would have killed both of us without a shred of compassion."

Parker smiled at Fay. "Thank you. No further questions, Your Honour."

Prosecution counsel, Alicia Braithwaite, rose to her feet for the cross-examination. "Dr Kendrick. How far away from your husband and Mr Wixx were you when this fight broke out?"

Fay thought for a moment. "About fifty or sixty feet, I think."

"Maybe more?"

"Possibly. It was hard to tell."

"And you could clearly see that Mr Wixx was attacking the defendant – your husband?"

"Yes."

"And at this time, you were trying to escape a burning building."

"Yes."

"How do you account for the fact that Mr Wixx and your husband were fifty or sixty feet away from the cabin at that time?"

Fay looked flummoxed. "I don't know. I guess they were trying to move away from the fire."

Braithwaite sneered – it was the growl of a Rottweiler with a pitiless will to win. "I put it to you, Dr Kendrick, that Mr Wixx was walking away from the fire – away from both you and your husband. He did not attack Daniel Kendrick as the prosecution asserts but your husband – the defendant – left you at the burning cabin, went after Mr Wixx and attacked him from behind with the rope." She turned to look at Daniel in the dock. "Daniel Kendrick attacked and killed Mr Wixx in a wilful act of revenge."

"No. No… that's not what happened. I saw Wixx attack my husband." Fay was gripping the rail of the witness box, leaning toward Braithwaite, glancing pleadingly at Daniel, then at the defence counsel.

The barrister continued. "And yet, you say yourself that you were at least fifty or sixty feet away and next to a burning building. There would have been smoke and flames that would have obscured your view of the two men, would there not? I put it to you that you did not even see the fight and that you are lying to the court in order to defend your husband." A smirk twisted along her scarlet lips.

"No… no, that's not true." Fay leaned further over the rail of the witness box. She was staring wildly at the barrister, shaking her head in defiance, her eyes darted toward Parker, pleading with him to interject.

Daniel looked on. It was heart-breaking to see his wife taking such a heartless pummelling by the prosecution, but a feeling of dread washed over him. He knew the volatile anger that Fay was capable of when pushed to her limits. Like Orion's red giant, Betelgeuse, she was becoming unstable, ready to go supernova. It might have been better not to call her to the stand. He glanced at the jury. They were all entranced at the drama enfolding before them.

Then abruptly, it was over – just as the prosecution counsel had the upper hand. "No further questions, Your Honour." Braithwaite smirked in self-congratulation and sat.

Judge Baron-Tomlinson turned to Parker. "Do you wish to re-examine the witness, Mr Parker?"

Parker stood momentarily, hesitated, then said, "Not at this time, Your Honour." He was biding his time, waiting for his final triumphant moment in court.

Fay was led to the witness bench and sat next to DS Harper. Harper put a hand on her shoulder as if to calm her down.

Fay glanced up at Daniel. He could see the wetness of her eyes, the frustration in her face. Things were not going well. By the time Daniel had regained his reeling senses, Parker was calling his final witness.

Colin Mathias, a short, heavy-set man in his late sixties, with a slight paunch and a ruddy complexion, was sworn in by the usher. His best grey suit looked tight and uncomfortable.

"Please state your name."

"Colin Mathias."

"Occupation?"

"Consultant general surgeon."

"And how do you know Dr Kendrick?"

"I am his senior colleague at Riverbeke General. The clinical lead." Mathias fiddled with his tie.

"Dr Mathias, you've written a glowing report of Dr Kendrick's character. Do you stand by this in court?"

"Yes, I do. Daniel Kendrick is a talented surgeon and a vital part of our team. His good character is recognised throughout the hospital. In fact, I have a 2,250-signature petition signed by staff and patients asking that he be acquitted and reinstated at Riverbeke General. I can't praise him highly enough." Mathias handed a sheaf of papers to the usher, who passed it to the jury.

"Would you say that Dr Kendrick is capable of murder?"

Mathias shook his head fervidly. "Absolutely not. Daniel Kendrick is well known for his extraordinary efforts when it comes to saving the lives of his patients. It would be totally out of character for him to harm anyone intentionally."

"Thank you, Dr Mathias."

"No questions, Your Honour," Alicia Braithwaite said.

Colin Mathias left the courtroom with a sympathetic smile and a nod in Daniel's direction.

Daniel returned the smile. He felt humbled that so many people would sign a petition on his behalf. He had more friends at the hospital than he had ever realised.

SEVENTEEN

Ricardo Estevez stood in theatre, scrubbed, gowned, gloved and ready for his patient, Lawrence Shaw. He loved the tense atmosphere in theatre, the smell of anaesthetic gases, the clatter of stainless steel, the rhythmic whoosh of the ventilator and what sometimes turned out to be pure electrifying drama. Perhaps today would be one of those days…

The anaesthetist had managed to stabilise the patient's crashing blood pressure with noradrenaline given via a syringe driver and he was now being anesthetised and intubated using a rapid sequence induction technique. Once he was unconscious, the theatre orderlies wheeled him into the operating theatre and transferred him to the table. He was draped with autoclaved green cotton, the HD-LED operating room lamps were adjusted, and the scrub nurse pushed a trolley laid out with surgical instruments to the operating table.

Rick had requested blood results urgently and, apart from a slightly low haemoglobin, everything was normal. The man's blood type was A negative, and four units had been cross-matched and on their way up from the blood bank.

One of the surgical SHOs, Lisa Jackson, a petite woman with piercing blue eyes and a slightly anxious disposition, had joined him to assist and they waited in silence while the anaesthetist hooked the patient up to the cardiac monitor. The electrocardiogram picked up a steady sinus rhythm and, although still low due to blood loss, his blood pressure was now stable. A ventilator delivered ten breaths per minute via an endotracheal tube.

"*Listo para ir?* Are we ready to proceed?" Rick said, looking directly at the anaesthetist.

"Yep, go for it," he said as he adjusted the oxygen levels on the ventilator.

Rick took the scalpel that was being offered by the scrub nurse and began to cut into the patient's abdomen – a midline incision but restricted to the upper gastric area. The skin glowed a sickly brown under the bright light, due to the iodine prep. The hole made by the metal railing had been cleaned and was gaping, revealing yellow fatty tissue beneath.

As Rick extended his incision, the SHO followed with a coagulative diathermy, cauterising the bleeding vessels. He could have used a cutting cautery, but Rick loved the feel of the scalpel in his hand – always had. He took the diathermy and dissected down to the yellow subcutaneous fat and superficial fascial layers as the nauseating smell of burning flesh and acrid smoke filled the air.

"It's the trial today," the anaesthetist said. "Wonder how it's going."

"Trial?" Rick asked.

"Yes, the murder trial of your predecessor, Daniel Kendrick."

"*Por supuesto* – of course. I'd forgotten it was today. Colin Mathias is giving evidence, I understand. Do you think he'll be sentenced?" Rick continued to cut down to the rectus sheath and applied clips to lift the peritoneum. One snip of the scissors and he was able to open the peritoneum and access the patient's visceral organs. The SHO assisted in pensive silence.

"No idea. Matt Clarke and Colin hope he'll be acquitted,

and he has a lot of support at the hospital. He's a good surgeon and a thoroughly decent bloke – I can't believe he would have murdered someone." The anaesthetist adjusted the intravenous infusion.

Rick examined the slippery, wet organs and could see the track where the metal railing had penetrated through the abdominal wall. He could see that it had pierced straight through the liver, leaving a large laceration.

"Retractors," he requested.

The scrub nurse passed them to the SHO, who applied the metal instruments and opened the incision to reveal the path of the laceration through the layers.

"Swab on a stick."

The scrub nurse slapped the handles of a forceps into his palm, a white cotton swab was clamped around the teeth of the instrument. He dabbed at the bleeding vessels and checked the slippery small bowel with gloved hands.

"Well, if he walks free, he's not having his job back," Rick said, examining the loop of the duodenum, which had a superficial tear but, luckily for the patient, had not been penetrated.

The anaesthetist glared at Rick but said nothing.

Rick pulled back some of the small bowel and palpated the left lateral lobe of the liver, then the left and right diaphragm to check if there was penetration into the chest cavity. It felt complete and normal.

"That's all fine," Rick said. He could feel the heat from the operating room lamps on the back of his head.

The surgeon plunged his hand deeper into the abdomen to palpate the right lobe of the liver. There it was – the laceration. He could feel it beneath his fingers. It was contained within the liver without penetrating the chest cavity. Thanks to the patient's efficient coagulation, the bleeding was now minimal. No dramas, no bleeding out, no cardiac arrest. Everything had gone smoothly.

"Suture, please," he asked the scrub nurse. "And let's have some music, shall we? How about Dire Straits? Something to liven up the place."

One of the theatre orderlies obligingly loaded up the CD player and the backbeat rhythm of "Sultans of Swing" blasted out as Mark Knopfler began his chilled yet invigorating guitar performance.

Rick was handed a round, blunt needle with a synthetic absorbable suture. He began to repair the laceration in the liver. He loved the cut and thrust of emergencies – the tension, the uncertainty, the power of having someone's life in his hands. But his earlier excitement had waned, and he secretly felt disappointed. What was a potentially thrilling operation had turned out to be dull and humdrum. Still – better that way for the patient and it had been more interesting than the laparoscopic procedures he had lined up for the afternoon.

EIGHTEEN

Judge Baron-Tomlinson turned to the prosecution benches. "Are you ready for your summing up?"

Alicia Braithwaite stood. "Yes, Your Honour." She turned to the jury. "Your Honour, members of the jury. The defendant, Daniel Kendrick, is charged with the murder of Damon Wixx and that he strangled, throttled with his hands and then drowned his victim. There are two main things that prove the defendant's guilt. First, that Daniel Kendrick himself admitted killing Mr Wixx. Indeed, he called the police shortly after the crime was committed and confessed to the killing. You have also heard the pathologist confirm that the DNA of Daniel Kendrick was found on the rope that was used to strangle Mr Wixx." She paused, scanning the faces of the jurors.

Daniel turned to watch the jury. It was impossible to discern their thoughts as they focused on the prosecution barrister.

Alicia Braithwaite continued. "Second, and most importantly, the ligature marks around Mr Wixx's throat indicate that he was attacked from behind – not the actions of someone who was acting in self-defence. Now, counsel for the defence would have you believe that the injuries sustained by both parties are proof that there was a fight and that Daniel Kendrick acted in self-defence. However, all this evidence relies on the confession of the defendant and his account of the events of the afternoon in question. Mr Wixx is no longer here to give evidence. Now, members of the jury, I ask you to consider how reliable the defendant's evidence could be."

The prosecution barrister again paused. "There is only one reason, and, in fact, this is the only reason that Mr Wixx was killed on 24 August. Members of the jury, I put it to you that Daniel Kendrick attacked Damon Wixx in an act of revenge. A pre-emptive and, at the time, unprovoked attack that caused the death of Mr Wixx. If you believe this, then I urge you to find the defendant guilty." The barrister looked at the judge. "Your Honour, that concludes the case for the prosecution."

Daniel again shook his head in denial and indignation. If only they could have been there – to see what really happened. To know how much he and Fay had suffered at the hands of that evil monster.

Judge Baron-Tomlinson then turned to the defence bench. "Mr Parker."

Daniel focused on his barrister. It was his last chance to prove his innocence.

Miles Parker rose to his feet and looked directly at each member of the jury in turn as he spoke. "Your Honour, members of the jury. The prosecution have tried to prove that Daniel Kendrick made a pre-emptive strike at Mr Wixx in an act of revenge for the murder of his six-month-old daughter. A vicious murder that Mr Wixx himself admitted." He paused for effect as he once more scanned the faces of the jury. "Dr Kendrick was forced to undertake his own investigations of his wife's disappearance and became involved with a dangerous psychopath. In fact, a serial killer, again by Mr Wixx's own admission."

Daniel winced. He knew that part – that Wixx was the serial killer – was not true. The secret that he and Fay shared, that *she* was actually the serial killer, must never be allowed to surface. Ever. Wixx would take it to his grave. He felt a deep pang of guilt.

Miles Parker continued. "Members of the jury, you heard evidence from the pathologist that the defendant's DNA was found on the rope. That is not in question. We already have Dr Kendrick's confession. You also heard that the ligatures across Mr Wixx's throat were consistent with an attack from behind and their accusation that Dr Kendrick made a pre-emptive attack. You also heard from the pathologist that there were other injuries on the body of Mr Wixx that were consistent with a fight between the two men. Indeed, Dr Kendrick suffered considerable injuries himself that prove the men were engaged in a physical struggle – a fight, if you will. Dr Kendrick had also been attacked with a sword shortly before the events at the lake." Parker avoided looking at the judge as she glared at him. "You heard that no firm conclusions can be drawn as to the cause of death and that strangulation by a ligature – a rope – would not necessarily be the cause of death. The marks on the body from throttling and the drowning were carried out with Dr Kendrick facing his opponent. Consistent with self-defence. The defence asserts that Dr Kendrick is not guilty of murder as the prosecution suggests but was acting in self-defence and is therefore not guilty." Parker paused and scanned the faces of the jury.

He looked at the judge and back at the jury. "Members of the jury, if you believe that there is any reasonable doubt that Dr Daniel Kendrick attacked Damon Wixx in a pre-emptive and wilful act of revenge, then you must find him not guilty." Parker's eyes once more swept along the jury benches. "The case for the defence rests." Parker sat.

Judge Baron-Tomlinson turned to the jury. "Now, members of the jury, the directions I give you as to the law, you must accept and apply. However, whenever I refer to the evidence, the position is quite different. All questions of evidence and fact are for you and you alone to decide. That includes the evidence that has been agreed between the prosecution and the defence and placed before you. This case basically boils down to who you believe? Do you believe the victim was attacked in an act of revenge, or do you believe the defendant was acting in self-defence? Now, it's important to remember that it is for the prosecution to prove the defendant's guilt. It is not for him to prove he is innocent. The prosecution must prove that the defendant is guilty beyond reasonable doubt. There are very few things in this world that we know with absolute certainty." She paused as she regarded the jury over her spectacles. "Now, I will ask you to retire to consider your verdict, remembering that a guilty verdict must be unanimous."

The clerk addressed the jury, then asked them to rise and follow him out of the court and into the jurors' room.

As the jury filed out of the court, Daniel felt numb. His life was in their hands.

NINETEEN

Daniel had been taken to the cells in the basement of the court building and given a plastic cup of lukewarm coffee and a fish paste sandwich on a paper plate, which he felt too nauseous to eat. He sat in the stark coldness of his cell, self-pity gnawing away at him. He had to find some self-worth, if only for the next few hours.

His sandwich dried and began to curl at the edges as he paced his cell like a condemned man waiting for a last-minute reprieve. *Back and forth, back and forth*, the trial churning over and over in his mind. The image of Fay being torn apart by the prosecution was playing before his eyes like a hologram in some alternate reality. Then there was Colin Mathias's glowing character witness statement, the chameleon scrutinising his every nuance, the grinding weeks of wretched misery in prison, the horrifying flashbacks of his hands around Wixx's throat as he looked into the inky depths of his malevolent soul…

Back and forth. Back and forth…

It was just forty-five minutes later that he was escorted back to the dock. The jury had reached a verdict.

As he walked, trembling, into the courtroom, he could see Fay sat next to DS Harper on the witness bench. He longed to rush over to her but, instead, he gave her a wistful smile from behind the reinforced glass of the dock. This was it. The decision that would seal their future. An icy chill clawed at him as if he had walked over his own grave.

The jury filed back into the court and took their seats; the sound of heels on the wooden floor and the rustle of clothes echoed in the courtroom.

"All rise," the usher announced.

Judge Baron-Tomlinson stepped into the courtroom and took her seat. Her expression was unreadable.

The clerk glanced once again at the public gallery, stood and looked at Daniel. "Will the defendant please stand?"

Daniel stood in the dock, his legs trembling, adrenaline coursing through his body.

The clerk turned to the jury benches. "Would the foreman please stand?"

One of the jurors closest to the judge stood and faced the clerk. The chameleon watched Daniel – a softness now evident in her swivelling eyes, the intensity of her demeanour thawing like a reptile in the sunshine.

"Have you reached a verdict upon which you have all agreed?"

"Yes."

"What is your verdict?"

Daniel closed his eyes as if to deny the dreadful reality. He was shaking and close to tears.

The foreman paused. "Not guilty."

Daniel's eyes snapped open and immediately found Fay. She was beaming up at him. Even DS Harper was smiling. Daniel was stunned, elated, relieved all at once. He tried to focus on the courtroom.

Judge Baron-Tomlinson smiled generously and looked directly at Daniel. "You have been discharged by the jury. You may now leave the dock."

Daniel's legs almost gave way as he turned to walk away from the dock – away from the court and the nightmare he'd endured. Astonishment morphed into sheer elation as he rushed into the vast stone foyer of the court building, searching for Fay. He could see her running toward him and they fell into one another's arms. He felt the warmth of her body and her sobs of relief. His eyes filled with tears of joyful release as he embraced his wife.

He was a free man. Acquitted, at last, of murder.

Then he saw Miles Parker striding toward him, his silk gown flapping behind him, his tatty brown briefcase under his arm. He extended a meaty hand toward Daniel and he took it eagerly.

"Thank you," Daniel said. "Thank you so much."

Parker smiled broadly. "A pleasure. You're acquitted now. Exonerated of any crime against Wixx."

"Thank God," Daniel said. "Just one question, though. Why didn't you call the other witnesses?" It had been bothering him.

Parker's mouth curved into a knowing smile. "Well, we had more than enough for an acquittal, and I know Judge Baron-Tomlinson well – she likes brevity of evidence. Too many witnesses and it often muddies the waters, in my view. Glad we got it sorted out for you in a day." He extended his hand once more to Daniel and then to Fay. "Best of luck."

Daniel felt elated. Finally, the sun had returned to his life. He turned to Fay. "Come on, let's get out of here."

TWENTY

Daniel and Fay spoke briefly with friends and work colleagues that had watched the trial from the public gallery, thanking them for their support. They had largely managed to dodge the press, although Daniel stopped under duress on the steps outside the court to give a brief statement to one of the national papers saying he thanked all those who had supported him and that he hoped to be able to resume his career as a surgeon in due course. He pleaded for privacy for himself and his family.

Daniel jammed himself into the passenger seat of Fay's Mercedes SLK and she drove them both home, weaving through Riverbeke's rush-hour traffic. Light rain splashed the windscreen, and the sky was dark with clouds that were threatening more.

Daniel couldn't stop smiling. "My God, the relief. I can't tell you how it feels."

Fay glanced at him; a happy grin spread across her lips. "I know. I feel it too. Now we can put the past behind us and get on with our lives."

"Yes, it feels amazing. Like we've finally turned a corner."

Fay smiled again. "Do you want to eat out tonight or stay home?"

Daniel didn't hesitate. "Let's stay home. I've wanted this for so long – just me, you, the dogs and Maisie."

"Yes, me too. I have some proper champagne in the fridge and a nice steak for you – oh, and I got you some custard tarts. I know you have a thing for custard tarts." She glanced at him. "I had to believe you'd be acquitted."

"Sounds wonderful." He relaxed back into the leather seat, basking in the sense of relief that washed over him. Life would be good again.

From the depths of Fay's handbag, a phone pinged a text message.

"That's yours. I brought it in case," Fay said.

"Thanks." He rummaged in the bottom of the bag and found his iPhone. It was from Colin Mathias.

Sorry I had to get back to work – things have been crazy here. Just heard you've been acquitted. Well done – that was the right verdict. We'll talk later in the week. I'll get things moving with the BMA!

Daniel texted straight back.

Thanks so much for your witness statement – must have done the trick! Let's talk soon.

"Colin… sounds hopeful but we'll have a chat in the week." There were several text messages and missed calls, but Daniel ignored them and put the phone in his jacket pocket. He would deal with them another day.

Fay turned into their street: a row of modern detached houses on a no-through road. A kissing gate at the top of the street led to woodland and open countryside. "You really need to get back to work, don't you?"

"Yes, I do. I'm a surgeon – it's who I am. I'd be lost without that."

Fay pulled into their driveway and parked behind Daniel's BMW. They went into the house – their sacred sanctuary from the crazy world their lives had become. Daniel took off his jacket and threw it over the back of a chair. It felt good to be home.

Daniel had been away for a little over ten weeks, but the place seemed smaller – that strange phenomenon where things seem to expand in your mind over time. Maisie was in the living room and purred loudly when he picked her up. "God, I've missed being home," he said, stroking her fur. It had become charged with static from the dry central heating and her polyester blanket.

Daniel looked around the living room. Fay had brought out the fleece winter throws and bought new cushions. There were a couple of new house plants in the corner, a new tiffany lamp in the shape of a butterfly and some candles on the coffee table. The log basket was full, the fire in the wood burner was laid and the hearth tiles had been re-painted in matt black. The place looked cosy and smelled faintly of lavender. His saxophone was on its stand, polished and shiny, and the dent in its bell had been fixed.

"It was the least I could do," Fay said.

"Thanks."

He walked out into the kitchen. Maisie was sitting on the kitchen counter watching him closely. She mouthed a silent meow, and he gave her a sachet of Whiskas. She stalked off, obviously not happy with the chicken flavour he'd chosen for her – he would have to do better next time. Then he grabbed a carton of orange juice from the fridge and took a big gulp straight from the carton, feeling the chill go right down into his stomach. He wandered out to the "Dog House". Rosie, their dog minder, hadn't yet brought Chester and Ella back from the dog creche and Daniel felt disappointed. He had been longing to see the dogs. Their toys and hide bones lay strewn across their beds – the wooden beds he had made himself. Their automatic ball-thrower had spat out a dozen chewed and very soggy tennis balls, which he gathered up from around the room and put back into the machine. People thought he was bonkers when he mentioned it, but he loved the doggy smell in there.

Daniel wandered into the kitchen. He smiled at Fay, and they fell into one another's arms once again. He could smell the sweet fragrance of mango in her hair, feel the warmth of her body and the rhythm of her breathing. They held onto one another in silence for some moments, their arms tight around each other, as if they were almost afraid to let go.

"It's so good to be home. I love you, sweetheart," Daniel whispered.

"I love you, too."

As they stood wrapped in each other's arms, Daniel felt the horrors of the past three months begin to melt away. It was finally over. The dreadful events were behind them at last.

He heard a car door slam outside then Ella's bark before the doorbell rang.

"The dogs are back," Fay said.

Daniel slowly released his embrace, his hands reached for hers. He looked into her green eyes and lightly kissed her lips. "Better let them in." He smiled, letting go of her long, delicate fingers. He went to answer the door.

Rosie was gathering up their leads and toys from the back of a bubble-gum-pink sign-written Escort van that was covered in large black paw prints: *Rosie's Pet-Sitting Service*. The dogs bounded toward Daniel, tails wagging gleefully at seeing him again. Ella was almost howling with excitement.

Daniel stepped into the front garden to greet them. There was a frenzy of tail-wagging from the dogs and an equal measure of gusto from Daniel. He'd missed Maisie, Ella and Chester, their non-judgemental acceptance of him, their easy companionship. He knelt on the grass, not caring that the knees of his suit trousers were getting muddy. He put an arm around each of the dogs and pulled them close.

"What would I do without you two?" He couldn't have been happier if he'd just won the EuroMillions rollover jackpot.

Fay chatted briefly to Rosie on the doorstep and told her they would contact her when she was needed again.

Rosie looked decidedly nervous as she walked back to the van. "Nice to see you home, Dr Kendrick."

"Thanks. It's great to be back." He wondered how long people would react with apprehension. Would they always be cautious, knowing he'd killed someone? He felt sad that the easy relationships he'd known with friends and acquaintances would be mired by the fact that he'd been in prison – even though he'd been found not guilty. Despite the apparent support and the petition for his reinstatement, he wondered what his colleagues would be feeling when – if – he got back to work. That was another hurdle to cross but, for now, he turned his attention back to the dogs.

They were starting to calm down. "Come on, you two." He ushered them into the house, closing the front door behind them all, enclosing them in their private sanctuary. The dogs made for the living room. Chester jumped up onto his blanket-covered sofa and Ella went to fetch her teddy bear. She brought back a new golden-coloured bear and dropped it at Daniel's feet.

"What happened to Eddie?" Daniel asked.

"I threw him out – she'd chewed him to bits." She shrugged.

Life had gone on without him and Daniel wasn't sure how he felt about that.

"Dinner? You must be famished," Fay said.

Daniel's stomach rumbled and he felt the dull ache of hunger now his nerves had settled. He'd been longing for a decent meal. "I'll get out of this suit and be right back." He couldn't wait to wash away the stench of prison. It seemed to stick in his nostrils and throat, but he managed with a quick wash. He would shower later – for now, he was famished. He threw his muddy trousers in the laundry basket and slipped on clean navy chinos, changed his formal shirt for a more casual, pastel-themed checked one, and slipped on his monster-feet slippers, complete with claws, that his son Richard had bought him. He failed to find his favourite old sweater.

Daniel went downstairs to the kitchen, Fay was sautéing potatoes and had Daniel's steak under the grill. She had cooked vegetarian sausages for herself. She'd made a large bowl of mixed salad and there was crusty bread, real butter and a bowl of olives for snacking.

"What happened to my jade sweater?" he asked, popping a couple of black olives into his mouth.

"It had gone bobbly, so I threw it out. We can get you a new one."

"But I liked my old one."

"There were big holes under the arms, Daniel. It was falling apart."

"Just a bit of ventilation." He looked crestfallen. He loved that old sweater.

Fay rolled her eyes as she turned his steak.

"Shall I open the champagne?" Daniel asked. It wasn't worth making a fuss and he had become wary of any type of conflict, knowing how quickly it could escalate into something much darker and out of control.

"Absolutely. We have some celebrating to do."

Daniel grabbed the champagne, a bottle of Pol Roger Reserve. He began working on the seal and Fay brought out their best crystal champagne flutes. The cork popped and hit the ceiling and Daniel poured the frothy liquid into the flutes. They clinked glasses and drank a toast.

"To your release," Fay said.

"To my freedom and to us getting our lives back."

"Come on, the dinner's ready," Fay said, forking the well-done steak onto Daniel's plate. "Do you want to sit at the table or have a tray and watch TV? We could watch the news, if you want to. I expect you'll be on it."

"No – no news. I lived through the whole damned nightmare; now want to forget about it. Let's be civilised and sit at the table. We haven't eaten a meal together for so long."

Fay lit a couple of candles and they sat at the dining table adjacent to the kitchen. It had a beautiful view of the garden during the day through bifold glass doors, but the November evening had drawn in and all they could see were Fay's solar lights shining dimly in the trees. There was a faint tinkling from a windchime as the breeze picked up speed.

Daniel poured a large glob of his favourite blue cheese dressing over his salad and ground sea salt over the potatoes. As they ate, they chatted about the family, Daniel's grandson and Fay's mother. Apparently, she had softened her attitude toward Daniel when Fay had explained how the grief of losing Sophie had affected them both and led to the killing of their daughter's murderer.

"You haven't told her, have you?" Daniel had a mini panic attack at the thought that Fay had told her mother about the four people she'd killed.

"God no, absolutely not."

"No one must ever know, Fay. No one."

"I know, Daniel, and no one ever will. Not from me."

Daniel nodded and speared half a baby plum tomato with his fork and dipped it into the dressing.

Their conversation turned to mundane matters to do with the house and the list of jobs that Fay had accumulated for him to do, neither of them wanting to spoil the evening with an intense conversation. Nor were they ready to test their relationship. Would his love for his wife overcome his abhorrence at what she had done? Could he ever reconcile the conflicting emotions he was feeling? For now, Daniel wanted to forget about the trauma of being in prison and celebrate his freedom. He sensed Fay wanted that too. He would try to bring some sort of normality into their lives. He had to.

"Well – that was bloody lovely," Daniel said as he mopped up the last of the blue cheese dressing with a hunk of bread. He topped up their glasses. The champagne had gone straight to his head after months with no alcohol.

"There's trifle for dessert."

"Bring it on," Daniel said, patting his belly. His sizeable appetite was returning with a vengeance. He'd put on a few pounds thanks to the unappetising stodge of prison food and the lack of exercise but tonight was not the time to be worrying about his figure – he'd soon shape up again.

Fay served up a large helping of home-made trifle and Daniel ate the lot, quaffed down with champagne. Then he went to the fridge and grabbed another bottle and a couple of custard tarts, relishing the taste of the cold custard and the spicy nutmeg.

Fay handed him a small package that was wrapped in silver and gold paper and finished off with a red ribbon. "Go on, open it."

"What's this?" Daniel asked as he took the package from her.

"Just a little welcome-home present."

Daniel ripped open the paper and inside was a brand-new stethoscope with red tubing.

"For when you go back to work." Fay smiled.

Daniel's heart melted. "It's still an *if* – we'll have to see if the BMA and the hospital board will approve it." Daniel turned the stethoscope carefully in his hands. More than anything he wanted to practise as a doctor again.

"I'm sure they will now you've been acquitted."

Daniel nodded pensively. "Thanks for the vote of confidence – and for the stethoscope, sweetheart. That was thoughtful..."

"Come on, let's leave the dishes and crash out on the sofa," Fay said.

Daniel left the stethoscope on the table, and they took their glasses into the living room. Daniel struck a match and lit the kindling in the wood burner. The logs spat and crackled as the fire consumed them. Daniel and Fay cuddled together on the sofa beneath the new winter throw. Maisie made a beeline for the fire and lay roasting herself in front of it, her legs stretched out to their full extent with just the end of her tail flicking occasionally.

"I don't know how cats can tolerate so much heat," Daniel said. "She must be half-cooked by now."

Fay topped up their champagne flutes and searched with the TV remote for one of their favourite sci-fi films. They were both keen *Star Trek* fans.

They spent the next two hours happily cuddled together on the sofa watching the J.J. Abrams *Star Trek* movie, with Chris Pine as Captain Kirk and Zachary Quinto as Spock. Above the sound of the film, just as Commander Spock accused Kirk of cheating in the Kobayashi Maru simulation, Daniel turned to Fay. "Let's get a puppy."

She shot him a look that said, *are you crazy?*

He decided not to pursue it and they watched the rest of the movie in companionable silence. Daniel had missed the things that made their house a home. Their shared interests, their pets. He'd craved that so much in prison; he just wanted more of it. A puppy would feel like a new beginning.

They let the fire die down and, like a heat-seeking missile, Maisie jumped onto Chester's sofa and curled around his neck like a fluffy scarf. He opened one eye briefly but went straight back to sleep. Soon, he was snoring again.

Daniel was still aware of the cloying smell of prison in his nostrils and throat – the awful stench that had pervaded his senses for months and was still clinging to him. He couldn't wait to grab a shower and get clean.

He stretched. "Well, I'm off for a shower."

"Why don't you have a soak in the bath?" Fay said. "Wash away that dreadful place. I'll run it for you."

"That sounds good. Thanks."

She went off upstairs. Daniel sat, immersing himself in the atmosphere of their home, hardly believing the nightmare was finally over. Then, he wandered upstairs after Fay. He could hear running water but there was no sign of her. Their huge corner bath was almost full of steaming water and bubbles. Fay had dimmed the lights in the bathroom and lit more candles around the edge of the bath, illuminating the conch shells that they'd brought back from the Turks and Caicos Islands, along with Daniel's yellow plastic ducks. Daniel stripped and stepped in. The water was warm and enveloping; his nerve endings tingled with the heat. He inhaled the heavenly fragrance of coconut and shea butter, turned off the taps and laid back in the bath, soaking away the dreadful memories of prison.

He heard a familiar giggle behind him and turned to see Fay standing in the doorway of the bathroom wrapped in just a fluffy white towel, her hair tied into a scruffy bun. In her hands, she had two fresh glasses of bubbling champagne. She handed him one and smiled seductively. Then, in one nifty move, she released her towel, letting it fall to the floor, the soft candlelight revealing a lean, toned body, the fullness of her breasts, the tight curve of her waist and endless tanned thighs. She stepped into the bath and lay back against his chest, their skin slippery and wet against one another.

They clinked glasses. "Welcome home, sweetheart," Fay said as she sipped her champagne.

Daniel sighed. It was so good to be home…

TWENTY-ONE

The killer had found a new confidence since Daniel Kendrick had been acquitted. He would be the perfect frame for their killing spree – a man capable of murder. Maybe they should wait for Daniel to return to work but here was a perfect opportunity to take a life. It was early evening; the staff were tied up with a handover meeting and the ward was quiet and dimly lit. The killer prepared their murder "weapon" and crept unseen toward their quarry.

Louise Barlow considered herself lucky to have survived a stabbing with a prison shiv. If it hadn't been for Daniel Kendrick's quick action, she would have died on the wing landing amid the pandemonium. For quite some time, she had been considering quitting as a prison officer and taking a year out to fulfil her dream of experiencing the wilds of nature. After the incident at HMP Ravenwood, she had categorically made her mind up. Life was too short and there was no way she was going back to that hellhole, risking life and limb to quell some pointless prison riot. She had her savings along with a small inheritance from her aunt and the world of wildlife beckoned – polar bears in Canada, scuba diving in the Galapagos, African safaris, snorkelling the Barrier Reef, orangutans in Borneo, turtles in Malaysia – she had a very long bucket list and longed to experience all she could before settling down. Now all she had to do was recover from her surgery, hand in her notice and make her dreams come true.

The killer drew the curtains around Louise Barlow's bed and smiled. "Time for your painkiller."

Louise returned the smile; she welcomed some relief from the throbbing pain in her abdomen.

The killer plugged the syringe into the bung that was attached to the canula in her arm and depressed the plunger, flooding her veins with three times the lethal dose of potassium chloride, a potassium salt that, in high concentrations, causes the heart to beat abnormally, followed by cardiac arrest and death. Quick and simple, there would be subtle, if any, findings at a post-mortem.

Louise felt her heart thump hard as the first of the palpitations hit. She clutched her chest as the potassium deranged the electrical activity in her heart, causing lethal arrhythmias.

She looked into her killer's eyes, pleading for help, her heart racing, her blood pressure plummeting dangerously. All she saw was the icy, callous stare of a pitiless murderer, indifferent to her precious dreams of a better future.

The ventricles in her heart began to flutter and fail. The image of her killer was the last thing she saw before she felt her heart stop and her consciousness drift away into the blackness of death and whatever lay beyond.

The cause of Louise Barlow's death would forever remain a mystery to all but her killer.

TWENTY-TWO

Daniel had slept more peacefully than he had in months – no nightmares, no images of Wixx's face invading his mind, just solid, blissful sleep. With nothing calling them, they languished in bed until after nine the following morning. Fay had got up earlier, let the dogs out, fed them and gone back to bed for a snooze. They snuggled up to one another like they had in the early years of their relationship, and it felt good. Daniel was beginning to believe that they were moving past their grief at losing Sophie. Maybe their enforced separation had done their relationship some good.

Daniel's rumbling belly eventually shifted them out of bed. "What's for breakfast?"

Fay stretched and yawned. "There's plenty in the fridge."

Daniel slipped on the navy chinos he'd worn the evening before and put on a fresh blue cotton shirt. He went downstairs to the kitchen, filled the kettle, flicked it on to boil, then rummaged in the fridge.

"Bacon sandwich?" he called up to Fay.

"Just toast, thanks."

Daniel prepared breakfast for them with a large mug of tea each. The dogs sat in the kitchen, patiently waiting for scraps.

Maisie sat on the windowsill, her paws neatly together, chattering at a blackbird turning over leaves in the garden.

Fay appeared in the kitchen wearing jeans and a colourful Fair Isle sweater. Her long blonde hair was loose and flowing around her shoulders in messy waves and she had subtly emphasised her green eyes with plum-coloured eye make-up and mascara.

Daniel gave her a kiss. "You look gorgeous."

"Thanks."

"Here, come and get your toast."

They sat on tall metal and cream leather stools at the central island in the kitchen and ate. Daniel slipped each of the dogs a crust. "Let's go out for a walk – I've missed the woods."

"Yes, definitely. Let's go soon while the sun is still out."

They finished breakfast, put coats and wellingtons on and Daniel double-checked the back door lock and picked up a couple of balls and the new ball-thrower that Fay had bought. He noticed the new windchime that had been tinkling annoyingly in the trees. He'd never liked the things.

They walked up the street to the woodland and the dogs twisted their bodies around the kissing gate and scampered along the path ahead.

"It's bracing to be outside again," Daniel said, breathing in the crisp, cold air. It smelled of damp grass and moss mixed with the faint whiff of farmyard manure. Sunlight filtered through sparse leaves in a fan of bright crepuscular rays that highlighted the landscape as it rolled into the distance. The intense colours of autumn immersed his senses and lifted his spirits as they walked along the familiar path. They heard the mewing cry of a buzzard overhead and looked up to see it effortlessly glide the thermals beneath wisps of white cirrus clouds. To their right, ancient woodland morphed into an open patchwork of countryside with fields, bordered by newly cut hedges and dotted with sheep. It was a perfect, crisp November morning.

Fay slipped her arm through his and they walked in silence for some minutes, Daniel absorbing the splendour of the countryside and revelling in his new-found freedom. Chester and Ella were bounding through piles of fallen leaves in the woodland, chasing one another without a care in the world.

"Let's get a puppy," Daniel said, trying again to persuade Fay. He'd have a whole pack of dogs if he had his way.

Fay glanced at him, her brows knitted into a frown. "No, Daniel. We've got two dogs already."

"A kitten, then."

"No."

"A hamster?"

"No."

"Goldfish?"

"No."

"Well, can we at least sponsor another guide dog puppy?"

Fay looked at him and grinned. "Yes, of course."

They looked at one another and laughed. Daniel let it go. Maybe he was getting carried away with the elation of his acquittal. They walked in amiable silence, taking in the beauty of the countryside. Fay threw balls for the dogs and they bounded through the woods after them.

But Daniel's thoughts inevitably returned to his horrendous experience of prison. It had been one hellish nightmare but now he faced a new challenge. Prison life had shielded him from the reality of life on the outside in a strange sort of way. Although unwanted, his prison cell had been a cocoon of routine without his usual responsibilities – to his patients, to Fay, to the wider family. He was relieved and happy to be out of there, but he now had to face another reality and there was a new feeling beginning to bubble to the surface. He was thinking of the future and going back to work. He wanted more than anything to be a doctor again – to save lives and heal the sick. It was his purpose in life – his reason for living; for being. That and Fay, of course. She meant the world to him, and he loved her more than ever, but he was truly driven to be a doctor. Yet, just as he'd sensed in Rosie the day before, he wondered if his friends and colleagues would treat him differently now that he'd been in prison. Would they be uneasy? Fearful, even? Would they only ever see him as a killer, even though it was in self-defence and under extreme duress? He should try to alleviate any misgivings they might have. He knew life could never be quite the same again – not any time soon – maybe never. Perhaps that's what life was all about – gaining experience on a journey of personal evolution, learning from mistakes and hopefully gaining a little wisdom along the way.

"You've gone quiet," Fay said. "You alright?"

Daniel looked at Fay and smiled. "Why wouldn't I be? I have you and my freedom back. What more could a man want?"

Fay squeezed his arm.

"Come on, let's head for home."

*

Daniel had made lunch – a small salad for Fay and a Marmite and crisp sandwich for himself. It was a guilty pleasure he'd sorely missed. Now Fay sat on their wooden bench near the ash tree in the garden with Maisie curled up next to her. The warm November sunshine had lasted well into the afternoon and, while Daniel caught up with correspondence and a heap of text messages and phone calls, she decided to make the most of it. She had tried reading but couldn't concentrate. She had been thinking about Sophie and what Felicia Grainger had said. It had played over and over in her mind since the psychic reading. *You must move on… Sophie needs to be at peace. You both do… You need to listen to her and start thinking about your future. Think of this reading as a warning…*

She couldn't talk to Daniel about it – he would think she was crazy – and there was nobody she wanted to share this with.

Not even her friend and colleague, Shelly Winters, to whom she told everything. This was something she had to deal with alone. Maybe Sophie – Felicia – was right. Maybe it *was* time to move on for her own sake, for Sophie and for Daniel. Her grief had gone on long enough. She'd had three months to come to terms with what she had done, and she couldn't go back and change a thing – even if she wanted to. Yes, she had killed four people but, if she was brutally honest with herself, she had no real regrets, despite what she had told Daniel. Those barely human creatures were evil criminals and killers and they had deserved to die in her estimation. Even so, it wasn't easy coming to terms with the fact that she had deliberately killed and got away with it.

But now it was time to take control of herself and put the past behind them. She couldn't live with her anger any longer. It had been destroying her and their marriage. *Sophie needed to be at peace.* She would do it for her, for her darling daughter. It would be hard to let go, she realised that, but she had to control her obsession with Sophie and try to focus on the future. Sophie was dead and she would never look into her beautiful baby-blue eyes again. She had to accept it. But, if Felicia was right, Sophie's soul, her spirit, would always be around her. She could take comfort in that. Perhaps the psychic reading had been cathartic and healing, as Felicia suggested it could. She had to admit, she did feel comforted in her belief that Sophie's soul lived on and that she was happy in the existence that lay beyond death.

Fay had longed for a baby, had tried for almost two years to fall pregnant with Sophie, only for her life to be cruelly snatched away. Maybe they *should* try for another baby. Was that what Sophie was telling her?

Follow your heart…

Her heart ached for a baby and her body was telling her that time was running out.

Maisie suddenly looked up, past Fay's head. Her green eyes were soft and unconcerned but curiously, were focused on one spot behind. Fay turned but could see nothing. Maybe Maisie had seen a bird. Or maybe it was a ghostly presence. A shiver inched down Fay's spine. Perhaps Maisie could see Sophie's spirit. She'd read that cats might be able to sense and see things that people couldn't. Maybe Sophie was giving her a message that she was right. That she *should* try for another baby. Maisie looked away and started grooming her fur. In her mind, Fay was now convinced that what she was doing was right. Another baby would bring them peace and heal the dreadful grief they had suffered. She felt a surge of joy – not least because she had made her decision.

"Hi, sweetheart."

Fay looked up to see Daniel walking toward her with two mugs of coffee. He handed her one and sat on the bench beside Maisie.

"Thanks. Finished your paperwork?" Fay sipped the hot liquid and cupped the mug in her cold hands.

"More or less. There was a lot to catch up with, but I've had enough of it for today." Daniel leaned back on the bench, his face turned toward the sun as it started to fall toward the horizon. He put his mug down and reached for Fay's hand and they interlocked their fingers the way they always did.

"Beautiful day," Fay said. She wondered if she should bite the bullet and ask Daniel about the baby thing.

"Yes, it is. I can't tell you how wonderful it feels to be out of that damned place and home again with you. Nothing can touch us now." He stroked the back of Fay's hand with his thumb.

They sat in companionable silence for some minutes, enjoying the garden and watching a squirrel eating an acorn. But Fay was buoyed with excitement and finally looking forward to the future. She took a deep breath. No time like the present…

"How about trying for a baby?"

"A baby what?"

"A human baby, Daniel. Our baby. Let's try for another baby."

Daniel pulled his hand away from Fay and sat upright on the bench. "God, Fay, the last thing I want right now is another baby. With all that's happened, I just want some stability and a boringly normal life without any complications."

"But you wanted a puppy. Why can't we have a baby?" She wasn't sure she could persuade him, but she had to try.

"A puppy is one thing but a baby…" Daniel ran the palms of his hands over his face as if he couldn't believe what he was hearing.

Fay looked at him pleadingly. "It would be good for us – to help us heal."

"Fay, I still don't know if I have a job to go to and surely you remember the trauma we went through trying for Sophie. I can't go through all that again."

She had to admit that the infertility treatment had been painful for her and their whole lives had been hijacked by just one issue – her trying to get pregnant.

"But, Daniel, I'm forty-five. Time is running out."

"I know, sweetheart, but not now. I can't contemplate another baby right now. I'm sorry but I can't."

"Will you ever? I mean, my biological clock is ticking ever louder. The longer we leave it…"

Daniel shot her a look that said the subject was closed.

They sat in awkward silence. Fay could feel a mood of bristling resentment brewing between them. She knew he had no intention of discussing it any further.

Typically, after they'd "had words", Daniel tried to lighten the mood. "Fancy going out for dinner tonight? How about that nice little French restaurant by the river?"

Fay looked up at him, her eyes a little softer. "Sure, why not?" She put her arm through his as if she'd forgiven their little disagreement. But she had no intention of giving up now she'd made up her mind.

She might have known what his reaction would be. It was understandable; he'd been through so much. But what if it took another couple of years to get pregnant? She couldn't wait that long. If they were going to have another baby, it had to be soon – very soon. There was no time to try and bring Daniel around to her way of thinking – he would just have to accept it once she was pregnant. She would make an appointment at the infertility clinic and discuss her options. She smiled – they still had several frozen embryos – one of them might soon be growing inside her.

TWENTY-THREE

They arrived at Le Petit Café de Jardin at 6.30pm. It was the earliest booking Daniel could get. He realised how institutionalised he'd become with mealtimes and was used to eating at 5pm. He was famished. Fay had driven, so Daniel could enjoy a few glasses of wine. The restaurant was just a couple of doors down from Tatiana's, Fay's favourite café. It was one in a row of converted old redbrick warehouses that ran alongside the river. They walked along the path between the buildings and the river, the lights from the windows reflecting on the water as it meandered past. A flotilla of mallard ducks had gathered for the night on the opposite bank, noisily quacking and flapping their wings beneath a cloudless black sky, replete with twinkling stars and the glow of a full moon.

Daniel had worn smart navy trousers and a pale lavender-coloured shirt left open at the collar under his best navy sports jacket. Fay was wearing a simple black knee-length dress with a three-quarter-sleeve bolero that was covered in silver-coloured sequins. She wore a turquoise gemstone on a silver chain around her neck that Daniel had bought for her when they were on holiday a few winters ago. She was struggling in her black high-heeled courts and Daniel offered his arm to steady her, which she gladly took. Their earlier disagreement had been forgotten.

"Feels like a date night," Daniel said, squeezing her hand. It was a long time since they had eaten at a decent restaurant together and a world away from his revolting prison rations.

They went in through French doors and were greeted by the head waiter, Marcel Beaulieu, whom they knew slightly from previous visits. He was an older man with wiry grey curls and matching eyebrows. He wore a long black apron.

"Good evening. *Bonsoir*, and welcome to Le Petit Café de Jardin," he said with a theatrical bow. He led them to a table next to the window, where they had open views of the riverbank garden with soft lighting illuminating the tree-lined river beyond. Daniel had requested the best table in the house. The restaurant was quiet and there was a low murmur of conversation and tantalising cooking smells coming from the kitchen.

They sat at their table and the waiter handed them each a wine list and a menu, then draped white linen napkins across their laps. The table was dressed in white linen, with silver cutlery and large crystal wine glasses. A candle flickered in a glass holder, its flame reflected in the glass of the window. Whitewashed stone walls were an original feature of the building that the owners had retained to give an arty, textured feel, and there was a large blackboard chalked with the special dishes of the day. A long oak bar ran along the length of one wall and there were several large mirrors in antique wooden frames adorning the walls, bouncing soft light around the room. The floor was decked in recycled oak floorboards.

The owner, Louis De la Croix, had retained many of the traditional French customs and the place had the ambiance of an authentic Paris restaurant. It reminded Daniel of a restaurant they had frequented in Montmartre in Paris before they were married.

Daniel was looking through the wine list as the wine waiter arrived. He wore a long black apron and had such a thick, bushy beard that Daniel decided something was surely nesting in there. "*Bonsoir*. My name is Andre Barrere. What would you like to drink – madame, monsieur?"

"A large Chardonnay for me, please," Fay said.

The waiter nodded. "Of course, madame." He turned to Daniel. "And for monsieur?"

Daniel gave up with the list. He loved his wine but was no connoisseur. A bottle of plonk from the supermarket was more his usual style. "Can you recommend a nice red wine?"

The man stroked his beard. "Ah, for monsieur, I think a Bordeaux. The 2015 Château Bourgneuf Pomerol."

Daniel checked the wine list – a bit pricy but hell, he was celebrating. "That sounds good. Let's have a bottle of that."

The waiter nodded and went off to fetch their drinks.

They perused the menu: a delectable selection of elegant French cuisine. The dishes were listed in French first but translated into English in italics.

"What do you fancy?" Fay asked. "I think I'll have the Roquefort cheese and caramelised onion tart to start – or maybe I should stick to the bistro salad."

Daniel chipped in. "You could have frog legs or escargot, or, if you can't make up your mind, there's a special *pour les indécis* menu for the undecided."

"No, I'll go with the tart followed by the ratatouille," Fay said.

"Well, I'm having the cognac shrimp with beurre blanc, followed by the poulet chasseur," Daniel said, licking his lips. The chef, Frederic Ducasse, had been trained in Paris under the iconic French chef Julien Gauthier and his cuisine was an inspiration.

The wine arrived. Daniel tasted it and approved without hesitation – a plush merlot with dark sweet-plum notes. He swirled the dark red liquid and quaffed a large mouthful. This was more like it. A bit of decorum and no more prison stew rotting his stomach.

Marcel Beaulieu took their order and came back with a selection of bite-sized hors d'oeuvres. "Amuse bouche while you wait – on the house," he said, placing a tiny platter of smoked salmon with dill sour cream on toasted French bread, along with some miniature smoked sausages wrapped in crispy bacon and skewered with a cocktail stick.

Marcel had a slight north eye and Daniel wasn't sure which one to look at, so he focused on the bridge of the man's nose. "Thank you, that looks delicious."

When he'd gone, Fay looked at Daniel. "You can have mine – I'm vegetarian now."

"Since when?"

"A couple of months ago."

"OK." Daniel popped a sausage in his mouth. "We can order something veggie for you." Daniel marvelled at the oxymoron. His wife had killed four people in cold blood but had since, apparently, become a harmless herbivore. An indication of her remorse, perhaps?

"It's OK. There'll be plenty of food." She smiled and sipped her Chardonnay; the diamond in her engagement ring sparkled in the candlelight. She gazed out of the window at the river, twirling the stem of her glass.

Daniel worked his way through the mini hors d'oeuvres. Fay was full of surprises. He had no idea she wanted another baby, or that she'd decided to become vegetarian. He wondered how well he really knew his wife, especially after that jaw-dropping confession in her journal. Yes, especially after that. He would have to confront her about the journal and about getting rid of the evidence but now was not the time.

Just as he finished up the last salmon bite, Marcel arrived with their starter.

Daniel sipped his wine and tucked into cognac shrimp, a combination of shallots, wine, cream, butter and cognac drizzled over pan-fried shrimp. It was mouth-watering. Fay seemed to be enjoying her savoury tarts but was struggling to twirl pea shoot tendrils around her fork. He'd missed her so much and yet something had changed between them. A seismic shift that hadn't fully played out. Something he didn't yet understand.

"I've been thinking about what you said last week about selling the clinic," Fay said.

"And have you made any decisions?" Daniel forked in the last shrimp and dabbed his mouth with his napkin.

"Well, it seems sensible to sell it. I'd like to take a break from work, and we can't afford to keep it going for months or even years without an income coming in from it."

"Are you saying you're going to give up forensic psychiatry?"

"For now, at least. It's been a traumatic couple of years, and I'm completely exhausted with it all."

Daniel was relieved. He'd been telling her for a long time she wasn't safe with all the psychos she had to deal with. "I think that's an excellent idea. So, you're definitely happy to sell the place?"

Marcel came to clear away their plates. They smiled and thanked him. Daniel poured himself another glass of wine.

"Yes, I think it would be for the best," Fay said.

"I could give Oliver Davenport a call tomorrow. I'm sure he would be interested in setting up a second cosmetic surgery clinic. He's been talking about leaving the NHS and I know he's good for the cash."

"Yes, why not? I'm ready to let it go now. And it would be the perfect place for Oliver." Fay sipped her wine.

Marcel arrived with their main course. "Ratatouille for madame and poulet chasseur for monsieur." He placed their dishes in front of them, gave a little bow and went to take the order from a couple at an adjacent table.

"This looks delicious," Daniel said as he tucked into hunter's chicken with a reduced chasseur sauce prepared with tomatoes, mushrooms, onions, white wine, brandy and tarragon. It was served with potatoes à la dauphinoise and a few artistically arranged green beans.

"Yes, mine is lovely too." Fay seemed to be enjoying her ratatouille, a colourful dish with aubergine and a variety of vegetables served with crusty French bread still warm from the oven.

"We could turn the nursery into a study for you to finish writing your book on biophilia," Daniel said around a mouthful of potatoes.

Fay was silent for some moments before she replied. "No, Daniel, I'd prefer to work in the kitchen and that beautiful view of the garden."

Daniel didn't pursue it. He sensed there was more to Fay's reasoning but didn't want the conversation to turn to Sophie or the events of the past few months. Not yet. They were enjoying their evening together.

They ate in silence for some minutes. Marcel checked that everything was in order and topped up Daniel's wine glass. Fay refused another Chardonnay.

"I'll give Colin Mathias a call, maybe tomorrow," Daniel said, spearing two green beans with his fork.

"Yes, it would be nice to know where you stand. Do you think you will get your old job back?"

"I hope so. I've only been away three months. I'm sure they would have managed without me for that long." Daniel finished up his chicken and mopped up the rest of the chasseur sauce with a hunk of bread that Fay had left.

"It would be nice if we could both take on something less demanding – at least for a while." Fay finished her ratatouille.

Marcel took their plates away but was back a few minutes later with dessert menus. There was a choice of apple tarte Tatin, clafouti aux cerises, chocolate mousse and crème brûlée, and there was a small selection of dessert wines.

"Not sure if I've got room for dessert," Fay said.

"Well, I'm going to push the boat out and have apple tarte Tatin. Go on, have something – it's not often we do this." Daniel knew Fay was watching her figure, but he loved her whatever she weighed.

"Go on then – I'll have a crème brûlée."

Daniel gave the order to Marcel. "Help me finish this wine, Fay."

"Alright, then, but just a small glass. I have to drive."

Daniel shared the rest of the merlot between them, and Marcel brought the desserts.

Daniel's tarte Tatin came with Chantilly cream, and he spooned it into his mouth, even though his stomach was uncomfortably full. "This is delicious. How's yours?"

"Gorgeous," Fay said around a mouthful. "By the way, I had coffee with Shelly last week at Tatiana's."

"How is she?" Daniel hadn't heard from Fay's friend and colleague in a few weeks but knew she had been recovering well from a kidney removal following a knife attack by Damon Wixx.

"She's doing well – physically and mentally. I'm amazed how she's managed to put it all behind her. Anyway, she was saying that Doug has a couple of openings for research projects, and I was thinking it would be nice to get into some research again. It wouldn't pay much, and I'd lose my salary, of course, but who knows what it could lead on to?"

"Well, it's always better to be at the bottom of a ladder you want to climb rather than at the top of one you don't. Know any details?"

"Not yet but Shelly said she would arrange a meeting with Doug. I'll find out more then."

Daniel felt a tinge of guilt at the mention of Doug. He was Shelly's husband, a university professor of psychology, and they hadn't hit it off particularly well, especially after Shelly had been stabbed by that psycho Wixx. He blamed himself. If he hadn't involved Shelly with all that business with Wixx, she might not have been harmed. "Fingers crossed, then," he said.

They finished up dessert and declined coffee. Daniel could hardly move he was so stuffed, and he asked for the bill. Marcel placed a large sheet of white paper on their table and scribbled down all they'd had with a pencil, totting up the prices of each dish in his head – another little touch of French authenticity.

Daniel paid and left a generous tip and they walked out into the crisp November evening. Daniel put his jacket around Fay's shoulders. The ducks had settled in for the night and the moon had moved further west in the sky.

"Let's go home and have a nightcap while we look at the stars. I've missed that too," Daniel said.

"That sounds nice."

Fay drove them home and they changed into warm clothes. Daniel wore navy chinos and a cream Aran sweater that was covered in Maisie's fur, and Fay changed into jeans and her Fair Isle jumper under a purple puffer jacket and a knitted scarf. Daniel poured them each a generous Cointreau and they went into the garden with the dogs and sat on the bench by the ash tree.

Daniel curled an arm around Fay's shoulders and she snuggled in to him. Chester and Ella wandered around the garden before settling on the lawn.

"This is lovely," she said.

"Yes, I've missed this – and you – so much. I can't tell you what a relief it is to be home and have this nightmare finally over with."

Fay smiled. "It's good to have you home."

They sat in companionable silence for some minutes, watching the night sky. A couple of pipistrelle bats flew alongside a hedge, hunting for insects. Stars glittered like washed diamonds spilled onto black velvet and a steely moon shone through the bare branches of the ancient oak tree. The air

was still and smelled of wood burners and damp
snuggled in together against the chill of the nigh'

"Look, that must be the square of Pegasus'
glass in the direction of the constellation.

Daniel followed her gaze. "Yes, and above it would
Andromeda. It's incredible to think our nearest galaxy is over two million light years away."

"Look, there's Betelgeuse, above Orion's belt."

They both looked heavenward, marvelling at the constellations that were gin clear against a black, cloudless sky. Even the bright band of the Milky Way was visible in a spectacular display of billions of twinkling stars, faraway galaxies and nebulae.

"It's beautiful," Daniel said. He felt quite emotional as the vastness of the sky reminded him of his new-found freedom. Nothing must take that away again. Nothing.

Daniel was reluctant to spoil their magical evening but he knew they had to talk. To be honest with one another and confront their demons. He had to get Fay to destroy her journal – to destroy the evidence of the serial killings she had carried out. Nothing must jeopardise their future.

Daniel sat for some time, wondering how to bring up the subject, but he knew there were things that had to be said. He'd cogitated endlessly in prison and waited three months to say what needed to be said. He couldn't wait a minute longer.

"You know, when I was in prison, I had plenty of time to reflect on all that's happened." He felt Fay stiffen slightly, as if she didn't want to hear his words. But he was determined to go on. "I realised that I had been in denial with the grief of losing Sophie and in doing that I also shut you out. I had no idea you were going through so much pain, so much torment, and I'm so sorry for that."

Fay twisted her head, looked into his eyes and gave him a pensive smile.

"I realised that, by letting myself grieve, I've learned what it is to live more fully. By having my freedom taken away, I realised how much I wanted to be part of life – to embrace everything, good and bad. Even killing Wixx." Daniel took a sip of his Cointreau, the fiery orange liquid warming his throat. Fay was listening quietly. "You know, sweetheart, we created the circumstances we are living today. We let our grief dominate and get out of control. I was stuck in denial and you in anger. Both of us – and others – have paid a heavy price for that." With their lives, he wanted to add, but didn't.

"I know," she whispered.

Daniel paused, remembering that he wanted their conversation to be positive and not to blame or dwell on their past mistakes – that would help no one. "But remember, our lives would have changed irreversibly if I'd been sentenced to a life in prison. We've come through that now. We must be grateful for it. We have a second chance – let's grab it."

"It's not going to be that easy, Daniel."

"But it could be if we want it to be. The future is up to us. Life doesn't stop for anyone, and everything comes to an end, after all – everything – good and bad. We mustn't put our lives on hold, living in the past. Fixated on what we've done. We can't go back and change it, much as we'd like to. But, especially, we can't keep clinging to Sophie's memory. Life will never be fair and sometimes we get to experience things we don't deserve – like losing our baby daughter – but life is still beautiful. It's still worth living."

"But, Daniel, I killed those people. I killed them and blamed someone else. How can we live with that? How can you forgive me? You must hate me for what I've done." Her eyes were wet with tears.

"Sweetheart, I love you and I always will. But no amount of guilt can change the past. I've thought about this endlessly in prison." He smiled and kissed her forehead. "It's impossible to be happy if you're constantly somewhere else and unable to fully embrace the reality of this moment. We both have to accept the past and make peace with it. It will never go away but it will end up helping to create the future if we don't. We must let it go."

Daniel had come to know that hate and anger are emotional parasites that destroy happiness. He'd witnessed that in abundance in prison. Forgiving someone doesn't condone their actions – it simply frees you from being an eternal victim. He had to forgive Fay – and forgive himself – or life wouldn't be worth living.

Daniel took a sip of his Cointreau and went on. "You know, we'll lament the chances we didn't take far more than our failures in the past. Think about it. What's the worst thing that can happen? Will it really, actually kill you?"

Fay nodded sombrely as Daniel went on.

"Even death isn't the worst thing that can happen – allowing yourself to die inside while you're still alive is far worse. We can't let what's happened dictate our future anymore." Daniel felt relieved to say the things he'd wanted to say for so long during those interminably lonely nights in his cell. There was no point in recriminations now; all he wanted was to heal the chasm that had opened between them since Sophie's death. To be, once more, the loving couple they used to be.

"I know… I know you're right. You're always so pragmatic. Always looking for the good in people and situations. I don't deserve you." Fay snuggled into his shoulder.

Daniel held her close, and they sat in reflective silence for several minutes.

"Fay, there's one thing we really must do…"

She cut in. "I know what you're about to say – that we should destroy the journal." She paused. "And I agree. We should put the past behind us and move on."

Daniel was astounded that Fay was so accepting. He had been ready for a lengthy and heated discussion, but it seemed as if she had done plenty of reflecting of her own.

She pulled away from Daniel and stood. "I'll be back in a minute."

Daniel sat on the bench, his eyes once more returning to the bright stars twinkling in the blackness of the sky. They had to put the past behind them. All they had were the endless moments of now but what they did and thought in those moments would shape their future, create their happiness. They could choose to surround themselves with a mental prison of their own making, oblivious to the wonder beyond its walls – or choose forgiveness, freedom and happiness. They could choose to embrace the future as two souls sharing that eternal cosmic journey of love and adventure.

Daniel looked back toward the house to see Fay return with her journal. It was a raw, visceral reminder of what she had done – what they had both done. Despite all he had said, he fleetingly wondered if they would they ever get past this.

Silently, Daniel walked across the lawn and lit a fire in the barbecue; briquettes burst into flames and glowed yellow and orange in the darkness of the November night. Fay joined him and put one arm around his waist. In the other, she held the journal close to her chest as if she was reliving all the raw emotions she had written about. The grief of losing Sophie; the anger that had turned a loving mother into a vigilante on a quest to rid the world of the evil depravity she saw in it.

The heat from the fire seared into their skin. They watched the flames for several minutes then turned, their gaze locked into one another's. Daniel could see the wretchedness in Fay's eyes and sense the regret in them for all that had happened. Then she turned and pushed the journal into the fire. The flames seeking out every word that she had written, every heartfelt emotion, from the devastating grief and the agonising longing for her baby to its transmutation into the hatred and rage that had driven her to kill.

Fay finally turned away from the flames, from the record of

her journey of grief and her confession of the killings. She fell into Daniel's arms and sobbed.

Had they begun to heal? Finally, Daniel could sense a beacon of hope for the future – their future. Somehow, surely, they would find their way back to one another…

TWENTY-FOUR

Rick finished his outpatients' clinic and decided to take the afternoon off. He'd worked more than twelve hours of overtime during the past week and badly needed to get out of the hospital, get some fresh air into his lungs and feel the raw power of nature. The weather was dry, cold and windy – perfect for jet-skiing, and he wasn't going to miss another opportunity to get on the water. He hadn't spent over £15,000 on a jet ski to have it parked in the garage. He'd called Isobel to see if she fancied joining him, but she was too busy crunching data and setting up the drug trial. A lame excuse as far as he was concerned. She wasn't exactly into the same things as he was and preferred a sedate dinner at an expensive restaurant or a drive in the country – far more leisurely pursuits than he enjoyed. Well, he was happy to go alone and, if he left now, he'd have a few hours of daylight.

Rick left the hospital and slipped into the driver's seat of the Huracan. He loved the feel and smell of the leather interior, the array of dials that lit up along the dashboard and the guttural sound of the engine as it roared into life. He nosed the car out into the traffic and turned up the volume of the CD player that was blasting out Black Sabbath's "Iron Man"; Ozzy Osborne's nonsensical lyrics belted out over the pounding kick drum and riffage that had kept heads banging over the years. Rick tapped out the beat on the steering wheel as he left the curtilage of the town and picked up speed on the dual carriageway that took him most of the way home.

He slowed for the final three miles along the country lanes that led past the cove and the lighthouse to his apartment block. He glanced at the beach – the sea conditions were a force four to five with a moderate to fresh breeze that was whipping up some decent swells. For Rick, that was perfect. He parked in the underground garage and nipped up to the flat to change and grab a can of Red Bull from the fridge that would give him the caffeine hit he needed to stay alert. The red light on his answerphone was flashing with three messages, which he ignored. He changed into his winter wetsuit, a Rip Curl Flash Bomb in black and grey, and slipped on jet ski boots, grabbed neoprene gloves and goggles and threw his phone and keys into a drybag.

Within minutes, he was back in the underground car park taking the cover off his jet ski as it sat on its trailer; a Kawasaki Ultra 310LX in ebony black and citrus yellow. He hooked it up to the towbar of his old white Ford Kuga 4×4. The offside wing had a dent that was starting to rust, and it had over 150,000 miles on the clock but it was good enough for towing the jet ski.

Within five minutes, Rick was reversing down the slipway of the cove and the jet ski was afloat. He parked, donned lifejacket and gloves, mounted, attached the safety lanyard and depressed the green starter button on the handlebar. The engine thundered into life and Rick couldn't resist twisting the throttle hard as he turned and roared off into the surf. He tasted the sea, drawing in deep breaths of bracing air and relishing the powerful kick of acceleration that left a rush of water behind him.

The onshore wind had picked up to a fresh breeze and the tide was coming in. The conditions were choppy, with big, crumbling waves leaving masses of whitewater as they broke and crashed over the sandy beach. Rick leaned backward and accelerated into the wall of an oncoming wave. Momentum took the jet ski upward and out of the water. He landed heavily on the seaward side and was drenched in water so icy it took his breath away, despite the protection of a wetsuit. Excitement was mounting as he accelerated into the surf. Again, he jumped a wave, the jet ski lifting over ten feet in the air and crashing down on the other side, like a breaching whale.

Once past the surf, the sea surface was lumpy and Rick sped offshore, performing several zigzags and tight turns, carving up the water and sending it spraying in all directions. He turned sharply, jumped over his own wake then accelerated to 50 mph, the jet ski's deep-V hull enabling the craft to manage the swells with ease, its impeller sucking in water and converting the power of the engine into almost 2,000 pounds of forward thrust. He relished the exhilaration, the soaring excitement of an adrenaline rush as he skimmed and bumped over the surface of the water. Then he slowed and performed a couple of donuts – spinning around in the same place – then picked up speed with another exhilarating high-speed skim over the water, before releasing the throttle to perform a 180-degree spin, a stunt he repeated twice more.

Rick accelerated across the open water, twisting the throttle to 30… 40… 55 mph: feeling the salty wind bite into his face. It was a welcome escape from work and the shadowy thoughts that churned constantly through his troubled mind. He decided it was time for some advanced tricks.

Rick had watched high-level pros do four or even five backflips in a row. He was nowhere near that level but had tried a few single backflips and was improving. Deciding it was time for another try, he sped back through the surf, slowed the jet ski, adjusted the trim and got into a standing position. He turned into the surf, leaned back and accelerated toward a large oncoming wave. As he rode the curve of the wave, he pulled the handlebars toward him; momentum took the jet ski upward and the nose flipped backward. He felt himself turning upside down, then the craft landed nose first in the water – but he failed to keep hold of the handlebars and was wiped out. Rick was plunged into the sea, lost his orientation for a moment while he was underwater but surfaced, taking a deep breath, tasting the salt, feeling the icy chill.

The safety lanyard had killed the engine and the jet ski sat pitching and rolling in the waves. He swam toward it, pulled himself onto the back deck, then sat, reattached the lanyard and started the engine, driving seaward once again. He savoured the sheer power and explosive acceleration of the beefy Kawasaki as it reached a gravity-defying 0–30 mph in just two seconds. The intense thrill from the rush of hormones was as addictive as heroin but a hundred times more powerful. Rick was well aware that he was an adrenaline junkie, addicted to the highs that his own body was producing. But, just like a drug addict, he needed more and more to get the same high – going higher, deeper, faster each time, pitting himself against nature and gravity and going to ever more extremes to get the head rush he craved. He'd participated in several extreme sports – ice climbing, kitesurfing, skydiving – but he relied on his jet ski to deliver an easily accessible adrenaline jolt.

Two hours later, the November sky was darkening as the afternoon drew on. The shore was now far in the distance and the cove looked deserted. It was time to head back. He turned and sped off toward the surf, his white apartment block stark and prominent on the headland against the grey sky. He accelerated hard, taking the jet ski to over 60 mph, enjoying another thrilling surge of endorphins.

He finally slowed and surfed the waves back in, disappointed the buzz was over for another day. He beached the jet ski and fetched the Kuga. It had been an exhilarating afternoon. Rick reversed the trailer down the slipway, secured the jet ski and drove back to the apartment just as the light was fading to dusk. He went up to his flat, peeled off his wetsuit and hung it out on the balcony to dry, then took a shower, the hot water tingling and thawing his frozen body. He dried off with a supersized rough towel, changed into shorts and a T-shirt and padded around the flat in bare feet. It was now dark outside, the only light coming from the old lighthouse. Turning on a few lamps, he poured himself a large gin and tonic, plopped a slice of lime into the glass and took a gulp, savouring the bitter taste.

The red light on the answerphone was still flashing insistently. He pressed play. There was a message from the garage about a part he'd ordered for the Kuga. There was a monotonous-sounding pitch from a double-glazing salesman, which he deleted part way through. Then he heard the soft, familiar voice of his sister, Clarissa. She'd left a message in Spanish and sounded excited.

Please call me the minute you get this, Rick. I must speak to you.

Rick checked the clock. Barcelona was an hour ahead. Maybe he should call her. It sounded urgent. He looked up her number in his address book and dialled from the landline. She answered after four rings.

He spoke in fluent Spanish. "Clarissa, it's me, Rick. *Que tal?* How are things?" He took his drink and wandered over to the picture window, watching the street lights on a distant headland.

"Rick – thanks for calling back. I have some good and bad news."

"OK… good news first." Rick pictured his younger sister, with her classically beautiful Andalusian dark straight hair and mischievous, brown twinkling eyes.

"Hugo and I are getting married. He proposed a month ago at the beach. It was so romantic. I wish you could see my engagement ring, Rick. It is so beautiful. A huge square diamond and two little sapphires."

"*Maravilloso!* It sounds lovely, and about time he made an honest woman of you. When is the wedding?" He sipped his gin.

"In two weeks. Rick – you have to come. I want you to be there."

Rick couldn't answer. He suddenly felt conflicted. There had been no contact with his family, apart from Clarissa, for four years following the crash that killed his wife, Maria, and their son Alessandro. The crash that he had been responsible for.

"Rick? Will you come?"

"What about father? You know the situation between us."

"I don't care what he says. You're my brother and I want you there at my wedding."

"But why so soon?" He was stalling for time.

"We don't want to wait. We can't wait. Rick, our brother, Lucero, is terminally ill..."

TWENTY-FIVE

Daniel had spent the past couple of days catching up with jobs that had to be done at home – working his way through the list that Fay had put together for him. He still had to get around to chopping logs for the wood burner, but he'd managed to trim the hedges in the garden, repair one of the kitchen cupboards, replace a leaking tap washer and finally hung the family portrait pictures in the downstairs loo – a comedic series of sketches of skeletons. He'd also tied string to secure the windchimes – the constant tinkling was driving him nuts – managed to get a decent haircut and was enjoying getting his life back to some sort of normality but he was starting to feel restless to get back to his career. Colin Mathias hadn't been in touch, and he was desperate to know if he had a job to go back to. Should he call him? Maybe leave it another day? No – he decided to call him straight away. There was no point in waiting and he needed to know.

Daniel dialled Mathias's direct line in his office at Riverbeke General. It was answered after three rings.

"Colin Mathias." His voice was blunt and to the point.

"Colin, it's Daniel. Any news?"

"Ah, yes." His voice softened a little. "I was planning to call you this afternoon. I've had a few meetings with the board, the BMA and the GMC. Can you come in this week, and we'll discuss it?"

"Can you tell me over the phone?" Daniel was impatient to know what was going to happen to his career and whether it was all about to go tits up.

There was a pause on the line and the sound of pages being turned. "Come in today, if you like. I'll be free by eleven."

"That's fine. See you at eleven." Daniel ended the call. At last, some progress. Fay had gone out to do the grocery shopping and visit her mother. He hoped he would have some good news to tell her later.

Daniel just had time to walk the dogs, feed them and put them in the Dog House. He changed into an open-neck shirt under a navy suit and polished his black work shoes. He absently listened to a dreary radio discussion about politics and the state of the economy as he drove through Riverbeke and circled the hospital car park looking for a space. Someone had parked a pretentious-looking silver Lamborghini in his consultant's space, a car that was obviously compensating for something. He finally found a parking space – nipping in just as someone was pulling out. He walked through the main entrance, through the concourse, and took the stairs to the surgical floor – he had become wary of enclosed spaces after spending months in a prison cell and didn't fancy the lift. As he walked along the corridor to his department, he saw a few faces he knew. Some smiled but others hurried past. No doubt the hospital gossip machine had been working overtime.

A porter held the door open for him and he went into the department and along the corridor. He was greeted by the familiar sounds of rattling trolleys, ringing phones and bonging heart monitors, and there was an amalgam of smells – disinfectant, ethyl alcohol and the cloying whiff of an infected wound. He almost tripped over a couple of yellow warning notices left by the cleaners – *Danger, Wet Floor* – then turned toward the nurses' station. He could see down the length of the Nightingale ward that almost every bed was occupied. Things hadn't changed one bit in the three months he'd been away. The place was as busy as ever, with nurses rushed off their feet, porters collecting patients for the operating theatre, phlebotomists taking bloods, pharmacists checking drug charts, doctors examining patients and performing procedures. It was good to be back in the hustle and bustle of hospital life.

"Hello, stranger." Stacie Taylor, a staff nurse, was sorting through a pile of patients' notes. She smiled but he could sense a tinge of apprehension.

"Hi, Stacie. I've come in to see Colin."

"He's in his office."

"Thanks." Daniel walked across to Colin's office. The sign on his door read, "Mr Colin Mathias, Clinical Lead." Daniel knocked and waited.

"Come," a voice boomed.

Daniel went in and closed the door behind him. Colin was sitting in his office chair peering at a computer screen. He swivelled around, the chair making a familiar squeaking noise. "Nice to see you, Daniel. Take a seat." He indicated a chair adjacent to his desk.

"You too. It's good to be back."

Mathias, a short, portly man in his late sixties, was a kindly person, believing in the goodness of human nature. Quiet and unassuming, he didn't seek the constant ego-stroking that many of Daniel's colleagues seemed to thrive on. Mathias removed his scratched reading glasses and began his habitual swivelling back and forth in his chair, his trouser legs riding up to reveal hairy shins and stripy socks that clashed with his suit. He was sitting with his hands interlocked over his growing paunch. "So, about your career at Riverbeke General – mixed news, I'm afraid."

Daniel's heart sank. He should have known it would be too simple to be able to sail back into his job. "OK, enlighten me."

Mathias went on. "I'd better bring you fully up to speed." He seemed to be oblivious of his squeaking chair. "About four weeks after you were remanded, I suffered a heart attack. It wasn't life-threatening but, of course, I was off work for a while. In fact, I've only just returned to full duties."

Daniel was shocked; he knew nothing of this. "I'm so sorry to hear that, Colin. Are you recovered now?" Daniel felt a surge of guilt. Colin had likely been under a lot of strain being left as the only consultant in the department. He felt responsible.

"I'm fine now, thanks, but of course we had to appoint someone to fill the vacuum. We were without a consultant for three weeks. Matt Clarke acted up from his registrar post, but he admitted himself he's not ready for promotion. Anyway, since I was on sick leave, someone was appointed to take on your role as consultant – you must realise we didn't know how your situation was going to be resolved." Mathias cleared his throat. "The new consultant, Ricardo Estevez, is a cardiothoracic surgeon but has extensive experience in general surgery. He's joined us from the Hospital Clínic de Barcelona. He has excellent credentials and has turned out to be rather a charming chap. Been here six weeks now and seems to be settling in nicely."

Daniel was deeply disappointed. It felt like someone had stolen his life while his back was turned. "So where does that leave me?" Mathias's swivelling and the squeaky chair were becoming irritating. Why couldn't he just sit still?

"Well, since you were acquitted and found not guilty, your career as a doctor is not in question. However, your old post is no longer available."

"Does this Ricardo bloke have a permanent contract, then?"

"Yes, I'm afraid he does. If I had been here, I could have pushed for a temporary arrangement or get a locum in until after your trial, but it was out of my hands, I'm afraid." Mathias seemed genuinely sorry.

Daniel didn't know what to say. He'd been desperate to

return to work, to practise as a doctor again, and now it was being snatched away from him.

"However," Mathias went on, "there is an opening in our new intensive care and high-dependency unit, and we could also use some help here on the ward."

Daniel could feel a "but" coming on.

"But it would be at the SHO level. Quite a demotion, I know, but in time a more senior position might become available."

Daniel nodded pensively. It had been years since he'd been a senior house officer and, yes, it would be a jump backwards – a giant leap, in fact – but it was work and a way back to the hospital he loved. It would be quite a drop in salary, too, and now that Fay was giving up her job it would be a stretch to manage the finances, even though Fay was selling the clinic.

"We need someone to float between ICU, HDU and the surgical ward. We could get you working in theatre as well – you would need to keep up your surgical skills." Mathias continued his rhythmic swivelling.

"I'm not sure what to say, Colin." Daniel was trying to reconcile the information in his mind.

"I know it could be damaging for your reputation but you're a damned good doctor, Daniel. I… we'd all hate to lose you."

"I'm not bothered about my reputation. That's already in tatters. I just need to get back to work." Daniel knew this was all there was on offer. Consultant posts were few and far between and he couldn't contemplate the effort it would take to find a post elsewhere. He and Fay liked living near Riverbeke and they had the rest of the family close by. It would be a disaster to be forced to move to another part of the country.

"Take a day or so to think about it. It's a big jump, I know."

"I'll take the job," Daniel said.

The ramifications of what he'd done just kept coming.

TWENTY-SIX

"Let me introduce you to Ricardo Estevez," Mathias said.

"Sure." Daniel followed him out to the nurses' station, toward his old office.

The door was ajar, and Mathias knocked once and pushed it open. Daniel followed him into the room. Sitting in Daniel's chair was the new consultant. He looked up from the computer screen, a questioning eyebrow raised.

"Rick, this is Daniel Kendrick, your predecessor. Daniel – Ricardo Estevez." Mathias said, introducing the men.

Daniel graciously leaned forward and offered his hand. Rick shook it firmly. "Mr Estevez. Nice to meet you," Daniel said.

"Please, call me Rick." He remained seated.

Daniel nodded. He felt like a stranger in his own life, with someone else sitting in his chair, doing his job, parking what must be *his* pretentious Lamborghini in his parking slot, depriving him of his career. It was like he'd fallen into a wormhole and been spat out into a parallel universe where he didn't belong. He felt a tinge of resentment, as if life had gone on without him and that he was completely expendable. And, to rub salt into the wound, Rick was ruggedly handsome and appeared to be supremely confident. From what Mathias had said, he was also more experienced, especially given his cardiothoracic surgical skills. He felt undermined and insecure.

"Daniel is going to join us as an SHO, floating between this ward, theatre, ICU and HDU."

A dogsbody, Daniel thought. Nothing more than a bloody gofer. He felt a stab of shame that this was what his life had become. Had they even created a job for him out of pity? If it were true, it would only serve to make him feel even more devalued.

"Nice to have you on our team," Rick said, a slight smirk discernible on his lips. He leaned back in the chair.

"I look forward to it," Daniel said. It was a strain to be pleasant, but he had no choice.

"Alright, let's go meet them on ICU," Mathias said. "See you for this afternoon's ward round, Rick."

With trepidation, Daniel followed Mathias out of the office, past the nurses' station and out into the familiar corridor. They fell into step alongside one another as they walked to the intensive care unit, dodging trolleys and porters pushing patients in wheelchairs.

"Rick's a nice fellow. You should get on well with him," Mathias said.

"Yes, I'm sure." Daniel hoped he would be able to overcome his uneasiness once he started the job.

Mathias let them into the ICU with his swipe card and they walked to the nurses' station, where a group of doctors and nurses were chatting. Among them was Angela Edwards, the unit manager – a friendly face from the past. She looked up and smiled at Daniel, appeared to be about to speak but hesitated and stayed silent. The others stopped talking and looked at Daniel. He could sense a prickly awkwardness.

Mathias broke the ice. "Some of you know Dr Kendrick. He'll be working with us as an SHO across the department. He's an excellent doctor and will be a valued member of the team."

He saw eyes widen in surprise, foreheads scrunched in confusion, and there were several forced smiles. One junior nurse gave him a lopsided look of contempt, another a whimsical smile. There was a grim and ominous silence. This wasn't going to be easy, he thought. Where was the support from the staff that Colin had suggested in the courtroom? Maybe, after all, he should be looking for a job in a different hospital, where his past would be less conspicuous. Maybe the anonymity of stacking shelves in Tesco would be preferable to suffering the contempt of his colleagues.

Angela Edwards finally broke the impasse. "Hey, Daniel, it will be lovely to work with you again."

"Thanks, Angela," Daniel said. They exchanged a warm, genuine smile.

There followed a slight murmur of assent, then Daniel could see Matt Clarke, his former registrar and friend, striding toward him. "Daniel, so good to have you back." He shook his hand warmly and gave him a manly slap on the back. It was a demonstration of acceptance, of Matt letting the team know that Daniel was welcome.

"When do you start?" Matt asked cheerfully.

Daniel glanced across at Mathias for confirmation.

"How about Monday? I don't see any point in waiting."

Daniel hesitated, not sure if this was what he really wanted anymore, given the frosty reception, but Matt cut in.

"That would be great. I'm sure we're all looking forward to seeing you first thing Monday morning." He looked at the group gathered around the nurses' station. They grudgingly nodded their agreement.

"Yes, Daniel, congratulations," Angela said. She leaned across the countertop and offered her hand. Daniel shook it, relieved to have the initial awkwardness mostly out of the way.

The group gradually began to resume their activities, discussing patients' treatment, writing up notes, scrutinising X-rays.

Daniel glanced along the length of the ICU. Beds were occupied by patients on ventilators, fighting for their lives. He wanted more than anything to be a doctor, to make a difference in the world. He would get through this for his patients. He had to. There was more at stake than his wounded feelings.

TWENTY-SEVEN

Daniel nosed the BMW out into the traffic and inched through town. He knew their finances would take a hit, but he had to be positive. They had some savings, he could downgrade the car and they could remortgage the house, if necessary, although he didn't relish the idea of taking on a hefty loan again. Still, they were in a better position than a lot of people and, somehow, they would find a way to cope. Perhaps he could do some moonlighting with Oliver Davenport at the cosmetic clinic. He didn't particularly fancy it – or seeing Oliver's wife, Melissa, again – but the money would be good, and it would help to tide them over until he could get a promotion. As Daniel drove home, he tried to tell himself that everything would be fine.

He pulled up onto their drive to find a black Range Rover parked behind Fay's Mercedes that he didn't recognise. He parked in the street. As he opened the front door, he could hear voices and laughter coming from the living room. He threw his jacket over the banister and went in to find Shelly Winters, Fay's friend and colleague, along with her husband, Doug, sitting on the sofas drinking his whisky; a half-empty bottle of Glenfiddich was on the coffee table. Chester was lying across Shelly's feet and Doug was squirming back into the seat as Maisie tried to curl up on his lap. Ella was stretched out on the rug in front of the wood burner, one paw on her new teddy.

"Shelly, how are you?" Daniel said. "You look well considering…" Daniel was referring to Damon Wixx's knife attack, which had cost her a kidney and almost her life. He leaned over the back of the sofa and kissed her cheek.

"I'm fine, thanks, Daniel. I've made a good recovery. Had a good nurse." She smiled at Doug, who looked a little embarrassed.

"Hello, Doug," Daniel said. He shook Doug's free hand, one of their best crystal whisky tumblers in the other. Doug looked awkward and geeky, his long, spindly limbs sticking out from sleeves and trousers that were way too short.

"Afternoon," Doug managed.

Daniel gave Fay a kiss, tasting whisky on her lips.

"Doug's been talking through some potential research projects with me," Fay said. "He has some funding from a grant, and I'd love to do something – get into studying again with the psychology department." She was smiling for the first time in days.

Daniel perched on the arm of Fay's armchair. "Sounds interesting."

Doug was a professor of psychology at the university that was amalgamated with Riverbeke General Hospital. He and Shelly worked in an adjacent building and shared a rather untidy office there.

Fay turned to Doug. "Tell Daniel which projects you have in mind." She took a sip of whisky and offered Daniel her glass.

Doug put on half-rimmed reading glasses, picked up a sheaf of papers on the seat next to him and juggled them with his whisky glass in a clumsy effort to avoid disturbing Maisie as she lay on his lap. "We have several ideas for projects." He cleared his throat. "Understanding Engagement with Digital Behaviour Change—"

Fay cut in. "Don't fancy that as Kim Jeffreys is the project lead – can't stand the woman. Anyway, go on, Doug."

"Modifiable Psychological Risk Factors for Psychosis in the Young—"

Fay cut in again. "That's about fake news on social media. Not sure about that one."

Doug continued. "A Review of Impulse Buying Behaviour…"

"You already have a PhD in that." Shelly laughed.

Fay rolled her eyes.

Doug adjusted his glasses. "The Psychological Study of Near-Death Experiences in a Hospital Setting, and, finally, A Comparative Analysis of Midlife Crisis in Women and Men."

Daniel finished Fay's whisky in one gulp and turned to look at Fay. "Fancy any of those?"

She looked up at him. "Well, if I did the one on near-death experiences, it would mean I could work in the hospital with you. We'd get to see more of each other…"

"True," Daniel said, "but isn't it a bit morbid?"

"Not at all," Fay said. "It would be fascinating."

"And Doug is the project lead on that one, so we could see one another more often too," Shelly added.

Daniel felt a little uneasy after all they had gone through. "Wouldn't the shopping one be more up your street? Maybe we could finally understand why you have a wardrobe crammed with clothes you never wear."

Shelly laughed and Fay tapped him playfully on the arm before grabbing the whisky bottle and topping up everyone's glass. She emptied the bottle into her own glass and gave it to Daniel for them to share.

"So, what do you think, Fay? Have you decided?" Shelly asked, shifting her feet slightly beneath Chester's head.

"Yes, I'll definitely go with the one on near-death experiences." She smiled up at Daniel.

He gave her a fretful smile back. He wasn't so sure it was a good idea for her to be embroiled in death day in, day out after all that had happened: Sophie, the serial killings and Wixx. But he had to concede, it was her choice, and it would be good to see more of her at the hospital – another comrade on his team.

Doug smiled and reached across to clink glasses with Fay. "Alright, it's a deal. Come to the office on Monday and we'll make a start."

"Excellent." Shelly said.

They chatted for a while about life at the university but declined Daniel's offer for them to stay to dinner. Finally, after edging toward the doorway for ten minutes, they left amid promises to meet for dinner at Le Petit Café de Jardin, after Fay recommended the meal they'd had there the other evening.

Daniel closed the front door after waving them off. "Shelly looks well."

"Yes, she's made an amazing recovery. She's already getting back to work and trying to put it all behind her." Fay wandered into the kitchen and Maisie followed her, ever hopeful for a bowl of food.

"I saw Colin today."

Fay turned to face him. "What's the situation?"

"They've appointed a new consultant in my place and offered me an SHO post. It was disappointing to say the least."

"Oh, Daniel, I'm sorry."

"Yes – not what I was hoping for at all. Still, it was all that was on offer, and we have to make the best of it."

"Maybe I shouldn't be giving up the clinic. You know there won't be much payment from the research project."

Daniel worried that they would be going from two substantial salaries to his reduced earnings to keep them both going financially. "Don't worry, sweetheart, it will work out – you'll see."

He would definitely have to moonlight at Oliver's clinic now.

TWENTY-EIGHT

Fay was pleased that she had made the decision to join Doug with some research. It seemed like light at the end of the tunnel – apt given the project she would be working on. She'd sensed some resistance from Daniel but maybe he was just feeling disappointed at being demoted at work. He had insisted she carry on with the research despite her offer to keep the clinic going.

It had been a pleasant distraction but, even so, she had spent the past couple of days feeling emotional after the ceremonial burning of her journal. It was if as if she was saying goodbye to her little girl, to all the feelings she had kept alive for the past two years. She wasn't sure if she had been ready for it, but she knew in her heart that Daniel was right. *We can't keep clinging to Sophie's memory.* She loved Daniel, and if she wanted her marriage to continue she had to move on somehow. "The future is up to us," he'd said. Nobody would ever stop her loving her baby daughter but, if Felicia Grainger was right and she had received a message from Sophie, she had to move on for her sake too.

She'd churned it over endlessly in her mind and was determined that trying for another baby was the right thing to do. Daniel would never agree to it, but she hoped he would come around to the idea eventually. For now, she was alone with it all. Daniel had been out in the garden all morning chopping logs for the fire. She could hear his chainsaw intermittently but, apart from a shrill car alarm in the distance, it had gone quiet for the past ten minutes. Through the kitchen window she could see him stacking logs and would be busy for a while. She looked up a contact in her phone and tapped out the number.

"Hello, Genesis Fertility Clinic, Amanda speaking, how may I help you?"

"Yes, hello. I want to make an appointment to see Dr Nancy Chan, please. Is she still with you?"

"Of course. Are you one of her patients?"

"Yes, I saw her for IVF about three years ago."

"Alright, let me check her diary."

Fay could hear the sound of computer keys tapping.

"Actually, we have an appointment this afternoon at 2pm – a cancellation. Is that any good for you?"

"Yes, that would be perfect. Thank you. The name is Fay Kendrick." She gave her address and date of birth and ended the call. She checked the clock. She would have to leave soon if she was going to make the appointment. The clinic was the other side of Riverbeke.

She freshened her make-up, brushed her hair, changed into a powder-blue shift dress under a black cardigan with opaque black tights and sensible kitten heels. She would have to tell a white lie as to where she was going.

Daniel was still stacking logs, so she called from the kitchen doorway. "I'm just off shopping – need anything in town?"

"Nothing, thanks." He blew her a kiss.

She waved goodbye, then headed for the Riverbeke ring road to avoid the town traffic, a route they had taken many times when she'd been trying to conceive with Sophie. It felt strange to be going alone but no one, especially Daniel, must know about it until she was pregnant again. By then it would be a fait accompli and there would be no going back.

She arrived at the private fertility clinic, a modern detached brick building on the edge of a quiet science and business park. She found a parking space easily and walked down a wide stone path to the front entrance. Above the doors was a tasteful copper sign that read "GENESIS FERTILITY CLINIC". The path was strewn with colourful autumn leaves from the trees that surrounded it. Automatic doors *swooshed* apart to admit her, and she stepped into a spacious and gleaming reception area with marble floors, mirrored walls, spot lights and a vast, curved reception desk finished in maple.

A young woman with long auburn hair, a strip of dark roots, heavily tattooed eyebrows and plum-coloured lipstick looked up from a desktop computer. "Good afternoon. Can I help you?"

"Yes, it's Fay Kendrick for my 2pm appointment with Dr Chan." The woman's cloying musk perfume hung in the air.

The woman checked the computer screen. "Take a seat; she'll be with you shortly."

Fay sat on one of the black leather sofas near an expanse of window overlooking the front lawn. A thirty-something couple sat on the opposite side of the room, the woman nervously twisting the handle of her handbag, her husband gazing nonchalantly out of the window. They were just like her and Daniel a few years ago, Fay thought. She picked up a magazine from the coffee table and absently flicked through it. Pictures of smiling couples with spotless, brand-new babies beamed back at her along with a plethora of sponsored features and adverts for baby equipment, formula milk and complimentary therapies. Yes, she wanted to be a mother again, more than anything. To hold a baby in her arms, to experience again the unique love between a mother and her child. Coming here had confirmed that in her mind. She remembered Daniel's words: "We have a second chance – let's grab it." This was *her* second chance.

"Dr Kendrick?" A familiar voice with a soft Chinese accent called from behind her. She turned to see a petite woman in her fifties with short, poker-straight black hair, plump cheeks and a pleasant demeanour. She wore a white lab coat with a name badge on the lapel. *Dr Nancy Chan. Genesis Clinic Director.*

Fay stood and walked toward her. "Dr Chan. Lovely to see you again." The women shook hands.

"On your own today? How is your husband?"

"Oh, he's busy with work – you know what it's like," Fay lied, as she followed the doctor into her consulting room.

"Take a seat."

Fay sat in one of the two armchairs on the opposite side of the desk and put her handbag on the floor beside her. The consulting room was huge, with white-painted walls adorned with colourful abstract art and sparsely furnished apart from a trolley housing medical equipment. In the far corner was an examination couch. There was a picture window partially obscured by shutters. Fay glimpsed the trees outside, moving with the breeze, a flurry of leaves falling onto the grass.

Dr Chan sat, put on frameless reading glasses and consulted a computer screen. "How is your little one – she must be three now? Time goes so quickly – I lose track of it."

Fay looked down at her lap. "I'm afraid our little daughter died. She was just six months old."

"Oh, my dear, I'm so very sorry to hear that. I had no idea." Dr Chan removed her glasses and looked sympathetically at Fay.

"Thank you. We're trying to get over it." She didn't elaborate and didn't feel like explaining things. They had been through enough of that.

Dr Chan paused briefly as if she was waiting for Fay to say more. "Alright… so what can I do for you today?"

Fay took a deep breath. "I… we… want to try for another baby. We've given it a lot of thought and the time seems right."

"Yes, of course. Let's see." She replaced her spectacles and checked Fay's notes on the screen once more. "Well, after your last IVF treatment, you had three viable embryos left over. They were at the blastocyst stage and frozen using our vitrification technique. Basically, they were put into a cryoprotectant solution, then rapidly frozen." She scrolled down the screen. "You opted to keep them frozen for up to ten years, so, of course, we still have them here stored in our liquid nitrogen tanks."

"So, I could use them now? Have them implanted?"

"Yes, we could try, subject to a consultation and an advanced ultrasound scan. We would have to carry out a few tests but, as long as you are healthy and the embryos are suitable, there's no reason why not."

"So, I wouldn't need to take fertility drugs again?"

Dr Chan consulted the notes and shook her head. "I see you are forty-five now and treatment in older women is less likely to be successful. I think a scan should help us decide how we should proceed. Do you have any other questions?"

Fay had plenty. "If there are three embryos, how many would you be able to implant?" She began to hope she might have twins – even triplets. Why not? She was healthy and, after all, time was running out. The ticking of her biological clock was becoming deafening.

"We usually only implant one due to the risk of multiple birth. We could try two but don't forget, you only have three embryos. Since you are among the thirty-two percent of couples with unexplained fertility problems and, given your age, I'm afraid this could be your only chance."

Fay liked the idea of twins. Twin girls would be nice. "What will happen to my embryos?"

Dr Chan took off her glasses again and placed them on her desk. "We would carry out a frozen embryo transfer – FET. Our team of expert embryologists will carefully thaw the embryos and assess their suitability. If all goes well, they will be transferred to your uterus just like a normal IVF cycle."

"What are the chances of the embryos surviving the freezing process?"

"Most do survive but there is a chance that not all of them will. The chances of success with the transfer are comparable to fresh embryo transfer these days. However, I must warn you that in your age group, the success rate is quite low, around six percent." Dr Chan looked sombre.

Fay was desperate to try. She had to believe it would work. "I want to go ahead. What sort of costs are we looking at?"

Dr Chan took out a pamphlet from the drawer in her desk and ran a finger down a list of prices. "The package comes to £2,360 and includes all the scans and consultations as well as embryo thawing and assessment."

Fay and Daniel had already paid thousands for infertility treatment, and she felt a twinge of guilt, especially as Daniel was facing a pay cut and they were supposed to be watching their spending. But she had her own savings, so he would never know, and by the time the baby was born things were bound to be looking up. "Alright, let's go ahead. I really want this baby."

"Shall I book you in for a consultation and get the scan underway?"

"Yes please – as soon as possible."

Dr Chan tapped a sequence of keys on her computer. "Dr Amy Williams is free soon. I'm sure she would be happy to see you."

Fay was elated. She couldn't wait to get the process started. "Yes, that would be wonderful."

Dr Chan stood. "Perhaps you'd wait in reception." She gave Fay a very large glass of water. "You will need to drink all of this – you need to have a full bladder for the scan."

Fay followed the doctor out to the main reception area and sat on a sofa overlooking the front lawn. Things had moved more quickly than she had anticipated. She could be pregnant within weeks. It was hard to contain her excitement and she felt a surge of happiness. She knew Daniel would disapprove of her doing this behind his back, but couples sometimes tried for years with fertility treatment only to give up and fall pregnant naturally. He need never know.

Fay tried to contain her excitement for some twenty minutes before Dr Amy Williams appeared. She was a tall, willowy woman with intense blue eyes framed with heavy-framed glasses. She wore a grey pencil skirt and pale pink blouse under a white lab coat. "Fay Kendrick?"

Fay stood. "Yes." They shook hands and Fay followed the doctor to a clinical room lined with white cupboard units. There were several stainless-steel trolleys housing various pieces of equipment, blood and urine testing kits, and stacks of lab forms. Along one wall stood an examination couch covered in white paper; next to it was a state-of-the-art 3D Doppler ultrasound scanner with a digital consul, monitor and various probes and attachments clipped onto each side.

"Just lie on the couch," Dr Williams said. "We'll do the scan first. It will take around twenty minutes."

Fay lay on the couch and exposed her lower abdomen.

"Where are you in your cycle?" the doctor asked.

"About midway."

"That's perfect. All being well we can start treatment soon." Dr Williams switched on the scanner and squirted KY gel onto the ultrasound transducer. She placed it onto Fay's lower abdomen and began twisting it in various directions as she studied the monitor.

Fay watched, fascinated. She remembered having her pregnancy scans with Sophie. Daniel had been with her when they first saw the miracle of their baby: a tiny six-and-a-half-week foetus. Then there were the subsequent scans that tracked her development. She'd kept printouts of them all.

The women were silent while the scan was being performed, then Dr Williams handed Fay a wad of paper towels to wipe away the gel. "OK, all done," she said with a smile.

"Is everything alright?" Fay asked as she sat up.

"Looks fine to me. Have a seat and we'll go through it." Dr Williams gestured for Fay to sit opposite her at a desk. "Everything is normal – no cysts, fibroids or polyps that could cause a miscarriage. The blood flow to the uterus is good and the thickness of your endometrial lining is just about perfect for the embryo transfer to take place in the next day or two. Would you be prepared for that?"

"Absolutely. Yes." Fay's excitement was growing by the minute.

The doctor took Fay through a health questionnaire and took several vials of blood.

Dr Chan came into the room. "All good, Amy?"

"Yes; once we get the bloods back, we're good to go ahead."

"That's excellent. Well, Fay, we'll see you back here in a few days and let's hope we can do the embryo transfer for you. I'll inform our embryologists and, providing all is well, they can begin the thawing process."

Fay made an appointment with the receptionist and left the clinic happier than she'd been in a long time. Things were definitely looking up.

TWENTY-NINE

Fay had been bubbling with excitement for two whole days. She could hardly wait to get to the clinic that afternoon for the embryo transfer. She wanted more than anything to bring another baby into the world. She had decided to ask for all three embryos to be transferred. If she ended up having triplets, then that would be three times the happiness. She couldn't stop thinking about the embryos in suspended animation. Tiny little souls waiting for a chance to be born, to experience the world. It had all happened so fast and yet it felt so right.

Fay checked the time. Two hours before she was due at the clinic. Daniel was out at a meeting with Oliver Davenport about the sale of her own clinic and she'd happily left all the business arrangements with him. She had more important things to attend to now. All she wanted was to be a mother. It had been hard to keep it from Daniel, but she couldn't take the risk of him finding out. He would try to stop her, and this meant everything to her now. Nobody must stand in her way.

Fay went upstairs to Sophie's nursery. Going in there felt different. Now there was hope, not grief. The months she had spent in that room, crying, longing for Sophie and wrestling with her anger seemed like a dream. Now, it felt, after seeing

Felicia Grainger, that Sophie had given her permission to love another child. She had told her to follow her heart. "Thank you, my darling little girl," she whispered. She felt a mixture of gratitude, happiness and anticipation. In nine months, there would be a baby in this room again – maybe two or even three. She looked around the room – yes, she could easily rearrange the furniture to get three cots in there.

She opened the drawers of the cupboards one by one, taking out Sophie's clothes and imagining her new babies wearing them. She smiled as she thought of Sophie and the fun of bath time, the amusement of watching Daniel trying to change a nappy. It was going to be wonderful. They would be a truly happy family again with a future worth looking forward to. She would join the mother and baby group and make new friends. She would bore Shelly stupid with baby stories and relish her own mother being a grandmother again.

She thought of baby names as she worked her way through more of Sophie's things: her pink matinee coat that her mother had knitted, the soft white babygrows, summer dresses, a floppy sun hat, her pink and white fleece rabbit, her soft-bristled hairbrush, her plush patchwork blanket. She could sense Sophie in that room, but raw grief had become subdued beneath the excitement of having another baby.

Fay looked in the long mirror on the wardrobe door. She turned sideways and patted her tummy. Then grabbed the teddy from Sophie's cot and stuffed it under her top. She posed, imagining herself pregnant, and it felt good – felt right. Then she glanced at the clock. It was time to go. Time to have her embryos implanted. She was ecstatic with happiness for the first time in years. How could anything come between her and the little souls that would be her babies? She was going to be a mum again. Everything in their life would change and it would be wonderful. She would feel the powerful bond of love that would carry her through sleepless nights and the contentment of having a sleeping baby in her arms. Before Sophie had been born, she had no idea how big her heart would grow to accommodate her love for another little person or how much she would wonder at the tiny, fragile infant with so many needs. Soon, she would feel that again. She wanted it with the whole of her being – her body, heart and soul.

Fay almost skipped out of the house having put Chester and Ella into the Dog House. She reversed out of the driveway and flicked on the CD player. It was playing a sweet country song, "You're Gonna Be", by Reba McEntire. The emotive melody lifted her spirits and Fay sang along as she drove to the clinic. Life was good at last.

Soon, she turned into the Genesis Clinic. She parked and practically floated through the doors into reception, her spirits soaring with joy and contentment. She was going to be a mum again with three little angels sent from heaven.

"I have an appointment at 3pm with Dr Chan. For my embryo transfer." A huge grin lit up her face.

The receptionist smiled back. "Take a seat. She'll be with you in a moment."

Fay felt an inner peace, a spiritual connection to Sophie and to the babies she would be bringing into the world. Daniel would love them too; she knew he would.

"Dr Kendrick." Dr Chan stood next to Fay, her expression unreadable.

"Hello, Dr Chan." She smiled and followed her into the large, white consulting room.

"Please, take a seat." Dr Chan sat opposite, her fingers clasped together on the desk in front of her.

Fay sat in one of the armchairs, expectantly.

"I've spoken to our team of embryologists. They have thawed your three embryos and checked a number of factors: the number of cells present in each one of the blastocysts, how fast they were dividing, whether the cell division is even and whether there are any fragments of cells present – in other words, whether some cells have degenerated."

Fay felt her heart lurch with excitement. These were her babies – the precious babies she was longing for.

Dr Chan paused and reached for Fay's hand. "I'm afraid none of the embryos have survived."

THIRTY

Fay stared at Dr Chan in disbelief, her mind numb, unable to comprehend the enormity of what had happened.

"I'm so very sorry," Dr Chan was saying.

Fay tried to speak but the words were trapped in her throat. She felt like the world had collapsed around her. How could this be true? She was convinced that she would be a mother again and that her three embryos would be implanted and start to develop into three wonderful children. She was devastated.

"We can offer you counselling. We have a lovely lady here, Julia Shaw. I can get her to come in and have a chat with you?" The doctor's voice was gentle and sympathetic.

Fay felt the warmth of Dr Chan's hand on hers, heard the compassion in her voice, but now all she wanted was to get out of there. Her babies were dead. Her dreams of becoming a mother were dead. She wished *she* were dead.

Dr Chan softly asked again, "Shall I ask Julia to come and have a word with you? It might help to talk things through with someone – with a professional."

Fay shook her head. "No… thank you but I can't talk about it right now. I… I have to go." She just wanted to get away from the place – to be alone with her thoughts, her feelings of desolation.

Nothing anyone could say to her would bring back her embryos – her babies. She stood, grabbed her handbag and made for the door. "I have to go…"

"We're here for you if you need to talk," Dr Chan called after her.

Fay got through the door and ran down the corridor, through reception and out onto the front lawn of the clinic. She felt the bitter taste of bile rise in her throat and retched. She fumbled in her pocket for a tissue and wiped her mouth. She felt desolated. Her babies were dead. Sophie was dead. She had wanted them all so much, had longed to be a mother again. How could she possibly go on now? She felt the empty hollowness in her heart, the aching, the longing, the crushing disappointment. Why had this happened? Why couldn't she be allowed to have some shred of happiness? All she wanted was a baby to love and that chance had been snatched from her again. Why? Was she being punished for what she had done? Was this her retribution?

Fay walked to her car, sat in the driver's seat and slammed the door. She closed her eyes and let her forehead rest on the steering wheel, her mind numb as she absorbed the silent solitude inside the car. She sat for several minutes not knowing what to do. She felt trapped. Even tears wouldn't come. Why couldn't she cry for her babies?

She had to get away from the clinic. Go somewhere to be alone with her thoughts. She couldn't go home – not yet. Daniel would sense she was upset and would want to know what had happened. She could never tell him. She could never tell anyone. It felt too raw, too private a thing to share with anyone – even her husband. She slowly put the key in the ignition and started the engine. Raindrops fell on the windscreen as she drove away, not really knowing where she was headed.

Maybe she shouldn't be alone. Maybe she should find somewhere where there were people – life. Strangers, so she didn't have to talk. She turned the car toward town and the river, needing to be somewhere familiar. She would have a drink and calm herself, gather her thoughts, then go home.

Fay parked close to Tatiana's café but walked past it to the Cellar, an intimate wine bar overlooking the river and next to Le Petit Café de Jardin. Now all she felt was a throbbing loneliness. She ordered a bottle of New Zealand Sauvignon Blanc from the bar, paid with her debit card and found a small table near the window. There were only two couples in there, each absorbed in their own cosy conversations. Fay sat and poured herself a large glass of wine, savouring the cold, sharp tang and the citrus notes of gooseberry, tempered by passionfruit. She took another gulp, then another until the effects of alcohol tingled inside her brain. She looked out onto the river, beyond the rain-soaked window. A woman and a small child were feeding the mallards. The child was wearing a raincoat and wellingtons – bright colourful ones with yellow flowers – and they both had umbrellas. The woman had a blue one and the child a smaller, red one. The ducks were quacking and racing to get the food that was being thrown to them. That's all Fay wanted. The simple pleasures of life shared with a child of her own. It didn't seem fair. Life wasn't fair.

She swigged her wine and soon she'd drunk most of the bottle. She couldn't drive home, and she didn't want to – not yet. She emptied the bottle into her glass and signalled to the barman to bring her another.

All she wanted right then was oblivion.

THIRTY-ONE

Fay had drunk over half of a second bottle of wine before she left the Cellar. She'd walked along the riverbank for over an hour – the grey clouds and dismal rain matching her mood. Her clothes were soaked, and she was cold, but had barely noticed. Her brain was churning the same thoughts over and over – her embryos; Sophie; the mind-numbing loss she felt. She called into Tatiana's for a strong takeaway coffee and sat in the car to drink it. Finally, somehow, she had driven home.

She pulled up onto the driveway and parked next to Daniel's BMW. She could see him in the window watching for her.

Shit.

How could she explain where she had been and why she had been drinking all afternoon? She walked up the driveway as Daniel opened the front door.

"Good God, Fay, you look like a drowned rat. Where have you been? You had me worried sick." Daniel sounded concerned.

Fay took her coat off and walked into the kitchen. Chester had gone to greet her, but she ignored him. She threw her coat over the back of a chair and placed her bag on the kitchen counter.

Daniel had followed her. He turned her to face him and leaned in to kiss her. "Have you been drinking?"

She looked up into his eyes and told a bare-faced lie. "I bumped into Shelly in town, and we had a couple of wines in the Cellar." At least part of it was true.

"Well, why don't you have a hot shower and warm up? You're soaked through."

"Yes, maybe I will. The heavens opened as I was walking back to the car."

"You didn't find anything you wanted in town, then?" Daniel said pointedly when he could see she'd come home empty-handed.

"No, nothing I fancied." Fay wandered upstairs to shower.

She stood under the hot water for over fifteen minutes, letting it soothe her senses. She sobered up and knew she must sort herself out or she'd have a lot of explaining to do. She wanted to be alone but maybe it was good that Daniel was there to stop her descending into the blackness of her desolation. She began to wonder if there might be other options she could consider. Dr Chan had said the embryos could be her last chance but surely there was a way for her to be a mother again. IVF using donor eggs and sperm? Surrogacy? Donor embryos? A tiny ray of hope began to cut through the shadows of her mind. Don't give up. Something will work out, she told herself.

Fay rubbed down with a huge fluffy towel and put on comfortable black velour trousers, a long-sleeved T-shirt and slippers. She couldn't be bothered to fuss with her hair or put on make-up. It was only 5.30pm but it was already dark outside and all she wanted was to conk out for the evening and watch some mindless drivel on TV. She went down to the kitchen to find Daniel rummaging through the fridge.

"Want to go out for dinner?"

Fay couldn't face the thought of going out and having to make conversation. "Why don't we order a takeaway?"

"Good idea. Chinese?"

She wasn't hungry but drinking on an empty stomach hadn't

been a good idea. "Why not? I'll have my usual sweet and sour stir-fried veg with rice." She thought of Dr Chan and the dreadful news she'd given her that afternoon.

Daniel fished out the takeaway menu for the Red Lantern, chose a chicken curry with rice for himself and called in the order, adding some prawn crackers and crispy seaweed. "They'll deliver within the hour. Time for a snifter – fancy a glass of wine?"

Fay couldn't face the thought of it, but Daniel would be suspicious about how much she had drunk if she turned it down. "Thanks." She would just have to sip it slowly.

Daniel poured her a cold glass of Chardonnay. She took it into the living room and flopped out onto the sofa next to Maisie, who stared into her eyes as if she was trying to hypnotise her. Fay stroked her soft fur; at least she could pour out her troubles to the animals, knowing her secrets were safe.

Daniel wandered in. "You alright?"

"Yes, I'm fine. Just tired, that's all." She could never tell him what had really happened that afternoon.

Daniel seemed to accept what she had said. "I went to see Oliver. He's definitely interested in buying your clinic in Park Road – he's going to talk to his solicitor and get the ball rolling this week."

"That sounds promising. So how was he with you?"

"Fine. He was his usual self – full of his own importance. He's still working at the hospital but planning to leave the NHS in the next month or so – he reckons he's making a fortune."

"Money is all they seem to care about," Fay said with a touch of resentment. She'd always thought Oliver and his wife Melissa shallow and self-absorbed.

"He's got the first clinic up and running and it looks great." Daniel smoothed Ella's head and scratched behind her ears. "Apparently business is booming. He had a long list of clients wanting Botox and fillers."

"I know a few people that could do with that," Fay said sarcastically. "So, what's the clinic like?" Fay wasn't really interested but it seemed rude not to ask.

"It's on the corner of Abbey Road, right next to the park and just down the road from your clinic. An old Victorian detached house that's been done up. The reception area is in one of the old sitting rooms, which has been knocked into the hallway and there are several treatment rooms for aesthetic treatments downstairs. The upstairs has been converted into a modern operating suite with a recovery room and several private bedrooms for patients. He's doing a lot of face lifts, boob jobs and tummy tucks at the moment with the help of a couple of moonlighting surgeons…"

Fay tuned out as Daniel droned on about the clinic. All she could think of was the embryos and her feelings of loss.

Daniel went on. "By the way, Oliver has agreed to train me to do some Botox injections. The money would be good."

Fay nodded. All she wanted was to be left alone with her thoughts.

The takeaway arrived and Fay listened while Daniel talked about Oliver's clinic and how disappointed he was not to be going back to his old job. Finally, they went into the living room to relax for the evening. The room felt cosy with candlelight flickering around the walls and the woody smell of a fire burning in the hearth. It was their refuge from the world.

Daniel sat next to Fay on the sofa, his arm around her shoulders. She nestled into him.

"Fancy a film?" Daniel asked.

"Sure, why not? You choose."

As the theme tune for another *Star Trek* movie started, Fay thought about her embryos, Sophie's murder and the pain of grief that never seemed to go away. More than anything, she wanted another baby, but did she deserve to be a mother? She thought about her journal and the anger she had poured into it. A primitive, visceral rage that had driven her to kill. How could she live with that? She had deprived four human beings of their life and, worse, had taken pleasure from it at the time.

She could feel Daniel's rhythmic breathing next to her and the weight of his protective arm around her. A man that had stood by her through the worst of times after Sophie's murder, even though he was struggling with grief himself. He had gone through so much because of her, had compromised his own moral principles so she could evade prison. He had killed Wixx but had owned his actions – confessed and gone through the process of justice. She felt conflicted about the killings, but she had to live with the shame and abhorrence of what she'd done. It might have been better if she too had confessed. And yet she knew that prison would break her. She would rather die than spend the rest of her life without her freedom. Without Daniel. Without the chance of another baby.

Like a pair of binary stars trapped in a gravity embrace, they shared a deadly secret that would bind them together forever.

Fay was beginning to wonder if she could live with it.

THIRTY-TWO

Ricardo Estevez had arrived early for work on Monday morning and was sitting in his office with a strong black coffee reading old news stories online about Daniel Kendrick. He'd heard the hospital rumours, of course, but it was only now that he'd met the man himself that he wanted to know more about him. He had shaken Kendrick's hand – the hand that had fatally crushed his victim's throat. What had driven him to that? He'd read that Damon Wixx had confessed to being the serial killer that had terrorised the Riverbeke area for months and, since the killings had stopped, it had been accepted as true. The murdered victims themselves had been killers and paedophiles – some would say they were no real loss to society. He wondered if that had influenced the jury's decision to acquit – but, whatever it was, Kendrick had been judged innocent and he had no problem with that.

Death had always held a fascination for Rick, ever since he had lost his wife and son in that fateful car crash on an *autovia* just outside Barcelona. He had been responsible for their deaths – had been texting while driving, despite Maria rebuking him for it just seconds before the crash. He had never forgiven himself for that. In a way, he understood the pain that Kendrick and his wife had gone through after losing their daughter. The aftermath of the crash had been the driving force for him leaving Spain after the damaging fallout with the family. His mother, Benicia, had been more understanding and, he had to admit, he missed her. But his father, Felipe, and to an extent his brother Lucero, had effectively disowned him. Maria's family wanted no more to do with him either and that was understandable.

Now Clarissa wanted him to attend her wedding. He'd managed to stall her, but she had texted him earlier that morning, prompting him for an answer. He'd ignored it, not knowing what to say. Their brother Lucero had been diagnosed with prion disease, a fatal neurodegenerative disease caused by the misfolding of proteins in the brain. He had less than three months to live, yet Rick couldn't face going back there with all the memories and the dragging up of the past it would entail.

Then Rick heard a commotion on the ward and went out to see what was going on. Halfway along the female side of the Nightingale ward, several nurses gathered around the bed of one of the patients, Jean Wyatt. The alarm on her heart monitor was going crazy.

"What's up?" Rick asked one of the senior staff nurses.

Jackie Hines, a tall woman in her thirties with a long horsey face etched with a permanently sad expression, was trying to calm her patient. "She's become really anxious, and her heart rate has skyrocketed. She has chest pains."

Rick glanced at the monitor. Her heart rate was 120 bpm, blood pressure just 90/50 mmHg, and her respirations were rapid. He grabbed her notes and quickly read the summary that she'd had lung cancer three years ago, treated with surgery and extensive chemotherapy but, despite this, she had recently been diagnosed with metastases and had been admitted for a liver lobectomy. He quickly checked her recent bloods and they were within normal parameters.

"OK, let's have a look at you," he said. He rubbed sanitiser into his hands and placed a reassuring hand on her arm.

Her eyes were dark and wide with fear, her breathing shallow and rapid. He placed a finger across her jugular vein. "We have an elevated jugular pressure, and her trace is showing electrical alternans – alternate height and beat to beat variation in the QRS complex."

Nurse Hines peered at the monitor. "So, what does it mean?" She stood at the opposite side of the bed, holding her patient's hand. With her free hand she silenced the persistent bonging of the alarm.

"Essentially her heart is wobbling inside a fluid filled pericardial sac – the sac around the heart." He felt the pulse at her wrist, then watched the heart monitor. "I can also feel a distinct paradoxic pulse – her blood pressure is dropping each time she takes a breath in." He looked around the room. "Aren't there any doctors on the ward?"

"They're busy with an emergency in one of the side rooms."

The patient was clearly frightened and struggling to breathe, her eyes darting between Rick and the nurse.

"I think it's a cardiac tamponade. We'd better get the on-call cardiothoracic surgeon up here." He turned to one of the other nurses. "Can you fast bleep them, please, and order an urgent electrocardiogram?"

The nurse nodded and rushed off to the phone at the nurses' station.

Rick glanced at the monitor, then back to his patient. "How are the chest pains, Mrs Wyatt?"

"Getting worse."

He turned to Nurse Hines once more. "I think, given her history of malignancy, elevated jugular pressure, chest pain and difficulty breathing, I'm certain it's a tamponade. She might need a pericardiocentesis – a surgical drainage of the pericardium."

Rick monitored the woman for a few minutes, keeping a careful eye on her vital signs. He listened to her heart with his stethoscope and could hear strange distant sounds, another indication of a tamponade. He knew only too well that the condition was a medical emergency and could be fatal if not promptly dealt with. "Where the hell is the cardiothoracic surgeon?"

The nurse rushed back to the bedside. "I've bleeped Mr Pendelton but he's not answering his bleep. Mr Abara is tied up in theatre."

Rick thought for some moments. The woman's chest pain was becoming more severe, her breathing was laboured, and the ECG was all over the place. His decision was made. "I'll have to perform an emergency pericardiocentesis." He turned to Nurse Hines. "Get me a surgical pack, please, and a pair of sterile gloves, size eight."

He turned to the patient. "Mrs Wyatt, you have what is known as a cardiac tamponade. That means you have some fluid in the sac that surrounds your heart and is causing your symptoms. I'm going to have to perform a surgical drainage of this fluid. We can do it here on the ward. I will have to insert a needle into the sac around your heart and draw out the fluid. That should relieve these symptoms."

The patient nodded. "Yes, go ahead," she said breathlessly.

Nurse Hines returned with a stainless-steel trolley holding a sterile pack, gloves, drainage needle and tubing. She drew the curtains around the bed and tried to reassure her patient.

Rick glanced at the heart monitor. The patient's blood pressure was falling dangerously, and her heart rate was erratic and climbing. He would have preferred to wait for the echocardiograph that would help to guide the needle to the pericardial sac, but the situation had become a medical emergency – he had to act now to save his patient's life.

"We'll have to go ahead without the echo," he told Nurse Hines.

She opened the sterile pack, filled the plastic pots with sterilising fluid and tipped out the drainage equipment from its packaging. Rick pulled off his tie and pushed it into his pocket, rolled up his sleeves and put on a plastic apron that was handed to him. Another nurse exposed Mrs Wyatt's chest and made her comfortable for the procedure. She once again silenced the bonging alarm on the heart monitor when the mute had timed out. The trace showed there was no time to lose; she was on the verge of a sudden haemodynamic collapse. A nurse was at her side, trying to reassure her.

Rick snapped on sterile gloves, cleaned an area of Mrs Wyatt's chest and began to insert the needle at a fifteen-degree angle between her xiphoid and left costal margin, plunging it toward her heart. He then expertly lowered the needle, advancing it toward the tip of the left scapular while aspirating. Once Rick was into the pericardium, he inserted a J-tipped guidewire and exchanged the needle for a pig-tailed catheter that was left on continuous drainage. Thanks to his skill and experience as a cardiothoracic surgeon he'd avoided puncturing her lungs or heart – all without the guidance of an electrocardiograph. He had saved his patient's life.

Within minutes, over 450 ml of pericardial fluid had been drained and, gradually, Jean Wyatt's heart trace was beginning to return to a more normal PQRS wave. Her systolic blood pressure began to climb above 110 mmHg and her breathing slowed a little.

"Alright, Mrs Wyatt. I've managed to drain some fluid away from your heart and things are settling down. Are you feeling a little better?"

Jean Wyatt nodded. "It was very painful but I'm grateful. Thank you, doctor."

Rick turned to Nurse Hines. "She'll need careful monitoring for a while. Will you order a portable chest X-ray, please?"

Rick Estevez basked in the thrill of performing a life-saving procedure, revelling in his skill as a doctor and the power of being able to bring someone back from the brink of death. It was only 9am and he'd already had his fix for the day.

THIRTY-THREE

Daniel had crept out of bed early, trying not to disturb Fay. All weekend, she'd seemed quiet and withdrawn. Her mood, like much of nature, fluctuated with the phases of the moon, but something had been bothering her. She didn't seem to want to talk about it, but he'd put it down to the emotional wrench of burning her journal and all the feelings of grief and anger that had been raked up all over again.

It was 7am, still dark, but dawn was just over the horizon. Daniel put on a headtorch and walked the dogs up the street and through the kissing gate, into the woods. They happily bounded off ahead in the gloom. Ella was panting with excitement. Daniel felt apprehensive. It was Monday morning and his first day back at Riverbeke General. It had been a deeply disappointing blow to be told that someone else had taken his job, but he understood that the needs of patients and the hospital had to come first. Somehow, he would make the best of his demotion and hopefully, in time, he might be offered a more senior post. He would just have to work hard to prove himself and regain the trust of his colleagues. With the extra work at Oliver's clinic, he might just make ends meet financially. He just hoped he and Ricardo Estevez would be able to rub along somehow.

He thew a stick for Chester and the Great Dane lolloped after it – his long, powerful legs covering ground effortlessly. Ella was engrossed in the smells at the base of a gnarled oak tree and was lagging behind. Sheep were lying in the fields, their eye shine reflecting the light from the torch. Ahead, a waning gibbous moon and Venus were bright in the sky and moving toward the western horizon and he could hear dairy cows lowing from the farm in the distance. They had been taken into the farmyard for the winter – prisoners themselves through the cold dark months. He checked his watch: 7.30am. He would have to get back. "Come on, you two." He whistled for the dogs to follow him and headed for home.

The horizon was glowing with a faint rosy luminosity as he headed back toward the kissing gate. He stood awhile to watch as the dawn painted banks of fluffy white clouds with a meld of intense colours. Shafts of pure, golden light burst from the sun as it lifted from the horizon and shone its life-giving radiance into the world, drenching the landscape and sending nocturnal animals to their daytime hideaways. Ragged wisps of cloud drifted along the sky as the Earth rolled into a new day.

Daniel had missed the rhythms of nature, the sheer spectacle of beauty and the magnificence of our planet. The sun rose every morning, life went on and he knew that, somehow, he would prevail.

He noticed a plane's contrail in the sky and briefly wondered where it was going. A winter holiday in the sunshine, perhaps. He would love to take Fay somewhere warm, to lift their spirits after the trauma they had been through, but his career had to come first. He needed to feel the security of a job and to rebuild the esteem and recognition at work that had been compromised by his time in prison. The dogs followed him through the gate and back home. He fed them and let them have the run of the garden. Maisie had brought in a mouse and had eaten most of it on the kitchen floor. The remains, a head, foot and intact stomach, lay as a gruesome reminder of the wild side of her nature.

"Thanks for that, Maisie," he said as she watched him disdainfully. He dutifully cleaned up the carnage, showered and put on black chinos with a blue stripped shirt, open at the collar, under a charcoal sports jacket. He grabbed his new swipe card and slipped the lanyard over his neck, checked he had his wallet and phone and went upstairs to say goodbye.

Fay was still in bed, only half-awake.

"I'm off to work now, sweetheart. The dogs are loose in the garden, but they've had a quick walk and been fed." He sat at the side of the bed and smoothed her wayward hair.

Still sleepy, she looked at him and smiled. "Have a good day. I'll be in to see Doug later about the research project."

"OK. See you at the hospital." He kissed her warm, soft lips.

Daniel inched the BMW through the rush-hour traffic but still managed to reach the hospital in good time to park and grab a takeaway coffee and a Mars bar from the kiosk. He took the stairs to the ward. He had no idea where he would be needed but Colin would, no doubt, let him know. Swiping himself into the ward, he walked along the corridor to the nurses' station.

"Just missed all the action," Nurse Hines said with a smile as she looked up from sorting through a pile of blood results.

"Oh? What happened?" Daniel asked.

"Jean Wyatt suffered a cardiac tamponade and Mr Estevez did an emergency pericardiocentesis."

"Crikey, is she alright?"

"Yes, it was touch and go for a while but she's recovering now. We'll send her to the HDU for monitoring."

"A good call, then." Daniel had missed a tamponade diagnosis a few years back but thankfully it had worked out alright.

Daniel wandered over to Colin Mathias's office. The door was open, and Colin was throwing his jacket over the back of his squeaky swivel chair. His hair was still damp from the shower, and he was wearing a lilac shirt that was pulled tight around his paunch.

"Daniel, come in. Looks like we missed the excitement this morning. Good job Rick was early."

"Yes, so I hear."

"I think we could use you on the ward here today." Colin fired up his laptop and flicked the kettle on in the corner of his office. "Rick has a full theatre list this afternoon and one of the SHOs has called in sick. High dependency is also busy so maybe you could float between the two."

"Fine," Daniel said. His demotion still felt weird, but he reasoned he could do without the pressure of a consultant's role right now.

"By the way, there's a clinical drug trial starting in the department today. It's being overseen by Dr Isobel Duncan. Not a medical doctor; she has a PhD in medicinal chemistry. I guess she will give you all a talk about it at some point."

Colin chomped on a biscuit as he made himself a cup of tea, tossed the used teabag into the bin and checked the clock on the wall. It was 9am. "Ward round with Rick and handover in thirty minutes, then," he said, spitting biscuit crumbs.

Suddenly, Daniel felt awkward. In the past, the two men would have chatted in Colin's office over their morning cuppa, but now he sensed he should know his place and join the other SHOs. "I'll acquaint myself with the patients. See you later."

Daniel made his way to the nurses' station and the trolley that contained the patients' notes, binning his half-drunk coffee on the way. He began leafing through, noting in his peripheral vision the stares of several of the staff. Would people only ever see him as a convict – being defined by his crime – even though he had been acquitted in a court of law? He felt judged all over again. What was going through the minds of these people? Were they feeling apprehensive? Morally superior? What would it take for him to be accepted again? He sensed someone behind him.

"Morning, Dr Kendrick." It was the Spanish lilt of Ricardo Estevez.

Daniel twisted his head to look at Rick. "Morning." His smile was not returned.

"I'd like you to join the ward round."

"Yes, of course," Daniel said, feeling undermined by the authoritative tone of Rick's voice.

"Dr Isobel Duncan is giving a briefing about the new drug trial in the main ward office at 11am. You will need to attend." Rick was clearly starting to assert his authority.

Like a pair of rhinos, they weren't entirely comfortable in each other's company.

Daniel spent the next twenty-five minutes flicking through the patients' notes before Rick appeared with his entourage of junior doctors, SHOs, and Matt Clarke, the specialist registrar, along with senior staff nurse Jackie Hines, to begin the ward round. Daniel trailed along awkwardly with the others, more used to leading than following.

Rick stopped at the first room near the entrance to the ward; in one of the four beds lay a sixty-five-year-old man wearing brightly patterned pyjamas. He had been reading a sailing magazine. Nurse Hines handed Rick the patient's notes and he flicked through, checking blood results and the report from a colonoscopy.

Rick looked at the patient. "So, Mr Jenkins, how long have you had diverticulitis?"

The patient looked pale and tired, his thick brown hair sticking out in all directions. "At least ten years but it's been worse lately." He rubbed a hand over his tummy. "I had a camera up the er… you know, my bottom." He looked decidedly embarrassed.

"Yes, I see you presented with a fever and pain low on your left side. Your colonoscopy and subsequent CT scan revealed quite severe diverticular disease and it doesn't seem to be responding to conservative treatment. I think we should perform a laparoscopic colonic resection to remove a small part of your bowel." Rick placed a hand on the man's lower abdomen and pressed down gently.

The man winced in pain. He glanced at Matt, then one of the junior doctors, Daniel and back to Rick, as if asking for a simple explanation.

"It's a very safe procedure, Mr Jenkins, and we should have you home in a few days. We could fit you in this afternoon."

The man still looked baffled as Rick moved on to the next patient.

Daniel signalled to the man that he would come back and explain.

Rick stopped again at another bed in the four-bedded room and was handed the patient's notes, which he flicked through. The patient, a man in his mid-twenties, was recovering from a laparoscopic appendicectomy. "How are you feeling, Mr Price?"

"It's a bit painful but otherwise I'm fine." The man had an expectant look on his face and was eagerly watching Rick's expression.

"Wound OK?" Rick asked Nurse Hines.

"Yes, clean and healing well."

Rick turned to the patient. "I think we can let you go home this morning."

The man thanked him profusely and texted his wife to fetch him.

The entourage dutifully followed Rick into one of the single-bedded rooms along the corridor. An elderly patient lay on the bed, the translucent pallor of his face almost as white as the pillow. He reluctantly opened his eyes at the disturbance. The room smelled of disinfectant and the untouched breakfast that had been left beside the bed.

Matt Clarke stepped forward to hand Rick the man's notes and give an update to the group. "This is Mr Ray Willet, a ninety-four-year-old man who had a surgical resection for a metastatic stage IV colon cancer six months ago. However, the cancer has spread and become inoperable. He's had palliative chemotherapy and is now waiting to go to St Anne's Hospice, when a bed becomes available, for end-of-life care. We are giving him diamorphine for pain." Matt smiled sympathetically at the man, who nodded a slight acknowledgement back.

Daniel's heart went out to the man. He looked exhausted and frail, his skeletal body ravaged by cancer. Nurse Hines gestured for one of the nursing assistants to remove the breakfast tray and she offered Mr Willet a drink of weakly diluted orange squash through a straw. He took a few sips before closing his weary eyes once again.

Rick closed the notes and handed them back to Matt. "OK, keep him comfortable."

The entourage moved on through the ward. Jean Wyatt's cardiac tamponade was reviewed by the cardiothoracic team, and she was transferred to the high-dependency unit for further monitoring. Daniel was given a stack of discharge letters to write. Great, he thought, he'd gone from running the show as a consultant to running errands and doing everyone else's paperwork. Still, he ought to feel grateful to have a job at all – it would all work out, he told himself, hopefully.

Rick was rounding up doctors and nursing staff for the briefing on the clinical trial. "Briefing starts in ten minutes," he told them.

Daniel remembered he had to explain to Mr Jenkins about the laparoscopic colonic resection he was about to undergo. He would just about have time before the briefing. He found the patient and explained the procedure, but he didn't seem happy about it. It took several more explanations before he understood what was going to happen to him.

"It's a very safe procedure, Mr Jenkins," Daniel told him. "Your recovery will be quicker with the laparoscopic procedure and there are fewer complications than with conventional surgery. Also, there is less chance of a wound infection." He waited for the patient to confirm that he understood.

"Yes, alright, thank you, doctor. It sounds like it's the best option for me."

"I think it is," Daniel said. He looked up at the clock on the wall: 11.07am. Shit, he was late for the briefing. "I have to go, I'm afraid, but do let me know if you have any further worries."

Daniel rushed to the meeting room, dodging trolleys and busy nurses along the way. The briefing had started, and everyone turned to stare as he managed to find a seat at the back of the room. Dr Isobel Duncan was just finishing up an introduction about herself and the project. Rick glared at him but said nothing; Oliver Davenport nodded from the other side of the room; Matt pretended not to notice. Daniel felt awkward but his patient's needs had to come first.

Isobel Duncan continued, unperturbed, to address her audience. Daniel just about caught the details before she flicked to the next slide on her PowerPoint presentation: a professional-looking summary of the clinical trial.

She was the head of a small biotech company, Regenex Biologics, who were developing a new antibiotic, Bravafloxacin. She also, on occasion, collaborated with Trevelyan, Madigan and Winslow Pharmaceuticals – TMW.

Isobel continued. "So, the first stage is the pre-clinical testing which involves two studies on at least two different non-human animal species – in this instance, rats and dogs – to determine the toxic effects of high single doses and investigate the longer-term effect of repeated doses."

Isobel was lean, beautiful and perfectly groomed. She had delicate features and her long blonde hair was swept up into a chignon, her make-up and jewellery tastefully understated. She wore a Valentino dusky pink business suit with a pencil skirt and a jacket that was nipped in at the waist over an ivory silk blouse. She stood in four-inch heels and was every bit the professional representing her company. Daniel thought she looked like an ice maiden.

She flicked to the next slide, titled *Phase 1 Clinical Trials.* "Then, we test to see how well the product is tolerated in healthy volunteers."

One of the doctors piped up. "Who are the volunteers and what is the risk to them?"

Isobel looked at him directly as she gave her answer. "Volunteers are usually healthy young men in the first instance. Any clinical trial is not without risk to health but in this case there were no major concerns."

Some bright spark interjected before she could continue. "How much did they get paid?" He chuckled for no apparent reason.

Isobel twisted on her heels to face the man. "They all received £1,500 each for their contribution to science." Without turning a hair, she carried on, clicking over to the next slide. "The next phase is where we are now. Phase 2 clinical trials. This is where we test the drug in selected patients known to have the disease the drug is intended for. We are looking for efficacy – in other words, does it work in the real world?" She clicked on to the next slide, a schematic of the drug's formulation.

Daniel glanced at Rick, who was standing near the front. He was watching Isobel intently. She smiled at Rick and he gave her a little wink back. They were obviously an item.

Isobel continued. "So, the drug we are testing, Bravafloxacin, is a broad-spectrum antibiotic and will be given as an intravenous injection or infusion."

There was a brief knock on the door and one of the junior nurses came in, scanned the room, saw Nurse Hines and summoned her with a hand. "Sorry – Jackie, you're needed on the ward."

Jackie Hines gave her apologies and left the room.

Isobel continued, clicking to the next slide. "Now, this will be a double-blind placebo-controlled trial. All this means is that some patients will get the actual drug and some will get a placebo – a harmless saline solution. This is standard procedure and is meant to remove bias and make sure the patients, clinicians or researchers don't know who is getting what until the end of the trial."

"So how will that work in practice on the ward?" one of the nurses asked.

"A computer gives each patient a code number, which is then allocated to the different treatment groups. The treatment arrives on the ward with the code number on it."

The nurse nodded but was still not happy. "If one of the patients had a reaction to the drug, how would we know if it was the experimental drug so that we could treat the patient accordingly?"

"In an emergency, researchers could find out which group the patient was in but, generally, no one knows until the trial has finished."

After thirty minutes, Rick pointedly looked at his watch and signalled to Isobel that she should wind up the briefing. She rushed through the final two slides, thanked everyone and reminded them that the trial was starting that day.

Daniel filed out of the room with the rest of them, then Oliver Davenport tapped his arm as he was dashing off. "Good to see you back. By the way, we must get you going with the Botox at the clinic."

"Sure. Let's talk soon." He wasn't relishing the idea but he would have to just get on with it if he was going to make ends meet.

Daniel walked the length of the corridor, dodging trolleys and a patient wheeling a drip stand, whose gown was flapping open at the back to reveal grimy boxer shorts and a pair of pale, skinny legs.

Then, in the corridor, he saw a familiar face. One of the cleaners was an ex-convict – he had served his sentence and had been discharged from prison a week after Daniel had arrived at HMP Ravenwood but not before the two of them had had a minor skirmish. Daniel's brain blanked for a moment before he recalled his name – Eddie Bates – that was it. He'd been sentenced to five years for manslaughter when a burglary had gone wrong. He'd shot and killed an elderly lady at point-blank range. She'd died instantly.

Bates looked up from mopping the floor and stared at Daniel, an acidic smirk of recognition spreading slowly across his ugly, pock-marked face.

THIRTY-FOUR

Fay had finally managed to drag herself out of bed and get to Doug's office in the new wing of Riverbeke General. She had talked herself into a brighter mood during the journey, but it had taken two strong coffees, a CD of feel-good songs and some bright November sunshine to get her there. Her thoughts kept going back to her three embryos and the loss she felt but she had to get her act together; she had work to do and maybe the project would take her mind off things. Now she was sitting with Doug Winters in the cluttered office he shared with his wife, Shelly – it looked like a poltergeist had been busy in there. Doug had been going through the research project they were embarking on, "The Psychology of Near-Death Experiences in a Hospital Setting".

"Alright, Fay, so the main thing is to find patients following a cardiac arrest or other near-death experience and go through the questionnaire with them. We're looking for any psychological issues, not necessarily proof of life after death."

"So, do you want me to put symbols up near the ceiling and stuff like that?" Fay asked.

Doug gave a small laugh. "No, we don't need that sort of thing. That's covered in other types of research. Just stick to the questionnaire."

"Fair enough," Fay said.

"Shall we go over to the ICU and introduce ourselves? I did warn the unit manager and she is expecting us." Doug stood and grabbed his battered briefcase.

Fay joined him and they strolled along the corridor, chatting about the study. They took the lift to the ground floor and walked the short distance through the hospital grounds to the main entrance, dodging several patients in hospital gowns puffing on cigarettes outside. They walked through the vast concourse lined with shops and cafés and took the lift to the third floor, turned left and found the ICU and HDU, which were within the same unit, separated by a short, internal corridor. Doug pressed the intercom and they were buzzed in. Within a few minutes, Angela greeted them. A tallish woman with an hourglass figure, sleek brunette hair swept into a ponytail with a heavy blunt-cut fringe, she had a soft, friendly face.

"Professor Winters." She extended her hand to shake his, then turned to Fay. "And you must be Fay – Daniel's wife. Good to meet you." The women shook hands. "So, you're going to do some research on near-death experiences, I hear."

Fay smiled. "Yes, if that's alright with you."

"Yes, of course. I've had a long chat with Professor Winters, and it would be a good thing to have some research done into this. Some patients welcome the opportunity to talk about their experiences and try to make sense of them, but the nurses don't always have time and our psychologist is on maternity leave for the next few months. In fact, we have one patient in the HDU who said she would be very happy to have a chat with you. Would you like to meet her now?"

Fay glanced at Doug, and he nodded his agreement. "That would be lovely."

They followed Angela into the unit and she filled them in on the patient's condition. "Mrs Jacobs had a cardiac arrest just yesterday and was very lucky to survive. She was clinically dead for six minutes during her resuscitation and has only just begun to tell us about the strange experience she had. She's recovering very well and should be able to go to the ward in a day or so."

They passed several beds, all with patients hooked up to heart monitors, some with oxygen masks and intravenous infusions, others with various drainage bags attached to the side of their bed. Then Fay noticed a woman who was obviously heavily pregnant, on a life support machine. She couldn't help staring – she looked so young and vulnerable. She wondered what awful tragedy had left her in that state.

Angela stopped at the bedside of a kindly-looking lady in her late fifties with short greying hair and a pleasant, rounded face. She was reclined in her bed with an oxygen canula in her nostrils, the clear plastic tubing tracing the line of her cheekbones and disappearing into her hairline. Her eyes, a striking ice blue, seemed to be scanning the room.

"Mrs Jacobs, I have with me the lady I told you about, Dr Fay Kendrick. She's a psychiatrist and would love to have a little chat with you, if that's alright."

Mrs Jacobs nodded, her eyes scanning Angela. "Yes, of course. I'd be happy to. It would break the monotony of being in here." She gave a little laugh.

Doug and Angela excused themselves and Fay found a chair and sat at the patient's bedside. She couldn't help glancing over to the young pregnant woman, who was opposite. She pulled out a sheaf of papers from a folder Doug had given her and selected the questionnaire and a blue biro. "It's nice to meet you, Mrs Jacobs. I hope you're feeling better now."

The patient reached out her hand as if she wanted to touch Fay. "Yes, I'm feeling fine now. These people do wonderful work here. Saved my life."

Fay instinctively put her hand over Mrs Jacobs's and gave it a little squeeze. She briefly looked at the questionnaire and decided to abandon it for now and just chat. "Why don't you tell me what happened?"

"Well" – she cleared her throat – "one minute I was having the most dreadful pain in my chest and the next I felt myself lifting upwards and out of my body. It was the strangest *whooshing* feeling. I could see everything around me, and the doctors and nurses were rushing to help me – it was absolutely astounding and very real. One nurse took my false teeth out and put them on the shelf behind me." She laughed. "I had to remind her where they were when I came around."

Fay laughed along with her and squeezed her hand once more. Mrs Jacobs didn't seem to want to let go, and Fay was happy to hold her hand while she explained her extraordinary experience.

"From above, I could see a very handsome doctor, tall, dark and quite rugged-looking. He had a heavy Spanish accent and was the one trying to save me. He was pumping my chest and shouting orders to everyone. He called for a crash trolley and the red-haired nurse went running off to fetch it. I recognised his accent – he had been with me just before I had my heart attack. It was lucky he was there just at the right time. He saved my life, and I can never thank him enough."

Fay smiled. "That's amazing."

Mrs Jacobs continued. "Anyway, all the pain had stopped, and I could see my body on the bed as I floated up through the ceiling. I could see the hospital grounds and the town all around me. It was the most incredible sight. Then, suddenly, I was in a dark tunnel whooshing toward a very bright light and all I could feel was love – the most intense, unconditional love and peace coming from the light. It was like nothing here on Earth." She paused and smiled as she recalled her experience.

Fay wondered if Sophie had felt that love and peace when she had died. She glanced again at the pregnant woman. Would she and her baby survive whatever it was they had experienced?

Mrs Jacobs's eyes were rolling back and forth as she continued her recollection. "Then the tunnel opened into a beautiful landscape, and I was greeted by my mother and grandmother and some of the pets I'd had as a child. They looked like beings of light and they spoke to me via their thoughts. I was guided through some vivid memories of my life; experiencing them again just as I had the first time but incredibly quickly and all at once. Then my grandmother told me that I couldn't stay – not this time. She said that I still had things to achieve. That it wasn't my time to die and that I would understand soon. Suddenly, I was whooshing back into my body, and I felt the pain in my chest again and a lot of noise and people around me."

"That's an amazing experience, Mrs Jacobs." Fay wondered if anyone had greeted Sophie. Her great-grandmother? An uncle that had died years before? Yet Sophie was too young to know anyone who had passed on. "Were you frightened at all?"

"No – not in the least. And now I'm not afraid to die. Where my spirit went was the most unimaginably beautiful place. It felt like I was going home."

"It must have been an incredible thing to see and experience."

"It was, my dear. It was a complete revelation – especially since I've been blind since birth."

THIRTY-FIVE

Daniel had sidled around Eddie Bates but didn't speak to him. He wondered how he managed to get a job in the hospital, so close to patients on the ward. Had he lied about his prison sentence? It bothered him as he made a start on the day's workload. He had replaced a patient's chest drain, written up some post-op medication and caught up with some of the discharge letters. Then he went to find Colin Mathias. This thing with Eddie Bates was bugging him.

Mathias's door was ajar, and Daniel knocked twice.

"Come," Mathias boomed.

Daniel went in, closed the door and sat when prompted.

"How are you settling in? Not too dull for you, I hope." Mathias sat in his squeaky chair and had been scrutinising a data set of recent hospital admissions.

"It's fine. Nice to be back at work. I just wanted to check something with you, Colin."

"Fire away," he said, taking off his glasses and looking directly at Daniel.

"One of the cleaners on the ward – Eddie Bates – he's an ex-con. Just wondering how he managed to get a job so close to the patients. It seems a bit risky to me."

Mathias stiffened and his bushy eyebrows flew upwards, crinkling his forehead into a series of deep furrows. "And have you wondered how you managed to get a job that allows *you* to have patients' lives in your hands?" He shifted in his chair, leaning forward slightly, obviously irritated. "I know you were acquitted but you admitted murdering someone – and you now have a job as a doctor here. Shouldn't we be wondering about that?" Mathias waited coolly for an answer.

Daniel was taken aback at Colin's response. Only the other day he had given Daniel his unqualified support. The irony had escaped him, but it hit him now with its full force. Did people think that he shouldn't be around patients? Did they feel the same preconceptions about him that he was feeling about Bates right now? He started to feel indignant; surely, he wasn't in the same category as Bates. "But, Colin, I was in prison with him briefly and he was a scumbag. Plus, he's made a career out of robbing innocent people – armed robbery at that – and he killed that defenceless old lady at point-blank range. Oh… he's also a known drug dealer and now he's around old ladies and drugs on the ward."

Mathias sighed, visibly trying to calm his annoyance. "Look, on release from prison, individuals can work and have full employee rights – including Edward Bates. We did everything on the level and work with the New Futures Network to interview prospective candidates before they are even released and we've chosen the best person for the job, in my opinion."

Daniel remembered Bates and his arrogant behaviour, but it was typical of Colin to see the good in everyone.

"But how do you know you can trust him? He's a thief."

"Look, Edward wants the opportunity to get his life back on track. Just like you." Colin shot him a warning look… *don't pursue this any further.*

Daniel still felt uneasy about Bates but maybe he was projecting his experience of prison onto Bates unfairly. After all, he knew him only slightly. "Alright, Colin," he conceded. "I didn't realise he'd been employed through the proper channels. I just wondered if he'd lied about his criminal record."

Colin seemed to relax. "It's OK. At least you brought it to my attention and we're on the same page about it now. Edward seems to be getting on well with his colleagues and is chatty with the patients. They need to see a friendly face around here."

"Well... I'll get back to it, then." Daniel stood and left Mathias's office. His instincts told him to be wary of Bates, but he would have to back down. At least he'd ruled out the possibility that Bates had got the job through deception.

He spoke to some relatives that were concerned about their daughter's operation and seemed to have been able to alleviate their fears, then he spoke with Isobel Duncan, the clinical trial lead, about some possible minor side effects one of the patients in the trial had experienced. Isobel had reassured him there was nothing to worry about and he relayed that to the patient.

He then went to find Matt to check the theatre schedule for the afternoon since there was a query about one of the elective procedures. He found Matt in a side room talking with Mr Ray Willet, the ninety-four-year-old patient with inoperable colon cancer. The door was closed but Daniel could see them through the window panel. Matt was holding the man's hand, obviously listening and nodding sympathetically. It looked like a private conversation and Mr Willet seemed in some distress. Daniel decided to leave them alone and go back later. He checked on a few of his patients and wrote up some alternative antibiotics for a nasty wound infection that hadn't been responding to treatment. Then he went back to Mr Willet's side room. Matt was still in there, about to give an intravenous drug into the canula in the back of the man's hand. Matt looked up and gestured for him to go in.

"Everything alright on the ward?" Matt asked as he gave the canula a saline flush prior to giving the drug.

"Yes, fine. I just wanted to go over the theatre schedule with you, but it can wait."

"Sorry I've been so long. Mr Willet and I have had a long chat. I'm just giving him some diamorphine."

"Any news on when we can transfer him to the hospice? I'm sure he'd be more comfortable there," Daniel said.

Matt's bleep went off. He checked it. "Sorry, I have to go – emergency on HDU. Can you finish giving this for me?" Matt stood aside to let Daniel finish administering the diamorphine and rushed off down the corridor.

Daniel stood by Mr Willet's bedside and slowly gave the diamorphine. The poor man looked exhausted, pale and emaciated. He had been given just weeks to live. Daniel noticed the man's notes open on the bed. There was a DNR order – do not resuscitate – which had been dated and signed by Mr Willet earlier in the day. Daniel felt sad for the man. He didn't seem to receive any visitors, and nobody had called the ward to enquire after him. No children or grandchildren; no nieces, nephews, friends or people from his community. Daniel knew there were desperately lonely people out there, just like him, with no one to care about them. It had been a long wait for a place at the hospice, which was dependent on someone dying to free up a bed. They had done their best on the ward to give him some dignity and privacy, but it was a busy place, and the hospice would at least afford him some peace and quiet with dedicated and skilled palliative care.

"Alright, Mr Willet. All done. Hopefully that should relieve your pain in a few minutes." Daniel withdrew the empty syringe. He gave the man's arm a gentle, reassuring rub and pulled the blanket up around his chest.

Mr Willet opened his eyes briefly. They were the eyes of a man desperate to be released from his suffering. "Thank you, I'm very grateful." His voice was weak and barely audible.

"That's alright. Get some rest now." Daniel began to gather

up the man's notes to leave but Mr Willet feebly grabbed at his hand.

"Please, doctor. Stay with me." His yellowing eyes betrayed a fleeting fear as he implored Daniel to stay.

"OK, Mr Willet, I'll stay with you. You'll be alight." Daniel dragged a stool close to the patient's bedside, sat and cupped the man's cold, fragile hand between both of his.

Mr Willet's face relaxed and he gave Daniel's hand a brittle squeeze, nodding his appreciation. Within minutes, the man's breathing became shallower and began to rattle in his chest. His half-closed eyes stared sightlessly ahead, and his lips worked inaudibly as if he was speaking to an unseen entity. His breathing was becoming barely perceptible, and his skin had turned ashen-grey. Daniel knew he was close to death but how did it happen so soon? His prognosis was that he had several weeks left to live and earlier, he didn't look as if death was imminent. His instincts were to try to rouse him but that would only prolong his discomfort. He looked so peaceful now and close to slipping from this world and into the next.

"It's alright, I'm here with you." He gave the man's hand a gentle squeeze, trying to reassure him. He would respect the man's wishes and the DNR order – he had no choice. This was no time for heroic life-saving actions. It was a time for dignity, peaceful acceptance and the compassion of one human being to another.

Ray Willet died peacefully on the ward amid the distant sounds of trolleys clattering down the corridor, the bonging of cardiac monitors and the constant hum of voices, his hand still cocooned in Daniel's.

THIRTY-SIX

Daniel had pronounced Ray Willet dead at 14.06 and Jackie Hines and an assistant nurse had laid him out after respectfully leaving his body covered with a sheet for just over an hour – an old ritual among many of the nurses. There were no relatives to call with the news, but the hospital chaplain was informed, and the man's body was taken to the morgue, or "Rose Cottage" as it was wistfully referred to. There would be no post-mortem, no enquiry. His was an expected death.

Matt had finally returned to the ward and Daniel asked to see him in the now empty side room. He closed the door behind them, lowering his voice, aware of people constantly passing in the corridor. "Matt, what's going on? Mr Willet died minutes after that IV. What the hell was in the syringe?"

Matt looked away and shifted awkwardly on his feet. He seemed reluctant to say anything. Finally, he spoke. "He'd been begging me for days to let him go peacefully – to give him an overdose of diamorphine. I only wanted to help him."

Daniel ushered Matt further into the room away from the door. "But surely you had his pain under control? He was meant to be going to St Anne's for a peaceful death. Matt… I gave him that injection." Daniel knew he should have double-checked the drug before giving it – now he felt just as responsible for their patient's death.

"You didn't have to listen to him begging me to help him. Daniel, he was desperate. He just wanted to die, to let go. He had nobody in the world. Come on – you've done it too, for someone you cared about." He paused and looked at Daniel pointedly. "Susan?"

Daniel felt an icy shudder blast through his body. Susan. His first wife. She had been dying with cancer and he'd been unable to save her, as a surgeon or as a husband. He remembered how she'd pleaded with him for weeks to help her to die. To relieve her of the agonising pain and distress. Eventually, out of love and compassion, he had given her a large dose of morphine and she died peacefully in his arms. He'd wept for days.

Daniel stroked his fingers across the three fine scars that ran across his left wrist. "Yes, Susan. But I could barely live with myself afterwards." He remembered the aching void that she had left in his life – the struggle to bring up their young son, Richard, alone; the crushing guilt at hastening her death and his subsequent suicide attempt, which, if successful, would have left Richard an orphan.

Matt put his hand briefly on Daniel's shoulder. "I know. I'm sorry."

Daniel looked up at his friend and colleague. "It might be a mercy killing – but it's still a killing. We can't play God. We just can't, Matt." He just wanted the nightmare to stop. First Susan, then Sophie – why did he have to lose the people he loved? And the killing of Wixx – he *had* played God through the veil of his rage. He felt a shuddering stab of remorse.

Matt cut into Daniel's thoughts. "At least Mr Willet is at peace now. We're meant to relieve suffering and he would have died soon – at least we spared him a few days or even weeks of pain and fear. We do that for our beloved pets, yet we can't help our patients. It doesn't sit right with me."

Daniel nodded pensively. Maybe he'd been around death too much and, since he'd killed Wixx for the murder of their baby girl, he was even more acutely aware of the morality around the issues of taking a life. He tried not to think of Fay's actions.

"Come on, Daniel, we have work to do." Matt shifted awkwardly again and cleared his throat. "I'm assuming this will stay between us?"

Daniel looked at the registrar. "Yes, of course." He knew as well as Matt did that they had both been complicit in Ray Willet's mercy killing.

They exchanged a glance that sealed their agreement. It was another secret that could never be exposed.

THIRTY-SEVEN

Daniel had finished up a few jobs on the ward and checked with Angela Edwards on the HDU as to whether they were alright for medical cover before he finished his shift, then handed over to the SHO who was coming on duty. He just wanted to get out of there. The disagreement with Colin over Eddie Bates and then Mr Willet's diamorphine overdose had been bothering him more that he'd realised. He'd bumped into Fay on the HDU and had time for a brief chat before she was called to speak to another patient who had been having nightmares. They agreed to catch up at home later.

Daniel found his BMW at the far end of the hospital car park and as he was about to start the engine his iPhone rang. It was Oliver Davenport from his cosmetic clinic.

"Daniel – how are things? I meant to catch you at work earlier but had to dash. How do you fancy coming over later for a spot of training on the aesthetics side of things? We're snowed under with clients."

Daniel wasn't really in the mood for it but knew he would have to start moonlighting soon if they were going to make ends meet. "Guess so, Oliver. When is good for you?"

"Couple of hours?"

"Fine, see you then." Daniel wondered what to do with the next two hours. It wasn't worth going home and he didn't want to go back into the hospital to get embroiled with more work. He cogitated for a while and decided it would be a good opportunity to do something about the car. He'd treated himself to the BMW when he got the consultant's post but, now that was well and truly down the pan, he needed something cheaper and more sensible given their new circumstances. He headed for Williams's garage across town. Maybe he could downgrade the car and clear the loan to give them some headroom with the finances.

He crawled through the rush-hour traffic, which was gridlocked in the centre of town, but made it to the garage. He spoke to the same salesman he'd bought it from less than a year ago and the man was very accommodating. In a little over an hour, Daniel had swapped his BMW convertible for a 1990s matt black Land Rover Defender 90 that he'd spotted at the side of the garage forecourt. He'd managed to pay off the loan and ended up with a few thousand pounds to spare. He'd always fancied a Defender, ever since they'd moved to the countryside. It had done nearly 180,000 miles but looked in good nick, had heaps of room in the back for the dogs and would be perfect for getting back and forth to work. It had alloy wheels, heavy duty bumper guards and a front power winch, which, although he had no idea what he would use it for, might come in handy sometime.

He thanked the salesman, arranged immediate insurance with his bank, filled her up with fuel and took her for a spin around the outskirts of town. The car felt weird – high off the ground compared to the sporty, low-slung BMW. It lacked the computerised dashboard, and the gear lever was much longer, taking a bit of manoeuvring to position the gears – but, all in all, he was happy with it. He could either lament the loss of his treasured BMW or be glad he'd saved some cash. He drove to Oliver's clinic, parked and made his way to the reception desk over marble flooring, past a vast black leather sofa and a long coffee table adorned with glossy magazines. He was greeted by a young woman in a grey pencil skirt and a white blouse with a badge fastened over her ample bosom. It was printed with the name Nadia Jackson. She had jet-black hair flowing in loose, shiny curls around her shoulders. Her brown eyes were bright and eager to please, but her face was wax-like and overly Botoxed.

"I'm here to see Oliver," Daniel said.

"Just a minute, I'll buzz him down."

Oliver appeared at the top of the stairs. A pleasant man with the heavy build of an endomorph, a soft rounded face lacking the lines of a man of his age, thick, slightly wavy greying hair and sharp, dove-grey eyes. He was dressed in charcoal suit trousers, tan Barbour Ouse brogues and an expensive tailored white shirt, open at the collar. "Good to see you, Daniel."

Daniel met him in the reception area.

"What's with the old banger?" Oliver asked, with a quizzical look.

"My new car – always wanted one."

"And you got rid of the BMW for that?"

"Yep." Daniel didn't see the need for explanations and Oliver, somewhat awkwardly, let it drop.

He followed Oliver into one of the clinical rooms – a large, white-painted room with oak flooring, pastel-coloured modern art on three walls and replete with a black leather examination couch, trolleys laid out with syringes and other medical paraphernalia and a row of white, glossy cupboards beneath a cream marble worktop. It had the air of an expensive Harley Street clinic, and Oliver had spared no expense.

"Nice," Daniel said as he looked around.

"Thanks." Oliver was obviously proud of his achievement. In less than a year, he had created the clinic from scratch and built up an impressive list of clients as well as working at his

NHS post. "The conveyancing solicitors are pulling together the contract for Fay's old clinic as we speak. Should have that up and running in the next few months. I'll move the aesthetics across and use this building solely for cosmetic surgery." Smugly, he swept a hand around the room.

"Sounds good," Daniel said. "We'll be glad to get Fay's clinic sold and move on from it."

"Yes, I can see you need the money." He twisted his head in the direction of the car park. "It was a shame you lost your consultant's post. You're a good surgeon and nobody can blame you for that ghastly business with the Wixx character." He slowly shook his head as if he was commiserating with Daniel.

Daniel stayed silent as he wandered around the room. He had no desire to talk things over with Oliver. For one thing, his wife Melissa was the first to spread gossip and he'd had more than enough of that.

"Alright, then. Let's get started. I have a client due in twenty minutes for Botox. She's a regular and won't mind if you observe. I have the instructions here for the treatment. Why not have a read-through and make yourself a cuppa in the kitchen?" He handed Daniel a sheaf of papers.

Daniel wandered off to the kitchen, a white-painted room with a row of brand-new kitchen units in duck-egg blue, a white Belfast sink and a round wooden table and six chairs near a window overlooking a small garden at the back of the clinic. The room smelled of microwaved pasta with a hint of bleach. Daniel threw his jacket over the back of a chair, sent a quick text message to Fay to let her know he'd be late home, made his coffee and sat at the table with the papers that Oliver had given him. Botox, he read, is a neurotoxin that works by preventing the nerves from functioning. There were several annotated diagrams of the facial muscles. It all looked straightforward, he thought, although he found it bewildering to think that anyone would actually pay good money to have the stuff injected into their face.

"Hello, Daniel."

He turned to see Melissa Davenport, Oliver's wife, standing in the doorway. She looked thinner than he remembered her back in the summer and her face was tired and drawn. Her platinum-blonde hair was still as immaculately coiffured as ever and worn in a side sweeping ponytail. Her make-up was, as usual, overdone and her long nails sparkled with glittery purple polish. She wore a simple sleeveless wrap dress in pale pink under a purple cardigan and cerise courts with towering heels. She was every bit the "lady".

"Melissa."

Awkwardness bristled between them. The last time they'd met had not been a pleasant experience and, since she had told him she was leaving Oliver, he was, frankly, surprised to see her there. He noticed she still wore her platinum wedding ring and an extravagant platinum and diamond solitaire.

Melissa's scarlet lips slowly drew out into a thin, almost regretful smile. "Nice to see you again. I hope prison wasn't too awful."

"I managed." He couldn't blame her for being spiteful before – nobody could have predicted how things were going to turn out or that he would end up being arrested for murder. None of it was her fault and he decided to forgive her minor transgressions – if only for the sake of cordial relations at the clinic. "So, how have you been?"

"Alright. It's been a busy time setting up the clinic. A bit stressful at times."

"Well, things are very different now Oliver will be leaving the NHS. It will take some getting used to when he's at the clinic full time." He could see Melissa wasn't her usual bubbly self, despite their unease with one another. There was a grey shadow lurking beneath her amiable demeanour.

Oliver joined Melissa at the door of the kitchen. "Ah… I see you've found my darling wife." He put a hand in the small of

Melissa's back. She stiffened slightly. "My client is just waiting in reception. Would you like to observe, Daniel?"

"Sure." Daniel followed Oliver into the clinical room to find a stainless-steel tray laid out with a vial of Botox, several small syringes already drawn up, some wads of white gauze and a tube of local anaesthetic cream.

Oliver went out to the reception area and returned with an elegant, athletic-looking woman in her early forties with long flowing auburn hair and intense hazel eyes. She wore tight black Lycra leggings, an oversized aquamarine cashmere sweater and black court shoes.

"Ms Cooper, this is Dr Daniel Kendrick. Daniel, this is Jessica Cooper." They shook hands. "Daniel will be observing today, if that's alright with you?"

"Of course." She threw her bag onto a chair in the corner of the room and lay on the couch as she had done many times before. She pushed her hair back from her face. Her pale, freckled skin was flawless, with barely a line or wrinkle.

Oliver examined her face, running his index finger across her forehead. "Just a top-up today?"

"Yes, but I could do with more of a browlift this time."

"I'll see what I can do." Oliver said, cleaning her skin with a wet cleansing wipe, carefully avoiding her eye make-up. Then he picked up the tube of anaesthetic cream and rubbed some around her eyes and forehead. He turned to Daniel. "So, we start with a little pain-numbing cream and let that take effect. Then Jessica has her upper face and eye area treated to eradicate frown lines and crows' feet. As you can see, it has worked very well and with three- to four-monthly top ups we can keep her looking youthful for many years." He smiled at his client. "OK, then, let's make a start."

Daniel grabbed his sheet of instructions and a biro.

Oliver snapped on latex gloves and picked up the first syringe. "Jessica, give me a big frown."

Jessica frowned as best she could against the residual effects of her last Botox treatment and Oliver gave a small injection between her brows. He glanced up at Daniel, who was leaning over Oliver's shoulder observing. "We give four units into the procerus muscle to alleviate glabella lines." There was a faint whiff of Clive Christian aftershave.

Daniel made a note on the diagrams.

"Now frown again, please, Jessica." He moved the needle to the top of her inner brow and gave two injections on each side. "So, Daniel, two injections of four units to each of the corrugator muscles. That paralyses that V section on the forehead and allows the frontalis to lift the lateral side of the brow."

"Relax, Jessica." He moved his hand up and down her forehead. "These vertical muscle striations cause the horizontal frown lines on the forehead, so we inject six to twelve units in four equal doses along the frontalis." He made four small injections across Jessica's already-smooth forehead.

Oliver picked up another syringe. "Now for the crows' feet area. Smile for me, Jessica."

She smiled and her cheeks crinkled into several small lines around her eyes.

"We need to focus on the upper, outer part of the orbicularis muscle surrounding the eye and we give about ten units on each side, spaced out." He administered several small injections around the outer part of her eyes.

"All done." He dabbed at some tiny spots of blood.

She smiled, sat up and shook her hair back into position. "Thanks, doc. I can face the world again now."

The two doctors watched as Jessica retrieved her bag and walked to the door. "I'll pay in reception."

"How much would that cost?" Daniel asked when she'd gone.

"Three areas come to £360. We don't do cheap offers here. She also has fillers and other aesthetic treatments. She's a good client and we have plenty like her. In fact, if you will take over some of my regular Botox clients then I can concentrate on lower face work, fillers and my latest cosmetic miracle, flab blaster."

"Flab blaster?"

"Yes, an injection that melts away fat. It's a bit *under the counter* – if you know what I mean." Oliver gave Daniel a wink and tapped the side of his nose like a rogue double-glazing salesman. "We can't advertise it but I'm quietly recommending it to my trusted clients. It's magic, Daniel – just melts away the fat – and the best thing is that clients will pay £1,500 a time. It's bloody brilliant."

Daniel looked down at his growing paunch. A fat-melting injection – why hadn't he seen it all over the news and featured in the BMJ? It sounded good, if it worked, but he wasn't sure he'd want to squander £1,500 on it.

"It's injected into fat deposits, an enzyme breaks down the fat cells and it miraculously melts away those double-chins, love handles, tummies, thunder thighs and eyebags. My clients love it and, as you can imagine, are more than happy to keep it a secret."

Daniel nodded trying to hide his scepticism. "Well, I'm sure I can manage a few of your Botox clients every week. How about an hour or two on my way home from work?"

"Yes, that would work out nicely. Sort out some appointments with Nadia in reception. Perhaps you could do the next couple under supervision and then get on with it under your own steam. I have to get back to the hospital soon."

Once Oliver had gone, Daniel worked his way through several Botox clients, perfecting his injecting technique before arranging a few appointments. He was heading back to the kitchen to retrieve his jacket when he saw Melissa climbing the stairs. She didn't see him but she'd taken off her cardigan and that exposed a large black bruise on her arm. It looked like she'd had a nasty fall or something. Probably tripped on those killer heels.

THIRTY-EIGHT

Fay had made some notes about Mrs Jacobs's experiences and told her she would speak with her again another day to go through the psychological questionnaire. She didn't want to tire her too much and Angela Edwards had asked her to see a patient who had been experiencing nightmares since he'd come out of a coma. One of the student nurses was writing on the chart of the pregnant patient opposite and Fay couldn't resist trying to find out what had happened.

She stopped at the foot of the bed. "How is she?"

The nurse glanced at the ID card that hung from a lanyard around Fay's neck. "She's not good. Been in a coma since the road traffic accident."

"Will she make it, do you think?" Fay could see the woman was being ventilated and on full life support.

"We don't know yet but she's stable."

"And what will happen to the baby?"

"Baby's fine for the time being but we're monitoring her closely."

"You know it's a girl?"

"Yes, she's due in six weeks. We're hoping she won't have to be induced prematurely."

Fay noticed the woman was wearing a wedding ring. "It must be awful for her poor husband."

The nurse slowly shook her head. "I'm afraid he didn't make it. He was killed in the crash."

"That's so sad," Fay said.

The nurse gave her a pensive smile and went back to her chart.

Fay couldn't help thinking of Sophie and how her life had been cruelly snatched away. She hoped mother and baby would recover as she wandered off to find the patient she needed to speak to. He was in the end bed by the window on HDU. "Brendon Wilson?"

The man opened his eyes. "Yes?"

"Mr Wilson, my name is Fay Kendrick. I'm a psychiatrist and I'm doing some research on near-death experiences. Nurse Edwards said you'd like to have a chat."

The man sat up in bed and reached over to shake her hand. "Yes, hello and thank you."

Fay found a chair and sat at the side of the bed. "I understand you've had a nasty experience."

"Yes, I've been having nightmares – people and animals chasing me, feeling trapped and frightened. It's been horrendous."

Fay listened for the next fifteen minutes as Brendon Wilson told her the details. She made some notes. "It sounds like you've been having some disturbing dreams rather than a near-death experience," she told him.

A low voice cut in behind her. "Probably induced by the sedation."

Fay looked up to see one of the doctors standing at the end of the bed. He was ruggedly handsome and dark-haired and spoke with a Spanish accent. "Yes, maybe," she said. She liked him instantly and sensed a rare charisma about him that she found rather alluring.

"Rick Estevez," he said, offering his hand.

Their handshake lingered a little longer than was necessary. "Fay Kendrick," she said.

"Yes… Daniel's wife. Good to meet you."

"Likewise." She noticed the way his eyes crinkled at the corners when he smiled and how his hair curled around his collar.

"Do you really believe the soul lives on after death?" His dark eyes were sparkling as they swept over her face.

He obviously wasn't into pointless small talk – she liked that. "Actually, I do. There have been many reports throughout history of people having these experiences and it's the closest we'll get to understanding it until we die ourselves."

Brendon Wilson was watching them both as the conversation continued.

"Indeed – but couldn't these NDEs simply be hallucinations, the effects of drugs or the result of anoxia in the brain after the heart has stopped?"

Fay could see Rick was playing devil's advocate and she was happy to play along. "No particular physiological or psychological model alone explains all the common features of NDEs, which raises some puzzling questions about consciousness and its relation to brain function. Hallucinations are usually illogical, fleeting and often bizarre, whereas most NDEs are logical, clear, very vivid, and memorable for decades after. Hallucinations are quickly forgotten."

Rick interjected, obviously enjoying their discussion. "But the evidence is purely anecdotal."

"That doesn't mean it's not valuable. Near-death experiences often lead to profound and permanent transformations in people's personality, attitudes, beliefs and values. That doesn't happen after hallucinations." Fay glanced at Brendon Wilson. His eyes were fluttering as he started to drift off to sleep.

Rick smiled and nodded slightly in recognition of what she had said. "But what about certain drugs? Surely they have been shown to produce strange mystical experiences."

Fay paused while she dug deep into her memory. "Well, ketamine and psilocybin do apparently trigger mystical experiences, but they are also different to hallucinations. There are some similar elements to an NDE, though. The most respected researcher on this, Karl Jansen, has concluded after twelve years of research into psychoactive substances that there is a soul that is independent of the body. Anyway, most patients who report an NDE have not taken these substances, so there is no correlation." She looked at Rick, satisfied with her account.

"Well, I don't believe in life after death, but you seem to know what you are talking about. It would be good to discuss this again sometime." He checked his watch. "I'm afraid I have to go now but it was nice to meet you." His eyes lingered on hers before he turned to go.

Fay watched as Rick wandered through the unit and disappeared into the corridor. So, *he* was Daniel's new boss. She was intrigued by him and hoped she would get the chance to see him again – there had definitely been some sort of spark between them: a professional rapport or maybe it was something more personal? She glanced at Brendon Wilson. He was fast asleep. She told Angela she would come back to finish her chat another time and decided to call it a day and go home. She found a text message from Daniel saying he would be late, but she didn't reply.

As she walked through the hospital toward the main entrance, she thought about the pregnant patient on the unit. It must have been a bad crash to put her in a coma. She inevitably began to think about Sophie and the embryos that were no longer viable. All she wanted was to be a mother again – nothing else really mattered to her. After meeting Rick, she was feeling upbeat and positive – dare she say excited? That wasn't a bad thing, surely, she thought. After all she had been through lately, she needed some happy thoughts and a more positive state of mind. She checked her watch. If she hurried, she might catch Dr Chan at the Genesis

Fertility Clinic – she had told her she could call back anytime and she wanted to talk through some further options with her. Surely, there had to be a way for her to become a mother.

Fay managed to get through the traffic to the other side of town and parked easily at the Genesis Clinic. The reception area was deserted.

"Any chance of seeing Dr Chan for a few minutes?"

"I'll check." The receptionist picked up the phone and tapped out a number. "Dr Chan, I have Fay Kendrick here. Would you be free to see her now?"

Fay looked around the reception area. There were several framed posters of smiling babies and their mothers. That was all she wanted – to hold a baby in her arms again. There had to be a way.

"Dr Chan is on her way."

"Thank you." Fay waited briefly before Dr Chan called her into her office.

Fay sat at the desk opposite the doctor.

"Are you alright, Dr Kendrick?"

Fay nodded. "I'm getting over it, but I wanted to find out if there was any other way for me to have a baby. I've been reading on the Internet about various methods – donated embryos, cytoplasmic transfer, cloning…"

Dr Chan held up a cautioning hand. "There are other methods, yes, but given your age and history of infertility we have to be wary. There are no easy or quick fixes. Now, you mentioned donated embryos. I'm afraid we must give them to women with the greatest chance of a successful pregnancy and there is quite a waiting list. That's not a viable option for you."

Fay wasn't going to be deterred. "What about IVF with an egg and sperm donation?"

"Again, not really a good option for you. We have a lot of younger women waiting and it is a long process. It would be the same for cytoplasmic transfer."

Fay was beginning to feel downhearted. "There must be something. What about cloning? That's had some success, hasn't it?"

Dr Chan slowly shook her head. "Dr Kendrick, cloning and the experimental technique of nuclear transfer are not procedures we can offer at this clinic and probably never will. I think you will have to accept that your options are very limited. Have you thought about adoption? There are lots of older children that are in need of a loving home."

"I really want a baby of my own."

"Then I really don't think we can help you here at the Genesis Clinic. I'm so very sorry." Dr Chan smiled sympathetically.

"Thank you. I just needed to go through the options with you." Fay stood, shook the doctor's hand and left the clinic. She tried not to feel downhearted – surely there was still something she could do.

THIRTY-NINE

Sandy Lewis lay in her hospital bed barely aware of the hubbub of the high-dependency unit. She bit down on the plastic tube in her mouth, panic rising in waves as she fought against the machine. She knew it was keeping her alive along with a cocktail of drugs that were being pumped into her veins but all she wanted was to get out of there, to go home to her husband and three children. The hope of that was all she had to cling onto.

In the past few days, fragmented memories of the accident were starting to flood back into her mind. The slow-motion crash as a delivery van ploughed into the driver's side of her car, the sickening thud, then spinning out of control across three lanes of the motorway. The restraint of the seat belt as a car smashed into hers from behind, the screech of metal against metal, the shattering of glass, the squeal of tyres against tarmac as a stream of vehicles skidded to a halt. The world spinning before her, then the jolt as she veered across the road into the back of a lorry. The juddering crash before slumping into the dark oblivion of unconsciousness...

The next thing she was aware of was being surrounded by medics in the emergency department, tubes in her throat, an immobilising neck brace. She tried to move her legs, but they were dead weights anchored to the bed. Her fingers moved slightly but didn't feel like her own.

She'd been in the HDU for weeks now and had heard the doctors say she might never walk again – something about damage to her spinal cord. But, even if that were true, she wanted, more than anything, to be at home with her family. Her husband had held her hand every day, told her he loved her and promised they would deal with whatever lay ahead.

But her future was about to be cruelly snatched away.

Sandy Lewis looked up into the eyes of her killer. They were familiar, kindly eyes but today they held a frigid darkness she hadn't seen before. There was no anger – just a cold reptilian determination to see her dead. She felt an intuitive flash of realisation and an icy chill ripple down her broken spine as she sensed she was about to die.

With cybernetic control, the killer reached up and silenced the alarm on her cardiac monitor, before reaching around the back of the ventilator and disconnecting the electrical power cable. The machine sighed as it delivered its final mechanical breath.

Sandy Lewis watched the killer, terrified, as she fought to breathe for herself. But her lungs were paralysed by a severely damaged spinal cord – they would never hold air again. She looked pleadingly into the killer's eyes – she had so much to live for – so much love to give to her family.

The killer watched as Sandy Lewis's life drained from her; smiled as her blood pressure plummeted, unable to sustain the arterial pressure to keep her heart pumping. The killer glanced at the monitor as her heart fluttered and failed, a series of flat green lines confirming she was dead.

The killer disappeared into the hubbub of the HDU.

Sandy Lewis's death would look like a terrible accident.

FORTY

Fay arrived home before Daniel. During the drive home, her mood had darkened considerably. She'd gone to the Genesis Clinic full of hope and now her dreams had been dashed again. Rosie had delivered the dogs back home after their day at the dog creche and she fed them and let them into the house. She was feeling too dejected to bother to take them out for a walk and Daniel would never know she hadn't. Maisie devoured a fish-flavoured sachet of Sheba, then groomed herself on the kitchen windowsill.

Fay was brooding about the visit with Dr Chan when she thought she heard something upstairs. She stopped and listened in the hallway for a while and realised it was a baby crying, softly at first, then more insistently. The sound was coming from Sophie's nursery. When she realised what it was, she flew up the stairs and flung open the nursery door. The room was in darkness, but the sound was still there. She flicked on the light and the sound vanished as suddenly as it had appeared. She stood in the doorway for several minutes, listening, but the sound had gone. Was it Sophie? She lingered a while, then left the door open and went downstairs. Perhaps it was her mind playing tricks on her. She had been preoccupied with thoughts of babies. Perhaps her disappointment at the news from the clinic had made her hear things that weren't there.

Fay decided to prepare the dinner. Daniel would be home soon and hungry. Cooking would take her mind off things, for a while at least. She prepared a pasta bake with salad and as she was about to put the pasta in the oven Daniel arrived home.

"Hi, sweetheart," he called out. "Come and see what I've bought this afternoon." He led her out to the driveway and pointed to the Defender. "Always wanted one of these. What do you think?"

Fay looked through the nearside window and glanced at the space in the back of the car. "You've only got two seats and it's ancient. The BMW was far nicer."

"Yes, and it was costing too much. It makes sense to save some money at the moment."

Fay didn't really care either way. She had other things on her mind and, if she did get pregnant again, they could always change it for something more family friendly. "It's fine," she conceded.

They went back into the house and Daniel made a fuss of Chester and Ella, then went upstairs to change. Fay heard him close the door of the nursery.

"How was your day?" he said when he returned dressed in old, creased chinos and a pastel-coloured checked shirt that had a rip in one of the sleeves.

"Fine. I spoke to a lady who had a near-death experience, Mrs Jacobs. She told me about the most amazing things she saw while she was clinically dead and what made it so incredible was that she'd been blind since birth."

"Amazing."

"How about you?" Fay washed the lettuce, celery and baby plum tomatoes.

"Oh, just the usual stuff – rounds, chest drains, mountains of paperwork. Then Oliver rang, so I went to the clinic. Been giving

Botox injections for the last couple of hours." Daniel rolled his eyes and fished out a couple of wine glasses and poured them both a glass of Sauvignon Blanc from the fridge.

"How's Oliver?"

"Good – he's got the clinic looking very classy and he seems to have plenty of clients. The solicitors are working on the sale of your clinic." He wandered into the living room to see the dogs.

"I met your boss today, Rick Estevez," Fay called from the kitchen.

"Oh yes – what did you think of him?" he called back.

"Seems like a nice bloke. We had a chat about my research."

"You know, he's seeing Isobel, the clinical trial woman from Regenex Biologics. It's so obvious they're an item."

"Can't hear you," Fay called; the tap was running, the washing machine was on full spin and the oven fan was rattling again, drowning out anything he'd said.

Daniel became immersed in playing with the dogs and Chester was growling as he tugged at a rope toy that Daniel was teasing him with.

"Oh, never mind," Fay said to herself as she chopped up a red onion, her eyes stinging and watering.

Ten minutes later, Daniel wandered back into the kitchen. "I'm starving."

"You're always starving." Fay smiled at her husband. They were happy enough, but she wished things could be the way they were when they'd first met and later, when they were expecting Sophie. Perhaps another baby would be good for their relationship. Even if he didn't think he wanted another child now – he would soon get used to the idea, she thought.

Daniel topped up their wine glasses and peered into the oven. "Smells scrummy."

"Help yourself to salad; it's just about ready." Fay put on an oven glove and transferred the pasta bake to a metal trivet on the table.

They ate at the island in the kitchen, chatting about work and Oliver's clinic. Daniel cleared up the dishes and they went into the living room to relax. Maisie curled up between them on the sofa and Chester and Ella lay next to one another on the hearth rug. Chester was snoring and twitching in his sleep.

Daniel flicked around the TV channels and settled on a David Attenborough wildlife documentary about lions. Fay logged on to her laptop and was searching through Facebook. She was a voyeur – rarely posting anything herself but interested in seeing what others were doing. She smiled at some of the funny animal antics and "liked" a couple of posts her aunt had put on there. Then she had a thought. In the search box, she typed "surrogate mothers".

Fay turned the laptop screen slightly so Daniel couldn't see what she was doing. He seemed engrossed in the TV and the sound of roaring lions reverberated around the room. She found several groups, most of them private. She kept searching and finally found a group with a website that seemed to be all about matching surrogates to people who wanted to create a family. She realised that it could cost around £30,000 and took at least a year on the waiting list before a suitable surrogate was found and an agreement signed. That was too long for Fay – she wanted a baby in her arms in that time. She hunted the Internet further and finally found a woman named Dianna Collins in her area who was offering surrogacy. From her photograph, she appeared to be in her early thirties, average build and height with short dark hair and a pleasant pixie-like face. She scrolled through her profile and discovered she had four children of her own and wanted to help other women to have a family. She seemed ideal. On a whim, Fay sent her a message asking if they could meet to discuss things.

She looked across at Daniel. He'd fallen asleep with Maisie draped across his chest, David Attenborough's voice still narrating the film. Surely Daniel would come around to the idea of having another baby. He had to.

FORTY-ONE

Clarissa had sent several text messages begging Rick to attend her wedding to Hugo in two weeks' time. He'd ignored all of them, as well as her calls. He felt conflicted about meeting up with his family after three years and bringing all the turmoil of the past back to the surface, just as he was settling into his new job. Their brother, Lucero, was terminally ill with a neurogenerative disease, Clarissa had told him, and he was not expected to live beyond the next three months. Rick would like to be at his sister's wedding, of course he would, and he wondered if he should go for Lucero's sake, but his brother had made it pretty clear he wanted nothing to do with him after the car crash. He'd taken his father's side and between them, they had effectively ostracised him from the family. Rick was much happier in the UK – a nice apartment by the sea, jet-skiing and, of course, a serendipitous consultant's post. He also had Isobel, wherever that was going. He wanted to keep things casual, but he was sensing she was itching for more. His relationships usually ended at the point when he was expected to make more of a commitment but, with Isobel, he felt obliged to keep things going. The benefits outweighed any discontentment. But Maria had been the love of his life and, if he was honest, he wasn't sure any woman would live up to her memory.

"*Mierda*," he said aloud – what the hell was he going to do? He had to settle on something. Since this thing with Clarissa had come up, he couldn't sleep, and, when he did, the dreadful nightmares had returned. His stomach was constantly churning with anxiety, and he was getting the same flashes of guilt he'd suffered after the crash. Survivor guilt, his GP had told him. Guilt that he had survived when his wife and son had died. The crash was his fault and his alone. He was the one that should have died – not them. They were innocent. He recalled his desperate yet futile attempt to save them both. He had failed as a doctor and as a husband and father.

Rick sat in his Lamborghini in the hospital car park and finally made a decision. He texted Clarissa.

Sorry I won't be able to come. Work is too busy for me to get away. I'll try to see you after the wedding. As soon as he had written the words, he knew his place was at Riverbeke General.

She texted back almost immediately. *What about Lucero? Don't you even want to see him before he dies? How could you be so cruel!!*

In another flash of guilt, he simply typed back. *Sorry, Clarissa.*

He imagined her flying off in a temper, begging their mother to persuade him – to make him go – but his mind was made up. He wasn't going anywhere. The prospect of seeing his father with all the inevitable angst would be too much.

His phone bleeped with another text from Clarissa, *I hate you!*

Rick felt bad but there was no going back now. He would send Clarissa and Hugo an extravagant wedding present to try to make up for it and perhaps he would bring himself to write a letter to Lucero and even to his mother. For now, he had work to do. He locked the car and headed for his office on the ward. The corridor was busy, and he passed a group of canteen staff gossiping and laughing. He swiped himself into the ward and was met by one of the junior doctors, who looked like she'd been up all night.

"Mr Estevez, would you have a look at one of the trial patients, please? I think he may be having a reaction. I've asked Daniel and he saw him briefly but was called away to see a post-op patient." She seemed flustered.

"Is it an emergency?" Rick asked.

"No but I think someone should see him. It's Bob Hackman in bed six."

"I'll be right there, just give me a minute." Rick went to his office to leave his jacket and briefcase, slung his stethoscope around his neck, then went into the ward to see Mr Hackman, rolling up his shirt sleeves as he went. There was no sign of the junior doctor or Daniel.

The man was in his early sixties, with the build of an all-in wrestler but way past the height of his career. His head was shaven and bristly, revealing several folds of flab across the back of his neck and his skin was covered in brown liver spots. He lay on the bed, his bare, flabby chest partially covered with a white sheet.

"Mr Hackman. What seems to be the trouble?" Rick asked, reaching for the patient's charts and notes, which had been left on the end of the bed.

The patient was awaiting surgery for a hernia repair and had been put on Isobel's clinical trial. According to his prescription chart, he'd received two doses of either the medication or placebo and was also on beta-blockers. "Are you allergic to anything?" Rick asked.

"Penicillin, I think," the man said.

Ricked checked his notes and charts. "There's nothing here about an allergy."

The man shrugged.

"So, what are your symptoms?" Rick began to feel a little tense. The staff had a heavy workload, but it was basic stuff to record allergies on the patient's records.

"I'm feeling faint and clammy, and my heart is racing." The man wiped his sweaty forehead with the back of his hand. "A bit hot too."

Rick felt the man's radial pulse and listened to his heart with the stethoscope. "Seems alright to me. It is rather hot in here – maybe it's that." He looked around the ward. Still no sign of the junior doctor, or Daniel. In fact, apart from the new cleaner, Eddie Bates, there appeared to be no staff on the ward. He would have to deal with it himself. He pondered for a few moments. "I'll be right back," Rick said, then went off to the clinical room and prepared a couple of injections.

"Thanks, doc," the man said, as Rick gave him one of the intravenous injections through the canula in the back of his hand. He left the other on a cardboard injection tray on the bed table.

"That should help. I'll be back in a minute." Rick kept an eye on the patient from the nurses' station as he was checking the theatre list. Bob Hackman was due in theatre that afternoon, but he would have to be reviewed considering this new development. He glanced across at his patient. He looked as if he was struggling to breathe. Rick went back to him. The man was clutching his throat, trying to speak but the only sound he could make was a hoarse, strangulated gurgle.

His breathing was rapid and shallow, and his face was turning purple as his oxygen saturations fell. Rick sat him up and reached for the oxygen and a bag-valve mask, placing it over the man's nose and mouth. He clipped a pulse oximeter onto his middle finger – his oxygen levels were falling to 90%... 85%... 82% as his airway began to swell. He was decidedly clammy. Rick was about to take the man's blood pressure when he lost consciousness. Rick laid him against the pillows and turned the oxygen flow to full, but his oxygen levels were plummeting to dangerous levels – 78%... 73%. His skin was turning purple. Rick checked the man's heartbeat. It was thready and just about audible through a stethoscope. He grabbed the second syringe and injected adrenaline into the man's thigh muscle. He was having a severe allergic reaction.

Rick switched on the cardiac monitor behind the bed and grabbed the ECG leads. He attached them to Bob Hackman's chest. The monitor picked up his heartbeat – over 120 beats per minute with irregular electrical activity. He was deteriorating rapidly. "Can I get some help in here?" Rick shouted.

Daniel appeared from one of the treatment rooms, snapping off latex gloves. "What's the problem?"

"He's going into VF. Could be anaphylaxis. Grab the crash trolley and the defibrillator."

Daniel ran off to get the equipment and called the crash team. Rick could see Hackman's heart rate had climbed to over 300 beats per minute and the ECG was showing grossly irregular activity. Rick felt adrenaline surge in his own body as he realised the man had gone into VF – ventricular fibrillation – his heart ventricles were fluttering uselessly, and he had to act quickly to save the man's life. He pulled the pillows away and laid him flat on the bed. Positioning his hands over the man's sternum, he locked his elbows and began rhythmically pummelling his chest – thirty cardiac compressions at two beats per second, sending life-giving blood and oxygen to his organs and tissues. Daniel arrived with the arrest trolley, twisted an airway stabiliser into his mouth, sealed a bag-valve mask around his nose and mouth, attached it to the oxygen and began bagging the patient's airways – two breaths after every thirty of Rick's cardiac compressions. After two minutes, Rick stopped and looked at the monitor.

"He's still in VF. We need to shock him." Daniel had already set the manual defibrillator to charge at 120 joules. Rick placed orange adhesive pads on the man's chest and applied the paddles.

"Clear," he shouted as he delivered the electrical shock into Bob Hackman's chest. The man convulsed but his heart failed to respond.

Daniel was already grabbing a syringe of adrenaline. "I'm giving 1 mg intravenously," Daniel said as he pushed the fluid through the canula and into his vein to increase the power of the heart's contractions.

Rick checked the monitor again. "Still in VF," he said. He began cardiac compressions again, but the man's face was turning purple and his oxygen saturations were down to 52%. "We need to intubate; his trachea is swelling."

Jackie Hines had arrived on the scene and was taking the headboard off the bed for easier access to the patient.

"I've got this," Daniel said as he reached for a laryngoscope from the trolley.

"No," Rick said, "I'll intubate, you get the tube ready." Rick snatched the laryngoscope from Daniel's hand and manoeuvred himself into position behind the patient's head. He lifted the man's neck and twisted the metal blade of the instrument into his throat. "OK, I can just about see the vocal cords. Pass me the ET tube."

Daniel passed the tube and Rick inserted it between the vocal cords and down into his swollen trachea. He inflated the cuff with air from a syringe and attached the bag-valve mask, squeezing it to deliver three rapid breaths to the patient. His oxygen saturation levels began to rise – but only slightly. "Daniel, take over here."

Daniel took the mask from Rick. Then Rick gave Hackman another intravenous dose of adrenaline before resuming cardiac compressions. After thirty compressions, he stopped while Daniel delivered two breaths via the bag, then continued compressions for a further two minutes.

"He's still in pulseless VF. Charge to 200 joules." Rick said breathlessly while Jackie Hines fast charged the defibrillator.

Rick applied the paddles to the patient's chest. "Clear."

Everyone stepped back while Rick shot 200 joules of electricity through the man's heart. He convulsed again, his chest rising stiffly from the bed. Rick, Daniel and Jackie turned to look at the cardiac monitor. He was still in VF.

There was a commotion on the ward as the cardiac arrest team began to arrive – an anaesthetist was first on the scene, breathless from running and carrying a holdall full of equipment.

"It's OK, I've got it," Rick said breathlessly, as he pounded the man's chest.

After five cycles of CPR, Rick checked the heart monitor. There were still no signs of his heart returning to a normal sinus rhythm. "Let's shock him again." Rick delivered a third jolt of electricity into the man's heart. "Try some amiodarone."

Jackie Hines passed Rick a syringe of the drug that would slow the heart and treat arrythmias such as VF. He pushed the drug through the canula and continued with CPR.

After forty minutes, Bob Hackman's heart had still not responded. The anaesthetist and another doctor from the cardiac arrest team pleaded with Rick to stop. Reluctantly, he had to concede.

"Time of death 09.50," Rick said breathlessly.

Eddie Bates was smirking at the far end of the ward as he pushed his mop around aimlessly. He'd been hovering near the scene like a wasp around a jam sandwich.

FORTY-TWO

The doctors had wandered away and the crash team went back to their posts while the nurses tidied up Bob Hackman's body and pulled the curtains around the bed. They would leave him for an hour before laying him out and getting the porters to take him to "Rose Cottage". Someone would have to inform his girlfriend and his parents and explain that it was necessary for him to have a post-mortem. There was a subdued atmosphere on the ward, with both staff and patients contemplating what had happened that morning. Daniel had finished treating his patient in the clinical room and as he was making his way toward the nurses' station he bumped into Fay. They had travelled into work together that morning in Daniel's new Defender.

"Hi, sweetheart. Everything OK? I didn't realise you were on the ward this morning – I thought you'd be in the HDU."

"No, Angela was busy and asked me to come here. You've had an emergency." She twisted her head toward Bob Hackman's bed. "I was keeping out of the way, but I could see what was going on."

"Yes, poor man. He didn't make it."

"That's sad. Listen, I must go. There's a lady I have to see.

She's had a strange experience, but it doesn't sound like an NDE to me. Better check it out, though."

"Well, let's catch up later." Daniel gave her arm a little rub and went off to find Rick. He still didn't like the fact that Fay was around death so much after all that had happened, but he realised it would be difficult to influence her. She was pretty headstrong when she made up her mind about something.

Daniel was just going into Rick's office when he heard Colin Mathias's voice behind him. "We should have a chat about your patient." He was obviously rattled.

They both went into Rick's office. Isobel was there but excused herself saying she had an important phone call to make. Colin closed the door. "Alright. Tell me what happened this morning and why we have another death on the ward." He folded his arms over his portly belly and leaned against the wall.

Rick explained what had happened. "We did everything we could – he just wasn't responding."

"And you think it could be due to the trial drug, Bravafloxacin?" Colin asked.

"Possibly. He'd had two doses of either that or the placebo," Rick said.

"Any other medication?"

Rick turned and looked pointedly at Daniel. "Did you give him anything, Daniel? You were the last one to examine him before he collapsed."

Daniel sensed a harder tone in the room. "No. I checked on him before you arrived, but he seemed alright. Just a bit hot and bothered. I had to leave him to attend to another patient." Daniel felt defensive. The man had been fine when he saw him, and he didn't like Rick's accusatory tone.

Colin said nothing but nodded reflectively. "This is a serious matter. We should at least find out whether he had the Bravafloxacin or the placebo. Ask Isobel to get that information for us, will you, Rick? We need to know if we should stop the clinical trial."

"Of course."

Colin left and there was an awkwardness between the two doctors. Daniel felt that Rick had undermined him in front of Colin but was unwilling to tackle him about it.

Rick broke the silence. "We have the ward round in an hour. Make yourself useful until then."

As Daniel was leaving, Rick added, "Perhaps you'd take over the post-op clinic for me this afternoon." It was a rhetorical question and evidently not up for discussion.

Daniel had no choice but to agree. He knew Rick was delegating the tedious routine work he hated, just as he delegated the minor procedures and the paperwork and anything else he didn't fancy doing. He was beginning to feel like a dogsbody. "Sure, no problem," he said.

Daniel strolled through the ward, checking his patients. Thankfully there were no issues, and the nurses were busy with medicine rounds and caring for their patients. He stood beside an elderly man, John Gardener, an emaciated gentleman with bony, arthritic hands, bright green eyes and a sunken face that was etched with a lifetime of disappointments. "How are you feeling after your operation yesterday?"

The man was in his nineties and had undergone a surgical debridement of a deep pressure ulcer to his buttocks that he'd acquired at home. He lay cautiously on his side. "A bit sore, to be honest, but I'm alright in myself," he said.

"The nurses will change your dressing today and let me know how the wound is looking." Daniel noted from his chart that he was on the clinical trial but had not received any drug or placebo so far.

The man appeared to remember something and started fumbling in his bedside locker. "I seem to have lost my wallet. It was here first thing this morning. I guess I nodded off despite all the commotion earlier and must have left it on the top." He leaned across and pulled out everything in the cupboard, piling stuff on the bed – a box of tissues, a battered old watch, a packet of sweets, an asthma inhaler, a pile of get-well cards, a bag of toiletries, a threadbare towel and a change of pyjamas – but no wallet. "I hope it hasn't been stolen."

Daniel helped him to search for it among his few possessions, but it was definitely missing. "Did you have a lot of money in it?"

"Not much – but there's a picture of my late wife in there that I'd hate to lose." The man sighed in defeat and flopped back onto the pillows, exhausted.

"Get some rest, Mr Gardener. I'll be back to see you later." Daniel glanced around the ward. Was there a thief around? He spotted Eddie Bates chatting with one of the patients. He always seemed to be lurking in the shadows. Could he have been responsible for the missing wallet? He didn't relish the idea of a confrontation with Bates. Colin was on the warpath about Bob Hackman's death and, with the tension between them, there was no way he'd bring this up with Rick. Security, he knew for sure, wouldn't be interested in pursuing it.

Daniel went into the clinical room that he'd had to leave unattended while he was busy with Mr Hackman. He checked the stock of syringes, and it looked like there were several missing along with a pile of needles. Yes, Bates. It must have been him – a known thief and drug dealer; it was obvious to him, but he doubted anyone else would believe him – especially given the irony of his own spell behind bars. He would have to keep an eye on him but for now Mr Gardener was missing his wallet and he felt obliged to do something about it. Daniel checked the time: thirty minutes yet before the ward round started. He told Jackie Hines he was going off the ward for a few minutes, but she could bleep him if he was needed, and took the stairs to the main concourse. He went into the small gift shop and managed to find a nice black leather wallet. He paid for it, then went to the cash machine and withdrew £50 cash and stuffed it into the wallet. He bought a tube of Smarties for himself, which he ate on the way back to the ward.

He went over to John Gardener's bed and gave him the wallet. "I know it's not the same, but I found you a new one."

Mr Gardener looked surprised. "I can't take this from you, doctor. It wasn't your fault."

"Please, I want you to have it. The ward can't take responsibility for patients' belongings, unfortunately, so there's nothing we can do, but please let us keep it locked up until you go home."

John Gardener had a tear in his eye. "Thank you so much, doctor – you're very kind."

Daniel asked Jackie Hines to bag it, label it and lock the wallet away until his discharge. He couldn't help thinking that, if he'd been more insistent with Colin about having Bates on the ward, it might not have happened.

FORTY-THREE

Fay had spent a couple of hours on the ward and had spoken to a patient who was having some weird hallucination-like dreams, but they decided it was caused by the drugs she'd been taking. One of the doctors changed the prescription and Fay said she would check on her in a few days. She went up to the HDU and had another chat with Brendon Wilson about his nightmares. She also spoke briefly to Rick Estevez before he dashed off to an emergency. She had to admit, she still found him attractive, and he seemed interested in her research, although finding patients that had experienced a near-death experience was proving to be more difficult than she'd realised, even though she knew that it was a relatively common phenomenon. She had read studies that showed around fifteen to eighteen percent of the population in some countries have had them and, in the US alone, some 774 NDEs occur every day. She just had to wait and talk to as many patients as possible – at least those that had been clinically dead and survived.

Fay had gone up to Doug's office to check in, but he wasn't there and neither was Shelly. The office was locked up. She felt at a bit of a loose end so decided to go to the university library for a while and catch up with some reading for her research. Just as she was settling down, her phone beeped with a message. It was from Dianna Collins, the surrogate she'd contacted the evening before.

Would love to meet for a chat. Pop over anytime today – I'm home with the kids.

Fay felt elated. At last, some positive news. She was desperate to meet up with Dianna. She replied immediately. *That's great. I can come around in the next half hour. I need your address.*

Dianna replied a few minutes later with an address and postcode. It was just south of the village of Catsash. She could be there in twenty minutes. Then she remembered she'd gone into work with Daniel that morning and didn't have her own car. She considered asking Daniel if she could use the Defender but dismissed the idea. He would want to know where she was going. She'd better get a taxi. She tapped out the number of the local taxi firm and they said they would be there in five minutes.

The taxi edged its way through the town traffic and out into the country roads, the driver chatting incessantly all the way. The sat nav directed them to a row of old country cottages down a narrow lane off the main road. Fay found Dianna's house, "Bramble Cottage". She paid the driver and walked through a wooden gate and up the short brick pathway to the front porch: a rustic wooden shelter with a slate pitched roof that was covered in Virginia creeper. She rapped on the door with the heavy brass knocker, and she could hear children chattering inside. The door was opened by a young woman who looked exactly like her photograph – average build with short dark hair and pixie-like features. Except, now, she was heavily pregnant. She stood in the doorway with three of her four children gathered around her.

"Ah… you must be Fay. Come in." Dianna ushered her in to a small, homely sitting room and gestured for her to sit on the sofa. The room was strewn with the children's toys and a Yorkshire terrier with a red glittery collar lay on the armchair near the window, an ancient tabby cat sitting on the windowsill behind, grooming his matted fur. Fay picked her way around the toys and sat, while Dianna manoeuvred herself around her cumbersome baby bump onto the sofa opposite. The children gathered quietly around their mother, staring wide-eyed at Fay.

Dianna put her arm around one of the girls. "Amy, tell Fay how old you are," she said to the little girl. The child shook her head and bit her bottom lip. Dianna turned to Fay. "She's a bit shy." She prompted the girl once more. "You're four. Tell Fay you're four and it's your birthday soon, isn't it?" The girl nodded but leaned into her mother and continued to bite her lip.

"They're beautiful children and they look just like you," Fay said, smiling. She craved a family like this. It was all she wanted. She wondered what Sophie would have been like at that age.

"And this is Annabel and Alex – they're two and six," she said, pointing to each of them in turn. "Antony is somewhere around – probably in his bedroom on his computer. He spends half his life up there." She rolled her eyes.

Fay tried to engage the children in conversation but none of them wanted to talk. Finally, Dianna sent them off to play.

"You have a lovely family." Fay felt emotional as she mentally projected the children into her own life.

"Yes, I'm very lucky. And now I have another one on the way. This one is for a childless couple. It's my second as a surrogate."

"It's a wonderful thing you're doing. We lost our little girl over two years ago and I'm desperate to have another baby." Fay needed to get down to business without seeming indelicate. "We've been through all the possibilities: IVF, frozen embryos – the works – but we seem to have run out of options. I wondered about surrogacy."

Dianna seemed to sense Fay's desperation. "Well, as you can see, I'm due in six weeks and after that I'll need a rest. If you're hoping for me to be a surrogate for you, there is actually a waiting list. It will be at least three years before we would be able to come to any sort of agreement but, if you're happy to wait, we could discuss it again nearer the time."

Fay wished Dianna had told her this before she'd made the journey to her home. She'd had such high hopes and now they were dashed again. Was there to be no prospect of her having a baby soon? "It's alright, I understand, but I was hoping to have a baby before then – I'm not getting any younger." Fay gave her a half-hearted smile. "Do you know any other surrogates that might be able to come to an agreement sooner?" She could hear the children playing in the other room – the sound of laughter and then one of the girls scolding her brother.

Dianna pondered for a few moments but shook her head. "I'm afraid I don't. My friend is a surrogate – or rather was. She had some complications with the last pregnancy." She gave Fay a sympathetic smile. "There are some agencies around but it's always a long process. Have you thought of adoption?"

Fay was tired of hearing that. All she wanted was a newborn baby of her own. "Maybe someday," she said.

"I'm sorry I can't help at the moment, but I'll let you know if I hear of anyone willing to help in the short term."

"Thank you," Fay said. "All the best with the new baby. I hope things go well." The women stood, shook hands and Fay glimpsed into the other room at the children happily playing together.

They said goodbye at the doorstep and Dianna went back inside the cottage. She wandered along the row of houses back toward the main road. She wondered whether to call the taxi to collect her, but she felt so downhearted and disappointed that all she wanted was to walk and be alone with her thoughts. She noticed a lane off to her right signposted to Hallbrook Manor and the Riverbeke Falls tearoom that was half a mile up ahead. She turned and walked down the lane. Maybe she would stop for a coffee at the tearoom before going back to the hospital. It was getting on for lunchtime anyway.

As she walked, Fay brooded on everything that had happened since Daniel had been released from prison – the message from Sophie via Felicia Grainger, her perished embryos, the infertility treatments that Dr Chan had rejected and now even surrogacy looked like it would be a very lengthy and difficult process. Yet, she desperately wanted a baby. Each step took her into a darker place in her mind. She was rapidly plunging into the depths of despair. Why was life so unfair? Was she being punished for the killings she'd carried out? Was she meant to suffer forever for what she'd done? All she had wanted was to rid the world of evil and find the monster that had murdered their daughter. She looked across the open countryside and at the woodland that lay beyond the river Beke. Her aunt's lake and log cabin were through those trees – the sanctuary she retreated to when she wanted to escape from the world. She was drawn there again but, now, images of Damon Wixx haunted her memories. The sight of him lying dead in the lake, the cabin burned to the ground. Would she ever be able to go there again? She wasn't sure.

The single-track lane soon became a fork. To the right was Hallbrook Manor and, to the left, the tearooms. Fay looked straight ahead to the meandering tree-lined river and headed across the field toward it. The river was drawing her to it. It was if she was hearing the voices of her lost babies – of Sophie and the three embryos that had been denied the chance of life.

They were calling her to the river.

FORTY-FOUR

Rick sat in his office, bitterly disappointed at the death of his patient, Bob Hackman. He'd tried his best to save his life, but he'd just not responded. With the heaviness of guilt, he remembered Maria and Alessandro and the desperate but futile efforts he'd made to save them. He'd suffered from a form of post-traumatic stress disorder – PTSD – with flashbacks, anxiety and abject depression. His mind was haunted by the terror in Maria's eyes as he tried to save their son's life – a terror that morphed into anguish as he died in Rick's arms just moments before she herself slipped into the blackness of unconsciousness and death.

For the past three years he'd managed to distance himself from the people that reminded him of the tragedy but Clarissa's call insisting he go to her wedding and Lucero's terminal illness had just brought it all back up to the surface. He had to stay in control.

His thoughts were interrupted by a knock on the door. His instinct was to ignore it, but it could be something important. "Yes, come in."

The door opened and Isobel stood in the doorway. She was immaculately groomed, with her hair in loose waves and wearing a powder-blue skirt suit over a white blouse with navy

Dolce & Gabbana heels. "Rick, I thought it was time we caught up. Have you been avoiding me?" She gave him a saucy wink.

"Not at all. Just busy." If he was honest, he had been avoiding her. With all that was going on with Clarissa and Lucero, his mind had been on other things.

Isobel sat on his desk in front of him and crossed her legs seductively, one expensive shoe dangling from her foot. "Shall I come over tonight? We could eat in and have a few drinks."

Rick wasn't in the mood for her company and the endless conversations about the office politics at Regenex. He scratched the back of his head, wondering how he could let her down gently. Their relationship was starting to become stifling and, although she was beautiful, the reality was that they had little in common. He liked excitement and a challenge, but Isobel was far too conservative for him. Yet it suited him to have her in his life. For now, at least, he would string her along. "Mind if we make it another time? I have a lot on at work and I'm dog tired."

"But I haven't seen you for ages. We could have an early night..."

She leaned across to run her fingers through his hair, but he pulled away. "Really, Isobel, I could do with some time to catch up with myself. Another time, alright?"

He was saved by another knock on the door. It opened before he could answer, and Daniel stood in the doorway. "Oh... sorry, didn't mean to intrude."

Isobel slid off the desk and stood, fumbling to put her shoe back on.

"What is it?" Rick sounded irritated. The truth was that Daniel Kendrick had felt like a threat ever since he'd started back at Riverbeke General – maybe because of the consultant's job or because he'd been in prison for murder and felt slightly intimidated by him – he wasn't sure but he had to deal with it; had to assert his authority, especially now with Colin Mathias, the clinical lead, sniffing around trying to clarify why Bob Hackman had died.

"Just to say I'm needed in the HDU. I've handed my patients over to Dr Adebayo."

"Fine. I'll be up to check on Mrs Wyatt, my tamponade patient, soon."

Daniel nodded and left them to it, closing the door behind him.

Rick turned to Isobel, who was standing against the wall. "Sorry, I have to go but Colin Mathias is asking whether Bob Hackman had the drug or a placebo. He was on the clinical trial but arrested and died this morning."

"Alright, leave it with me. I guess he'll be having a post-mortem?"

"Yes. They are just about to take him down to the morgue."

"Right, I'll sort things from here… are you sure about tonight?"

"Yes. Sorry – another time, OK?"

Isobel shot him a look of disappointment but left graciously.

Rick replied to a couple of important emails and had a chat with Mani Adebayo, the SHO who had taken over from Daniel, then made his way across to the high-dependency unit.

He swiped himself in, chatted briefly with the unit manager, Angela Edwards, and wandered into the main part of the unit. There were eight beds: mixed male and female patients, with only one empty bed. The sound of bonging alarms from cardiac monitors, syringe drivers and dialysis machines pervaded the room and there was a pungent smell of floor cleaner tinged with a microwave ready meal coming from the adjacent nurses' coffee room. Rick could see Fay at the far end, near the window, speaking to Brendon Wilson about his nightmares and Daniel was checking Jean Wyatt's chart. Rick went over to him.

"How is she?" Rick asked.

"Seems to be stable. The cardiothoracic team have been monitoring her tamponade, but she needs a liver lobectomy for metastatic cancer, so she's still your patient." Daniel handed Rick the notes and ambled off to see another patient.

Rick stood at the side of the bed and skimmed through the notes, checking blood and echocardiogram results before turning to the MRI images of her liver cancer. "Mrs Wyatt, I see you've been treated with anti-inflammatory drugs and your blood pressure seems to have been stable. How are you feeling?"

"Not too bad, doctor. A bit of chest pain and an aching tummy but I'm alright." Jean Wyatt smiled through pain-induced gritted teeth.

Rick pondered for a moment over her medication chart and checked the unit for available nurses, but they were all busy. "I see your ibuprofen is due – that's the medication we give you for inflammation and pain – I can give you that now. It might help."

Rick took the prescription chart into the treatment room, prepared an intravenous drug and drew it into a syringe. He took it back to his patient and began to give the drug through the canula in the crook of her arm.

Mrs Wyatt looked puzzled. "I normally take a tablet."

"This will work more quickly and is not so harsh on your stomach. You're written up for both." Rick smiled. He finished giving the medication and disposed of the syringe in the yellow sharps disposal box. "There you are – all done. Hopefully we can get you to a ward soon."

"Thanks, doctor – you've very kind." Mrs Wyatt lay back onto her pillows.

Rick wandered off to say hello to Fay. She'd finished chatting with Brendon Wilson and was flicking through some papers. "Any more near-death experiences?"

Fay looked up and smiled. "No, not today."

Rick returned her smile. She had stunning green eyes and soft, feminine features. He glanced along the curves of her slender figure, accentuated by a tight-fitting jersey dress. Yes, he thought, she was definitely his type and a bit more of a challenge than Isobel. It would be rather fun to try and lure her away from Daniel – it would give him a sense of control, of power. Even a thrill.

Fay cut into his thoughts as she continued. "Mrs Jacobs told me about her NDE. She's been blind since birth, but she saw you resuscitating her."

"She saw me? And did she see a light at the end of a dark tunnel and a bunch of angels as well?" Rick knew he was being facetious.

"Actually, she did go through a tunnel and experienced a bright light. I believe her. These NDEs are very real, deeply emotional, and can be life-altering to the people that experience them." Fay seemed defensive and a little feisty. Rick liked that.

He smiled at her, his eyes darkening. "I see you take your research very seriously, Dr Kendrick."

"Yes, I do. You know, Mrs Jacobs watched you as you called for the crash trolley and shouted orders to the medics. She said you had been with her just before she had her heart attack."

"Really?"

Fay's expression softened. "Yes. And she's very grateful that you saved her life."

Rick grinned. "Well, we'll have to discuss your research further sometime." In his peripheral vision, he caught Daniel watching them from the other side of the unit. Then he glanced across at Mrs Wyatt. She seemed to be in some distress. "Excuse me," he said, "I have to go."

Rick strode across to Jean Wyatt. Her blood pressure was stable, but she was showing cardiac arrythmias on the monitor. She seemed very distressed and was clutching her chest. The canula in the crook of her arm had dislodged and crimson blood was pouring from her vein, soaking the white sheets and pillows.

Daniel rushed across. "Is she alright?" He felt her pulse. "Her heart rate is all over the place – could be another tamponade." He grabbed a wad of paper tissues and compressed the bleeding vein in her arm.

"I don't think so," Rick said, listening to her heart with his stethoscope. "Her blood pressure is OK, and I can't discern a pulsus paradoxus. She's been on anti-inflammatories, so I suspect her tamponade has resolved. She's been stable so far."

They both watched the monitor as her heart rhythm deteriorated further. A nurse had torn off a length of surgical tape, added another wad of gauze and taped it to Mrs Wyatt's bleeding arm, then pulled out the pillows and laid her flat on the bed. Another nurse had unbuttoned her nightie to expose her chest.

Rick watched the monitor and listened to her heart rate again. "She's going into ventricular tachycardia – VT. Get the crash trolley, we need to shock her."

The nurse grabbed the trolley and defibrillator from the far side of the unit and hurried back with it, two other nurses following behind her. Daniel was trying to get a canula into the back of her hand, but her veins had collapsed – it was impossible.

Rick charged the defibrillator to 120 joules, slapped the pads onto Jean Wyatt's chest and applied the paddles. "Stand clear," he shouted. The electrical charge surged through her heart but failed to restore her heartbeat. Rick gawped at Daniel. "Can you get IV access?"

"No," Daniel said, trying another vein. "It's not looking good."

Rick started charging the defibrillator to 160 joules, but he needed to get some adrenaline into her circulation quickly in order to concentrate blood around her vital organs – especially her brain and heart – and to stimulate the heart muscle. "Get me 1 mg of adrenaline and a spinal needle," he said to one of the nurses.

Daniel looked aghast. "You're not going to give an intracardiac injection, surely?"

"If we can't get IV access, what choice do I have? It will be faster than intubating." Rick was already probing between Mrs Wyatt's ribs for the fourth intercostal space with the fingers of his left hand and taking the syringe from the nurse, armed with a 9 cm needle, in his right.

"Stand clear," Rick held the syringe in his hand as if he was poised to stab her with a knife. He thrust the needle between the patient's ribs and rapidly pushed the plunger of the syringe with his thumb, delivering the adrenaline directly into the chamber of the left ventricle of her heart. He withdrew the needle and watched the monitor for signs of a heartbeat.

Daniel was about to step forward with the defibrillator when Rick stopped him.

"She's back," Rick said.

They both looked at the cardiac monitor. Mrs Wyatt's heart was beating again in a normal sinus rhythm.

FORTY-FIVE

Fay had walked across the field to the river. The water was flowing fast downstream as it made its way south toward Riverbeke town before turning east and on to the estuary. In the babbling currents, Fay could hear the sounds of children laughing and the sweet gurgling sounds Sophie used to make as she splashed in the bubble baths she'd so loved. She stood on the riverbank for more than thirty minutes, mesmerised by the eddies and currents as the river flowed by. Countless thoughts collided in her mind – Sophie's birth, the blissful six months of her life they'd shared, the police woman telling them they had found her little body, the dark pit of despair and grief that had fuelled her anger… then the weight of the knife in her hand as she slit Robert Horton's throat in his own garden, the pleasure she felt as she watched Jack Butler convulse and die after she spiked his drink with ketamine, the terror in Paula Bishop's eyes as she suffocated to death from inside her own body – the torrent of rage that tore through her as Wixx callously told her he'd killed her darling Sophie…

The sound of laughing children coming from the river morphed into horrifying screams; Sophie's terrified screeches and the cries of her three little embryos. Her precious babies. Fay took a small step toward the river…

"Are you alright, miss?"

Fay turned slowly to see a tall man in a raincoat with a brown cocker spaniel at his side. "Sorry… I… umm…" Her own words seemed like echoes that came from the river and not from her.

"Are you OK? You seem troubled." There was a look of concern in his eyes as he took a step closer.

"I… I don't know." The thoughts in her mind became jumbled and somehow clumped together into an incoherent mess before seeming to melt away into the water. Then she realised where she was. She was on her way to get herself a coffee and some lunch. Yes, that was what she must do. She turned to thank the man but there was nobody there. She looked into the distance but there was no man and no dog.

Bewildered, Fay turned from the river and began to walk robotically toward the tearooms, her mind numb, uncomprehending, as if her thoughts had emptied into the river and been washed away along with the sounds she thought she'd heard. It was warm inside and there were several groups of people sitting at tables, engrossed in conversation. A woman looked up as she went past – could she see what had been going through her mind? Did she know she had killed those people? Fay glared at her but went on to the counter when the woman looked away.

"Yes, what would you like?" A pleasant middle-aged woman in a navy apron over a light blue bobbly jumper smiled at her.

Fay was befuddled for a moment, then remembered she wanted coffee. "A latte, please."

The woman tapped her order into the till. "Anything to eat?"

"A toasted sandwich, I think." She checked the fillings on the menu. "Cheese and red onion marmalade." Fay handed the woman a £10 note.

The woman gave her some loose change and a number on a wooden stand. "We'll bring it over to you."

Fay wandered over to an empty table near a woodburning stove. She didn't realise how cold she'd become. She shivered and sat as close to the fire as she could get, then placed the number on the table and put the coins into her purse. There was a view of the gardens across the adjacent table with the river beyond. Had she really heard voices coming from the water? They seemed so real but now she wasn't sure. Maybe she was just tired. There had been a lot going on lately, with Daniel being released from prison and her giving up the clinic and starting her research project.

A waitress brought her order. Fay sipped the coffee but left the sandwich – she didn't know why she'd ordered it. She wasn't hungry and pushed it away. She sat for twenty minutes, staring out of the window, relishing the warmth from the fire – her mind still numb and unable to make sense of the sounds she'd heard or why the man had appeared and brought her back to reality. She heard a police siren in the distance and her thoughts turned to Daniel and the hospital. She checked the time on her phone: 2pm. Where had the past couple of hours gone? She ought to get back to work. She tapped out the number for the taxi and waited outside. A different driver pulled up and she asked him to take her to Riverbeke General.

They made the journey in silence.

Fay went up to the high-dependency unit. She wanted to check one last time on Brendon Wilson. She had to get a grip, she told herself, as her mind started to wander back to Sophie and her lost embryos.

"Ah, Fay. I've been looking for you." Angela Edwards caught up with her. "Mrs Wyatt wanted to have a chat. You might remember she had a cardiac arrest this morning. Sounds like she has an interesting story to tell."

"Sure", Fay said. She could see Brendon was asleep, so she made her way straight to Jean Wyatt. She didn't have her briefcase with her, but she grabbed a notebook and pencil from her handbag, took a deep breath and tried to calm her rambling mind.

"Hello, Mrs Wyatt. I'm Fay Kendrick. I understand you'd like a chat." The two women shook hands. Fay hid behind her professional façade.

Mrs Wyatt looked pale and drawn as she lay in her bed, but she smiled and her eyes were shining with what seemed to be elation. "Yes, I would. Thank you, doctor. I had the most amazing experience." She gestured to the chair at the side of her bed and Fay sat.

"Apparently, I was clinically dead for several minutes this morning, but I saw everything that happened. I was suddenly outside my body and floating upward. I saw you talking to Dr Estevez and then I saw him and another doctor with three nurses around my body. Then..." Mrs Wyatt smiled and closed her eyes momentarily as if she was reliving the experience in her mind. "There was a white light surrounding me and I felt the most incredible sense of love and peace. My grandfather was there with me, and I could see the most amazing swirling colours of light. Then I was floating with my grandfather toward a stunningly beautiful meadow packed with wild flowers – more wonderful than anything I've ever seen on Earth. We reached a gate and my grandfather said that, if I went through the gate, there would be no going back to my life here. That it would be my choice whether I stayed or came back to my body. I wanted to go..." She reached out for Fay's hand.

Fay took her hand in both of hers. "Go on, Mrs Wyatt."

There was a tear in her eye as she spoke. "I really wanted to go through that gate and stay in the most beautiful place I've ever experienced but I was suddenly pulled back and woke up in my body again. Dr Estevez had brought me back to life."

"And how do you feel about that now?" Fay had been fascinated with Mrs Wyatt's account, finally forgetting, for the moment, about her own troubles.

Mrs Wyatt held Fay's gaze, the shadow of sadness in her eyes. "Conflicted, if I'm honest. I wanted to stay with my grandfather.

That place felt like my real home. I've never experienced such love and acceptance. Never..."

"But you have a chance of a longer life now with your family." Fay squeezed her hand.

"I know and I should be grateful, but I have cancer and I won't live much longer. To be honest, I can't face the pain and distress that's coming. I was so happy in that place this morning – I just want to go back." She paused and looked into Fay's eyes. "Is it bad of me to feel that way?"

"No – not at all. It's good to be honest and recognise those feelings."

Mrs Wyatt gripped Fay's hand firmly and pulled her toward her. "Please don't tell anyone. I don't want to seem ungrateful."

"It will be our secret, I promise," Fay whispered softly.

FORTY-SIX

Fay stayed awhile with Mrs Wyatt. Her mind had been wandering back to Sophie. Had her little girl experienced the love and light that her patients had described? It was comforting to think of her in a beautiful place. She looked across at the pregnant woman, still in a coma – there had been a group of doctors around the bed for some time. They had attached a cardiotocograph – CTG – to her abdomen and the sound of the baby's heartbeat could be heard around the unit. It was fast one minute, then slowed before speeding up again. The doctors had been in deep discussion but abruptly seemed to come to an agreement. The nurses gathered around her bed, attaching her to a portable ventilator and cardiac monitor, the CTG sound was turned down but continued to record the foetal heart rate. Fay could hear it faintly and it reminded her of when she had been pregnant and the wonder of hearing Sophie's heartbeat. Within fifteen minutes, the woman was being wheeled away.

"Perhaps you should get some rest now, Mrs Wyatt," Fay said. "I'll come and see you again tomorrow." She patted the woman's hand, gathered up her notes and handbag and wandered over to the student nurse that was tidying up the area around the woman's bed. She was the same nurse that she'd spoken to previously.

"Is she alright?" Fay asked.

"They've decided to do a caesarean. One baby is getting a little distressed – late decelerations on the CTG. It's probably the drugs."

"One baby? Do you mean there's more than one?"

"Yes, they discovered from an earlier scan that Megan is having twins. It's best they get the babies out soon. They have a good chance at 32 weeks."

Fay was astonished. Twins – what she'd always wanted. "Where will they do the caesarean?"

"They've rushed her to theatre one, I think." The nurse was absently tidying and wiping down surfaces with antibacterial spray.

Fay thanked her and wandered away, her mind now occupied with thoughts of the woman and the dreadful situation she was in. Would she survive to see her babies? And, if she did survive, how would she cope with twins as a widowed mother?

Fay could still hear the echo of the baby's heartbeat in her mind and on impulse, she headed toward the theatre suite. Maybe she could see the babies as they took them to the neonatal unit – to see for herself that they were alright. She stood outside the entrance for some minutes, then a doctor came out and she could see thought the doorway that there was nobody manning the reception desk. She adjusted her name badge – unless someone looked closely, nobody would tell whether or not she was one of the medical staff. She straightened her back and walked purposefully past the reception area and down a long corridor. There were staff changing rooms on the right and offices and equipment rooms on the left. Then she was in the operating theatre area. She found theatre one and a signpost that indicated a viewing room. She crept up the stairs to the door and opened it a crack. The room was in darkness and there was nobody inside. She went in and closed the door. Ahead was a large viewing window that looked down onto the operating theatre and in front of that a row of chairs. She sat and watched as the woman was wheeled into theatre and transferred to the operating table. She was covered in green drapes and an orderly adjusted the operating room lamps, while a nurse swabbed the woman's swollen abdomen with a brown liquid that seemed to glow under the LED lights. Behind her a ventilator and a bank of syringe drivers pumping drugs into her body was all that was keeping her alive.

The swab nurse wheeled a trolley, laid out with stainless-steel instruments, next to the operating table and the anaesthetist was busy adjusting the ventilator settings. Then, in strode one of the doctors Fay had seen on the unit, followed by two others, all gowned, masked and gloved. They gathered around the woman. Fay couldn't hear what was being said but could see glimpses of the operation from her vantage point above. Other medical and nursing staff in scrubs came into the room with a Resuscitaire and an incubator. Within minutes, the obstetrician had cut through the skin and muscle layers and into the uterus. Through a gush of amniotic fluid, he reached inside and delivered the baby's head. He gently manipulated her shoulders and brought the rest of the tiny body out onto the woman's stomach. His assistant cut the cord. The baby was covered in blood and vernix but wasn't moving or crying. She looked pale and limp. Fay held her breath as she watched, willing the baby to cry.

The newborn was handed to a midwife, who placed her on the Resuscitaire's warming platform and rubbed her down with a hospital towel. Another pushed a suction tube into the baby's throat while another held an oxygen mask near her face. Then Fay saw the baby's arms and legs move and could see her skin had turned pink. The midwife wrapped her in a clean towel and placed her in the incubator. Fay couldn't hear her, but she could see the baby was crying.

After a tense few minutes, the obstetrician delivered the second baby's head, followed by a twist of the shoulders and finally the body. It looked like a boy. The assistant cut the cord and the baby was handed to the midwife. He looked blue and wasn't moving. Again, the midwife rubbed the baby down with a towel and suctioned his throat. Another administered oxygen but the baby didn't seem to be responding. Fay watched anxiously for the second twin to breathe. It looked like they were going to intubate and get him onto a ventilator. One of the nurses wheeled the first twin from the theatre and into the anaesthetic room but the midwife called to her and she rushed back in, leaving the incubator behind.

Fay watched for a few moments, then, compelled to act, she crept out of the viewing room and made her way back down the stairs and along the corridor to the double doors that led to the anaesthetic room. She peeped inside and there, in the incubator, was the baby girl. The sound of her cry overwhelmed Fay with a flood of maternal feelings. She ached to hold her and comfort her. The baby's chubby little face was crumpled in her distress and her chin was quivering. White vernix and a few spots of dried blood were stuck to her forehead and a shock of dark hair. She was a perfect miracle of life. Fay's instincts overwhelmed her. She had to hold the poor little soul, to comfort her. She had to.

Fay opened the porthole of the incubator, unfolded the towel she was wrapped in and held the baby's hand, but she was still crying. She needed to be cuddled, to have human contact and to realise she wasn't alone. Fay unclipped the front of the incubator and dropped the front fap. Then she reached in and lifted out the tiny baby and held her close. It was the most wonderful feeling – to be holding a newborn again. To feel the weight of her body in her arms, to breathe in her smell, marvel at the softness of her downy skin and touch her tiny fingers. She was perfect – just as Sophie had been. As her embryos would have been had they survived.

"*Shhhh*… little one," she whispered. Fay cuddled the baby closer to her, wiping away some of the white vernix from her face with a corner of the towel. "It's alright now. You're safe." She instinctively rocked her back and forth and tucked the towel in around her quivering little chin. The baby started to settle, and her wailing cries gradually turned to sobs then little intakes of breath. Soon, she was asleep in Fay's arms, content to be held and welcomed into the world by another human being.

Fay walked back and forth in the small room, rocking the baby in her arms. She began to hum tunelessly as memories of Sophie came flooding into her mind. "It's alright, little Sophie," she whispered, "Mummy's here. I've got you all safe and sound. Nobody can hurt you now." She blocked out the memories of Sophie's murder, filling her mind instead with the familiar sensations she was feeling – she was actually holding a newborn baby. "Little Sophie. My precious sweetheart – I love you so much. I'll never let them take you from me again." Fay rocked the baby, drenched in the feelings of motherhood – of love for this little life she held. She closed her eyes and projected herself into Sophie's nursery. The cot was there waiting for her, the teddy waiting to be cuddled. There were clothes in the wardrobe, plenty of nappies and toys – everything a baby could need. She imagined herself bathing her, then singing a lullaby as she rocked her to sleep in her arms. Fay began to quietly sing "You Are My Sunshine", not realising the poignancy of the words…

She was swept up in a soothing world of motherhood once again. A cocoon from the dreadful grief that had shattered her life.

Then Fay realised she would have to get away from the hospital – get the baby home to the nursery before they stopped her. Would she be warm enough in a towel to get her to the car? She looked around the room – there was a hospital blanket folded on the end of the patient's trolley. She grabbed it and gently wrapped it around the baby.

She had to get her home before anyone saw them.

FORTY-SEVEN

Daniel and Rick had stayed on the unit for a while after Mrs Wyatt's cardiac arrest. She seemed to have recovered well and had been talking to Angela and then Fay.

The ICU doctors had been monitoring the enlarged spleen that Megan Foley had developed since the road traffic accident. Delivering the twins had been their only option.

Rick was on his way back to the ward and Daniel was still in the HDU when his bleep went off. He called the number displayed on the bleep from the phone on the unit.

"Dr Kendrick, you're needed urgently in theatre one. Megan Foley has a splenic rupture, and we need a general surgeon – stat."

"I'm on my way," Daniel said.

He ran to the theatre suite and into the scrub room, put on his theatre cap, a surgical mask and began washing his hands and forearms as quickly as he could.

The obstetrician, still gloved and gowned, spoke to him while his assistant sutured Megan's uterus. "Thanks for coming so quickly. This lady is thirty years old, been in an induced coma for the past two weeks following an RTA. We just C-sectioned her and delivered twins at thirty-two weeks gestation. We picked up a subscapular haematoma on scan and it looks like it may have ruptured. Probably a trauma injury from the accident."

"OK, I'll be there in just a minute." Daniel finished scrubbing, wiped his hands with a sterile paper towel and thrust his arms into a gown a nurse was holding for him.

Daniel heard Rick's voice behind him. "I'm scrubbing in… Daniel, open her up and I'll take over."

Daniel realised Rick must have been bleeped as well. Plus, Dr Nnamani Adebayo appeared in the scrub room, ready to assist.

The obstetrician continued. "It could be an intra-abdominal haemorrhage judging by her vital signs."

Daniel snapped on powdered latex gloves and followed the obstetrician into the theatre. The midwives were still working on the second twin. The scrub nurse was organising a pack of surgical instruments for a laparotomy. The obstetric SHO moved aside to let Daniel in, and he quickly assessed Megan's condition. He needed to move quickly.

"Scalpel please." The scrub nurse slapped the handle of a number eleven blade into his palm. He made a midline incision and quickly worked though the fat and muscle layers before dividing the peritoneum and reaching the abdominal cavity. As suspected, there was a large subcapsular haematoma in the spleen, with blood rapidly filling Megan's abdomen.

The mood in theatre was strained with midwives battling to save the second twin and surgeons now working to save their mother. The sound of ventilators and monitors, suction and the whirring of syringe drivers the only sounds in the tense atmosphere of the operating theatre.

Daniel managed to find the ruptured artery as Rick, gowned and gloved, strutted into theatre. "Alright, Daniel, I'll take over from here." He held his hand out, waiting to take the artery clips from him.

Without looking up, Daniel said, "It's alright, I've got it." He clipped the artery and the bleeding stopped. The obstetric

SHO suctioned blood from the abdominal cavity; a pink froth moving up the tube into the receptacle.

Rick was insistent. "Move aside, please."

Daniel glanced at Rick. He was bullish and meant business. Reluctantly and with a dash of resentment, he moved to the other side of the patient and took over from the obstetric SHO, who stood by, observing. Rick was still refusing to acknowledge his experience. Only months ago, he'd been in the same consultant role as Rick and was perfectly capable of dealing with a ruptured artery, yet he was being treated like a doctor just out of medical school. Was it a deliberate attempt to undermine him or was Rick just an arrogant piece of work?

Daniel dutifully assisted as Rick repaired the spleen. The tension between them was palpable and others in theatre seemed to sense it too. Like a couple of tigers, they were prowling around one another and, instead of the usual chatter between the theatre staff, there was an edgy silence. The midwives had been joined by a paediatrician and were still trying to resuscitate the second twin. They worked as a team, each anticipating the other's next moves. The baby looked floppy, blue and unresponsive as he lay on the Resuscitaire. Daniel desperately hoped they could save him, but it wasn't looking good.

Rick finished repairing the artery and, over his surgical mask, he shot Daniel a look that bordered on contempt. "Would you suture up, please?" Without waiting for a reply, he strode out of theatre via the scrub room, snapping off bloodied gloves and removing his cap and gown, throwing them all in a metal bin on his way out.

Daniel was left with no choice but to complete the routine part of the operation – suturing up the layers of tissue. "Yep – I'm just your bloody dogsbody," he whispered beneath his mask. Still, at least Megan Foley was alive and had a decent chance of recovery now the twins had been born. Daniel got on with the job in hand.

FORTY-EIGHT

Fay had wrapped the baby as best she could ready for the cold walk to the car. She was desperate to get her home to the warmth of the nursery, and quickly. She would bathe her and dress her in one of Sophie's newborn babygrows that she'd put away. She looked through the glass panel into the theatre and she could see Daniel and the other doctors still operating on Megan and the midwives and the paediatrician working on the second twin. This was her chance to get away. But as she crept out of the anaesthetic room, she heard the dulcet Spanish tones of Rick Estevez behind her.

"Dr Kendrick – what are you doing here?"

She turned and saw Rick's eyes widen as he noticed the baby in her arms. Her mouth flew open, dumbfounded.

Rick grabbed her arm and steered her back into the anaesthetic room, closing the door firmly behind them. "What the hell are you doing?"

Fay still couldn't speak.

"This baby needs to go to the neonatal unit. It needs to be in an incubator. Look, the poor thing is freezing." He put a hand on the baby's head.

Fay finally found her voice. "It's a little girl. My Sophie."

She pulled the baby closer to her, pushing Rick's hand away indignantly.

"Dr Kendrick – Fay – you shouldn't be in here. What on Earth were you planning to do?"

Fay hesitated for a moment. "She was crying. She needs a mother. I can look after her." She saw the puzzlement in Rick's eyes turn to silent recognition.

"You lost your little girl, didn't you?" He steered her toward the patient couch and they both sat, perched on the edge.

Fay nodded slowly. "She was… murdered." She looked down at the living, breathing baby in her arms. "Nobody can take her away again."

Rick put his hand on the small of Fay's back, trying to soothe her. "Fay, this baby belongs to Megan. You do realise that, don't you?"

Fay glanced at Rick. "This is my Sophie – she's mine." Her eyes were wet with tears, her mind a jumble of incoherent thoughts.

Rick seemed to sympathise with her. He gave her a sad smile. "You know, I lost my little boy too. He was just five years old."

Fay looked at him wide-eyed. "You did?"

"Yes, his name was Alessandro. He died in a car crash in Spain a few years ago. I lost my wife, Maria, as well. It's something you never get over. Grief can make you do irrational things."

Fay just looked at Rick blankly, rocking the baby in her arms.

"Let's get her back into the incubator." He went to take the baby from her.

"No…" Fay stood and clutched the little girl tightly. "She's mine now… mine." Fay heard the screams again that had come from the river. Faintly at first but growing louder.

"Fay – she's Megan's little girl – she has a mother and a twin brother too. You must give her back."

Fay stood shaking her head, clutching the baby ever tighter. "You can't have her… she's mine. My little Sophie…" Fay desperately needed to get out of there, to take the baby home, to stop the screams echoing in her head. Her eyes darting around the room for an exit, she tried to get past Rick, but he stood and blocked her way out.

"Fay, please – you must give her back. She's not Sophie. She belongs to Megan – not you. You're not thinking straight. You're still grieving for your little girl, but this won't help." He bent his head to look into her eyes. "Please, you have to put the baby back."

Fay was sobbing now, not wanting to listen to Rick, yet knowing somewhere in the depths of her troubled mind that he was right. She could see compassion in his face – his smile, the way he looked at her with dark, benevolent eyes. He seemed to understand her pain like no one she had ever met before. Without thinking, she blurted out, "I've done something really bad."

Rick continued to smile and look into her eyes. She trusted him – she could see a kindred spirit. She had to unburden herself of the terrible things she had done. The things that had haunted her for long lonely months. Without thinking, she had said it, "I killed four people – murderers and paedophiles – I killed them, Rick..."

Rick frowned, his eyes darkening. "I don't understand..."

"I was the serial killer the police were after in the summer. I killed those people – they were my patients and I killed them." Fay clutched the baby in her arms, the screams in her head starting to recede.

"But I thought that Wixx character had confessed to the killings."

"It was me. We blamed Wixx but it was me. I was trying to rid the world of the evil monster that killed Sophie." A stab of anger mixed with guilt flashed through her.

Rick simply nodded slowly, taking in this new information.

The screams in her head had finally stopped and a wave of relief at having finally released her deadly secret washed over Fay. But it was tinged with the fear of what Rick would do now he knew the truth. She looked into his eyes and saw a brooding acknowledgement of what she had said. She saw no judgement – not yet – perhaps that would come later.

Fay stiffened. She shouldn't have told him. It was a moment of madness – of extreme pressure. It was a secret only she and Daniel knew but now she had betrayed her husband as well as herself. What the hell would become of her now? She imagined Rick calling the police, her being arrested and put in prison for the rest of her life for what she had done. But in that moment she didn't care – all she wanted was to rid herself of the burden she carried around constantly. The guilt that she had killed those four people compounded by shame that she had taken such pleasure from it. She clutched the baby – all she wanted now was to take her home – to be a family. To be a mother…

Again, she gazed steadily into Rick's eyes and saw only compassion. No horror at what she had done, no revulsion or rejection of her – only empathy for another human being and an understanding of her frailties.

"I think we should put the baby into the incubator. She will need a feed soon and she needs to go to the neonatal unit to be checked out." He gently tilted her chin toward him and held her gaze. "Will you do this, Fay? You know it's what's best for the baby and best for you."

Fay knew he was right. He wanted what was best for them both. He wasn't judging her – just trying to help. She began to come to her senses and realise what could have happened if Rick hadn't stopped her from stealing the baby. It didn't bear thinking about. Rick gently took the baby from her arms, and she let him. She watched as he unwrapped her from the blanket, leaving her in the towel, and placed her in the incubator. He fastened the front flap and secured the porthole. The baby stirred slightly but settled again to sleep.

"Thank you," Fay said, her face wet with tears for the emptiness and loss she felt.

Rick turned and took her in his arms – an act of friendship. Understanding. Compassion. She felt safe there – protected from her own volatility. She nestled her head into his shoulder and sobbed. For a while, he said nothing – just held her, his strong arms around her like a refuge from the storm raging in her mind. There was an unspoken bond between them now. He stroked her hair as she sobbed until she could cry no more. Only then did he break their embrace.

"I'll get Daniel. You need to go home…" His voice was quiet, reassuring, firm. He gently wiped her tears with his fingers and led her to a chair in the corner of the room. "Stay here. I'll see you again soon and we'll talk. Alright?"

"Thank you…"

Then, after wheeling the incubator into theatre, he was gone.

FORTY-NINE

Daniel was starting to suture the skin on Megan's wound when Rick came into theatre, with the incubator containing the first twin. He parked it near the Resuscitaire without comment, then walked over to Daniel.

"Let Dr Adebayo finish up – I need to see you in the anaesthetic room."

Daniel wondered what the hell he was going to belittle him for now but dutifully handed the needle holder and forceps to Mani Adebayo and followed Rick, snapping off his surgical gloves, then removing his gown and mask.

Rick closed the door of the anaesthetic room behind them and gestured to Fay, who was sitting, dazed, in the corner of the room. "She needs to go home. I narrowly managed to stop her abducting the baby."

Daniel looked aghast at his wife. "Shit…" was all he could manage.

"She needs help. Take her home and take the rest of the day off." Rick sounded uncharacteristically empathetic.

"Are you going to report this?" Daniel could barely believe what he'd heard. The repercussions were only just beginning to dawn on him.

"No," Rick said without hesitation. "Just take her home." He gave Fay a sad smile and left.

Daniel looked at Fay. She watched him like a startled fawn, her eyes red and swollen.

"What happened?"

She hesitated for a moment. "I thought she was Sophie… I had a moment of – I don't know…"

"Madness?" Daniel stood in front of her, one hand on his hip.

She nodded sombrely. "It felt like that…"

"I thought you were feeling better – you know" – he lowered his voice to a whisper – "now we got rid of your journal. We said we would put the past behind us."

"I know… I'm sorry."

Daniel stood for long moments, wondering if there was anything constructive, he could say. Fay seemed to have lost her mind for a while, but he had no idea how to deal with it. He had really believed they were moving on from the grief of losing their little girl. "Come on, let's get you home."

Daniel drove them in silence. Fay seemed subdued and lost in her own thoughts and Daniel was struggling to come to terms with what she had done. It had to be Rick bloody Estevez that had found her – why couldn't it have been him or even his friend Matt? But Rick, of all people.

They arrived home and Fay looked tired and overwhelmed. "Why don't you go to bed for a little sleep?"

She nodded her agreement and went upstairs. Daniel followed her, partly drew the curtains and settled her into bed, tucking the pillow under her head.

"Stay with me," she said softly.

Daniel lay on top of the bed next to her and she nestled her head against his chest, their arms around one another. He gently stroked her hair and soon her breathing slowed and deepened as she fell asleep. Maisie had come into the bedroom and was curled up on the end of the bed.

Daniel's mind went over and over Fay's behaviour since he'd been released from prison. He hadn't noticed anything troubling – not since they had burned the journal. Either she was hiding her true feelings or this was just a reaction to the trauma that Megan Foley had gone through – the car crash, losing her husband and fighting for her life along with her twins while in a coma. Fay must have empathised with her, and it had dragged up the trauma of losing Sophie all over again. But to nearly abduct a baby from the hospital – shit, that was serious. If it ever got out… he couldn't bear to think about it. He just had to hope that Rick was true to his word and wasn't going to report it. It was his word against Fay's. Luckily, she hadn't taken the baby outside the theatre suite. If she had – the consequences would have been serious.

What the hell could he do? He was trying his best to be a good husband. Perhaps they should go to Shelly for the counselling she had promised but it seemed risky. If it ever came out that Fay had committed the murders…

He blocked the thought from his mind. Their secret could never come out.

Never.

He lay on the bed as Fay slept in his arms, their breathing now synchronised. He felt the warmth of her body and the fragrance of her hair as he absently stroked her long blonde tendrils. All he wanted was to be a doctor and a good husband, but he wondered if they would ever get over losing Sophie.

Or Fay's vigilante killings…

Would the secret they shared bond them together or tear them apart? He thought about the rage that had led Fay to kill. Was she still stuck in the furious anger of her grief? He couldn't see signs of it. When she'd visited him in prison, she'd been upbeat and coping – or was that a façade for his benefit? Today, she seemed sad, lost and vulnerable but what had prompted her to want to abduct Megan's baby? Perhaps she'd struggled to cope while he'd been in prison – just when she needed his support – but she'd seemed alright until now.

Or was she?

Perhaps he was sliding into denial again – as he had after Sophie's death – unaware of the inner turmoil his wife was going through and unwilling to confront it.

A visceral panic began to rise from deep in his belly. From a happy couple in love, expecting their first baby a few years ago, they had since lived through the harrowing abyss of losing Sophie, the threat of losing one another and then the deadly secret of Fay's killings. Their secret – a life sentence of its own – kept them trapped in an endless cycle of betrayal, remorse, shame, confusion and fear. Was he strong enough for this? A life tarnished by the actions of someone he loves.

And what of his own actions?

In the end, the act of killing Wixx had not relieved him of the feelings of injustice or anger he'd felt at the time – they had simply merged with the later turmoil of self-recrimination and regret. Wixx should have been tried in a court of law, just as he had himself. He should have been subjected to society's judgement of his actions. Taking the law into his own hands, even in a deranged fit of rage, was wrong – Daniel knew that. And yet Wixx had pitilessly murdered their beloved daughter. That monstrous act could not go unpunished.

The raw brutality of retributive justice – an eye for an eye, a tooth for a tooth, a life for a life? Or the flawed dictates of a society that can allow murderers to go unpunished or hand the innocent a lifetime of wretched and unjust incarceration. Either way, they are futures that are decided at the hands of others. A lifetime in prison is, ultimately, death. The slow death of a life without hope. A soul trapped in a material world, aching for its final release.

Daniel had lost control in the moment he killed Wixx – besieged by the raging anger of grief – and for that he would have death on his hands forever. A court might have acquitted him of killing his daughter's murderer, but his soul would never let go. He had deprived another human being of the chance to redeem himself; to realise for himself that what he had done was wrong. Wasn't all life sacred and equal in the eyes of God? Didn't we all have the right to learn from our mistakes?

Daniel felt a karmic justice hanging over him like the sword of Damocles – demanding the payment due for his blood debt – a debt he can never repay. There was no escape from himself. Silently, he was being consumed by shame.

He stroked Fay's hair and gently kissed the top of her head as she slept. What inner torment must she be going through? Would love be enough to hold her mind together? Could they really find their way back to one another as he so desperately wanted?

The fading winter sun was casting shadows around the room as he felt her slipping out of reach.

"Don't leave me, sweetheart," he whispered.

FIFTY

Daniel glanced at the alarm clock. Almost 5pm. He was due at Oliver's clinic in an hour and Rosie would be bringing the dogs back any minute. He gently pulled his arm from beneath Fay's neck. She stirred briefly but went back to sleep. He changed into a pair of grey suit trousers and a tailored blue shirt and went downstairs just as Rosie arrived on the doorstep. He opened the front door and Chester and Ella bounded in, tails wagging their usual frenzied greeting.

"Thanks, Rosie." He smiled at her, and she returned the gesture, seemingly a little more comfortable in his presence now.

The dogs followed him into the kitchen and Ella made a beeline for Maisie's dish, walloping down the last of her dried food and tipping her water over the floor in the process. Daniel managed to mop it up and clear the mess she'd left. Then he grabbed a bowl of muesli drenched in coconut milk – it would have to do for dinner as there wasn't time to cook. Maybe he and Fay could eat together later.

He was about to write a note to Fay when she appeared in the kitchen. Dishevelled; her hair looked like it had been brushed with a hand grenade and her mascara was smudged under her eyes. She looked vulnerable and Daniel was reluctant to leave her after the drama that had unfolded that afternoon.

"Hello, sweetheart. Feeling better?"

Fay yawned and dragged her cardigan around her. "Yes, I'm fine. Sorry about this afternoon – I don't know what came over me."

Daniel kissed her. "I have to get to Oliver's. Will you be alright for a couple of hours? Should I get Shelly to come over and keep you company?"

"No – I'll be fine. Honestly. You go, I'll cook when you get back." She sounded like her normal self again – either that or it was a good pretence.

Daniel hesitated. "Maybe I should call Oliver and put it off for this evening."

"No – go. You'll be letting your clients down. Really, I'm OK. Just feeling like a prize idiot now."

"Did you really try to take the baby, Fay?" Trying to rationalise things, Daniel wondered if Rick had exaggerated what had happened – he wouldn't be surprised if he was trying to score points and Fay was certainly playing it down.

"She was crying, and I was just trying to soothe her – that's all. It must have looked like I was about to snatch her, but I wouldn't have done that." She looked straight into Daniel's eyes. "You know I would never hurt a newborn baby."

"Of course, you wouldn't. Maybe it was just a misunderstanding." Daniel held her for a few moments then kissed her lips. She was warm and soft and sleepy. He wished he could stay but he'd made a promise to Oliver.

"I have to go…"

Daniel drove the Defender to the clinic and spent over two hours giving Botox injections. Melissa had been around and had not engaged in conversation, but he had heard her and Oliver arguing upstairs complete with slammed doors and raised voices. He decided to mind his own business and Nadia, the receptionist, had rolled her eyes as if it were a regular occurrence.

He'd bought Fay a bunch of mixed roses and lilies from the supermarket on the way home and she had showered, dressed and applied fresh make-up. She'd also cooked a vegetarian lasagne with salad and crusty French bread and there was a glass of merlot waiting for him on the kitchen counter. It had seemed like a miraculous transformation since Rick had called him into the anaesthetic room and accused her of abducting Megan Foley's baby earlier that day. They'd spent a normal sort of evening together and she seemed bright and bubbly again – in fact, Daniel thought she seemed quite animated. A total transformation. Perhaps the sleep had done her good.

All the agonising he'd done that afternoon and she seemed fine. Perhaps Rick had overreacted after all.

FIFTY-ONE

Daniel had arrived on the ward for work the next morning but was asked to go to the high-dependency unit. He was reviewing a few of the surgical patients with Matt. There had been no sign of Rick, although he'd been on the unit minutes before – perhaps he'd been called away to an emergency. Colin Mathias had been in back-to-back meetings on the ward all morning and had asked not to be disturbed. Daniel noticed Eddie Bates hanging around one of the patients and glared at him as if to warn him off. He still hadn't spoken to him about the theft of John Gardener's wallet and wondered if he should. He had no actual evidence that he had stolen it and was reluctant to cause trouble. Bates seemed to get the unspoken message and went back to mopping the floor.

Daniel had got caught up with examining a patient's laparotomy wound when Matt called him from the other side of the unit. Daniel put his head around the curtain to see Matt struggling to lay Jean Wyatt flat on the bed. Her cardiac monitor was alarming amid the constant cacophony of bonging and bleeping – cardiac monitors, ventilators, syringe drivers and other life-saving medical equipment.

"Sorry – have to go," he said to his patient, snapping off his gloves and squirting hand sanitiser onto his hands.

He rubbed it in as he rushed to Mrs Wyatt's bedside.

"She's crashed." Matt said.

Daniel looked at the monitor. Her heart rate was absent – just a flat green line running across the screen. "Shit – she's in asystole."

"I've no idea what happened – just found her collapsed."

Daniel started cardiac compressions "One… two… three… four…" He counted to thirty and stopped to allow Matt to deliver two breaths via a bag and mask.

A nurse checked a dose of adrenaline with Daniel and handed it to him. He gave it intravenously, via the canula. "Still in asystole," he said as he started another cycle of cardiac compressions. It was a pulseless electrical activity that would not respond to defibrillation.

Matt delivered two breaths. "Not looking good," he said.

"Keep going," Daniel said breathlessly as he started another cycle of CRP. He glanced at the nurse beside him. "More adrenaline, please."

The nurse grabbed another syringe and Matt checked and administered it.

Daniel continued giving cardiac compressions for several more cycles but after forty-five minutes there was still no heartbeat. "I think we should call it," he said. He looked at Matt for approval.

"I agree. It was an unwitnessed cardiac arrest – she was probably gone before I got to her."

Daniel nodded solemnly. "Time of death 11.46."

The monitor sounded one long piercing alarm that confirmed Jean Wyatt's death.

FIFTY-TWO

Colin Mathias had been informed of the recent deaths in the department. Daniel and Matt were summoned into his cramped office. Rick was already there, sitting nonchalantly in the best chair in the room.

"Sit, please," Mathias said. His voice was uncharacteristically harsh.

Matt closed the door behind him and found the only other vacant chair. Daniel perched on the windowsill as Mathias took off his reading glasses, cracked his knuckles and clasped his hands across his paunch. He glanced at Daniel, then Matt. "Look, I'll get straight to the point. The death rate on this ward is worryingly high lately." He looked pointedly at Daniel. "What the bloody hell is going on?"

Daniel squirmed. Was he being blamed for the deaths? Why pick on him? He started to feel defensive. "Jean Wyatt's heart was weakened from her tamponade and subsequent cardiac arrest. We tried everything we could." He looked at Matt for support.

Matt cleared his throat. "Yes, we tried several cycles of CPR and adrenaline, but she didn't respond. We couldn't shock her – there was no shockable rhythm – she was in asystole."

Rick piped up, a hard tone to his voice, "it's not just Mrs Wyatt, though, is it? We've had several deaths in the past few days alone… all your patients."

"Mr Willet's death was expected," Matt said, looking at Daniel, then at Rick.

Daniel simply nodded his agreement.

Colin interjected. "What about Sandy Lewis – another patient found dead in her bed?"

Matt piped up. "It looks like there was a loose power cable on the ventilator. We've sent it off for repair. It was a tragic accident."

"An absolute tragedy for this young lady and her family. So why didn't anyone notice an alarm? Surely there wasn't a fault with the cardiac monitor as well." Colin sounded exasperated as he looked around the room.

Matt shrugged; Rick shook his head. Colin looked at Daniel.

Daniel felt obliged to answer. "I wasn't around, so I don't know, but apparently the alarm was muted."

Colin slowly shook his head. "Unbelievable…" was all he could say.

They all knew there would be an investigation.

Colin Mathias turned to Rick. "Any news on whether Mr Hackman had the drug or the placebo in the clinical trial?"

"Not yet, but Isobel is looking into it." Rick shifted in his chair and loosened his tie. "Mr Hackman did seem to be having some sort of allergic reaction."

"Well, if he did have this experimental drug, we'll have to stop the trial. Was Mrs Wyatt on the trial as well?" Again, he looked pointedly at Daniel.

"I believe she was, yes."

Colin shook his head slowly, mumbling to himself, "I really don't know why we allow so many of these damned trials in this department." His chair gave out a long, brain-cramping squeak as he swivelled.

"I'll get Isobel to look into it," Rick said.

"Yes, thank you, Rick." Again, he turned to Daniel. "We really must up our game here. The stats are not looking good and the whole department will be under fire if we're not careful." He put his glasses back on. "I don't want to hear about another death – am I clear?"

"As a bell," Matt said.

Mathias glanced at Daniel, Matt, then Rick. "Alright, get back to work," he said dismissively.

Matt and Rick stood and filed out of the room. Colin looked at Daniel as he walked toward the door. "I hope I haven't misplaced my trust in you."

Daniel felt a flash of indignation. Why the hell was he in the firing line? "You haven't," Daniel said.

As he went out into the ward, he saw Rick smirking as if he'd overheard Colin's comment.

Daniel ignored it and went back to work but his mind wasn't on the job. Was Colin giving him a thinly veiled threat of dismissal? Because that's how it seemed. He couldn't contemplate losing his job after less than a week. More than that, he didn't want to lose Colin's trust or his friendship. He'd done nothing wrong, and those deaths had nothing to do with him, yet he seemed to be in the firing line. A hierarchy of blame that ended with him getting a kicking like the proverbial cat. Had Rick said something to Colin – trying to deflect the blame because of the tension between them? Were Colin and Rick inferring the death rate rose only after he started back in the department? Then there was his spell in prison – the constant elephant in the room. He tried to forget about it. There would be an investigation into the deaths with post-mortems. Hopefully, they would know soon, and Colin would quit with the thinly veiled accusations. In the meantime, he had work to do.

Daniel checked on his patients. John Gardener was making progress; his bedsore was starting to heal. He had also been seen by the social services liaison officer, who had found a place at the Hamilton Court Nursing Home for his recovery. Matt had offered to speak to Mrs Wyatt's family and try to answer the questions raised by her death. Now, he had another clinic to run and, after that, more Botox clients at Oliver's clinic before he could go home and check on Fay.

"Hey, Daniel."

Daniel turned to see Matt racing to catch up with him.

"What's up, mate?"

"A couple of things. I found out that Megan Foley is improving and starting to come out of her coma. The twins are doing well too. They are still in the neonatal unit, but the prognosis is good."

"Excellent." Daniel sighed with relief.

"Also, I just heard from Rick that both Bob Hackman and Jean Wyatt were taking the placebo, so their deaths had nothing to do with the Bravafloxacin in the trial."

Daniel's heart sank. Now, as the apparent ward scapegoat, the wretched finger of blame would be pointing directly at him.

"I think he's upstairs – at least, he was ten minutes ago."

Daniel thanked her and went upstairs. He could hear voices coming from one of the offices and recognised Melissa's, then Oliver's. He knocked and waited. Oliver opened the door.

"Ah, Daniel. Everything alright?"

Daniel looked past him and could see Melissa dabbing at her eyes with a tissue. She caught him and turned away. "Yes, fine. Penny Henderson is waiting in reception. She's having Flab Buster with you?"

Oliver nodded. "Yes, of course. I'll be there in a minute."

Daniel glanced into the room again and saw Melissa putting on sunglasses. Perhaps she'd been having some sort of treatment. He decided to mind his own business and went back downstairs to see Isobel Duncan standing at the reception desk.

"Penny, Oliver will be with you soon," he said, then turned to Isobel. "Fancy seeing you here..."

Isobel looked a little embarrassed. "Daniel... I didn't know you worked here."

"Just a bit of moonlighting."

Oliver appeared at the top of the stairs and spotted Isobel. He raced down and greeted her with a hug, air kissing both cheeks. They were obviously well acquainted.

"I didn't know you were coming in today," Oliver said to her.

"I managed to get a cancellation. It's just for Botox, that's all."

Daniel cut in. "I can do that for you, Oliver, if you need to see to Penny."

"No – Isobel is a very special client." He smiled ingratiatingly at her. "I'll administer her treatment. I'm sure Penny won't mind."

Penny looked up from her magazine. "That's alright," she said.

"No," Isobel said determinedly, "I'm happy to take my turn." She gestured to Oliver for him to deal with his client and walked, in towering heels, to the sofa. She sat, scrolling on her iPhone.

Oliver escorted Penny into his treatment room and closed the door. Daniel's next appointment had cancelled due to a work commitment, Nadia informed him. He contemplated hanging around in reception to chat to Isobel but decided against it, not really knowing what they would talk about apart from the clinical trial – or Rick. He went into the kitchen for a quick break and found Melissa sitting at the table with coffee and a chocolate digestive.

She looked at him from behind her sunglasses. "Hi, Daniel. How are you getting on?"

"Fine – bit of a gap between clients. How are you?" He wondered why she was wearing sunglasses indoors in November. Either he'd missed the latest hot fashion trend or she was hiding something. "Everything alright?"

Melissa seemed to hesitate for a moment, then stood, closed the kitchen door and removed her sunglasses. She had a nasty bruise under her left eye. She simply looked at him as if she was inviting him to comment.

Daniel took a step toward her, peering at the bruise. "How did you get that?" Now he knew something was wrong.

"I could say I walked into a door but I'm not going to – this is a little present from my darling husband," Melissa said acidly.

"And is this a regular thing?" He knew she was telling the truth but was shocked at Oliver's behaviour. He didn't have him down as a wife beater. A money-grabbing con man, perhaps, but not a wife beater.

"Regular enough," she said.

"I'm sorry to hear that, Melissa, I really am. Is there anything I can do?" As that last sentence involuntarily left his mouth, he regretted it. The last thing he wanted was to get involved in their marital problems.

Melissa put her sunglasses back on and slowly shook her head. "Thanks, but I'm not sure there's anything anyone can do… I either live with it or get out, I guess."

"And is that what you want – to get out of your marriage?"

"I don't know, to be honest. Sometimes that's all I want – to be at peace – but I don't know what I'd do or where I'd go…" Her words trailed off, leaving an awkward silence.

Daniel backed away slightly. There was no way he wanted to get involved – not in this. Melissa would have to deal with it herself. Surely, she had friends that would take her in and support her. It wasn't his problem.

His mind was racing to come up with a tactful way out of the situation when they heard a commotion in the treatment room next door and Oliver shouting for help. Daniel rushed into the room, closely followed by Isobel and Melissa.

Penny Henderson was clutching her throat and obviously struggling to breathe; there was a high-pitched rasping noise as she gasped desperately for air.

"Her throat's closing up," Oliver said.

Daniel rushed to her side. "It's an allergic reaction." He turned to Oliver. "Have you got adrenaline?"

"Yes, upstairs."

"Get it quickly. Several doses."

Isobel stood opposite Penny. "It must be a reaction to the Flab Buster – shit."

Penny's skin was becoming red and blotchy and her breathing more laboured by the second. Daniel tried to reassure her and laid her flat on the treatment couch, propping her legs up with a pillow to help counteract low blood pressure due to shock.

Melissa stood in the corner of the room watching intently, her hand covering her mouth, her sunglasses abandoned. Isobel seemed to be in panic mode, unsure what to do.

Oliver rushed in and handed a syringe to Daniel, then lifted Penny's skirt to expose her thigh. Daniel checked the injection and stabbed the needle into her quadriceps, injecting 1 mg of adrenaline.

"Alright, Penny – this will help. You seem to be having an allergic reaction. Try to relax." Daniel was trying to reassure her, but she was wheezing dangerously and obviously distressed.

Daniel turned to Oliver. "We should call an ambulance."

Oliver reacted immediately. "No… no, she'll be fine. Just let the adrenaline work." He glanced furtively at Isobel.

"But her airway is swelling – look at her." Daniel was insistent. "We can't just let her go into respiratory arrest."

"No – let's try another dose of adrenaline." Oliver grabbed another syringe and injected the drug into Penny's thigh.

Daniel wasn't happy. "She needs to be in hospital." He took Penny's hand in his, trying to calm her.

Isobel cut in. "We can manage it here – there's no need for hospital." She scowled a *back off* warning at Daniel.

Melissa was still in the corner of the room, obviously shocked by what had happened.

"She's breathing a bit easier," Oliver said.

"Yes, panic over," Isobel added, rather too jovially.

Daniel watched Penny. Her breathing was becoming less laboured and the rasping noise as she inhaled had disappeared. "Are you feeling a little better now, Penny?"

Penny nodded and tried to sit up. Daniel helped her and Isobel place a pillow in her back.

"I still think she should go to hospital," Daniel said.

Oliver dismissed the idea again. "It was just a minor reaction."

Daniel eyed him suspiciously. This was more than just a minor reaction. "What the hell is in this stuff?" Daniel snatched the packaging from the Flab Buster injection. He read the long list of dubious active ingredients, then turned the package over.

It had been developed by Isobel's biotech company, Regenex Biologics.

FIFTY-FOUR

Fay had made an excuse to Doug and spent the day at home. After the episode with Megan Foley's baby, she couldn't face the hospital again so soon and was desperately trying to rationalise what she'd done. She'd called Rosie and told her not to collect Chester and Ella for the dog creche and had taken the dogs for a long walk in the woods. After feeling so depressed the day before, she was much brighter now and when she got back from the walk she spent hours cleaning and polishing – normally, she loathed housework. She'd even cleared out some cupboards, throwing out two bin bags full of clutter, including some of Daniel's old clothes, books for the charity shop and a tattered old bed of Maisie's. She'd prepared food for the freezer in the afternoon, making fruit pies and cheese scones ready for the oven, keeping some back to cook for Daniel for when he got home.

By the time Daniel arrived just after 8pm, she felt frenzied and restless.

"Daniel – how was your day?" Without waiting for an answer, she launched into an excited monologue about the cleaning, cooking and sorting-out she'd been doing. The dogs seemed hyped as well, as if her mood was rubbing off on them.

"Hey, slow down – you sound like something possessed. Are you alright?"

"Yes, I'm fine – never better. What shall we have to eat – want a scone?" She leaped across to the oven and put the scones in to cook. "See, I've cleaned the oven too – come and see."

Daniel dutifully inspected the oven. "Are you sure you're OK?"

"Yes, I said – fine. What else do you want to eat?" She went to the fridge and started pulling out half the contents. "Look – cheese, potatoes, tomatoes, ham, butter, chocolate – what would you like?" She seemed wired – like she was on steroids or something.

Daniel was frowning and caught her around the waist, turning her to face him. "Sweetheart – slow down."

She wriggled free. "Come on – let's make some dinner. Have you eaten already? You must be starving."

Daniel looked perplexed but went along with her. "OK, how about a jacket potato and some salad – that would be easy. It's getting late for a heavy dinner."

Fay looked at him with wild, staring eyes. "Yes... yes... yes... let's have that." She quickly pulled out the salad stuff from the fridge and washed a couple of large potatoes, pricked them with a knife and put them in the microwave. Then darted around the kitchen as she prepared the salad and put it on their plates.

"Fay – you haven't taken any drugs, have you?"

"Drugs? Drugs? What do you mean?" Fay continued bustling around the kitchen, not really achieving very much but compelled to keep moving.

"Well, you seem hyped up today. I just wondered if you'd taken anything."

"Don't be daft. No, I haven't taken anything – just full of energy, that's all. Isn't it great? I've managed to get so much done." She took the microwaved potatoes and put them to finish cooking in the oven. The scones were done so she took them out and put them on the kitchen counter to cool.

Daniel seemed to accept what she'd said. She rarely took medication, not even a painkiller for a headache.

Daniel poured them both a glass of chilled Sauvignon Blanc. "The scones smell nice. You haven't cooked anything like that for ages."

"Here – have some." Fay passed him a couple of scones on a plate. "So, what have you been up to today?" She finally slowed her relentless jumping about the kitchen and leaned against the counter tapping her foot and constantly fiddling with her hair.

Daniel buttered the scones. "Bit of drama at Oliver's this evening. One of his clients had an allergic reaction to the Flab Buster injections. Thankfully she was alright, and Isobel gave her a lift home."

"I remember you said the Flab Buster sounded a bit dodgy," Fay said, picking Daniel's crumbs off the worktop, her foot still tapping on the floor.

He talked around a mouthful. "Well, I won't be recommending it – that's for sure. Looks like Oliver is pushing the boundaries of his client's safety for the sake of making money. He seems driven to make a profit at all costs."

"What does Melissa say about it?" Fay threw the crumbs into the sink and sipped her wine, her foot still jiggling and tapping the floor.

"Looks like she's just going along with things – did you know Oliver has been hitting her?"

"That doesn't surprise me. I think it's been going on for a while, from what she told me when she was coming to me for therapy."

Daniel nodded pensively. He passed a piece of his scone to Chester, who was sitting next to him, drooling. "I'm trying not to get involved."

"A wise move," Fay said. She checked the oven. "Ten more minutes."

Daniel finished his scones, giving a last morsel to Ella. "Jean Wyatt died this morning."

Fay looked dejected at the news. "That's sad. I was talking to her yesterday after she'd had a near-death experience." Fay didn't tell Daniel the details – about how she'd wanted to stay in the wonderful place she'd found herself in when she was clinically dead. Maybe she just gave up living. Could someone do that? Just stop living when they'd had enough?

They sipped their wine and Daniel made a fuss of the dogs, slipping them both a couple of bone-shaped biscuits, which they devoured in seconds. Maisie came in from the garden through the cat flap and made a beeline for her dish, tail straight up in the air.

Fay thought about Sophie and the peace and light some of her patients had described. Was Sophie happy as Felicia Grainger had told her? Had she really relayed a message from her baby girl from beyond the grave? And what about the four people she had killed – were their souls also in a beautiful place full of love and light or were they in some sort of purgatory or even hell? Had they been judged for the killings, rapes and crimes they had committed? Would she be judged for what she did?

"Colin is getting twitchy about the high death rate in the department lately. It feels like I'm the scapegoat…" Daniel smoothed Chester's head.

Fay nodded absently, her foot finally slowed and stopped its relentless jiggling and tapping. Her mind drifted elsewhere as Daniel told her about the meeting that morning with Colin, Rick and Matt. She thought about Wixx – the evil bastard that killed their daughter – he should be roasting nicely in hell now after what he did. She couldn't bear the thought of him enjoying the love and peace Mrs Wyatt had told her about. Not him. He should be judged and sentenced to eternal damnation.

Daniel checked the oven. "The spuds are done," he said, putting one on each of their plates. "Come on, let's slum it tonight and watch TV."

They took their dinner into the living room on trays and Daniel flicked around the channels and settled on a Netflix programme about the solar system.

"By the way, Megan Foley is coming out of her coma and both twins are doing alright," Daniel said.

"That's good," she said. Daniel didn't seem to realise how serious she had been about taking Megan's baby. She hoped he wouldn't find out – especially from Rick.

Rick.

She recoiled as she remembered she'd told him their deadly secret – a moment of sheer madness. Daniel mustn't find out.

Ever.

She would do all she could to make sure he didn't.

Then, in her head, she heard Sophie's voice again – her infectious giggle when Daniel used to blow raspberries on her tummy, her cooing, and the way she had just started to babble, almost saying "mama" just weeks before she was murdered. Then happy laughter turned to cries, then desperate screams…

Fay's mood abruptly fell over a cliff face. From hyped up and fidgeting all day, she plunged headlong into the darkest, deepest ravine.

Sophie.

FIFTY-FIVE

Daniel arrived on the ward the following morning having left Fay in bed. She seemed to have the weight of the world on her shoulders once again. He was at a loss as to what he could do about it and, if he was honest, had enough problems of his own to deal with – settling into his new job and dealing with the prejudice he still sensed from some of the staff, not to mention the tiring extra hours moonlighting at Oliver's clinic. Perhaps Megan Foley's baby had made her think about Sophie again, he reasoned, although he still wasn't sure why she had been in the anaesthetic room in the first place. He thought better than to question her on it and he reasoned it was best left alone now. Rick had implied she was trying to abduct the baby, but it could well be an exaggeration on his part. Just another ploy to get at him.

He passed the side rooms near the entrance to the ward and heard the shrill cry of a patient in pain. He glanced through glass panel of the room that Ray Willet had occupied and saw an elderly woman being given an enema by one of the junior nurses. He turned the corner into the nurses' station. Matt was going through patients' blood and CT results.

"Hey, Matt. Got dressed in the dark?" Daniel was referring to the registrar's brightly coloured Hawaiian shirt.

“Very funny,” Matt said, rolling his eyes. “Want to give me a hand with these?”

“Sure.” Daniel sat, took a wad of papers from Matt, and started checking the results for abnormalities. He glanced up to see Eddie Bates lurking around one of the female patients, a frail-looking lady in her seventies who was sleeping off an anaesthetic. Daniel continued checking the results but kept an eye on Bates. He was hanging around the sleeping woman, surreptitiously looking into a handbag that was on top of her bedside cabinet. Daniel glared at him. Bates caught his eye and wandered off, pretending to dust the surfaces. It was obvious to Daniel that he’d been up to no good.

Jackie Hines was on duty and was starting her medicine round, assisted by a junior nurse. Daniel watched as she handed out medication. Bates was still lurking on the sidelines.

“You in theatre this afternoon?” Matt said absently.

“No, I think I have to be in the HDU later, although with this floating around arrangement it’s anyone’s guess where I’ll end up.”

Rick appeared behind them. “Right, let’s get started.” He’d made no reference to Fay and the events in the anaesthetic room two days before and appeared to have let it go.

Daniel and Matt grabbed a pile of notes and followed Rick as he started his ward round. They were joined by a couple of junior doctors and a staff nurse, a short, plump woman in pale blue scrubs, her dark hair scraped into a ponytail.

They approached the first patient, a man in his early twenties, who was sitting on the side of his bed in two-toned grey pyjamas. He’d been rushed to A&E with a ruptured appendix three days ago. Mani Adebayo had operated.

“Mr Jackson. How are you feeling after your operation?” Rick smiled at him.

“It’s a bit painful but I’m getting about alright now.”

Rick looked through the notes and checked the blood results. “Well, I think we can let you go home later today.”

The man beamed. "Thanks, doc."

They moved on to the next patient, but Daniel was still watching Eddie Bates. Jackie and the junior nurse were with John Gardener, the elderly patient with a pressure ulcer to his buttocks. He seemed to be having problems sitting up to swallow his tablets and they had left the medicine trolley unattended while they helped him. Daniel watched as Bates slyly strolled past the trolley, reached in and grabbed a handful of boxes. As far as Daniel could tell, they were painkillers. Bates disappeared down the ward toward the exit.

Daniel tapped Matt's shoulder and whispered, "I need to go off the ward for a while."

"OK, I'll cover for you," Matt said.

Daniel slunk off unnoticed by Rick and the rest of his entourage and followed Bates out of the ward and into the corridor. He could see Bates scurrying away and hurried to catch up with him, dodging trolleys, wheelchairs and groups of people. Bates disappeared down four flights of stairs toward the basement of the hospital, an area that Daniel had never visited. It was dingy and cold, an industrial-looking rabbit warren of concrete corridors lined with huge steel pipes. Daniel could see Bates as he swerved and disappeared into a room on the right.

Daniel stopped and peered through the open doorway. Bates was squirrelling the stolen boxes away in one of a line of lockers. He locked the door and pocketed the key. The room was dingy, with one small, frosted glass window with an old metal frame, and three dining chairs arranged around a battered coffee table.

"Caught you, Bates," Daniel said breathlessly.

Bates turned, speechless, disbelief etched into his face.

"Come on, hand back the drugs you stole." Daniel hesitated, then stepped into the room.

"I didn't steal anything."

"I saw you. What was it – painkillers? I knew you were up to no good."

Bates seemed to dither for a moment, then took a step toward Daniel. His expression had changed from surprise to grim determination with a trace of hatred. Daniel remembered their skirmish in prison. Bates had been intimidating but had backed down eventually. He hoped he would do the same now but there was no telling how he would react. Daniel knew he had to stand up to him – *don't show weakness.*

Bates pushed his face up close. Daniel could smell his foul breath, tinged with garlic, see the pock marks pitted into his skin. His eyes were burning into his. He grabbed a handful of the front of Daniel's shirt and pulled him further toward his face. "I never stole anything – got it?"

Daniel snarled though gritted teeth. "I saw you – you won't get away with this. And I know you've also been stealing from the patients as well as medical supplies from the treatment rooms."

"Yeah – and wot you gonna do 'bout it?" Bates spat the words into Daniel's face.

"Call the police – lose you your job here."

Bates laughed bullishly. "You ain't got no evidence. It's just your word against mine and besides who's gonna believe an ex-con like you… a murderer." His eyes shone with glee.

"I can have you removed from your job once our clinical lead hears about this."

"Ha – you mean dear old Colin Mathias? Well… just try it."

"He won't stand for petty thieves on the ward."

Bates just smirked and let go of Daniel's shirt. His eyes locked with Daniel's for several uncomfortable seconds before he strode out of the room, slamming the door behind him. Daniel could hear the hooting of laughter receding down the corridor.

He went to Bates's locker to retrieve the evidence, but it was locked. Maybe he should just call security and let them find it in Bates's possession. That would be a stronger case against him. Daniel went to open the door of the room, but the handle was missing from the inside. He searched around but couldn't see it or anything he could use to prise the door open. He reached into his pocket for his iPhone to call security, but it wasn't there – he must have left it in his jacket back on the ward.

Shit. He was trapped in this grimy room. It stank of sweat, garlic and smelly feet. He called out a few times, but the place seemed deserted. The only way out was through the small window that didn't open. He had no idea where it would lead to but, unless he wanted to stay there until someone happened to come along, the window seemed to be the only chance of escape.

Daniel picked up one of the chairs by its backrest and weighed it in his hands. It should be robust enough to break the window. He heaved it back, then lunged forward, hitting the glass with the chair's legs. The window cracked but was still intact. One more blow and it shattered, sending shards of glass skittering across the room. Daniel turned away to protect his face, then placed the chair in front of the window and stood up onto the seat. He could see the back end of the hospital and a small car park. To his left was "Rose Cottage" – the mortuary. He could walk to one of the side entrances of the hospital.

Daniel hauled himself through the window, sustaining several minor cuts to his hands in the process. He jumped down a six-foot drop the other side onto an area of rough ground set below the road. He looked up to see a familiar figure coming out of the morgue – it was Isobel Duncan, closely followed by one of the mortuary technicians – tall and lanky with a man bun and a cigarette clamped in his mouth. What the hell was Isobel doing in there? He instinctively crouched close to the wall and watched. Isobel walked over to what he presumed was her car; a brand-new Bentley Bentayga in gleaming black. She opened the boot. The technician hefted a bulky black refuse bag into a cool box she had in there. Isobel reached into her handbag and passed him a thick envelope. They shook hands and he went back to the morgue. Isobel got into the car, reversed out of her space and drove off.

Daniel contemplated what Isobel was up to as he walked around to the side entrance of the hospital and down a long, convoluted corridor. He had to conclude that he had no idea. He arrived back at the ward. Rick had finished the ward round. He washed the blood from the small cuts to his hands and found Matt.

"Did I miss much?"

"Just a few post-op discharges and a change to the elective surgery list. Oh – and Rick said he wanted to see you in his office."

Shit. Was this going to be about Fay? Should he tell Rick about Bates or just let security deal with it? And what about Isobel? Best left alone, he decided. "Thanks Matt." He walked across to Rick's office. The door was ajar, and he knocked once.

"Yes." Rick's voice sounded slightly irritated.

Daniel went in to find Rick tapping at the keys on his laptop. He had several tabs open, and it looked like the computer had frozen. "You wanted to see me?"

Rick looked up. "Daniel, can you do a night shift tonight? Mani Adebayo has called in sick and he was supposed to be covering it."

Daniel hated nights but what choice did he have? It would mean cancelling his clients' appointments at Oliver's clinic, but he couldn't let on to Rick he was moonlighting. "I guess…"

"Well, you'd better finish up and go home now – come back in at 6pm for a handover."

"OK." Daniel hesitated to mention Bates. It was a matter for security or the police. Rick wouldn't be interested in knowing about a cleaner that was pilfering.

"How is your wife now?"

"She's fine, thanks." Daniel shifted uncomfortably, unsure where Rick stood on the matter.

"Good. See you tonight, then." Rick sounded strangely glib as turned back to his laptop.

Daniel left feeling relieved. He'd obviously misconstrued the situation. Now all he had to do was deal with Bates. He told Matt there was a change of plan with his shifts and called into the security office on his way home. He explained the situation to a young security officer and was assured they would deal with it and replace the broken window.

He drove home hoping for a quiet afternoon with Fay but, when he arrived, her car was gone, the house was empty, and Rosie had obviously collected Chester and Ella for the dog creche. Fay's briefcase was missing, and he guessed she'd gone back to work. He sent her a text letting her know he would be working that night and not to expect him home – she replied and confirmed she'd gone into the hospital.

He decided to spend the afternoon reading up on some new surgical techniques, but his mind kept wandering to Isobel. She was obviously in cahoots with Oliver, and he remembered that Melissa had told him they had shares in a pharmaceutical company. Maybe that was Trevelyan, Madigan and Winslow or the biotech company, Regenex Biologics, but what the hell was Isobel doing at the mortuary earlier?

FIFTY-SIX

Fay had woken in a brighter mood and decided to get back to work. She felt useless at home and needed to catch up with Doug about the research project. She drove her Mercedes across town through lashing rain. The November sky was solid grey. She managed to park close to the university wing of the hospital, dodged around the puddles in the car park and took the lift to the first floor. She strolled down the corridor to the office to find Doug and Shelly engrossed with their respective computer screens.

"Hello, you two," she said.

Shelly looked up and smiled. "Hey, good to see you. How's it going?"

"Fine, thanks. Keeping busy." Fay could hear a radio playing in the background with people talking over one another as they had some sort of discussion. Fay found it irritating – how could anyone work with that racket going on?

Doug stood and pulled a chair next to his desk for her and cleared away a heap of papers and folders. "Any progress with the research?"

Fay sat and told him about the experiences of Mrs Jacobs and Mrs Wyatt and the few patients that had had nightmares and strange dreams. She had also updated the psychology questionnaires for each patient and handed a copy to Doug.

"Well, it sounds like you're making progress, although it could be years before we get enough data to get a paper published."

Shelly turned the radio off and handed her a mug of coffee. "We must go for lunch one day and catch up properly."

"Yes, of course," Fay said hesitantly. She enjoyed Shelly's company and she'd been a good friend to Daniel too. But somewhere in the dark recesses of her mind she felt as if she was being watched – as if Shelly was spying on her. She tried to shake off the creepy feeling, realising it wasn't rational.

They chatted about research, Shelly's recovery from her kidney operation, the dogs – but the subject of Damon Wixx was tactfully avoided as it had been since Daniel had been sent to prison on remand.

Fay drained her coffee mug. "I'd better get over to the ward and see what there is to do," she said.

"Don't be a stranger." Shelly stood and the women hugged briefly.

Fay turned to Doug. "I'll come in next week with an update."

Doug waved a dismissive hand and turned back to his computer screen, lost in a world of spreadsheets and datasets.

Fay left the office, walked down the corridor, took the lift to the ground floor and headed out into the busy throughway that led to the main hospital building. She headed for the ward and swiped herself in to be greeted by the rancid smell of vomit. There was a pool of lumpy orange liquid on the floor in the four-bedded room surrounded by yellow hazard signs. Eddie Bates and another cleaner were busy mopping up. She turned toward the nurses' station to find Jackie Hines speaking on the phone, her long, horsey face a picture of frustration. Fay waited until she hung up.

"Bloody great – they've managed to lose Mr Taylor's CT results – just what we need today," Jackie said to anyone within earshot. She turned to Fay. "Sorry; having a bad day."

"No problem. I was just wondering if I need to interview anyone for the NDE research?"

Jackie thought for a moment. "Actually, yes. Jayden West – he attempted suicide and almost succeeded by all accounts. Tried to hang himself, for the second time, in his prison cell and was brought to A&E unconscious and barely breathing. He's been rambling about dark tunnels and lights – could be an NDE." She stopped and looked at Fay as if she'd just realised something. "Would you be alright with that – that he's a convict? In for murder, I think. A prison officer is with him – I think it's safe."

Fay smiled. "Yes, of course. I'm a forensic psychiatrist. Or at least I used to be. I'm well used to working with prisoners." She grinned at the irony. If only she knew.

"Well, if you're sure. He's in the first side room – can't miss him." Jackie went off to see one of her patients.

Fay made her way back toward the entrance to the ward and found Jayden's side room. She went in and introduced herself to the uniformed prison officer who was sitting with him, an older man with a white goatee beard.

He extended a hand to shake hers. "Rivers – Frank Rivers."

"I'm here to have a chat with Jayden about the experience he had while he was unconscious."

"Be my guest," he said, indicating a chair near the bed.

She looked at Jayden. He was propped up in bed wearing a hospital gown that made his pale skin seem translucent. A fringe of dark blond hair covered one side of his face but he swept it back and looked at Fay.

"I'm doctor Fay Kendrick, a psychiatrist doing some research into near-death experiences. Would you like to have a chat about what happened?" She warmed to him – he seemed so young, and she saw a sad vulnerability in his eyes.

Jayden gave her a thin smile and nodded.

Rivers piped up. "You must be Daniel Kendrick's wife?"

"Yes, that's right."

"I know him from Ravenwood prison – he was very kind to Jayden. Top bloke. I'm glad he was acquitted."

News obviously travelled fast. "Yes, you might see him later – he's on the night shift."

"Maybe I'll catch him before I go off duty."

They exchanged a friendly smile and Fay turned to Jayden and sat on the chair next to the bed. "So, I understand you tried to kill yourself – is that right?"

Again, Jayden simply nodded.

"Tell me what happened…"

Jayden cleared his throat and leaned closer to Fay. They both glanced at Officer Rivers, who was now glued to his mobile phone in the corner of the room.

"I… I was outside my body, looking down. It was weird seeing myself hanging like that from the bed sheet." He frowned and shook his head as if he was trying to dislodge the memory. "Then I seemed to whoosh away from the prison but couldn't make sense of where I was. I seemed to be floating for ages, then I was in a very dark, frightening place."

Fay touched his hand. "It's alright, Jayden."

He paused and looked into her eyes as if he was seeking her trust. He gave an imperceptible nod before continuing. "But then I saw a tiny spec of light in the distance and felt myself flying toward it. I seemed to be in a narrow tunnel. It got bigger and bigger and when I came out I was surrounded with light and a beautiful old lady was there. She told me that she loved me and that she was always watching over me – it felt so peaceful, and I'd never felt so much love in my whole life." He paused, closing watery eyes briefly, obviously reliving the memory.

"Did you recognise her?" Fay asked.

"I don't know who she was, but she seemed familiar somehow." His face softened, his eyes now glistening with tears. "She said I must live out my natural life – that I had an important lesson to learn. She showed me a review of part of my life – my stepfather's abuse, the trouble I've been in as a teenager, going to prison. Then I was pulled back into my body and woke up as I was being taken to hospital."

Fay smiled. "I'm glad you survived. Has it changed how you feel about trying to kill yourself?"

"I guess… at least I'm not afraid to die anymore and I know now that I have a reason for living."

"That's good, isn't it?"

"But how am I supposed to live in prison for the rest of my life? I can't bear the thought of it…"

"Perhaps that's part of the lesson you have to learn, Jayden: how to cope in prison – in a place you don't want to be."

Jayden shook his head decisively. "No, I can't face it. I'd rather be dead."

"But life is so precious. Listen to me, Jayden, we can get you some proper help and you'll find a way to cope. You can do it." Fay thought about some of the other vulnerable patients she'd helped in the past. Some had developed coping mechanisms and some hadn't, but she knew Jayden needed professional counselling. "I'll help you, Jayden. You can't give up – especially now you know someone who loves you is watching over you."

She looked into his eyes and saw a tiny ray of hope there.

"Don't give up. You can do this, and I'll get you the help and support you need – do you promise me you won't give up?"

Jayden nodded and gave her a sad smile.

"And I promise you I'll do my best for you." Fay took his thin, bony hand in hers and they shook on their promise to one another.

FIFTY-SEVEN

Fay had spent the rest of the afternoon sitting at the nurses' station on the ward, liaising over the phone with the forensic psychiatry staff that served HMP Ravenwood. They had readily agreed that Jayden needed treatment and support following his suicide attempts after being handed a life sentence. She felt needed again and was upbeat and happier than she'd been in days. She had discovered that Jayden had killed his stepfather after a childhood of sexual and violent abuse – it was no wonder he was so utterly depressed and disenchanted with life. He'd been desperate to escape one world of torment only to find himself trapped in another.

She checked the time on her phone: 5pm. Time to call it a day. She wondered about getting a takeaway on the way home since Daniel would be working all night. She stood and grabbed her bag, ready to leave.

"Fay – leaving so soon?" Rick Estevez was behind her.

She turned to see him smiling at her. His hair was dishevelled, and a dark, three-day stubble shadowed his jaw. He wore a charcoal-grey suit over a white open-necked shirt and was carrying an old brown leather briefcase.

Fay suddenly felt nervous. The last time she had seen him

was when she had attempted to steal Megan Foley's baby. She felt foolish now – what the hell had got into her? "Rick…"

He drew closer and she caught a faint whiff of Gucci Guilty with its bold woody fragrance. "Off home?"

"Yes, had enough for today," Fay said.

"Me too – I'll walk you out."

They fell into step as they left the ward and walked the length of the corridor dodging John Gardener in a wheelchair as he was being taken by a nurse and an ambulance driver to the Hamilton Court Nursing Home.

"Bye, Mr Gardener," Fay said. "Good luck." She bent toward him and smiled.

He waved a dismissive liver-spotted hand and mumbled, "Just want to go home…"

Rick steered her into the lift and hit the ground floor button and the lift doors closed. There was a jerk as the lift began its decent.

Rick cleared his throat. "How are you feeling after the other day?"

"A bit silly, if I'm honest." Fay was cringing – he must have thought she was crazy.

Rick shrugged. "We all do silly things sometimes and no harm was done."

She gave him a coy smile. "You're very kind."

He smiled back – his eyes were twinkling in the dim light of the lift. "You know, both the twins are doing well and Megan is improving slightly, as far as I know."

"Yes, Daniel told me. It's very good news."

The lift stopped and the doors opened. They walked through the bustling concourse toward the main entrance.

"Will you join me for a drink? I'd like to hear more about your research," Rick said.

Fay hesitated, suddenly feeling shy. "I should get home really." She was also feeling nervous about her moment of madness and her stupid confession about the vigilante killings. What if he wanted to talk about that?

"Well, Daniel's working a night shift tonight and you'll be home alone."

"I'll have the dogs for company."

"Just one drink. I know a nice little wine bar in the high street – it's easy walking distance."

She realised she was out of excuses, and she had to admit that now she had told Rick her secret and he hadn't freaked out about it – or told Daniel. Or, worse, the police – she was beginning to believe she could trust him. "Alright – just one drink." What harm could it do? It was just an after-work drink with a colleague.

"Good." Rick gestured for her to turn left out of the hospital entrance, and they walked along the main street to a row of shops, cafés and restaurants, then turned left again into a narrow-cobbled side street. They chatted awkwardly about the weather, then Fay told him about Jayden West and the psychiatric support she had managed to arrange for him at the prison.

They arrived at a very contemporary wine bar and restaurant, called "Number 39". The front of the building was one huge window that seemed to beckon them in. Rick held a glass door open for Fay and she brushed past him and into a huge double-height room with soft lighting, a span of enormous mirrors, recycled oak floor, coffee tables and squashy sofas. The place was deserted apart from a tall, dark-haired barman behind a redbrick and oak bar that ran the length of one wall.

"What would you like?" Rick asked, reaching into the inside pocket of his jacket for his wallet.

"A New Zealand Sauvignon Blanc would be nice. Let me pay."

"I won't hear of it; it's on me." Rick ordered a large glass of wine for Fay and a gin and tonic for himself. They found a squashy cream-coloured sofa piled with cushions in a candlelit corner. They sat angled toward one another, a long coffee table in front of them, on which Fay placed her bag. Rick put his briefcase on the floor.

Fay twirled her glass by the stem, taking small sips of the chilled wine. "Very nice. Thank you," she said, savouring the tart taste of gooseberries, softened by passion fruit.

Rick swirled his G&T, the ice clinking against the glass. "It's a pleasure." He took a sip. "So, tell me about your research – have you come across many patients that have had near-death experiences?"

"A few," she said. "Most people seem to have strange dreams or nightmares – probably due to sedatives – but I've heard at least three cases that seem to be genuine near-death experiences. You know two of them, I think, Jean Wyatt and Mrs Jacobs. Both saw you while they were out of their bodies." She smiled at him and at the weirdness of it all.

Rick looked away. "Yes, sadly, Jean Wyatt died. Daniel was looking after her. Such a shame after all she'd been through with the cardiac tamponade."

"Yes, so very sad." Fay hesitated for a moment. "Interestingly, Mrs Wyatt hadn't wanted to come back after her experience. I think she was dreading the pain of her cancer and was so happy and serene during her NDE. I like to think she is at peace now and in a beautiful place surrounded by love." She hoped Sophie was in a place like that too.

Rick smiled at Fay, his dark eyes fixed on hers. He took another sip of his drink and relaxed into the sofa. "Do you think she wanted to die?"

"It did cross my mind, yes. I'm sure people just give up the ghost when they've had enough. You must have seen that too…"

Rick nodded pensively. "Yes, it's true. I've seen people who refuse to eat or drink and just want to end the pain and torment. It's like a slow suicide."

"Jayden West has attempted suicide several times."

"Ah, yes, the prisoner from Ravenwood. Didn't he have some sort of NDE as well?"

"Yes, he did – quite a vivid one."

"It must have been harrowing after trying to kill himself."

"Actually, no. Jayden did have a frightening part at the beginning when he was in total darkness, but he too went through the classic tunnel toward a bright light filled with love. He also had a partial life review – another classic element. Actually, I've been reading the research and there's no correlation between the life history, beliefs, behaviour or attitudes of a person and the likelihood of having a harrowing NDE. Also, there is no correlation between the means of coming close to death, including suicide, and having a bad experience." Fay sipped her wine, looking into Rick's warm brown eyes. Was he going to ask her about the killings she'd carried out? Should she bring the subject up or just ignore it, pretending it never happened?

"Don't you think anoxia – a lack of oxygen to the brain – at the time of death could be responsible for these experiences?" Rick swirled the G&T in his glass, the clear liquid reflecting the soft light of the candles.

Fay noticed Rick's hands – they were the strong, clean hands of a surgeon. "No, I don't – and the research backs me up and discredits that idea. In fact, people having an NDE can actually have higher oxygen levels than people who don't have an experience and people who have perfectly healthy brains with no anoxia can have an NDE – during childbirth or in accidents for instance. In cases where anoxia is involved and monitored, such as in a cardiac arrest, the effects of low oxygen are disorientation and poor memory – the opposite of the experiences reported by people having an NDE after a cardiac arrest. Both Jean Wyatt and Mrs Jacobs, for example." Fay was starting to feel more relaxed and mellow now the wine was working its magic. She drained her glass. She was enjoying their conversation – and Rick's company. But they were talking about death – the killings would surely come up sometime.

Rick seemed determined to find a logical, medical explanation. "Alright, then, what about the different locations in the brain – haven't neuroscientists found areas that produce NDE? I'm sure I read that the temporal lobes, frontal lobe and hippocampus can produce these experiences."

"They also suggest the amygdala along with other areas and, as a psychiatrist, I'm aware of their research, but there is no empirical evidence that any one of these areas or any combination of them produce an NDE. Parts of the brain may well be involved but that doesn't mean brain activity caused the experience."

"But I'm sure there was some experiment that proved stimulation of part of the brain triggered an out-of-body experience."

"You're right, there was. A Swiss neuroscientist, Olaf Blanke, claimed that stimulation of the right angular gyrus can trigger an out-of-body experience, but his experiments involved only one patient and their experience was fragmentary, distorted and very, very different from the out-of-body experiences that occur during an NDE."

"Well, you seem to know your stuff." He gestured to her empty glass. "Another?"

"Why not?" It was still early. Daniel would have already started his night shift. Besides, she was intrigued with Rick and flattered by his interest in her research.

Rick took their empty glasses back to the bar and ordered another round of drinks. Fay felt calm and happy – a contrast to the past few days when her mood had been so up and down. He brought their drinks over and settled into the sofa, a little closer to her than before.

"So, tell me, what sort of aftereffects do people get following one of these experiences?" He was looking directly at her, his eyes dark and alluring.

"Well, if there's one thing that is common to all NDEs, it's that they transform the people that have them. Raymond Moody, one of the first scientific researchers into NDEs, found this back in the 1970s and it's been corroborated since in many other studies. Nearly everyone who reported an NDE lost their fear of death and believed in life after death following their experience. People who commit suicide do not generally attempt to take their lives again – so there is hope for Jayden. After an NDE, people report a higher sense of purpose in life, show a more loving attitude and are more interested in spiritual growth."

"But there must be some challenges as well."

"Of course – and some are considerable. Divorce is more common, major changes in personal values, career and relationship stresses are reported. Many are afraid to admit they've had an experience, especially if it was distressing."

"It must be risky to admit something like that. People can be so judgemental."

"Yes, they can."

They exchanged a knowing look. Was he trying to reassure her that he wasn't judging her?

Rick glanced toward the bar. "I'm hungry – how about you? We should get something to eat."

Fay wasn't sure she should be having dinner with Rick. A drink or two was one thing but dinner… "I should probably be getting home now."

"Go on – they do nice tapas here. I can highly recommend it – I come here quite frequently after work."

Fay checked the time on her phone. It was gone 7pm. "I can't believe we've been here all this time. I really should be going."

"Please – another hour won't make any difference and you do have to eat, don't you?" His eyes were smiling at her.

She thought about the dogs – Rosie would have taken them home by now but, knowing them, they would be napping as usual. They would be fine until she got home. "Alright, just another hour."

"Excellent. I'll grab some menus." Rick went off to the bar and came back with another round of drinks.

"Are you trying to get me tipsy, Dr Estevez?" Fay said coyly.

Rick smiled and gave her a cheeky wink. "What do you fancy? I can recommend the calamari fried in tempura batter and the lamb stew." He handed her a menu.

"I'm vegetarian," Fay said, searching for something suitable.

"Well, in that case, the vegetarian paella is very good here and there's the vegetable skewers and olives, of course."

"I think I'll have the paella, olives and a salad," Fay said.

"Right, I'll go and order. Are you alright here or would you prefer a table upstairs?"

"It's nice here." Fay liked their cosy corner and Rick sitting next to her. She felt a stab of guilt, thinking about Daniel working all night while she was having dinner with his boss, but it was too late to back out now. She might as well enjoy it.

Rick went to the bar to order and came back with a bowl of olives to share.

"So, tell me about your family in Spain," Fay asked, keen to find out more about this intriguing man.

"Ah – family. A sore point, to be honest. Haven't seen them since shortly after Maria and Alessandro died in the car crash. They have never forgiven me for that."

"But it wasn't your fault."

"It was – I was driving." A shadow fell across Rick's face. It was obviously still painful for him to talk about it.

"I'm so sorry," was all Fay could say. She could sense his pain.

"So, you see, we've both lost people we love. I understand something of what you've been going through, losing your little girl." Rick took a large swig of his G&T. "Do you think children have these near-death experiences?" He looked into Fay's eyes as if he was searching for comfort.

"I thought you believed it was all a consequence of brain activity and not a real phenomenon."

Rick shrugged.

"Well, from what I have read, yes, children do have near-death experiences. Some eighty-five percent of children that have cardiac arrests have an NDE and, with better resuscitation techniques, more and more are surviving and reporting these experiences." She thought of Sophie. "Children of any age can have an NDE, and I read just yesterday that, as soon as they can speak, very young children have reported NDEs they had as they were being born."

Rick's eyes widened. "Really?"

"Most reported a comforting experience of peace and love and a feeling of being safe. Many saw another being – a dead relative or a pet – and reported being out of their body. Only a tiny minority – two to three percent – had a distressing or hellish experience." Fay hoped Sophie hadn't been one of them.

Rick nodded pensively. "Well, it's certainly interesting."

"Do you believe in life after death, Rick?"

"I don't know. I really don't – but I *am* fascinated with death…"

Fay wasn't sure what he meant but, just as she was about to ask him, a waitress brought their order.

"Come on, let's eat; we're getting very morbid here," Rick said. He had opted for Galician octopus topped with smoked paprika and sea salt, along with a bowl of paella.

"This is delicious," Fay said. Maybe he wasn't going to bring up the subject of the killings. Had she just imagined she'd told him? The way her mind had been so fuddled lately; she wouldn't be surprised.

"So where do you live?" Rick asked before pushing a forkful of octopus into his mouth.

"Just outside town, in a small hamlet. It's lovely – just on the edge of open countryside and woodland. It's perfect for walking the dogs." She dug her fork into her paella. "How about you?"

Rick chewed for a moment before answering. "Right on the sea – a little cove near the lighthouse. I have an apartment there."

"Sounds great."

"Have you ever been jet-skiing?"

"No – you?"

"Yes, I have my own jet ski. You must come with me someday – take your mind off things for a while. It's fun."

"Maybe I'll take you up on that. It does sound exciting."

Rick smiled, finished his octopus and washed it down with the last of the gin and tonic. Fay was just finishing her salad.

Rick leaned toward her and gently took her hand in his. "You know, I do understand – about what you told me the other day..." He lowered his voice to barely a whisper. "The killings."

Fay swallowed a mouthful of wine. Shit – she *had* told him and now she had to face it again. She simply looked at him aghast.

His eyes darkened. "I won't tell anyone. That's a promise. It will be our little secret..."

Rick leaned toward her, slowly running his hand up her arm. He looked into her eyes, leaned further in and kissed her. She could taste warm gin on his lips, feel his rough beard against her face, smell the woody notes in his cologne. He ran a palm along her jawline and pulled her closer to him as his kiss deepened.

She didn't resist.

Then he pulled away. "That is, if you won't tell anyone about this..." he whispered.

All she could do was shake her head as he kissed her again.

Neither of them had noticed Isobel Duncan watching them through the window from the rear-view mirror of her Bentley.

FIFTY-EIGHT

A waitress cleared the table and Rick ordered himself another G&T. He sat alone in the wine bar after Fay had left. She seemed to have enjoyed their kiss but spooked and went off home with some lame excuse about the dogs. He let her go. He could never resist a challenge – it would be a deliciously slow burn. He thought about their conversation. There was something about her that resonated deeply with him – she was drawing him in like no woman ever had. Especially now he knew her deadly secret…

He heard the clatter of heels on oak flooring and looked up to see Isobel striding toward him in her dusky pink business suit. She stood over him. "Well – this is cosy, isn't it?"

"What do you mean?"

"I saw you – in here with Fay Kendrick. What the hell is going on?"

"Why don't you sit and calm down? Nothing is going on." He patted the sofa next to him, where Fay had been sitting.

"Don't tell me to calm down, Rick." She manoeuvred herself around the coffee table, sat and snatched his drink, taking a big gulp, leaving pink lipstick on the glass.

"Would you like me to get you a drink?" Rick asked sarcastically.

"I want you to tell me the truth. I saw you kiss Fay; now, what the hell is going on?"

Rick swallowed nervously and tucked one hand under his thigh. "Oh, that. Look, she was upset about a patient, and I was just trying to offer some comfort, that's all. She's a married woman – I'm not interested in her. Not in the least." He tried to look her in the eye.

Isobel glared at him, her lips forming a tight line across her face. "Ha – she was upset – that's a good one. You don't need to kiss someone if they're upset." She took another big gulp of his G&T.

"Well, that's the truth. Look, Isobel, we're in a public place, in case you haven't noticed, and she's not here now – she's gone home to her husband. Does that look like there's something 'going on'?" He managed to hold a steady gaze. He could see she was softening slightly.

"I'm not sure if I believe you..."

"Well, that's up to you but it's the truth. I guess we'd had a couple of drinks and it just happened. I'm sorry, I'm a failure; I wasn't thinking. There was nothing in it and it won't happen again."

Isobel glared back, unsure what to say.

Rick took her hand. "It was just a kiss, for pity's sake."

Isobel pouted. "It better not happen again."

"I love you, Izzie – you know that." It was all he had left. If he was honest, he didn't care one way or another if she stayed with him or not, but he was getting something he badly needed out of their relationship and he couldn't let it go – not yet.

Her eyes softened and he detected a tiny micro-smile at the corner of her mouth.

"Would you like that drink now?"

Isobel nodded. "OK – a Prosecco, please. Make it a large one."

Rick smiled at her, gave her hand a squeeze and went to the bar. That was a close shave, he thought. He cleared his throat and licked his lips – his mouth had suddenly gone dry. If he wanted to take things further with Fay, he'd have to be more careful. He paid for the Prosecco and took it back to Isobel.

"So, what brings you here anyway?" he asked nonchalantly.

Isobel looked at him mystified. "Didn't you get my text? I suggested we meet up for dinner at our usual place. When I didn't get a reply, I thought I'd come anyway, in case you were here."

Rick checked his phone and sure enough, he'd missed Isobel's earlier text while he'd been talking to Fay. "Sorry, Izzie." If only he'd checked his bloody phone.

Isobel sipped her Prosecco. "Anyway, I wanted to tell you I've had a preliminary unofficial result on the toxicology tests on those two patients from the post-mortem. It's not official yet but they've found an antibiotic and it's likely to be the Bravafloxacin."

"Didn't you tell Colin that they were on the placebo?"

"Yes, I did…" She paused while she sipped her drink. "Rick, I can't have the trial closed down – not now."

"Do TMW Pharmaceuticals know about it?"

Isobel shook her head. "No, we're running the trial from Regenex. I can sort that. The blood and tissue samples will be sent to our metabolism group, and we'll look at the pharmacodynamics. Biomarkers will pick up any drugs along with synergistic reactions with other drugs, but I can falsify the results – no one will ever know. TMW are only contract manufacturers. At the moment their interest in Bravafloxacin is only cursory, so they need never know either."

"Aren't they pushing for clinical data results?"

"Yes, but I've told them we're not ready. I can hold them off."

"And what about the Flab Buster? How are the trials going on that?" Rick wiped the lipstick from his glass with a napkin and took a swig.

"You mean the unofficial trials? Not too good at the moment. Another woman at the clinic had an anaphylactic shock the other day – it was touch and go, with Daniel insisting on calling an ambulance. She was alright in the end, and we managed to avoid her going into hospital. It'll be OK – these clients are happy to keep it quiet, although I'm not sure they realise they are being volunteered as guinea pigs. Still, that's none of my business."

"Daniel? What the hell was he doing there?"

"Moonlighting. Probably short of cash now he's been demoted."

"Is Oliver still cool with the Flab Buster reactions?"

"Of course – he'd do anything for money – you know him. He's making a fortune between lucrative under-the-counter cosmetic procedures and his skyrocketing shares in Regenex. He's about to open a second clinic and guess who he's buying the premises from?"

"Tell me."

"Fay Kendrick."

"I didn't know she had a clinic."

"Well, you do now."

Keen to change the subject of Fay, Rick probed further about Regenex. "What about the anti-ageing drugs – any progress with them?"

"Early stages yet. Mostly in vitro studies in the lab and a few animal trials, but when we get to the human trials I'm sure Oliver will oblige."

"No doubt; with an industry worth billions he's after his share by whatever shady means he can."

Isobel finished her drink. "So, shall we order dinner here or shall we just go back to your apartment?" She tilted her head to one side and smiled seductively, seemingly over the incident with Fay.

Rick felt trapped. Maybe, if he kept her up late, she would want to go back to her own place and leave him alone. That meant eating another dinner and he wasn't sure he could stomach it – the octopus was starting to repeat on him.

"I'll get the menus," he said.

FIFTY-NINE

Daniel had called Rosie and asked her to bring the dogs home early. He had walked them in the woods during a brief respite from the rain and fed them when he got home. Typically, Maisie had been asleep on the sofa all afternoon but now she was parading around the kitchen. He gave her a small cube of cheese and made himself two thick slices of cheddar on toast and drenched them in tomato ketchup. It would have to do – he could eat again later in the hospital's twenty-four-hour-a-day refectory if he managed to get a long enough break. It was 5.15pm and time to leave for his night shift. He shut Chester and Ella into the Dog House, changed into navy chinos and hunted for his favourite checked shirt. He couldn't find it anywhere.

"It's like the bloody Bermuda Triangle in this house," he said aloud. He guessed Fay had been having another chucking-out session. He would have to try and retrieve that shirt – he'd had it for years and loved it, even though it was frayed. Instead, for now, he settled for a pale blue one left open at the collar.

He locked the back door and checked it twice, turned out the lights, leaving the hall one on for Fay, put his jacket on, pocketed his wallet and phone and left for the hospital. He had hoped to get some rest before the long night ahead, but he'd been unable to sleep. No doubt exhaustion would catch up with him, as usual, in the dead of night.

The rain eased off as he drove the Defender through town and the busy rush-hour traffic. The hospital car park was empty, with clinics and office staff finished for the day. He parked near the main entrance and made his way through the corridor and up the stairs to the ward. He still couldn't bring himself to use the lift.

Daniel swiped himself into the ward and noticed Frank Rivers sitting at the bedside of a sleeping patient – Jayden West. The prison officer had spotted him and gave a friendly wave. He felt obliged to put his head around the door to say hello.

"Nice to see you back at work, Dr Kendrick," Rivers said.

Daniel didn't mention the demotion. "Yes, it's good to be back."

Rivers jabbed a thumb in Jayden's direction. "Remember him? Jayden West."

"Yes, I do. How is he?"

"Tried to top himself again and narrowly escaped. Been talking to your wife and she's arranged some psychiatric treatment back at the prison."

"Well, let's hope it helps." Daniel checked his watch. "Better go. Catch you later."

Rivers gave him a dismissive wave. Daniel realised how far he had moved on. It had only been a matter of weeks since his release from Ravenwood but his days in prison already seemed like a world away. He felt a rush of gratitude wash over him. Things could have been so very different…

He took the handover from Matt, who'd had a hectic day in surgery and was glad to be going home. Colin Mathias and Rick had left earlier and Hazel Colton, another SHO, would be based on the ward all night with a couple of junior doctors. Daniel was asked to float again wherever he was needed between the ward, ICU and HDU.

Hazel was a pleasant woman in her mid-thirties, but she was a chatterbox – constantly yapping about nothing of any consequence, leaving everyone frazzled. Daniel was hoping he'd be called away from the ward.

By 2am, that hope materialised when ICU bleeped him and asked for help. He let Hazel know and walked toward the exit, past Jayden's room. He was sleeping and a different prison officer was slumped in the armchair in the corner. He let himself out of the ward and made his way to intensive care, swiping himself in. He was greeted by a cacophony of alarms bonging and whining for attention – cardiac monitors, ventilators, syringe drivers, infusion pumps, kidney dialysis machines. The unit was practically at full capacity but seemed to be under control. There was a line of widely spaced beds along two walls with patients hooked up to ventilators and various machines with banks of syringe drivers delivering infusions of drugs and fluids. Nurses were giving one-to-one care and working flat out.

Daniel noticed Kitty Pemberton, the ICU consultant, still on duty from earlier that morning. She looked shattered. She was at Megan Foley's bedside speaking to her parents and younger brother. Her mother was sobbing and gripping onto Megan's hand, her husband trying to comfort her. Her brother looked on helplessly. It didn't look good.

He checked the office but there was nobody there, then he noticed Angela Edwards at the other end of the room.

"Hi, Angela. How are things up here?"

Angela looked up from suctioning a patient's airway, white froth slithering up the tube. "Daniel. Nice to see you. Kitty asked me to bleep you – it's hectic here tonight and we have another patient due to be admitted any minute, straight from A&E. A drunk driver crashed on the motorway. Apparently, there were two dead in the other vehicle, but he just about survived. They never learn, do they?"

"No, Angela, they don't. Nobody thinks it will happen to them."

Angela reattached the patient's ventilator tubing. "Not sure if he's going to make it – but, as ever, we'll try our best."

Daniel nodded. "So, what can I do to help?"

"Not sure what Kitty has in mind. Might be best to ask her when she's free. In the meantime, you could give me a hand to turn this lady, if you don't mind – the nurses are all tied up with patients."

"Of course, no problem at all."

Between them, they managed to turn Angela's patient onto her side without dislodging a tangle of tubes, drips and catheters.

"Thanks, Daniel – you're a star."

"Any time." He glanced across to see Kitty Pemberton walking toward him. A slim woman in her late forties with long, auburn hair swept back into a low ponytail. Her pretty hazel eyes were emphasised with smoky blue eyeliner and black mascara. She wore pale blue scrubs and training shoes.

"Thanks for covering," she said. "It's been a busy night. Come into the office and I'll fill you in."

Daniel followed the consultant into a small, windowless office. She perched on a cluttered desk. "I think you know Megan Foley?"

"I helped with the repair of her ruptured spleen the other day but I'm not really familiar with her case."

"OK, well, you know she had the twins, and they are doing well on the neonatal unit."

"Glad to hear it."

"However, we got Megan back from theatre and began reducing her sedation. She started coming out of her coma and we thought she would recover but we've discovered she has a brain injury, probably caused by a high-velocity impact during the car crash. Her head CT shows an extensive intracranial haemorrhage. There has probably been a slow, persistent bleed for a while that's gone undetected due to the coma." Kitty stifled a yawn behind her hand.

"Is it operable?"

"No, the neurologists have seen her, and they think not. She also has locked-in syndrome, with complete paralysis of voluntary muscles except for eye movements. We've tried communicating with her, but she is in and out of consciousness, probably due to the bleed. I've talked to her parents at length about the options and they want her life support switched off – they say she wouldn't want to live like this."

"But couldn't we leave it a while and give her the benefit of the doubt?" Daniel felt deeply saddened. A young mother with newborn twins that she hadn't even had the chance to meet, and now people having to make decisions about whether she lives or dies.

"The neurologists don't hold out much hope. Most patients with locked-in syndrome don't live beyond the early acute stage and she does have several complications. It doesn't look good, I'm afraid."

"Yes, one set of problems compounded by another. So, what's the plan?"

"Well, we'll probably leave her overnight and let the family say their goodbyes but if there's no improvement by the morning..."

Daniel slowly shook his head. It was never easy losing a patient. As doctors, they should be used to it, but they were hard-wired to save life, not let patients die.

"Anyway, that's Megan. We have an RTA coming in and several very ill patients on the unit at the moment." Kitty gave Daniel a brief review.

"Thanks. So, what would you like me to do?"

"Basically, just be around to help where needed. Perhaps you could keep a special eye on our surgical patients, but I need someone with consultant experience. I must try and get a few hours' sleep – I'm absolutely exhausted." Kitty looked as if she could sleep right there on the edge of her desk.

"Yes, get some sleep."

"Thanks, Daniel. I'll be in the on-call room if you need me." With that she wearily dragged herself out of the unit.

Daniel spent the next few hours helping the other doctors. The RTA patient, Graeme Buckley, was brought up from A&E having suffered several broken ribs. He also had a suspected spinal cord injury, for which he'd been referred urgently to the neurosurgeons. The unit finally quietened down and by 4.50am some of the nurses were able to cover one another while they took a short break. Daniel had managed to grab a sandwich from a vending machine in the corridor and sat in the staff room for ten minutes with a strong coffee before being called to assess a patient with an abnormal heart rhythm. Thankfully, it seemed to resolve without intervention.

Megan Foley's parents had gone to the refectory to get a coffee, and her nurse was busy with another patient, so he went over to check on her. This could be the final few hours of her life if they switched off her life support. Was there really no hope? He glanced at her cardiac monitor. Her vital signs were within normal parameters; her ventilator was on normal settings. Her neurological responses were untestable due to her locked-in syndrome, but she had briefly opened her eyes to commands earlier, according to her chart. She looked so small and defenceless in the bed surrounded by machines and medical equipment.

Daniel looked at her face – she could have been sleeping, not about to die from a catastrophic brain injury. He swept a lock of dark hair away from her forehead. "Megan, can you hear me?"

There was no response, but he tried again, a little louder and more firmly this time. "Megan, open your eyes."

Megan's eyes fluttered, closed, then half opened. Her eyes swivelled slowly toward him, and she seemed to be trying to focus.

"Can you hear me and understand what I'm saying?"

She just looked at him, dazed.

"Blink once if you can hear me. Once for yes, Megan."

Megan blinked slowly but he wasn't sure if it was in response to what he was saying. "Megan, blink once for yes. Twice for no. Can you hear me?"

Megan blinked once. It was more definite this time, but he wanted to check she understood both responses.

"Can you move your arm?"

Her eyes widened as if she was trying to move her arm. Then she blinked twice.

"Are you comfortable?"

She gave one slow blink.

Daniel knew she was conscious and was able to think and reason. Surely, she had a right to decide for herself if she wanted to live or be allowed to die. It would be a difficult conversation but one he felt compelled to have with her.

"Megan, my name is Daniel. I'm one of the doctors here. I need to know that you understand what's happening to you."

She blinked once.

"You know that your babies have been born by caesarean section just a few days ago?"

Megan blinked once.

"They are beautiful: a girl and a boy, and they are both doing well in the neonatal unit."

She blinked once.

Daniel continued. "You've been in a coma for a while but, now that you've come round, the doctors have found a bleed on your brain that they can't operate on. You also have what is called locked-in syndrome. It means that you can move your eyes but all the muscles in your body are paralysed. Do you understand?"

Megan blinked once.

Daniel had to go on. "There's no cure for this and nobody knows if you will ever recover from it. You could be on a ventilator for the rest of your life. Do you understand this?"

Megan stared at him, her pupils dilating, then she deliberately blinked once.

Daniel swept away another stray lock of hair from her forehead. "Now, in the long term, it's possible that you may regain some movement in your muscles, but this is by no means certain. You would be trained to use your blinks and eye movements to help you communicate more easily and there are some electronic and computer interfaces that can help as well but you need to know there is no cure or treatment for locked-in syndrome. Do you understand what I've just told you?"

She blinked once.

"Alright, Megan. Now I need to know how you feel about this." How the hell was he going to ask her if she wanted to live or die?

He looked into her soft blue eyes and took a breath. "Now I'm going to ask you a very difficult question but it's important."

She stared at him, the ventilator giving her the breath that was keeping her alive. The same machine that could be switched off in just a few hours if she lapsed into unconsciousness again.

"Megan… do you want to carry on living in this condition?"

She gave one very definite blink.

SIXTY

The sound of a single high-pitched continuous bleep signalled that someone had suffered a cardiac arrest. Daniel looked around to see that it was the new patient – the drunk driver from A&E, Graeme Buckley.

"I have to go, Megan, but I'll be back."

He dashed across to the other end of the unit and joined one of the ICU doctors and Angela as they fought to resuscitate him.

Daniel bagged the respirations while the doctor and Angela took turns giving cardiac compressions. Another nurse had joined them and administered adrenaline every five minutes, followed by amiodarone.

Fifty minutes later they got him back.

As the nurses were starting to go back to their own patients, Daniel's bleep went off. It was the ward.

"You go, Daniel – we'll be fine," the doctor said.

"Kitty wanted me to stay."

"It's fine," the doctor insisted. "Kitty will be back soon, and the day shift are due in any minute. Go – it could be urgent."

"OK – I do need to speak to Kitty, so I'll be back up as soon as I can." He had to tell her himself not to switch off Megan's life support.

Daniel made his way back to the ward and swiped himself in. As soon as he'd reached Jayden West's side room, he could see what had happened as several staff had gathered in the room, arms flailing, voices raised.

Hazel Colton spotted Daniel and pulled him into the room. "He's gone missing, and God knows how long he's been gone."

The prison officer looked sheepish. "I fell asleep…"

"Well, wasn't he handcuffed to the bed or something?" one of the nurses asked.

"No, I'm afraid not," the prison officer said.

"Shit, what are we going to do? I've called security but they're busy with some incident in A&E. They could be a while yet and we've got a bloody murderer on the loose." Hazel was almost beside herself.

Daniel tried to calm things down. "I know Jayden; he's not a danger to anyone but himself. I'm sure there's no cause for alarm."

The prison officer ran a hand over his face. "Yes, but he has been sentenced for manslaughter and is unpredictable – we need to find him and quick."

Daniel wasn't sure why they had called him, but it looked like Hazel had panicked.

"I'll go and look for him," Hazel said.

"No – I'll go with Officer…" Daniel checked the prison officer's name badge. "Morgan. You stay and look after the ward. You know what's going on here and you'll have to give the handover soon. Jayden knows me – he might be more cooperative."

"Alright – and I'll try security again." Hazel rushed off to the phone.

Daniel turned to Prison Officer Morgan. "Come on, let's go and look for him."

They went out into the corridor. "You take the west wing, I'll take the east," Daniel said, pointing the man in the right direction.

The hospital was basically one long building on four floors with a central corridor running west to east. Apart from the main entrance at the front, there were several side entrances and doors leading out into the car park on the ground floor. Jayden could have gone anywhere. Daniel guessed he would be trying to make a bid for freedom and ran down the corridor and down the first flight of stairs he came to, following the exit signs. He glanced around, then made for the main entrance and out into the hospital grounds – there was no sign of Jayden. Maybe he'd slipped out the back way.

Daniel ran back into the hospital and along the main corridor to another exit near the blood bank that led to the back of the hospital. Just before he turned into the doorway, he noticed a skinny man in a hospital gown way down the corridor in the distance – it could be him. Daniel sprinted down the corridor, thankfully deserted at that hour of the morning. As he drew closer, he could see it was Jayden. He was trying to get something out of a vending machine.

Daniel slowed to a walk, trying not to spook him. "Jayden, it's me, Daniel Kendrick," he said breathlessly.

Jayden looked up, his eyes wide and staring, he looked as if he was about to scarper but had changed his mind. He seemed so fragile – bony and naked under a thin hospital gown; his feet were bare. He was fumbling with the keypad on the machine.

"You must be freezing. Come on, let's get you back to the ward." Daniel reached a hand out to the man.

Jayden looked back at the machine.

"Are you hungry?" His heart went out to him. The image of him in that prison cell with a bedsheet around his throat had stayed with Daniel. He'd had nightmares about it. Jayden didn't belong in prison.

Jayden nodded.

"So, what would you like?" Daniel reached into his back pocket for his wallet and took out some change.

He pointed to a Cornish pasty.

Daniel fed the machine with three £1 coins and made the selection. The packet fell out into a tray, and he handed it to Jayden. "How about a coffee to wash it down?"

Jayden nodded. "Please."

Daniel moved along to the next vending machine and got two coffees, glad of one for himself – he was flagging after a busy night shift. He handed one to Jayden and gestured to a bench nearby. They both sat.

"What made you run off like that?"

"I can't face spending the rest of my life in prison," he said.

Daniel didn't know what to say. He understood how he felt. He was so young and killing his stepfather had been about survival and escape from the torture of constant abuse – not a deliberate act of evil. It would be so easy for Daniel to simply let him go, to pretend he hadn't found him. He could get him some warm clothes and a pair of shoes and just let him go free.

"Where were you planning to go?"

Jayden shrugged.

"Do you have any friends?"

"Not really."

"You'd end up on the streets, wouldn't you?"

He shrugged again. "Probably."

Daniel felt torn. Without support, Jayden would be even more vulnerable. Frank Rivers had told him that Fay had organised some psychiatric help at the prison and, much as he wanted Jayden to be a free man, he knew he would be better off getting professional treatment and support. Surely there was a way he could help him too.

Daniel thought for a moment. "Jayden, I think you would be better off getting that professional help that my wife has organised for you. I really do. That's why I want you to come back to the ward with me."

Jayden looked at Daniel, his eyes saying no.

"But I have an idea. How about we get you a good barrister – someone who has a reputation for winning appeals at murder trials? We could ask the barrister that got me acquitted. His name is Miles Parker. He's brilliant and I'm sure he'd take you on."

Jayden looked at Daniel wide-eyed. "I can't afford something like that."

"Don't worry about the cost. Just come back with me to the ward and I'll call Miles and get him to see you."

"I don't know..."

"Please, Jayden. If you are acquitted, you'll be a free man and you'll get the help you need to find a job and make a home for yourself. If you go on the run now, you'll always be looking over your shoulder and you said yourself you'll probably end up on the streets. This is a much better way."

"I promised Dr Kendrick I wouldn't give up."

"And will you promise me that you'll go back to prison and talk to Miles Parker?"

Jayden thought for some minutes then nodded pensively. "Alright, I will."

Daniel had no idea how he was going to pay for Jayden's legal fees, but he'd find a way somehow – even if it meant extra work at Oliver's clinic. "Let's get you back to the ward and into a nice warm bed."

Jayden walked alongside Daniel like a lamb. He was shivering and clutching onto his coffee cup for warmth. As they got to the stairs, the day staff were starting to file in, and Daniel saw Prison Officer Morgan rushing along the corridor toward them. They waited for him to catch up.

"Thank God – you found him," he said gasping for breath.

They walked together a while, then Morgan took Jayden back to the ward.

"Don't forget what I said, Jayden," Daniel said with a warm smile.

Daniel checked the time. It was almost 8.45am. The night shift would have gone home by now and he desperately needed to get to the ICU to stop them turning off Megan Foley's life support.

He dashed back up the stairs and along the corridor to the ICU, swiped himself in and made straight for Megan's bed. Ominously, the curtains had been pulled around the bed and Daniel opened them to see Kitty Pemberton at Megan's bedside along with her parents and her brother. Her mother was sobbing, her face buried in the bed covers; her father was hugging her brother as he sobbed on his shoulder.

Shit – it looked like he might be too late…

SIXTY-ONE

Fay had made an excuse, left the wine bar and gone straight home after Rick had kissed her but she couldn't stop thinking about him. She felt a mixture of guilt and nervousness tinged with schoolgirl excitement. She shouldn't have let him kiss her like that and it must never happen again – and yet she couldn't help but image being in his arms, or his bed.

She'd drunk almost a bottle of wine after she got home, then slept until gone 8am. She had picked up a text message from Doug, via Angela Edwards, telling her a patient on ICU had suffered a cardiac arrest during the night and would she check if he wanted to talk to her. She replied that she would.

She showered, moussed her hair into beachy waves and dressed in a skirt, blouse, and cardigan, then changed her mind and opted for a clingy wrap-around jersey dress with tiny white flowers on a black background. She put on her best gold necklace with a tear-shaped turquoise gemstone and black high-heeled court shoes.

She fed the dogs and shut them into the Dog House ready for Rosie to collect them. Maisie was nowhere to be seen but she left a fresh dish of turkey-flavoured cat food for her and changed her water. She contemplated breakfast but decided that the cereal she liked tasted rancid, so she skipped it.

She drove her Mercedes through town. The rain had eased, leaving blue sky and banks of fluffy white cumulus clouds. She wished she'd put on a cardigan, but it was too late to go back now. She turned up the heater in the car and put on a CD of upbeat Motown songs. She sang along with Diana Ross's "Chain Reaction".

She arrived at the hospital feeling wired and managed to park in the main car park, a good walk from the main entrance. She made a note to get there earlier in future – before the clinics started. Music filled her mind as she made her way to the front entrance and headed straight for the ICU. She swiped herself in and looked for someone to ask about the cardiac arrest patient. All the nurses looked busy, but she managed to catch one of the junior doctors.

"I'm Dr Fay Kendrick. Angela Edwards asked me to speak with a patient who had a cardiac arrest during the night. I'm sorry, I don't know the name."

The doctor looked puzzled for a moment, then pointed to one of the beds. "It must be Graeme Buckley. The neurologists are with him now but if you can hang on a few minutes…"

"Sure, no problem." She waited near the entrance, trying to stay out of the way.

*

Daniel tapped Kitty Pemberton's arm and she turned to face him. "What's happening?" he asked tentatively. He could see the ventilator was still working.

"We're about to switch her off," Kitty said sombrely.

Daniel pulled her aside. "No, you can't – I managed to communicate with her last night, and she wants to live. I asked her and she definitely said she wanted to live, even with locked-in syndrome."

"But she's completely unresponsive this morning. Daniel, this is what her parents want."

"But *she* wants to live. People do live with locked-in syndrome and there is plenty of help and support available for her to live at home. You said yourself that she's in and out of consciousness – surely we can give her a chance. She can still enjoy a good quality of life and she has two children to live for." Had she really gone beyond the point of no return? She was still technically alive – Daniel was desperate for them to give her a chance.

Kitty looked perplexed for a moment and looked at Megan, then her family and back at Daniel. "Alright, let's give her a reprieve for now and monitor the situation. I'll tell the family."

Daniel felt relief wash over him. It would have been tantamount to murder if they had switched the machine off, knowing she wanted to live and had the chance to. After Wixx and the deaths on the ward lately, helping to save a life felt good. "Thank you, Kitty."

"Why don't you go home and get some sleep? You look shattered."

"That sounds like a good idea." He'd been running on nervous energy since the early hours.

Daniel made his way to the exit and saw Fay standing there, smiling at him.

"Hey, sweetheart. You look nice this morning."

"Hi, Daniel. Thanks. I'm just waiting to see Graeme Buckley." She twisted her head in the direction of the patient.

"Ah, yes – we resuscitated him last night."

"You must have had a busy shift. I thought you'd be fast asleep in bed by now."

"Yes, it's been quite eventful but I'm finally off home."

Fay glanced across to the patient. The neurologists were still discussing his case at the bedside. "I guess I could come back later."

"Fancy some breakfast? I'm starving." Daniel was suddenly craving a full English.

"Sure – why not."

Daniel ushered her through the door, and they headed for the concourse. They queued at the cafeteria, the bright lights over the stainless-steel counter illuminating a selection of cooked sausages, bacon, mushrooms, eggs, beans, tomatoes, hash browns and toast. Daniel ordered a mega-sized cooked breakfast for himself, a chocolate muffin for Fay and a pot of tea for two.

They found a quiet table near the front window, overlooking the hospital grounds, and Daniel told her about Jayden escaping from the ward and then Megan's fight for life.

"What will happen to the twins?" Fay asked.

"I don't know – I guess that depends on what the grandparents want. She might also have godparents or other family that will take them in. Of course, if she survives, she might live with her extended family or have someone to live in and care for her and the babies. I don't know, but it will be for them to decide."

"We could adopt them," Fay said, looking at him pleadingly.

"That's not going to happen, Fay." Daniel speared a couple of fried mushrooms and some bacon and shoved them into his mouth.

"We could go through the proper channels and adopt them legally. What's wrong with that?"

Daniel gave her a look that said, *are you real*?

Fay continued. "If Megan dies, those babies will need a mother and, if she survives, she will need someone to care for them."

Daniel looked her in the eye. "No, Fay – it doesn't work like that and, if I remember rightly, we had this conversation about having another child. It's not on at the moment."

Fay had her sulky face on but seemed to know when to stop talking.

They sat in silence while Daniel finished his breakfast. Fay had eaten half her muffin and given up on the rest.

"You going to eat that?" Daniel asked.

Fay pushed the plate across the table to him. He finished her muffin and washed it down with the rest of the tea.

"Right – I'm off home to bed," Daniel said.

"What are your shifts today?"

Daniel thought for a moment. "I'm off tonight then back in the morning but I'll have to check if I have any appointments at Oliver's. I'll let you know."

"OK, see you later."

Daniel kissed her and left for home.

*

Fay sat awhile in the cafeteria. She watched Daniel walk away with a stab of resentment. Those two babies needed to be cared for and she was desperate to look after them – how did Daniel know that Megan's family would step in? She wondered if she should make some enquiries. If it was possible to adopt the twins, surely Daniel would come around to the idea eventually. She pictured the little girl in her mind and the warm feeling of holding her in her arms. Perhaps she'd be allowed to visit. It wouldn't hurt to try, and she had nothing else on for the rest of the day. The patient on the ICU wasn't going anywhere.

She grabbed her bag and headed for the neonatal unit, dodging trolleys and a cleaner operating a floor polishing machine in the corridor. Would they even let her in? She rang the intercom on the door of the unit and waited. A woman's voice crackled through the speaker.

"Yes?"

Fay took a deep breath. "I'd like to visit Megan Foley's twins please."

There was a pause, then a buzzer sounded and the door clicked. Fay pushed the door open and went inside. It was hot, bustling with activity and the smell of disinfectant was pungent.

Fay could see the intensive care room through a large window behind the nurses' station, with several incubators and tiny premature babies on ventilators.

A pleasant-looking woman in a dark pleated skirt and colourful top greeted her – her name badge told her she was the ward clerk. "Can I help you?"

Fay flashed the official ID card on a lanyard around her neck. "Dr Fay Kendrick. I promised Megan Foley I'd call in and see how the twins are getting along and get a few photos for her. That's alright, isn't it?"

The woman glanced at the ID. "I guess so, but I'd better check with sister. One moment." She wandered off, looking in various rooms, then came back. "I can't find her – she's probably on labour ward or in theatre." She glanced at Fay's ID again. "I guess it will be OK. Just a few minutes, though."

"Thanks," Fay said. She followed the woman's directions into a small, dimly lit room with three cots and two incubators. One of the incubators was empty but the other contained the twins with Megan's name attached to it. One of the nurses had put them in together and they lay wrapped in white sheets facing one another.

Fay gasped when she saw them – they were adorable. She recognised the little girl. She looked healthy and bonny. The boy was smaller, thinner and had a nasal oxygen cannula, the clear tubing taped to his rosy cheeks and attached to an oxygen point on the wall. They both had dark hair and the girl was gripping the boy's hand with her chubby little fingers. They seemed to be breathing in unison, although the boy was a little snuffly. Fay watched, overwhelmed with warmth and affection for the tiny infants. If only she could take them home and love them as if they were her own. She watched them breathing for long minutes, then took her phone out of her bag and took several photographs. She remembered Sophie at that age and how perfect she was.

She put her phone back into her bag, rubbed her hands with sanitiser, then opened one of the portholes on the incubator and put her hand in. She just wanted to touch them. She placed her hand gently on the little girl's back. She felt so warm and delicate.

Then she heard a woman's voice behind her. "Excuse me – I don't think you have permission to be in here." It was the ward sister, dressed in navy scrubs. Her name badge read *Janice Brownlow*.

Fay startled and pulled her hand from the incubator, shutting the porthole. "I'm visiting on behalf of Megan. Just wanted to get some photographs for her."

The sister scowled. "We had no prior notice. I'm afraid we must have Megan or her parents' permission to allow visitors – even family members, I'm afraid."

"I didn't mean any harm."

"I'm sure you didn't but we still can't allow anyone to visit without express permission."

"That's fair enough." Fay picked up her bag, glancing into the incubator. "Do you know what will happen to them?"

"I'm afraid I can't discuss that with you."

Fay was bitterly disappointed but followed the woman to the exit and left. At least she'd seen the twins and had a few photographs.

She strolled slowly toward the main entrance again – not really knowing where she was going or what she was going to do next. She felt lost and confused – her head full of images of the twins, her heart aching with longing to take them home. She pulled out her phone and looked at the photographs she'd taken. The little girl looked just like Sophie had at that age. She picked a close-up photograph of the baby's face and saved it as her home screen. She replaced her phone in her bag and wandered aimlessly around the concourse for twenty minutes, browsing the gift shop, the bookshop, then the chemist, before a text from Doug pulled her back to reality.

Did you find the patient in ICU?

Fay remembered she had to see Graeme Buckley – of course, she'd meant to go back there but had forgotten. She texted back.

On my way.

Why was Doug checking up on her? First Shelly and now him. Did they know where she was? Could they see what she'd been doing? Did they know she'd been to see the twins? She tried to rationalise but couldn't help feeling slightly paranoid. She tried to shrug off the feeling and focus on getting herself to the ICU. Work would take her mind of things and she needed a distraction.

She swiped herself into the unit and one of the nurses directed her to Graeme Buckley's bed. He was propped up on pillows and wide awake. Matt Clarke was pushing fluid from a syringe into his canula. She waited until Matt had finished.

He gave her a stiff smile. "How are you, Fay?"

"Fine, thanks. Just wanted a chat with your patient."

"Sure – be my guest," he said as he dropped the syringe into a sharps box and wandered away to check on another patient.

Although Matt was Daniel's friend and she'd seen him plenty of times around the ward, they knew one another only slightly. She stepped up to Graeme Buckley's bed.

"Hello, I'm Dr Fay Kendrick. I wondered if you wanted to have a chat about your experience last night." She swore she could smell boiled cabbage but couldn't see anything that could account for it.

Graeme Buckley sat up in the bed. "Ah, yes, the lady doing the research into near-death experiences. Nurse Edwards said she'd get in touch with you."

"May I sit down?"

Graeme indicated a chair next to the bed. "Please."

Fay sat and took a notebook and pen from her bag. "How are you feeling now? You took a turn for the worst last night."

"Yes, apparently, but I don't remember anything about that. It was after the crash that I had a strange experience."

"Why don't you tell me about it?" She was expecting a classical NDE: light at the end of a tunnel, being met by relatives, surrounded by love…

"I crashed the car – pulled out in front of someone on the motorway. I just didn't see them. I felt the collision and heard an almighty bang. The airbag deployed but I didn't have my seat belt on and slammed into the steering wheel. My head hit the windscreen and then – nothing. No pain. I couldn't hear anything. I felt myself lift out of my body and could see the crash from above – just a mangled heap of metal and shattered glass – along with a trail of traffic skidding across three lanes and coming to a standstill behind. I knew the two people in the other car were dead. There's no way they could have walked away from that…" He paused and looked away.

"Go on, Mr Buckley."

He thought for a few moments, shaking his head, then slowly turned to look at Fay, his eyes dark and fearful. "Then I was trapped in a dark place. It felt so lonely. So horribly lonely – like I was the only living soul left in the universe." He looked down and pulled the sheet up, smoothing it over his belly as if he was trying to distract his mind from the terror he was reliving. "I was shown a series of images – things that had happened in my life – as if I was living through them again…"

"What sort of images?"

"Nasty things I had done – hurting animals as a child, bullying other children in school, cheating in exams and then in my adult life – other things…"

It was the first distressing NDE Fay had come across and she wasn't sure how to deal with it. She waited while Graeme composed himself.

"I seemed to be in this cold, black place for a long time. I couldn't sense anyone else there, but these images kept coming. I've done plenty of good in my life, but this was showing me all the bad stuff. I experienced what I had done to other people as if I was living their experience myself. I cheated on my wife, and I lived through her heartbreak and despair; I felt the pain I had inflicted on those defenceless animals and the humiliation I caused those children. I felt the disappointment of my parents and the anger of my boss..." He smoothed the sheet again, slowly shaking his head. "How can I ever put those things right?"

Fay still didn't know how to respond but managed to say, "I'm so sorry."

Graeme looked at her with terror in his eyes. "Then it got worse... I was underground, fighting my way through soil, trying to breathe... trapped... buried alive. There were rats scurrying above me and giant worms burrowing into my body with razor sharp teeth – they were like aliens. I couldn't get away." He shook his head. "It wasn't a bad dream or some sort of hallucination – I was there, and I really was trapped. I tried to call out, but I couldn't – nobody was there to hear me."

Fay just looked at the man. She could sense his anguish.

"Then I was being dragged through this black soil and was suddenly back in my body in the ambulance being blue-lighted to hospital." He looked at Fay, horror etched into his face.

Fay paused, taking in what the man had said. "How do you feel about that experience now?"

The man looked down at the sheet again. "Terrified to die..." He shook his head as if he was trying to dislodge the memories, to rid himself of the awful things he'd done. "Bloody terrified..."

Fay just wanted to get out of there. She didn't know how to deal with the man's distress or contemplate that her daughter might have had an experience like that, however unlikely. She had been violently murdered and God only knew what Wixx had done to her before he'd killed her. Felicia Grainger had said that she was happy now, but she could have had a horrendous experience. How could she possibly know?

He looked at Fay again, now a ray of hope in his eyes. "But you know what, doc? It's made me want to be a better person

– to try and make up for what I've done. Two people are dead because of my breathtaking stupidity but when I get out of here I'm going to do some good in the world, turn my sorry, sordid life around. I want to dedicate the rest of my time on Earth to helping others. I've seen what a monster I had become and the effect I was having on other people. Now I just want to be a decent human being and do something worthwhile."

"Then maybe this experience has been a good thing?"

"Maybe." He smiled reflectively. "I hope so."

In her peripheral vision, Fay could see Rick walking toward her. She smiled. It was good to see him, but the heat of embarrassment flushed her cheeks as she remembered their kiss in the wine bar.

He stood on the opposite side of the bed. "Fay, nice to see you." He smiled at her, his eyes roaming her face and hair, then turned to Graeme. "I hear you had a close shave during the night."

"Yes, I'm lucky to be here."

Rick turned awkwardly and knocked a syringe driver off its stand with his elbow. It clattered to the floor and the syringe became unclipped from the driver. He bent to pick it up but seemed to drop it again.

"You OK there?" Fay asked, mildly amused.

"Sure – got it." Rick reassembled everything and pressed the start button on the infusion, slightly flustered. He turned to Fay. "Got a moment?"

"Excuse me, Graeme," Fay said as she stood and followed Rick out of earshot of the patients.

"Fancy coming jet-skiing with me sometime? I think it would do you good to get away from here for a while," Rick said.

Fay hesitated, not sure if she should commit herself. Then she thought about the twins and caught a glimpse of Megan Foley at the other end of the unit and decided that life was too short. Rick was right – she could do with a distraction, and it was only jet-skiing, for goodness' sake. Just a bit of fun after all that had happened. Rick was very alluring, and she was finding him hard to resist. "Alright – that would be nice."

"How about tomorrow? The weather looks perfect."

Tomorrow – Daniel would be working all day so she could get away. She decided there and then not to tell him, especially given the friction between the two men. He would never approve of her spending time with his boss but what he didn't know, he couldn't fret about. "OK, but I don't have any kit."

"Don't need it – I have wetsuits and all the clobber you'll need. Why don't we meet at the riverside car park just outside town at 9am and we'll go in my car? I'll get you back there by the end of the day."

She hesitated again but fleetingly this time. "Sounds good to me."

"Good. You'd better give me your mobile number, just in case."

They exchanged numbers and Fay put Rick's straight into her contacts. "I'll see you in the morning, then." She smiled and turned to go back to Graeme Buckley, but she could see he was struggling to breathe and his heart monitor was alarming.

"He's arresting again," Rick said, pushing past her to get to him.

She stood aside and watched Rick, two nurses and another doctor work on Graeme, Rick frantically pushing his chest with cardiac compressions, barking orders to the others. He had taken control of the situation.

"He's in VF," Rick said, glancing at the cardiac monitor.

A nurse handed him the defibrillator paddles and he slammed them onto the man's chest. Graeme convulsed as a 150-joule bolt of electricity shot through his heart muscle.

Rick continued with another cycle of cardiac compressions. "Charge to 200," he said.

Again, he shocked the man's heart, but the monitor showed one long flat line. His heart had stopped.

"I think you should call it, Rick, it's his second arrest in twenty-four hours." Kitty Pemberton stood at the foot of the bed.

"No – keep going with CPR," Rick said breathlessly, pumping the man's chest.

Fay watched in awe as Rick tried his best to resuscitate the man. He was giving it his all. She willed him on. He had to save him – Graeme was terrified of dying and he had things to do with his life. Good things. It would be a tragedy if his distressing NDE was in vain.

Twenty minutes later, Kitty Pemberton put her hand on Rick's arm. "Call it, Rick."

Rick reluctantly stopped and looked into Graeme Buckley's lifeless eyes. He glanced at the clock on the wall. "Time of death 12.25."

The monitor sounded one continuous alarm.

SIXTY-TWO

The following morning, Daniel was up before dawn after the night shift had disrupted his sleep. He left Fay in bed, crept out and walked the dogs on the path alongside the woodland. A waning crescent moon and its companion, Venus, were gliding toward the horizon with a complement of stars still glittering in the blackness of night. In the beam of his headtorch, Daniel saw a young fox crossing the pathway. It turned to face him, its eyes reflecting the torchlight like tiny headlamps. Tawny owls were hooting from the trees, and he caught a glimpse of a wing as it flew silently through the woodland. Sheep were calling to one another in the field and after the rain, the air was cool and refreshing.

He threw a ball for Ella, and she bounded after it. Chester had missed it in the dark and continued to bounce expectantly on his front paws. Daniel threw another for him, and he chased after it. He wondered if he could get luminous ones.

He turned at the end of the woodland path, where a wooden bridge crossed the stream. He whistled to the dogs, and they made their way back home just as an arch of sunlight was edging into the dark horizon. They arrived home to find Fay up and making toast for herself. She had showered, applied eye make-up and styled her hair into glossy curls. She was wearing a knee-length cream skirt and a skimpy pink camisole.

"Won't you be cold in that?" Daniel asked as he let the dogs off their leads.

Fay looked down at her outfit. "Cold? No. Don't you like it?"

"It's fine," he said, not wanting to make a big deal of it. What did he know? Maybe goosebumps were fashionable these days.

Fay looked as if she were pouting. "I'll take a cardigan."

Chester went to his bowl and took huge laps of water; his pink tongue splashing it all over the floor. Ella sat panting, waiting for Daniel to fill her bowl too. Maisie looked on disdainfully from the doorway. Daniel put two slices of bread in the toaster for himself.

"The kettle has just boiled," Fay said. She grabbed his favourite mug: pint-sized with the legend *Don't grow up – it's a trap*. She made him a black coffee. "I think the milk's gone off."

Daniel sniffed the milk in the carton, checked the use-by date and poured some into his mug. "Seems alright to me – we only bought it the other day." He pushed Maisie off the kitchen table when she tried to lick the butter. "So how was work yesterday? Sorry I fell asleep on the sofa again – these night shifts are knackering."

"That's alright. Work wasn't too bad. Did I tell you Graeme Buckley died?" Fay asked around a mouthful of toast and strawberry jam.

"The bloke we resuscitated in the night?"

"Yes, I was talking to him one minute and the next he collapsed and died."

"Crikey," Daniel said, slathering his toast with butter and lemon curd.

"Rick tried his best to resuscitate but it was hopeless," Fay said.

"That's sad – another death in the department." Daniel didn't say it but at least nobody could point the finger of blame at him for that one. Maybe he was being paranoid, a consequence of spending time in prison, more than likely. It would take him a while to put that particular part of the past behind him.

Daniel glanced at the time, then at Fay. "Better get to work. Would you be able to get the dogs sorted?" He took a gulp of his coffee and grabbed his jacket, wallet, iPhone and keys.

"Sure – go," Fay said.

Daniel kissed Fay on the cheek before hurrying out of the house. "Bye, sweetheart – see you later."

Daniel drove the Defender across town as the sun was rising into a clear blue sky. It was going to be dry and sunny with a stiff south-westerly breeze, according to the weather forecast on the radio.

He arrived at the hospital, found the only parking space left and what seemed like a two-mile trek to the main entrance. He took the stairs to the surgical floor and let himself into the ward. Jayden West had been transferred out – probably back to the hospital wing of the prison. He hoped he would get the help he needed and made a mental note to call Miles Parker.

There was no sign of Rick, but Colin was making tea in his office and Matt had followed Daniel into the ward.

"Hey, mate – how's it going? Are you on the ward today?" Matt asked, giving Daniel a friendly slap on the back.

"Yep – I think I'm here unless someone tells me otherwise."

They walked to the staff changing room to dump their jackets, then back to the ward to take the handover and prepare for the round.

Daniel could see Isobel coming out of Rick's office, immaculate as usual and dressed in a slim-fitting blue skirt suit over a white blouse along with a pair of black killer heels. There was no sign of Rick. She gave him a cursory smile as she went past but Daniel was still puzzled by the fact that he saw her coming out of the mortuary the other day. Should he ask her? Not a chance, he thought. Her haughty demeanour could be quite intimidating at times and he'd enough animosity to contend with.

"Any more news on the clinical trial?" Daniel asked Matt.

He was flicking through a pile of patients' notes. "Nothing at all. I guess it's still going on in the background."

"No more side effects or reactions?" He remembered Bob Hackman's anaphylaxis and Isobel's reassurance that he'd taken the placebo.

"Not that I know of." Matt said absently.

"Do we have the results from Regenex's metabolism group report yet?"

"Don't know," Matt said, only half listening. He showed Daniel a CT scan result. "Look at this tumour. Not sure if it's operable but what do you think?"

Daniel focused on the job in hand and looked carefully at the CT scan of Adrian Clifford's liver. He could see a large cancerous growth and there were several metastases. "We could excise the liver tumour, but the cancer has spread to both lungs and probably the small bowel." He pointed to the metastasis. "Maybe we should ask Rick since he's god or, should I say, boss in this place."

"You don't like him much, do you?"

"No, not much – there's something about him." Daniel couldn't put his finger on it, but Rick rubbed him up the wrong way.

"Maybe it's just because he took your job, mate – a bit of competition between you. He's not so bad once you get to know him. Anyway, he's taking the day off today, so Colin will be in charge."

Daniel was relieved. He could do without having to kowtow to him all day. "Great. Let's ask Colin about the tumour before the round."

*

Colin had decided that they should perform a laparotomy, excise the liver tumour to keep Adrian Clifford comfortable but assess the metastatic tumours once they had opened him up. Both Matt and Daniel had been assigned to theatre that afternoon. Matt took the lead and Daniel assisted. The outcome had been better than expected and the metastasis could be held at bay with chemotherapy and radiotherapy. For a while at least.

Daniel had spent the rest of the afternoon checking on surgical patients and clerked a new admission – a referral from her GP for acute cholecystitis. He then did a check of all the patients who were on the clinical trial. None of them had reported any reactions – except, of course, for Bob Hackman and Jean Wyatt, who had both died. Still, it couldn't have been caused by the trial drug if they'd had the placebo. He knew they would have to wait for the metabolism group report from Regenex – and that was in Isobel's hands.

He had given Dr Mani Adebayo a handover for the night shift, retrieved his jacket from the staff room and was getting ready to leave when he saw Eddie Bates striding across the ward toward Colin Mathias, who was standing near the nurses' station.

As bold as a baboon, Bates faced Colin square on and said something that Daniel couldn't hear. There seemed to be a slight skirmish between them, with Bates flailing his arms, before Colin reached for his wallet, took out a wad of notes and handed them to Bates, who pocketed the cash and strode off.

What the hell was going on? Daniel's instinct was to ask Colin if everything was alright but when he approached him he was fobbed off.

"It's nothing – just leave it." Colin shot Daniel a look that said *back off*.

He saw Bates in his peripheral vision as he was leaving the ward and decided on a whim, to go after him. If Colin didn't have the courage to stand up to him, then he would have to.

He was getting sick of Bates stealing from the patients, the treatment rooms and the medicine trolley. Now it looked as if he was throwing his weight around with colleagues and it was not on. He'd heard nothing more from security about the stolen painkillers – he would just have to confront the man himself.

Daniel let himself out of the ward and checked each end of the corridor. He could see the back end of Bates disappearing down the stairs. He rushed to catch up but kept a good distance behind. For the second time that week, he was trying to stop the thieving hound. Bates went through the concourse and out into the hospital grounds, turning right toward the main multi-storey car park. Daniel followed him and watched from behind a concrete pillar as he got into a battered blue Fiesta. He took a note of the registration plate.

As Bates drove toward the exit, Daniel was running to his own car. He fired up the Defender and followed. He could see Bates's Fiesta four vehicles ahead and managed to keep up as he drove through town. Two of the cars in front of him turned and he found himself a comfortable distance behind. Bates took the ring road out of town, then two miles west he took the slipway toward Dilport, then, another mile on, a left and through the lanes toward the village of Carrick. Daniel slowed as Bates pulled into a large building; a sign at the front gate read "Hamilton Court Nursing Home". Daniel remembered that John Gardener had been discharged here. He felt a stab of indignation. Surely Bates wasn't brazen enough to go after the elderly man again; he'd already stolen his wallet. He wished he'd confronted him at the time.

Daniel waited on the main road while Bates parked and went into the home. What the hell was he up to? Was he preying on elderly people? Conning them out of their money? It had to stop. And now. Daniel had no choice but to follow him and confront him – to catch him red-handed and call the police. DS

Harper would deal with him, he was sure. He would end up back in prison for this.

Daniel drove into the grounds and parked, then walked up to the main entrance – a large open stone porch with a half-glazed door with blue and red stained glass. There was a security camera to one side. He would have to ring the bell and have a good reason to be there if he wanted to be let in. He thought for a moment. It wasn't his style to go in all guns blazing, demanding to see Bates, and, anyway, he would just deny everything if he was confronted. He had to catch him stealing for it to stand up. He was a doctor – he could say he was coming to check on John Gardener. That would do it. He fished out his ID card from his pocket, slung it around his neck on the lanyard and rang the bell. He waited while a woman walked to the front door, her short, rotund frame distorted behind the coloured glass.

"Can I help you?" the woman asked. She had rosy cheeks and transparent, ice-blue eyes that locked onto his.

"Yes, thank you. I've come to check on John Gardener – he was discharged from Riverbeke General. I'm Dr Daniel Kendrick, one of the doctors on the ward." He showed her his ID card.

"Oh, that's nice of you but his GP has already been to see him. Is there something wrong?"

"No, nothing wrong but Mr Gardener was on a clinical drug trial at the hospital and I'm just following up on that. There's no problem."

"Well, you'd better come in then."

The woman stood aside to let Daniel through. She walked him to John Gardener's room along a freshly decorated, carpeted passageway. Several rooms led off it with the names of the residents on the doors. They reached John's room and the woman knocked twice and opened the door. The room was sparsely furnished with a window overlooking a large formal garden. John was sitting in a high-backed armchair on a ring doughnut-shaped pillow, reading a newspaper.

He looked up and beamed when he saw Daniel. "Ah, Dr Kendrick. How lovely to see you." He tuned to face the woman. "Mavis, this is that kind doctor I was telling you about."

The woman smiled. "I'll leave you to it." She went out, leaving the door open.

Daniel wandered around to the window, where he could get a view of the open doorway. He made polite conversation with John and asked how he was settling in.

"I'd much rather be at home, doctor, but it's only temporary and everyone is very kind."

John thanked Daniel for the cash he'd left in his new wallet, then they chatted about the weather and John's family for several minutes. Daniel thought he heard Eddie Bates's voice along the passageway.

"Well, I'll be off now, Mr Gardener. I'm glad you're alright." He edged toward the door.

"Thanks for coming, doc. Visit anytime." He waved him off and went back to his newspaper.

Daniel crept out of the room and down the passageway in the direction he'd heard Bates.

The door to one of the rooms was ajar and he peered in to see Bates with a frail-looking elderly woman, her neck bent, lank grey hair hanging around her face. She was propped up in bed wearing a pale blue bed cardigan over a yellow nylon nightie. There was a colourful, hand-crocheted blanket over the bed and the room was chock-full of antique furniture, ornaments and knick-knacks. She seemed to be arguing with him but he was gently trying to persuade her to drink from a plastic beaker.

Should he go in? Was Bates trying steal from her – to con her out of her life savings or sign her home over to him? He glanced around – the passageway was deserted. If he watched a while longer, he might catch him red-handed. Then he heard Bates.

"You have to drink something, it's your favourite blackcurrant squash." He was holding the beaker to her mouth. "Please, you have to drink…"

The woman swiped the beaker from his hand, and it clattered the floor. "No – no – no," she shouted, "You're trying to poison me. Stop it… help… help." She was lashing out at him with bony, arthritic hands, scratching his face with her nails. Her eyes were wild and staring.

Daniel stiffened – maybe now was the time to intervene. He was about to push the door open when he heard Bates again.

"Mum, please. You must drink." Bates was as calm as a clam. He wasn't retaliating.

"They all say that," the woman hissed.

"You'll make yourself ill if you don't eat and drink. Please, Mum…" He retrieved the beaker from the floor, wiped the spout and gently tried again.

Daniel looked at the name on the door. "Dorothea Bates."

She obviously suffered from dementia. Daniel had completely misread the situation.

Then he was startled by a voice in the passageway.

"Do you need to see Mrs Bates as well, doctor?" It was Mavis.

She came up behind him with a pile of pink towels and neatly folded nighties under her arm. She pushed Mrs Bates's door wide open. "Come in, doctor. This is Edward, Mrs Bates's son. He's such a good lad – always here helping to look after her." She smiled at Bates, and he proudly grinned back.

Daniel was ushered into the room before he could protest. Mavis plonked the clean laundry onto a cupboard. "There you are. I'll change the bed later."

With that she'd gone, leaving both Daniel and Bates shellshocked.

Bates stared at Daniel with disbelief, one hand holding the beaker, the other trying to ward off his mother's flailing hands. "What the hell are *you* doing here?"

"I think I owe you an apology," Daniel said sheepishly.

Bates waited, eyebrows raised, his mother starting to calm down.

Daniel felt foolish but there had been a reason he'd followed Bates. "I saw you on the ward demanding money from Colin Mathias and I followed you here. I jumped to conclusions..."

Bates smirked. "Yes, you certainly did."

"After you stole those drugs – and I know you've been stealing from the patients and the treatment rooms as well – I thought you'd robbed Colin and I followed you here."

"What are you gonna to do about it?" Bates asked.

"Colin may want to press charges and the police should be involved."

Bates sat on the edge of his mother's bed and looked at Daniel, a softer expression on his face now. He sighed. "Look, Daniel, you might as well know the truth. Colin is my father, and he gives me money to help pay for Mum's care here."

Daniel looked aghast. Bates was Colin's son? Suddenly his boss's ardent defence of prisoners in employment made perfect sense. His own son had been in prison.

Bates went on. "Mum and Colin met over thirty years ago and had a brief affair – I was the result. Dad didn't want to see me until a few years ago and by then Mum's dementia was getting worse. Maybe he pays up out of guilt – I don't know – but it's never enough. I admit I steal – money, drugs, whatever I can get my hands on to sell – but it's all to help pay for Mum's care. We've already used up most of the money we got for her house. Do you have any idea how much nursing home care is these days?"

Daniel remembered Bates's beaten-up Fiesta. It did make sense. He was arrogant, argumentative, defensive and a dealer but, as far as he knew, wasn't into taking drugs himself. He was probably just selling whatever he could steal. He looked around the room. "Can't you sell some of this? There must be some money's worth here and it's better than stealing."

"This stuff is what keeps Mum from going over the edge. It's her world in here and she's surrounded by the things she knows. Without this..." His words trailed off.

Daniel noticed several framed photographs – a young Bates with his mother, a more recent one of them smiling together at the home and a black and white photograph that was obviously Colin Mathias in his younger days. Daniel didn't know what to say.

Bates looked at him with pleading eyes. "Please, Daniel – don't tell the police. Mum needs me. I can't get banged up again."

Daniel suddenly felt sorry for Bates. What would be the point in getting him arrested? Would it help him? His mother? Society at large? Daniel decided to cut him some slack. "Alright – but you must stop stealing from the patients and the ward. Get another cleaning job or something if you need the money but you must stop stealing or I *will* have to tell the police. Do we have a deal?"

Bates nodded. "It's a deal... and thanks."

Daniel drove home from Hamilton Court Nursing Home realising that Bates was going out of his way to help his mother, yet she didn't even recognise her own son.

SIXTY-THREE

Fay had said goodbye to Daniel and waited while he pulled off the driveway. She put Chester and Ella in the Dog House, ready for Rosie to collect. She changed her mind about the cami top and skirt and put on some black cotton trousers and a lavender-coloured cashmere sweater over a long-sleeved T-shirt instead. She didn't want it to look obvious that she'd made an effort for Rick.

She pulled out a bag she'd packed the night before when Daniel had fallen asleep watching a James Bond film. It contained her travel hairdryer and a brush, a towel, bathing suit, her make-up bag and various toiletries. If she was going jet-skiing, she couldn't go home with wet hair and no make-up. That would just arouse suspicion.

She left the house and drove her Mercedes to the riverside car park to wait for Rick. She parked behind some bushes, just in case Daniel should drive past for some obscure reason. Ten minutes later, Rick arrived in his Lamborghini Huracan.

She gave him a little wave as he parked next to her. She locked the Mercedes and walked around to the right-hand side, realising the Huracan was a left-hand drive. Rick leaned across and opened the door for her and she slipped into a sumptuous leather seat that seemed to reach around and hug her.

"Hello, Fay. So glad you came." Rick was smiling, his eyes welcoming her into the car.

"Did you think I wouldn't?"

He gave her a little wink. "Not for a minute."

Rick shifted his medical bag out of the way behind her seat. "Sorry," he said, "that's my trauma team kit."

"I didn't realise you were on that."

"Yes, we do quite a few helicopter emergency call-outs too."

Fay was quietly impressed. She placed her bag in the endlessly long passenger well and clipped her seat belt on. The Huracan had a yellow leather interior and was a perfect fusion of bristling technology and unashamed luxury. She breathed in the smell of leather mixed with the woody fragrance of Rick's cologne. She felt the powerfully sensual roar of the V10 engine as Rick flicked the automatic gear shift into "drive" and pulled off.

He kept glancing across at her as he took the ring road, then headed east toward the coast. He drove way too fast for her liking, but the Huracan stuck to the road and cornered as if it was on rails. Her anxiety soon morphed into exhilaration. Led Zeppelin's "Stairway to Heaven" blasted out of the speakers, the acoustic introduction intensifying into a hard rock anthem mixed with the deafening vocals of Robert Plant. It wasn't Fay's favourite music genre – she preferred the gentler tempo of soul or rhythm and blues, but it got her foot tapping and the adrenaline flowing. Led Zeppelin was followed by Thin Lizzy, "The Boys Are Back in Town", then Deep Purple, "Smoke on the Water". By the time they had reached the coast, Fay felt wired.

Rick steered the Huracan off the main road onto a narrow lane that tracked the rocky headland and the cove just past the lighthouse. The tide was midway up a golden sandy beach and a blue sky was adorned with fluffy cumulus clouds drifting north-eastward. He glanced at the sea and turned the music off.

"Sea conditions are perfect," he said, "about a force three to four."

Fay didn't know what that meant but the sea looked calm enough. She hoped it wouldn't be too cold. She hated being cold.

Rick pointed ahead to a white apartment building with contemporary curved walls and vast expanses of glass; each apartment had a balcony and a sea view.

"That's home," he said.

Fay was gobsmacked. "Wow – looks amazing." The only time she'd seen a place like this was in a glossy magazine.

Rick simply smiled and drove through the gates and into the underground garage, the Huracan's throaty engine echoing around the concrete walls. He pointed to the jet ski on its trailer. "That's the beast over there but we'll need to go upstairs and get kitted up."

Fay grabbed her bag and followed Rick into the elevator and up to the second floor. She waited while he unlocked the door and followed him into a huge open-plan apartment with double-height, vaulted ceilings and a vast expanse of windows opening onto a balcony. The sea views were breathtaking.

"Stunning," Fay said, taking in the seascape.

The apartment was white, minimalist, with a whole wall of shelves groaning with books. There were two oversized white leather sofas either side of a long coffee table strewn with medical books and a sheaf of papers, which Rick gathered up and shoved into the bookcase.

"Would you like a drink? Tea, coffee?"

"Black tea would be nice, thanks." Fay wandered into the kitchen area while Rick filled the kettle with water.

"You have a lovely home," she said, her eyes roaming around the bright, airy kitchen.

"Thank you. I've been here about three months, and I love it. It's so peaceful."

She perched on a stool at the large island unit. "And you moved from Barcelona?"

"Yes, to get away from the memories and the family."

Rick handed her a mug of tea and opened a packet of shortbread biscuits.

"It must have been hard for you," she said, declining a biscuit.

"It was but things are better now." He smiled, his warm brown eyes gazing into hers.

Fay felt slightly uncomfortable. Would he kiss her again? Suddenly she realised she shouldn't be there – she'd allowed herself to get carried away. It was wrong of her to come and now she was stuck there with no car, relying on Rick to get her back to Riverbeke. What if Daniel found out?

Rick interrupted her thoughts. "You must have had a hard time too after your daughter."

She sipped her tea, tracing the raised geometric pattern on the mug with her fingers. "Yes, it's been awful but let's not talk about that." The last thing she wanted was to break down in front of Rick. She had to keep her composure and was feeling upbeat and excited after the ride in the Lamborghini and the anticipation of the jet-skiing.

"Whatever you want is fine with me." He dunked a biscuit in his tea.

They chatted about work and the death of Graeme Buckley. Fay wanted to tell Rick how impressed she'd been, watching him tirelessly resuscitate, but decided it would make her sound like she had a schoolgirl crush on him. They finished their tea and Rick put the mugs in the dishwasher.

"OK, I've found a couple of winter-weight wetsuits for you to try. I have others if these are not suitable," Rick said, wandering into the bathroom.

Fay followed him, glimpsing through the open bedroom door.

Rick pointed to the wetsuits. "There you go – shout if you need a hand." He gave her a little wink and she smiled.

The bathroom was huge with a free-standing bath and a glass-walled shower with black slate tiles. Thrown over the back of a white wicker chair in the corner were the wetsuits. She locked the door and stripped, put on her swimsuit and wiggled into a Billabong women's full wetsuit in two-tone blue. She pulled up the back zipper and it fitted perfectly. She scraped her hair up into a messy bun and went out to the living room to show Rick.

"What do you think?" She did a little pirouette.

Rick went over to her and smoothed his hand over her waist. "Yes, looks good. What size shoes do you take? You'll need some booties as well."

"Size five."

He went into the spare bedroom and found a pair of Gul neoprene jet ski boots with a reinforced sole. "These should be alright – they're nice warm ones."

She tried them on. "They're fine," she said, wiggling her toes.

"Right, well, hang on five minutes and I'll get my kit on too." He went into the bedroom.

The door was open a crack and Fay could just about see him undress. His body was firm and muscular. He slipped into a black and grey wetsuit and boots just before Fay dodged over to the picture window in the living room, pretending to study the view.

"Shall we go?" Rick said. He handed her a pair of neoprene gloves and some goggles. "You'll need these too."

She followed him into the lift and down into the underground garage. He took the cover off the Kawasaki jet ski and hooked the trailer to the Kuga.

"Jump in," he said, getting into the driver's seat.

Fay got into the car and Rick drove the short distance to the cove. "Stay here for a minute," he said.

Fay got out of the car and watched as he reversed down the slipway until the jet ski was floating, got out of the Kuga, removed the safety chain, released the winch strap and pushed the craft free of the trailer.

Then he waded into the sea and walked it to the beach, gesturing for Fay to join him.

She walked over to the shore and paddled into the waves up to mid-thigh.

"Here, hold on to this while I go and park."

Fay grabbed the handlebar of the jet ski and held on tightly as it bobbed in the waves. The water felt cold on her legs as it seeped through the wetsuit.

Rick returned, mounted the jet ski and gestured for her to mount behind him. He attached the safety lanyard – the kill cord.

"Ready?"

"I… I think so," she said, suddenly feeling nervous.

"Hold tight onto me." He depressed the green starter button and the engine thundered into life.

Fay put her arms around Rick's waist and held on as tightly as she could, gripping either side of the seat with her knees. She felt the powerful engine revving beneath her and slipped slightly as Rick turned the jet ski and pulled away. She felt cold seawater splash her face as they roared off through the surf, then the kick of acceleration and the wake of water as the jet ski ploughed through the incoming tide. She took a deep breath as the wind rushed past them, tasted the salt and felt the blast of cold water on her legs and feet. She gripped onto Rick, sensing strong muscles beneath his wetsuit.

She couldn't see ahead but, to the side, the waves were getting deeper, with a mass of whitewater heaving beneath them. She felt Rick lean backward into her as he accelerated into an oncoming wave. She felt the jet ski lift out of the water, then land with a thump. She gasped as she was drenched in icy water from the splash but held on tight as Rick accelerated through the surf. Again, he leaned backward, and they jumped an oncoming wave.

He twisted his head and shouted above the roar of wind and water, "OK?"

"Fine, thanks," Fay shouted back – not quite sure if she really meant it but unwilling to spoil Rick's fun.

"Hold tight," he shouted.

Fay gripped onto Rick as if her life depended on it, unsure what was coming next. Then she felt the force of acceleration as he twisted the throttle and sped off across the sea. The jet ski bounced over the waves and Fay gripped the seat harder between her thighs until they ached. She caught a glimpse of the lighthouse and the headland as they sped past. Part of her wanted to shout to him to stop so she could get her breath, but she held on as he zigzagged and made tight turns, carving up the water. Adrenaline flooded her body as they sped across the surface of the sea. A scream of excitement stayed trapped in her throat as the wind took her breath away. Gradually she realised she was beginning to enjoy the speed, the cold wind rushing past, the powerful engine beneath her, Rick's body next to hers. She loosened her grip around Rick's waist slightly. He must have sensed her excitement and accelerated, performing zigzags, then donuts. Fay giggled as they spun around and around, shifting her weight in the seat to match Rick's.

"Hold tight," he shouted.

Fay held on as he twisted the throttle again and they sped over the water, the salt air stinging her face, her hair drenched. She felt exhilarated.

As the jet ski made a sharp turn, she slipped in her seat and lost her grip. She flew through the air and felt a hard bang against her back as she hit the water's surface. Then the cold water enveloped her completely and she was lost in a sea of froth and bubbles. She was disorientated but aware of her flailing limbs and the icy water around her head.

Then, in her mind, she heard Sophie's voice babbling, "ma-ma, ma-ma…"

Fay looked through the veil of water but all she could see was diffuse light through the turbulent surface… frothing water all around her… cold clinging to her body as she sank deeper into the sea.

"Ma-ma, ma-ma…" Sophie's voice seemed to grow louder and more urgent, drowning out everything around her.

"Ma-ma, ma-ma, ma-ma…"

Fay's lungs were crying out for air – she had to reach the surface. She kicked her legs, but the water was rolling her back and forth. She tried to push upward with her arms and felt a stab of fear threatening to swamp her, her lungs now desperate for air.

Then a strange calm immersed her senses. She stopped struggling and let herself float under the water, surrendering to the forces of nature.

Sophie's face was clear in her mind. Her baby was smiling and gurgling, as she finally said her first words, "ma-ma, ma-ma."

She felt strangely tranquil as the countless shattered fragments of her being seemed to coalesce like a hologram playing before her. Splinters of her childhood, her adolescence, her first love, her work, meeting Daniel… unbounded thoughts colliding in her brain.

"Ma-ma…"

Then memories of Sophie saturated her consciousness as if Sophie's soul was entwined with hers as her body began to sink further into the icy water. The wretchedness of a mother's love denied, a thousand dreams unrealised…

Then she felt strong arms around her waist, pulling her upward toward the surface. She felt the wind on her face, spluttered and coughed; she took a big gulp of air, then another. She looked into Rick's eyes. They were brimming with concern… then relief.

She could see the jet ski bobbing in the water close by. Rick swam toward it, dragging her behind him. She spluttered as salt water splashed her face.

"Hold on here," Rick shouted above the roar of wind and water. He placed her hand on the foothold, checked she was gripping tightly, then lifted himself out of the water and mounted the jet ski from the back. Then he grabbed her arm and heaved her up to sit sideways across the seat in front of him.

"Shit – are you OK?" he asked, his arm around her back.

Fay coughed and nodded. "I think so…"

Rick waited while she composed herself. The jet ski was drifting with the current, taking them out to sea. "Do you want to carry on or call it a day?" Rick asked gently.

"Could we get back?" Fay was visibly shivering in the cold.

"Of course, let's get you warmed up." He smiled at her, his warm brown eyes melting into hers.

"Sorry to spoil the fun," Fay said.

"No – it's my fault. I forgot the life jackets." He shook his head reproachfully.

Rick held on to her as she manoeuvred herself toward the back of the jet ski and sat astride the seat behind him.

"Hold tight – I'll take it slowly this time," Rick said.

He reattached the kill cord, started the engine and steered the craft toward the shoreline. Fay began to relax as they made slow but steady progress toward the cove. The sense of Sophie's presence and the images that had been so vivid in her mind were fading to ethereal wisps, like the remnants of a dream. She wrapped her arms around Rick and rested her head on his back, taking comfort from the solid, grounding reality of his body.

By the time they reached the beach, Fay was calm and detached from the experience she'd had in the water. She dismounted from the jet ski and Rick beached it while he fetched the Kuga. Fay stood shivering on the sand, wondering if Sophie really had been there in the water with her. Rick would think she was crazy if she told him.

"Jump in; I'll get this onto the trailer," Rick said.

Fay climbed into the passenger seat, water dripping from her wetsuit. Five minutes later, Rick jumped in, wrapped a large blue towel around her shoulders and started the engine.

He looked across at her. "You alright?"

She smiled. "Sure – I'm fine." His eyes seemed to see right into her soul, and she realised in that fleeting moment that she was bewitched by him. She saw something in his eyes that she recognised in herself. Something she couldn't describe but, whatever it was, he captivated and mesmerised her the way no other man had ever done.

Rick drove the Kuga back to the apartment and parked in the underground garage, not bothering to unhitch the trailer. They peeled off their wetsuits and boots and left them in the back of the car, then, barefooted, Fay followed him up to the apartment.

"Go ahead and take a hot shower. There are plenty of clean towels," Rick said. "I'll fix us a drink."

"Thanks." Fay went into the bathroom, stripped off her swimsuit and stood under the warm water of the shower until she had thawed out. It was still early, their day having been cut short by her fall into the water.

She dried herself and realised she'd left her bag of toiletries in the living room. She wrapped a towel around herself and crept out to retrieve it.

"Feeling better?" Rick asked. He was standing in the living room with a towel around his waist.

"I just need my bag," Fay said, feeling slightly embarrassed.

Rick stepped toward her, trailing his fingers along the soft, damp skin of her naked shoulder. His eyes darkened as he looked into hers. "*Mujer Hermosa*," he said, "you are a beautiful woman."

Fay knew she should go. She should never have come. It was stupid and silly and…

She felt his fingers slowly move up her neck and along her jaw. She shouldn't be here – it wasn't too late to tell him she had to go…

Rick bent his head to kiss her. She felt the warmth of his lips, tasted the saltiness of the sea as his right hand gently guided her face toward his, his left snaking around her waist, pulling her close.

She shouldn't be here… she shouldn't be, yet she was hopelessly captivated by this intriguing man.

He slowly propelled her toward the bedroom, and she didn't resist. Then, she almost tasted the words he whispered as his lips brushed softly against hers.

"You know, Fay, we both have a little secret…"

SIXTY-FOUR

Adrian Clifford lay in his hospital bed recovering from palliative surgery to remove a tumour in his liver. The surgeon had told him when he woke from his anaesthetic that afternoon that the operation had been a success. It wasn't a cure, he was aware of that, but it would give him precious time to say goodbye to his wife and their three-year-old daughter. Adrian's younger brother was flying home from Australia to spend time with them after five years apart and his parents had organised a big family get-together at their home. It would be an emotional time, but he was looking forward to it. He had meticulously planned the last few months of his life – trips with the family to make memories they would treasure after his death. A week in the wilds of Scotland, a beach holiday in West Wales and, if he was well enough, a week in the sun, somewhere exotic with his wife and daughter.

His wife had struggled to believe he was dying, and his surgery would give her time to accept the inevitable. They had so much to say to one another, so much love yet to share – they needed the extra time the surgery would give them. He needed to put his finances in order, to know she would be able to bring up their daughter without money worries. There were so many things he needed to do and say before the end came.

Adrian's wound was sore now the painkillers had worn off, but the effects of the anaesthetic were making him drowsy, and he drifted off to sleep, not knowing it would be for the last time.

The killer was looking for the next victim and had Adrian Clifford in their sights. The killer reasoned in their callous, pitiless mind that Adrian was a man who was about to die before his time anyway. What difference would a few months make to him? They were doing him a favour and saving him from a slow and painful death.

The killer had come prepared with a lethal cocktail of intravenous drugs. The staff on the ward were tied up with an emergency on the main ward and Adrian's side room provided a perfect lair for a murderer. The killer moved in, creeping quietly toward the bed, so as not to wake their quarry. There were no monitors, no alarms to silence – it would be simple and quick.

The killer retrieved a syringe containing the lethal mixture from a pocket and gently plugged it into the canula in the back of Adrian's hand. They pushed the plunger and flushed 20 ml of clear fluid into the man's veins – double the lethal dose of warfarin, the anticoagulant in rat poison, along with three times the lethal dose of sodium thiopental, the rapid-onset barbiturate used in euthanasia.

Within thirty seconds, the sodium thiopental rendered Adrian unconscious while the warfarin did its work. Adrian was struggling to breathe – the sodium thiopental alone would have killed him within minutes. But the killer administered warfarin for good measure and smirked as Adrian's blood thinned dangerously and began seeping through the sutures in his liver. Within minutes, his abdomen was bloated with blood, while his brain suffered a massive subarachnoid haemorrhage. His blood pressure plummeted and, seconds later, his heart quivered and stopped beating.

Adrian Clifford died without ever regaining consciousness. There would be no goodbyes to the family, no more memories –

for them, just the pain and emptiness of their unexpected loss.

The killer, satisfied their work was done, slipped out into the deserted corridor.

SIXTY-FIVE

Daniel arrived home a little late after the strange encounter with Bates at the nursing home. He was expecting to see Fay but there was no sign of her, and Chester and Ella were still in the Dog House with a note from Rosie saying she'd walked and fed them. He guessed Fay must have been tied up with a patient or perhaps she was catching up with Doug and Shelly. He thought about calling her but, when he checked the time, he realised he'd have to go straight back out to Oliver's clinic. He'd almost forgotten about the clients he had booked in.

He left a note for Fay to say he'd grab them both a takeaway on the way home. He left a light on in the hallway, jumped into the Defender and drove to Oliver's, just as his first client was reporting to Nadia in reception.

"Be with you in just a minute," he said.

He found the client's notes, placed a couple of syringes and antiseptic wipes on a metal tray and took the Botox out of the fridge. Then he called the client in: a tall, athletic-looking man with thick dark hair and the shrunken demeanour of someone who struggles with shyness.

"Mr Barclay, nice to meet you. What can I do for you today?" Daniel asked, gesturing for him to lie on the couch.

The man lay back and looked at Daniel's hairline. "I'd like to get rid of my frown lines and this crease here." He pointed a finger between his brows.

Daniel peered at the man's face. There were four shallow frown lines and a small crease running horizontally across the bridge of his nose. "No problem. Have you had Botox before?"

"Yes, once, a few years ago but not since." He stared at the ceiling.

Daniel took a short medical history and checked for allergies. "Alright, just relax there for a minute." Daniel prepared the Botox injections and wiped the man's forehead. "Can you frown for me, please?"

Mr Barclay frowned, and Daniel injected four units of Botox into the procerus muscle between his brows, then he gave a series of injections into the frontalis muscle in the man's forehead. "Alright, you can relax now," Daniel said.

The man sat up and swung his legs over the side of the couch. "Thanks, doctor."

Daniel smiled. "No problem. That should start to take effect in a few days, and we'll see you in three months for a top-up if you need it."

Daniel walked the man out to reception and went back into the clinical room to dispose of the syringes but stopped when he heard banging and crashing upstairs and Oliver's raised voice. He went back into the reception area to see Nadia rolling her eyes and shaking her head.

"What the hell is going on?" Daniel asked her.

"I've no idea but they've been at it hammer and tongs all afternoon since Oliver got back from the hospital."

Daniel listened for a minute, then heard a loud thump against the door of Oliver's office and the piercing sound of Melissa's scream. Daniel couldn't ignore that. He ran up the stairs two at a time and barged into the office without knocking. Oliver was standing over a cowering Melissa, his clenched fist poised to punch her, contempt etched into his face.

"Stop that," Daniel shouted.

Oliver looked at Daniel, pure hatred in his eyes, his fist frozen in place above the side of Melissa's face.

"Don't you dare…" Daniel warned.

Oliver slowly brought his arm down and Melissa scurried away from him. Her eye was badly bruised and there was a cut across her cheek that was dripping blood onto her pink chiffon dress.

"What the hell do you think you're doing, Oliver?" Daniel glanced at Melissa. "Are you alright?"

She nodded and reached for a tissue to dab at the cut.

Oliver was bristling with anger. "What's that got to do with you?"

"It's got everything to do with me – I can't stand by and let you attack a woman like that. Look at her. You did that."

Oliver just glared at Daniel, his eyes dark with anger.

Daniel went to help Melissa, but Oliver lunged at him, pushing him against the door frame. He glared into Daniel's eyes. "Stay out of it…" he growled through gritted teeth.

"Oliver, leave him alone," Melissa shouted.

Oliver marched across to Melissa and roughly grabbed her arm, turning her to face him. "And you, you venomous bitch. Why don't you go to hell?" He spat the words into her face as she squirmed to get away from him. He tightened his grip on her arm and she yelped in pain.

Daniel tried to push Oliver away from her, but he turned on Daniel, his hand still around Melissa's arm. "Mind your fucking business – or do you think you can kill me as well? You're just a bloody lowlife murderer. You belong behind bars like some deranged animal. A rabid dog…" His mouth twisted into an ugly gesture of contempt. "Woof woof."

Melissa tried to pull her arm free, but Oliver slapped her face so hard her head snapped sideways. She shrieked.

Daniel had to intervene. He lurched toward Oliver and pulled him off Melissa. Oliver turned and punched Daniel – an uppercut to his left jaw. Daniel felt the crack of a tooth but managed to retaliate with a hard punch to Oliver's solar plexus. Oliver doubled over, groaning and clutching his belly. Daniel pulled out a splinter from a molar that had broken off.

Daniel went to help Melissa once again, but Oliver came back at him with a karate chop across his upper back. Daniel almost fell but managed to turn and punch Oliver square in the face. He couldn't tell if he'd broken his nose, but it was bleeding profusely. Oliver staggered backwards into a chair and then a desk and Daniel went after him again, grabbing a handful of his shirt with his left hand and pushing him backwards against the desk, his right fist poised to punch him again.

"Are you going to leave her alone now?" Daniel waited for an answer while Oliver cowered against the desk.

Oliver gave an almost imperceptible nod and held one hand up in surrender. His face was etched with the indignation of a lion cornered by a cackle of hyenas.

"If you try anything like that again – I will be calling the police. Got it?"

Oliver nodded again.

Daniel lowered his arm and shoved Oliver onto the desk. Finally beaten, the man lay still, watching Daniel warily as blood poured from his nose.

Daniel straightened and walked over to Melissa. "Come on, let's get you out of here."

Melissa picked up her bag and coat and scowled at Oliver. "I won't be coming back."

Daniel led Melissa out of the office, past Nadia, who had been watching the whole thing from the landing, a look of horror on her face.

"If you're wise, you'll leave too," Daniel said to her. "I'll have to let the rest of my clients down and please don't book any more in – I won't be back either."

He led Melissa down the stairs and out into the car park. They got into Daniel's Defender. In the quiet of the car, he turned to her. "So, what now?"

She looked at him with eyes that held the pain and sorrow of years of abuse. "I don't know…"

Daniel had been reluctant to get involved in their marital problems but, now he'd been dragged into it, he had no choice. "Do you have anyone you could stay with?"

"Not really."

Daniel hesitated but felt compelled to offer. "You can stay with Fay and me for a while until you decide what to do." Daniel rubbed his painful jaw and could feel a sharp edge on his tooth where it had broken.

Melissa shook her head. "That's very kind of you but no – I can't do that."

"I'm sure Fay will be fine with it."

"No, honestly, I need some time alone anyway. I'll stay in a hotel for a few days, then fly out to the beach house."

"Barbados?" Daniel saw another side to Melissa. Gone was the coquettish, flirty posh girl and emerging instead was a mature woman, growing in wisdom and self-confidence.

She looked at him, a spark of hope in her eyes. "Yes, just outside Bridgetown. I have good friends there. I could do with a long holiday and time to think things through. Oliver can't get at me there – he wouldn't dare try." She gave him a thin smile.

"Well, I guess you'll need some stuff from the house. I'll drive you home and then on to wherever you want."

"Thank you, Daniel. Just get me home and I'll drive myself – my car is in the driveway." She seemed to perk up a little. "I think I'll stay at Hallbrook Manor and charge it to Oliver's credit card."

"Yes, and treat yourself to some of those expensive spa treatments and a bottle of their finest champagne while you're at it."

She smiled. "Absolutely I will." She dabbed the cut on her cheek again. It had finally stopped bleeding.

"Things will work out for you," Daniel said softly.

"I know – I should have left years ago."

Daniel started the car and headed for Melissa's house, a large detached Georgian mansion in four acres of immaculately landscaped gardens just north of Riverbeke.

"Want to tell me about it?" Daniel asked.

"He's a bully. One of those patronising types and so damned full of his own self-importance. All he cares about is making money and he doesn't care how low he sinks to get it either."

"What do you mean?"

"He's got no morals, Daniel. I don't know exactly what's going on but there's something very fishy about Isobel and her company – whatever it's called…"

"Regenex Biologics. It's a biotech company."

"Yes, that's it. Her and Oliver are up to no good and someone is going to get hurt, I know it."

"What makes you think that?"

"You saw that woman – Penny Henderson. She had a reaction to the fat treatment Oliver had given her."

"The Flab Buster – yes, I remember."

"Well, that's not licenced to give to patients. They are using people as guinea pigs without their consent. It's why Oliver and I have argued so much lately. It's not right, Daniel, and he's making a fortune out of other people's misery."

"I did wonder about it. I should have done some digging around."

"You weren't to know, and Oliver is so slimy, he's an expert at covering up. Him and that bloody Isobel. There's something going on with her. Something bad but I can't get to the bottom of it."

Daniel turned north toward the village of Catsash and through the country lanes. "I wondered about her too. I saw her coming out of the mortuary the other day. She was obviously paying the technician for something. Maybe there is something dodgy going on – drugs, theft, blackmail – who knows?"

"It will be something illegal, I'm sure of it."

"Maybe we should call the police. I have DS Harper's number."

"I had thought of it but with no evidence or at least something more concrete to go on there's not much they can do. If Isobel and Oliver get even a faint whiff of the police, they'll just cover up whatever it is they're up to. They might be up to no good but they're not stupid either."

"Yes, I see what you mean."

Daniel turned into Melissa's driveway. With gravel crunching under the tyres, he pulled up outside the front porch. "Need a hand with anything? Want me to wait to make sure Oliver isn't lurking about?"

"I'll be fine, thanks, Daniel. Oliver won't be home for hours yet and by then I will be long gone." She leaned across and kissed his cheek. "You're a good friend."

"Take care and let me know how you get on in Barbados."

"I will." She smiled, got out of the car and let herself into the house.

Daniel pulled away and drove home. He was beginning to think that, whether he liked it or not, he would have some investigating to do.

SIXTY-SIX

Daniel arrived home and realised he'd forgotten to call in for a takeaway. His mind had been occupied by Melissa and the shenanigans that had been going on at Oliver's clinic. He thought about going back into town but decided not to bother – it was getting late and, surely, they could find something quick and easy to eat at home. Fay's Mercedes was in the driveway and the lights were on in the house.

"Hi, sweetheart," he called out as he went into the hallway. Ella grabbed her soggy teddy in her mouth and bounded out to greet him, closely followed by Chester. He dumped his jacket on the balustrade and made a fuss of them both.

"In here," she shouted from the living room. She'd obviously had a few glasses of wine, by the glazed look in her eyes. Maisie was curled up on her lap.

"You got my note? Sorry, I forgot to get the takeaway with all the drama at Oliver's this evening." He kissed Fay and could smell the alcohol on her breath.

"Drama? Tell me more." She took a gulp of her wine, pushed Maisie off her lap and followed Daniel out to the kitchen.

Daniel explained what had happened as he rummaged in the freezer. "Pizza?"

"Fine." She poured him a glass of Sauvignon Blanc.

He put two spinach and ricotta pizzas in the oven and perched on a kitchen stool. "So, now I'll have to do some digging around and try to figure out what Oliver and Isobel are up to." He stroked Chester's head and played with his ear.

"So, you're not going back to the clinic?" Fay sipped her wine and sat on the stool opposite Daniel.

"Too right. I'm not getting involved with Oliver again – ever. He's bad news by the sound of things."

"Did he pay you for the work you've already done?" Fay sounded indignant.

"No and I don't want his dirty money." He realised Oliver owed him over £1,650 but there was no way he was going to take it after the way he'd treated Melissa. He'd just have to find another way to make up the shortfall in his salary now he'd been demoted.

Daniel checked the pizzas. "Five more minutes," he said. He got some plates out of the cupboard and put them on the kitchen counter. "So how was your day? You weren't home earlier – I guessed you were tied up with a patient."

Fay looked away, her eyes shifting around the room; her foot started jiggling. "Yes, but it was someone that was having bad dreams. Nothing came of it." She brushed an imaginary bit of fluff from her cardigan. "How was work?"

"Alright. Rick had the day off, so it was a bit less tense than usual. Isobel was there, though, so I guess they weren't planning to spend the day together – I really must try and find out what she's up to at Regenex."

"Isobel? What do you mean?"

Daniel got the pizzas out of the oven, put one on each plate and cut them into slices. "Her and Rick are an item – I told you."

Fay looked bewildered. She twiddled with her ear and squirmed backward in her seat.

"Here, let's eat in front of the TV – I'm shattered." He handed her a plate, grabbed his own along with his wine and went into the living room. He flicked around the channels and settled on a news programme.

Fay followed him and sat in the armchair. She picked at her pizza and left most of it. She seemed to be in another world, but Daniel's mind was on what Melissa had said about Oliver and Isobel.

Fay's phone pinged with a text message in the kitchen, and she went to check it, taking the leftovers of her pizza for the dogs. She seemed to be out there for ages. Daniel took his empty plate and put it in the dishwasher.

"Everything OK?" he asked. "You're not eating much."

"Tastes funny," she said.

"Mine was fine." He remembered she'd said something the other day about the milk being off when there was nothing wrong with it.

She checked her phone again, then gazed at a photo, but he couldn't see what it was. "How are Megan Foley's twins?" she asked.

"I meant to tell you – Megan's parents are going to look after them. They should be going home with them in a few days and, so far, Megan is holding her own. I have every hope she'll be alright."

Fay didn't answer but stared at her phone.

Daniel was feeling uncomfortable. Fay seemed distant and moody lately. One minute she seemed elated – the next she was down in the dumps. Now she seemed morose. He put his hand on her back.

"OK, sweetheart?"

She shrugged him off. "Please – don't."

"What's the matter, Fay? You seem strange lately." He wondered if she'd been like this all the time he'd been in prison. With the few brief visits, they'd been allowed, it would have been impossible for him to tell.

"Nothing's the matter. Just leave me alone." She was staring intently at her phone.

He wondered if she was still upset after they had burned her journal. Perhaps it had been more traumatic for her than he'd realised – it was as if they were dismissing the grief she'd poured into it. Then there were the killings she'd carried out. Maybe she was unbalanced after an experience like that – after all, she wasn't some evil, cold-blooded serial killer – she was a mother in pain after losing her child. All she'd wanted was to rid the world of the monster that had killed Sophie. He remembered the rollercoaster of emotions he'd felt in the weeks after he had killed Wixx. Shocked, confused, guilty, ashamed, angry. God only knew what Fay must be going through after killing four people, who turned out to be innocent of their child's murder. At least he'd gone through the process of seeking justice in the eyes of society. He'd had some sort of closure, but Fay was still carrying all those feelings.

Daniel fleetingly wondered if she was killing again, then dismissed it.

"You hate me," Fay said. She finally looked at him, an unreadable expression shadowing her face.

"Of course, I don't hate you. Why would you say something like that?" Daniel was stunned at such an accusation, which had come out of the blue and was clearly not true.

"Well, you don't love me. I know what you're thinking, and you don't want to be with me anymore. You hate me – hate what I've become."

Daniel went to hug her, to reassure her that he cared, that he still felt the same about her, but she pushed him away. "You despise me – I know you do."

"Fay, I love you. I always have – no matter what. Surely you know that."

"You don't know what I've done..." Fay looked down at the floor.

Daniel felt an icy chill shoot down his spine. That sounded ominous – perhaps his fleeting suspicion had been right – that she *had* killed again. He tried to control the jumble of thoughts that were racing through his brain.

He had no idea what she'd been up to during the ten weeks he'd been in prison and then there was the high death rate in the department, which, when he thought about it, coincided with her starting her research project. The patients that had died – Mrs Wyatt, Don Hackman, Graeme Buckley – she was around them all before and during their deaths. And her research – she is obsessed with death and near-death experiences. Then there was Megan Foley's twins and if what Rick said was true – that she was prepared to steal one of those babies. That wasn't normal behaviour.

He had to know – had to confront her and stop her before she killed any more innocent people, or those deaths would be on his conscience too.

"Fay, what do you mean – what have you done?" He hesitated but knew he had to ask. "Have you killed again?"

She glared at him with a vehemence he'd never seen in her before. She looked as if she was ready to rip his head off.

She slammed her phone down on the kitchen counter just as it pinged another text message. "No, damn you, I haven't killed again. But do you know what? This bloody secret is tearing us apart – just like Sophie's murder tore us apart nearly three years ago."

"Fay, please..." He felt like he'd unleashed some malevolent spirit that had suddenly possessed her. She sounded unhinged.

"You never cared about Sophie... you never wanted her... you never wanted me... you hate me..." Fay was hissing the words through gritted teeth.

"That's not true. I love you both. Please, Fay – calm down, let's talk." He'd never seen such anger in her. It was as if she'd repressed these feelings for years and they had finally found an outlet.

"Calm down? Don't you tell me to calm down. This… this *thing*… is never going to go away, is it? It will always be between us." Fay was visibly shaking, her wild, staring eyes betraying her anger, hurt and resentment.

Daniel tried to reach out to her again, to hold her, comfort her, but she'd already shrunk back into herself – into a private world of torment and paranoia. An isolated, desolate place in her mind that he couldn't reach.

"I'm going to bed," she said bluntly, grabbing her phone and disappearing up the stairs.

Daniel knew he was banished to the spare room.

SIXTY-SEVEN

Daniel had a crick in his neck and there was a weight on his chest. He lifted his head to see Maisie lying across him, scrutinising him with disapproving green eyes. He tried to sit up, but she pressed the tips of her claws into his chest, daring him to disturb her.

He'd slept fitfully on the sofa, Fay's harsh words playing over and over in his mind. What had possessed her to say those things? Was she unbalanced? Did she need professional help? He thought of Shelly. Her experience as a psychiatrist, not to mention her friendship with Fay, would make her the obvious person to talk to. He would get Mani Adebayo or Matt to cover for him and take the morning off. He had to get help for Fay.

He'd let the dogs stay in the house all night and Chester was on his sofa, twitching in his sleep; Ella was curled up in the armchair, her head resting on her teddy. He sat up and Maisie stalked off. The dogs woke and followed him into the kitchen, bounding off into the garden when he unlocked the back door for them. They disturbed two noisy crows that were pecking food from the bird table.

He made himself a mug of strong tea, deciding to leave Fay alone for the time being. He hoped her mood would lift through the day, as it had so many times recently. It was 8.30am. Shelly would be up and about by now and probably on her way to work. He took his iPhone off the charger and tapped her contact number, taking the phone into the garden in case Fay was awake and listening.

She answered after three rings.

"Hello, Daniel, what's up?"

"Shelly, sorry to bother you. Fancy a coffee? I could do with a chat."

"Sure. Want to get together this morning? I'm having a well-earned couple of days off. It'll be nice to see you both – I've been meaning to catch up with Fay."

"Actually, it'll be just me. I need to pick your brains about Fay – I'm concerned about her."

"Oh… OK. That sounds worrying."

"I'll tell you more when we meet. So when and where? Up to you entirely."

There was a short pause and the sound of jazz playing in the background. "We could do breakfast if you haven't already eaten. Tatiana's do a nice full English. Bring the dogs; we could take a walk along the river afterwards."

"Sounds good. I can be there in forty minutes and I'm buying."

They rang off and, rather than disturb Fay, Daniel had a quick wash in the kitchen. He grabbed a clean shirt from the ironing basket and gave it a shake. It would have to do, and Shelly wouldn't care if he looked creased.

He left a note for Fay – "out with the dogs" – grabbed their leads and they followed him to the Defender, leaping excitedly into the back.

Daniel drove through unusually light traffic into Riverbeke town and parked close to Tatiana's. Shelly was already there and gave him a wave from the dog-friendly conservatory. He clipped Chester and Ella's leads on and walked them into the café. Shelly had found them a table in the morning sunshine with a good view of the river. There was a flotilla of ducks on the far bank and a pair of swans glided gracefully downstream. The willow trees were dipping their branches into the water to the rhythm of the breeze and the air carried the sound of cooing wood pigeons.

"Hi, Shelly." Daniel kissed her cheek. "Thanks for meeting me."

She smiled and made a fuss of the dogs. "Hey, you two – haven't seen you in here for ages." She looked bright and fresh in faded jeans and an aquamarine cotton sweater with a colourful chiffon scarf that highlighted the sapphire blue of her eyes.

An Alsatian growled from the far corner, but his owner tapped him firmly on the muzzle with a rolled-up newspaper and he settled down.

"Lie down, Chester," Daniel said. The dog obeyed immediately, and Ella followed suit, keeping her eye on a springer spaniel lying under the adjacent table.

"Shall we order and then you can tell me what this is all about?" Shelly said, passing Daniel a menu.

He glanced at the list, already knowing what he wanted. "I think I'll have a full English breakfast with toast," Daniel said.

"Then I'll have the same and a coffee."

Daniel went up to the counter to order and pay for their breakfasts and came back with two frothy coffees and a number, written on a wooden spoon, for the table. He passed one of the coffees to Shelly, stepped over Chester and sat.

Shelly stirred her coffee and smiled at him. "So, what's up, doc?"

Daniel chuckled but became serious as he tried to explain what was happening with Fay, without mentioning the fact that his beloved wife was a serial killer. He would never betray their secret.

"Well… Fay seems strange lately. She's not herself at all and I don't know what to do about it. I thought, as a psychiatrist, you might be able to fathom out what's going on." Ella laid her head on Daniel's foot and he absently reached down to stroke her back.

"Why don't you list her symptoms and I'll have a go?" Shelly sipped her coffee.

"Her mood seems to be up and down all the time. One minute she's down in the dumps, the next she's excitable and almost manic. Then she gets quite morose and can be argumentative." He remembered her outburst the evening before.

"Would you say she's depressed when she's down?"

"Yes, I guess so."

"Anything else you've noticed?"

Daniel thought for a moment. "Yes, actually, she thought the milk was off the other day but there was nothing wrong with it and last night she said her pizza tasted strange but mine was alright."

"And does she seem to see things that are not there?"

"You mean, is she hallucinating?"

"Yes, or hearing voices."

"I don't know but she seems paranoid. Yesterday, she said she knew what I was thinking, and she believes that I hate her – which is blatantly not true. I try my best to be a good husband and show her how much I care. I don't know where she's getting that idea from."

"And how long has she been like this?"

"I've only noticed it since I got home from prison, but it could have been months. I just didn't see it during our visits when I was staying at Her Majesty's pleasure."

"I haven't noticed either – but then I haven't seen much of Fay recently."

A waitress arrived with their breakfast. A short, slight woman in her early twenties with a wide smile and impossibly white teeth. They thanked her.

Daniel buttered his toast and poured baked beans from a small round dish over sausages and bacon. Chester was sniffing the air and the spaniel sat up and was watching his plate like a hawk while her owner read a book. Shelly dipped toast in her egg yolk and took a bite.

"Any ideas about what could be wrong?" Daniel asked.

"I'm afraid to say it sounds to me like she could be suffering with bipolar psychosis, although I would have to assess her to make a proper diagnosis, of course."

"That sounds serious."

Shelly's fork was poised over a fried egg. "It's a mental disorder characterised by alternating periods of elation and depression. It used to be called manic depression but is now termed bipolar disorder. Around fifty percent of patients with bipolar disorder experience psychosis and it does sound like Fay is one of them, if she is experiencing changes in the way she thinks or is losing touch with reality."

"She certainly seems different to me." He wondered if he should mention that she tried to abduct Megan Foley's baby.

"Sometimes patients believe they can read people's thoughts and feel ill-treated, so that fits in with your experience of her yesterday. It can cause significant problems in work and personal relationships due to confusion and false beliefs. I don't know how she's been at work and Doug hasn't been supervising her research. He's let her get on with things."

Daniel nodded pensively, looking at Shelly.

"People with psychosis hear, see, feel, taste or smell things that don't really exist, so that would explain the milk and the pizza. They can also be pretty paranoid, believing they are being watched or that people are plotting against them. It can start with hearing positive and agreeable voices, but some can be quite negative."

"Yes, that explains a lot." Daniel slipped the dogs a titbit of sausage each. The spaniel was still watching from the next table. "So, what causes it?"

"Research hasn't been able to uncover just one single cause

of bipolar psychosis – it could be multifunctional. Various biological and psychosocial factors could be to blame." Shelly cut the rest of her sausage in half and fed it to the dogs.

"Such as?"

"Well, one good model that explains the development of psychosis is called the 'vulnerability–stress model'. The idea behind it is that some people are genetically predisposed to psychosis and develop it during specific situations such as puberty, falling in love, separation, loss of a loved one, pregnancy and so on. Even environmental factors or traumatic events can trigger bipolar psychosis."

"Fay has had a stressful time of it lately, especially with me being in prison and the trial. Her life could have looked a lot different now if I'd been sentenced. Plus, she's given up her career and the clinic. There have been a lot of changes in her life."

"Yes, but I think losing Sophie would have been the main trigger. It's probably been developing since then."

And, Daniel thought, led to her killing four people. "I think you're right. It was an horrendous time. I'm not surprised she's become unbalanced." He thought for a moment. He recalled all they had experienced after Sophie's murder and the way they had each gone through the grieving process so differently.

"You know, Daniel, psychosis can intensify and become extreme and even life-threatening. If she is suffering from this, and I think she could be, she will need professional help."

Daniel realised it may have already become serious. "Shelly, she tried to abduct a baby from the hospital the other day."

Shelly looked aghast. "Shit, Daniel. What happened?" She put her knife and fork down and dabbed her lips with a napkin.

"One of the other surgeons found her and, to be honest, I don't know if she would actually have done it, but it looks like she tried."

Shelly shook her head in astonishment. "Daniel, we really

must get some treatment for her as soon as possible. It will become harder to treat the longer we leave it."

"What sort of treatment do you suggest?"

"I would recommend antipsychotics, as a first line of treatment. Drugs like chlorpromazine or haloperidol, for instance. They alter brain chemistry by blocking the effect of dopamine and help to reduce symptoms like hallucinations, delusions and disordered thinking. They can also prevent them returning, although, I have to say, they are not a cure. Then, as a longer-term intervention, we could try psychological therapies, including behaviour or family therapy."

"How can I get her to accept treatment, though? The way she was last night, I don't think she'll listen to me."

"The most important factor is for her to be willing to accept her condition and undergo treatment. You can't force her to do anything. You must realise that. She must be a willing participant, or it won't work."

Daniel knew there would be one hell of a challenge ahead.

SIXTY-EIGHT

The killer knew that time was of the essence and was already hunting the wards for another victim. Emboldened by success, the killer was driven to act out a fantasy role of executioner by lethal injection. With an intravenous dose of phenobarbital, the victim would be rendered unconscious in less than thirty seconds. Next, a dose of pancuronium bromide would quickly lead to complete paralysis of the muscles and itself would cause death by asphyxiation. But, to be sure, a final syringe of potassium chloride would cause the victim's heart to flutter and fail. The drugs would cause unconsciousness, cessation of breathing and cardiac arrest due to a lethal arrythmia – in that order. A procedure that has executed thousands of prisoners on death row.

The killer had the next victim in their sights.

Megan Foley.

She was likely to die anyway, the killer reasoned. This would just speed up the process and the medics would suspect nothing. On the one hand, the killer could simply disconnect the ventilator and her locked-in body would expire of its own accord – the way nature had intended before the life-saving intervention. But the killer thought it would be fun to act out the role of executioner and had already prepared the drugs. It would be a shame to waste them.

*

Megan Foley was slipping in and out of consciousness thanks to a bleed on her brain, but she wanted to live; she had dreams and aspirations that were burning inside her. She was grateful to Dr Kendrick for having the courage to have that difficult conversation about whether she wanted to live or let nature take its course. If it hadn't been for him, she knew for sure that her life support would have been switched off. She heard everything that was going on around her when she was conscious and sometimes even when she was unconscious. She would feel her soul slipping from her body and was able to see and hear and move around. She never ventured far from her body, but she knew she could, and it gave her a sense of freedom.

At first, when she had awoken from a coma, being locked in had been terrifying – like being buried alive in her own dead body. Abject panic had seized her mind in the most distressing living nightmare she could have ever imagined. She couldn't move any part of her body – even her face was paralysed – with no means of speaking or making her feelings known. She had no way to let anyone know if she was uncomfortable, in pain, or frightened. No one could have comprehended the petrifying nadir of terror she had found herself in. Only her eyes were able to move and, at first, even small movements were completely exhausting. She tried desperately to communicate with someone – anyone. Even her parents couldn't recognise how consciously aware she was. Death was her only way out of this horrifyingly claustrophobic prison.

One of the nurses, Angela Edwards, would quietly talk to her, as if she realised that she could hear and understand. "Try not to be frightened," she would say. "We're looking after you

– you're safe here." Her soft, gentle kindness soothed Megan's terror. Gradually the panic subsided, and, in its place, a sense of peace and acceptance began to grow.

One day, Megan woke, and Angela had told her that her babies had been born. She softly stroked her hair and described how beautiful they were. She looked into Megan's eyes and smiled.

It was then that Megan decided she wanted to live. A primeval instinct to survive kicked in. She wanted to be part of this world, whatever the future held. She had to live to see her children grow up. But she was well aware that the doctors had been talking about switching off her life support, with the assumption that her quality of life would be so poor that her life was not worth living. It seemed only a matter of time – that was, until Dr Daniel Kendrick had pleaded on her behalf. He understood she wanted to live. He understood that people with locked-in syndrome could have a meaningful and dignified quality of life. Megan wanted to live, to bring up her two children, and with the help of her parents she could fulfil that dream.

Thankfully, she remembered little of the accident that had so cruelly taken the life of her husband. They had been married just over a year and were happily looking forward to the birth of their twins. They knew they were having a boy and a girl and had decided to name them Heather and William. Megan had been training to be a veterinary nurse and was enjoying every minute of her new career. She had planned to go back to work part time when the twins were a few months old. That dream was shattered, but she still had so much to live for.

But the killer was minutes away from callously snatching all that away. The syringes of lethal drugs were poised to wrench the life force from her body. She moved her eyes to see a familiar face looming over her but there was a blackness in their eyes – the cold blackness of evil intent. The killer pulled the first syringe from a pocket, ready to inject the phenobarbital that would render her unconscious. She felt the cold liquid surge into her vein and within seconds she slipped into a black void.

The killer smiled and retrieved the second syringe containing pancuronium bromide that was meant to stop her breathing. Again, the liquid surged into her vein, paralysing her muscles.

Then behind, a voice…

"Ah… there you are. You're needed on the ward urgently." It was the soft Spanish lilt of Rick Estevez.

The killer had no choice but to abandon their task.

The ventilator continued to give Megan life-saving breaths while her body processed and eliminated the drugs. Without the final drug, which caused a lethal cardiac arrythmia, she would live to see her dreams fulfilled, of seeing her children grow up.

From just outside her body, she watched as the killer walked away. One day, she would find a way to tell someone…

SIXTY-NINE

Fay had heard Daniel leave the house with the dogs but lay in bed for hours, churning things over and over in her mind. The day before with Rick, the jet-skiing, her strange experience in the water and then, later at his flat, when they'd made love. She felt a stab of guilt at her betrayal of Daniel, but Rick had changed her world and she needed him in it. They had poured out their secrets to one another and now they were bound together like twin souls amid the chaos of life. It was as if they had found one another across the vast oceans of time and space. She pulled the covers up, closed her eyes and thought of Rick – his soothing voice, the adoration in his eyes, the warm comfort of his body next to hers. She had felt at peace. Nobody understood her like he did. He seemed to know what she was going through after losing his own son – understood the pain and torment and the things that grief could drive a person to do. There was no judgement from Rick about her killings, no accusations that she'd killed again, like Daniel the day before. Daniel told her that he cared and that he understood her pain but all he really cared about was that their secret – her secret – would never be revealed.

But now Rick knew all her secrets and she knew his and she trusted him with her life.

Daniel had lied to her, she knew that. About Rick and Isobel. He must have guessed she had been seeing Rick and had lied in a futile attempt to turn her away from him – but he couldn't stop her wanting to be with Rick. She was falling in love with him and nothing in the whole world could stop that. Daniel hated her – she was sure of it. He'd never stopped loving his first wife, Susan, so how could he love her? And how could he say he loved her after she had killed those people? How could he understand her like Rick did? She pulled the covers up tight around her neck as she saw the faces of her victims appear like a ghostly apparition before her. They were laughing at her, mocking her. She flailed her arms to make them go away but they kept swirling around and around in front of her face.

"Go away," she shouted, "leave me alone... please... please... leave me alone."

She turned on her side, pulled the covers over her head and closed her eyes, trying to fill her thoughts with something else. Anything to block their faces from her mind. She thought of Rick – his strong arms around her, comforting her, soothing her with his soft Spanish words.

"*Esta bien, estas Seguro conmigo* – it's alright, you're safe with me."

She wrapped her arms around herself and imagined she was with Rick. Imagined they were his arms around her, the soft, comforting warmth of his body next to hers, his voice humming a gentle melody. Gradually the faces faded away and she fell into a dreamless sleep.

*

She woke – a shaft on sunlight on her face. She looked at the time. It was midday. She should get up, get something to eat and do something with her day. She should go to work, act as if nothing had happened, but she hesitated. She was convinced that Doug was watching her every move and that he had spies watching her too. He wanted her to fail and so did Shelly. She was supposed to be her friend, but she knew they would both do all they could to destroy her career. She knew it because the voices in her head had told her. Everyone was plotting against her and the only place she felt safe was in Rick's arms.

Fay picked up her phone and looked at the photograph of the baby on her home screen. Was she really Megan Foley's baby? Or was she Sophie? Bright light through a gap in the curtains reflected off the screen into her eyes. She couldn't tell but as she stared at the little girl's face it became Sophie's face. She could hear Sophie's voice all around her babbling, "ma-ma, ma-ma." Then Sophie began to whimper and cry. She needed her mother. All Fay wanted was to reach out to cuddle and comfort her baby. The anguished pain in her heart was unbearable. There was an aching, empty chasm between her and her dead baby and all she wanted was to be with Sophie, with Rick. A tear rolled down her face and she began to sob. Why wouldn't the pain go away?

Why?

There was so much love in her heart and yet she felt so desperately alone. She buried her face in the pillow and howled and sobbed until her throat hurt and her eyes were swollen and sore.

Sophie…

SEVENTY

As he sat in Tatiana's with Shelly, Daniel's phone pinged with a message. It was from Mani Adebayo.

Sorry, I have to get home to the kids. Can you come in and relieve me before the theatre list this afternoon?

Daniel replied that he would. "I need to get to work, I'm afraid, Shelly. I'll be tied up in theatre all afternoon, so I'd better get the dogs to Rosie."

"Don't worry about the dogs. I'll take them for a walk along the river and get them over to the dog creche."

"Are you sure?"

"Yes, I'd love to."

"Alright – that would be great. Thanks. I'll be in touch again about Fay. I'll try and talk to her tonight."

"Yes, we must get some treatment for her as soon as possible." Shelly took Chester and Ella's leads, and they walked out to the car park together.

Daniel made a fuss of the dogs, slipped them each a mini bone-shaped biscuit from his pocket, gave Shelly a peck on the cheek and left Tatiana's, knowing she would keep their conversation confidential, even from Doug. He drove the Defender back through town and into the hospital car park.

He made his way up the stairs and along the corridor, passing Eddie Bates and another cleaner sweeping the floor. They exchanged a stiff smile.

Daniel swiped himself into the ward and dodged a woman in a burgundy uniform slopping out a plateful of cheese and potato pie with tinned tomatoes from a heated trolley – it was almost midday and the patients' lunchtime. The smell of food wafted around the ward.

Daniel found Mani Adebayo sitting at the nurses' station chatting to Jackie Hines. "Mani – everything alright?" Daniel asked.

"Thanks for coming in. The school rang – one of the kids is sick and I have to pick her up. My wife is away this week at her mother's."

"No problem." They exchanged a warm smile and Mani left for the school.

Daniel checked Mani's theatre list for the afternoon. There were several elective procedures – an inguinal hernia repair, a breast abscess excision, a large bowel obstruction for an anastomosis and a laparoscopic cholecystectomy. He would be in theatre for hours. The first patient was booked in for 2pm so he had two hours before he was due in theatre. He sat at the nurses' station and reviewed the patient's notes. It all looked straightforward enough. He glanced across at the small office that Isobel had been using when she was in the hospital. The door was open but there was no sign of Isobel. He knew she must be around because her laptop was open on the desk and there was a heap of papers next to it.

He turned to Jackie. "Where's Isobel?"

"I think she's gone for lunch. The refectory, I think, with Rick." She said as she went past with the medicine trolley.

It was too good a chance to miss if he was going to do some digging around on the Regenex thing. He wandered over to the office, eyes darting around to check the coast was clear. He half-closed the door so he could watch for Isobel, then sifted through the papers on her desk. In the middle of the pile, he found a sheet of handwritten notes. He struggled to read her scribble but saw the names of patients that had been on the clinical trial but had died recently. Jean Wyatt, Don Hackman and Graeme Buckley were listed, along with a few others he didn't recognise. Against each name, Isobel had noted whether they'd had the placebo, Bravafloxacin or a similar drug. Against them all, she had written "Bravafloxacin". He checked a printed report beneath what looked like an official document from the metabolism group at Regenex, led by Isobel herself. It had "placebo" against the same names.

He dug further and found a list of clients from Oliver's clinic, some with Flab Buster, some with C5HL2 and others with Regenebose written in Isobel's handwriting next to them. He had no idea what the last two were.

Then he heard the clatter of heels and quickly replaced the papers. He could see Isobel coming toward him, but it was too late – she'd spotted him.

"Hello, Daniel," Isobel said in a sickly-sweet tone. Her platinum-blonde hair was loose and ironed straight and her face was plastered in make-up. She wore a rose-pink business suit over an ivory silk blouse and four-inch nude heels.

Daniel was flummoxed after being caught out but managed to mumble, "Isobel – I was looking for the autopsy report for Jean Wyatt, since she was my patient."

Isobel smiled, seemingly unperturbed by his nosing around in her office. "I don't have that but, since you're here, I have a little proposition for you." She closed the door.

He was cornered. "Really? What sort of proposition?" It sounded ominous.

"Well… I've been thinking, since you are working with Oliver, if you might be interested in making a nice sum of money on the side? Regenex Biologics could do with a doctor like you."

A doctor like him. He wondered what she meant by that. A doctor who had been in prison? A doctor who had killed someone? A half-decent surgeon? Daniel saw the look on her face and sensed whatever was coming next would be something dodgy. Then again, it might shed some light on what she and Oliver were up to. He didn't tell her they'd fallen out over his treatment of Melissa and that he had no intention of going back to the clinic.

He perched on the desk. "Go on."

Isobel wandered over to her chair and sat, crossed her endless tanned legs and hitched her skirt to reveal toned thighs. "Did you know that by 2050 there will be almost ten billion people on the planet and two billion of them will be over 60 years old?"

"No, I didn't know that." Where the hell was she going with this?

"At Regenex, our aim is to help people stay as healthy as possible into old age. Not only for the benefit of the individual but for the planet and health services as well. We can do a lot of good, Daniel." She tilted her head and smiled at him, her eyes roaming down his body.

"What's all this got to do with me?"

She fixed him with baby-blue eyes. "We're carrying out clinical trials on a couple of anti-ageing drugs we have in development and we're looking to recruit volunteers to test them. You could be part of that at the clinic. Science as it stands today has four anti-ageing candidates – two are drugs already in use for other conditions. Rapamycin is used to block the growth of certain cancer cells but has also been shown to be effective at extending the healthy lifespan of mice by more than twenty percent. Studies are underway in healthy dogs and human volunteers to determine whether rapamycin can stave off diabetes, cancer, cardiovascular disease and extend lifespan."

Daniel listened, trying to hide his scepticism. Just because it works in mice didn't mean it would extend life in humans.

Isobel went on. "Another drug is acarbose, used in some countries to control diabetes but in mice, again, it can extend lifespan by up to twenty-two percent. Metformin, also used to control diabetes, can extend lifespan and is being studied in humans."

Daniel nodded; he was well aware of Metformin.

Isobel flicked her platinum hair behind her shoulder. "The fourth drug is an experimental chemical, 17-a-estradiol, that has also been shown to extend lifespan in mice. Then, of course, there are other ways to extend lifespan such as calorie-restricted diets, genetic mutation and stem cell therapy…"

Daniel knew these approaches were unproven, but he played along for the sake of gleaning information about her biotech company.

"But what we haven't got is a novel drug that will tackle all age-related diseases as well as reduce the visible signs of ageing. At Regenex, we have two life-changing drugs in the pipeline, Regenebose and C5HL2, that promise to be the best anti-ageing drugs on the market. People will look and feel twenty or thirty years younger than their chronological age; they will live to be 150. We'll also be able to regenerate and grow new organs cheaply."

Daniel didn't buy these science-fiction, overinflated claims. She was beginning to sound like a snake oil saleswoman. He nodded for her to continue.

"It will all happen in the next ten years and there's a lot of money to be made. You could have your share of that, Daniel. The anti-ageing industry is literally worth hundreds of billions." She ran a palm along the length of her thigh.

Daniel had no intention of getting involved in what sounded like a very shady enterprise but if he went along with it he could learn more about what she and Oliver were up to. "So, what would my role be in all this?"

"We would want you to recruit volunteers into the research from Oliver's clinic and give them the drug as part of an anti-ageing cocktail. It is given by subcutaneous injection."

"So, what's in this cocktail?"

"Human Growth Hormone – HGH, mainly, along with one of our experimental drugs, Regenebose or C5HL2."

Daniel had read about healthy people taking HGH. It was unproven and can prove lethal.

"As you know, HGH declines as we age and boosting the levels with injections can reduce body fat, build muscle, increase energy and take years off our looks, amongst other benefits."

Daniel nodded in agreement, but he knew full well that there is no scientific proof of that and some studies he'd read showed that increasing HGH levels without clinical need can lead to heart disease, diabetes and cancer.

"The patient pays £12,000 per year for the treatment," then she added quickly, "but we can take that in monthly instalments."

Daniel nearly choked. Not only was she using people for her experiments, but she was charging them for the privilege at an extortionate £1,000 per month. It was an outrageous exploitation of people's insecurities and, normally, it was the volunteer that got paid, not the researcher. Those profit margins far exceeded what the average cocaine dealer could expect per client. Still, he went along with her so-called proposition.

"And what about the pharmaceutical company, Trevelyan, Madigan and Winslow – are they involved in the research?" Daniel knew them to be a well-respected company. Her answer would be very telling.

Isobel shifted back in her chair and crossed her arms. "No, this is strictly a Regenex project. TMW wouldn't touch it because drugs are so costly and time consuming to produce. We'll be doing all the research and development in-house and look at the manufacturing later. If you come on board with this, Daniel, it must be top secret and I'll expect you to sign a non-disclosure agreement."

Interesting indeed. He decided to push it. "Well, perhaps I could come to your site and have a look around. We could discuss things further."

Isobel squirmed. "No, I don't think that would be a good idea at this stage. Let's see how things progress once you're on board. Do we have a deal?"

Now, his suspicions were definitely aroused, not so much by what she said but by her obvious discomfort at having him look around their facility. He'd hit a nerve by the look of it. Still, he played along – it would buy him some time.

"It all sounds very enticing, and I certainly could use some extra cash." He hesitated but decided to go for it. "One more question."

"Certainly."

"Obviously, Oliver's clients will need information before they get involved in the trial, so what do I tell prospective volunteers about the research and the drugs they will be taking?"

Isobel smiled. "Nothing, Daniel. Absolutely nothing. They are enrolled into a course of treatment that will make them look and feel much younger – that's all they need to know."

She was using people as guinea pigs without their consent. Right there was the proof he needed that she was up to no good.

SEVENTY-ONE

Daniel was exhausted after five straight hours in theatre. Mani owed him a big favour. It was time to get home, get some dinner inside his rumbling belly and relax. He changed out of his scrubs, handed over to one of the other SHOs and made his way to the car park. He cursed when he found a parking ticket under the windscreen wiper of the Defender. He'd only bargained for being in work until 5pm but it was gone 7pm and there was no way he could have stopped excising a bowel tumour to feed the damned ticket machine. He stuffed it in the glove compartment indignantly and drove home, his mind replaying the conversation with Isobel that morning. He'd told her he would consider her offer – it would buy him time to investigate further but there was no way he was going to get involved in underhand, illegal activities at the clinic – especially with Oliver. He needed to know more. Why the discrepancies in the placebo verses Bravafloxacin with the clinical trial? What was she doing at the mortuary? Why didn't she want him to see the facilities at Regenex? What the hell was she hiding? There were more questions than answers.

As tired as he was, Daniel decided to do a quick drive-by and set the sat nav for Regenex. It was only a twenty-minute detour, but he would see the place for himself. He followed the directions and turned off the ring road and past the Genesis Fertility Clinic on the science park, along a wide, straight, tree-lined road. There it was on the right – a huge single-story redbrick building in its own grounds with black-tinted windows enclosed by security fencing. A modest sign above the entrance read REGENEX BIOLOGICS. He drove past slowly; the whole building looked impenetrable. The back was just as secure behind high fencing. How could he get in there without Isobel knowing? Bluff his way past reception? Invent an excuse to be there? Break in?

Around the side was another entrance and he slammed on the brakes when he saw Isobel's Bentley. He was just about to do a three-point turn and get out of there when he saw a man in a white boiler suit and white wellington boots. He came out from the side entrance, walked across to her car, took a large cool box from the boot and carried it inside. It was the same box he'd seen outside the mortuary.

Whatever it took, Daniel knew he had to get into the Regenex building.

Daniel retraced his route back to the ring road and drove home. Melissa had been right, something dodgy was going on and, for the sake of the patients, he had to find out. Should he call the police? At the moment he had nothing to tell them. He needed evidence and the only way he was going to get that was to get inside the facility.

Daniel pulled up in the driveway behind Fay's Mercedes. He sighed; now, he had to tackle his wife's mental health and get her to agree to have some treatment with Shelly. It wouldn't be easy. He wondered what sort of mood she was in.

He let himself in and could hear guns shooting and cars tyres squealing on tarmac coming from the TV. There was no sign of the dogs, but Maisie trotted into the hall to greet him, rubbing around his legs and meowing as if she were starving.

He went into the living room. Fay was lying on the sofa texting someone on her iPhone, a large glass of wine on the coffee table. She closed her phone screen abruptly when he came in.

"Daniel – I didn't hear you come in." She sat up and pushed her phone into the back pocket of her jeans.

"Hi, sweetheart – are you alright?"

"Yes, why wouldn't I be?" she snapped.

"Did you go into the hospital today?" He went to give her a kiss, but she turned her head away.

"Had a day off," she said acidly.

He realised this was going to be hard going. "Where are the dogs?"

"In the Dog House."

Chester and Ella must have been in there since Rosie brought them home around 5pm. He wandered through the kitchen – there was no sign of any dinner being prepared and Maisie was still meowing, so he opened a tin of pink salmon for her, and she raced to her dish and tucked in as if she hadn't been fed all day. He went out to the Dog House, made a fuss of the dogs and let them into the garden. Their dishes were clean; they obviously hadn't been fed either and it looked like there'd be no dinner for him tonight unless he did the cooking. He was exhausted – all he wanted was to sit down and relax. He tipped out some dried food into each of the dogs' bowls and mixed in a couple of spoonsful of tinned meat. They came racing back and sat obediently waiting for the command.

Daniel stroked both their heads and whispered, "Thank heavens for you two." They looked back at him with trusting brown eyes. Then he gave the command, and they gulped down their dinner in seconds.

"Well – that didn't touch the sides. You must've been ravenous."

They followed him into the kitchen then went into the living room to settle down for the rest of the evening.

"What do you fancy for dinner?" Daniel called to Fay. "Let's have something easy tonight." He rummaged in the cupboard and found a jar of pasta sauce and a packet of tagliatelle. Then pulled out a frozen garlic baguette from the freezer.

Fay wandered into the kitchen. "I didn't get around to cooking. Wasn't sure what time you'd be home."

He realised he should have called before he went off to Regenex. "That's alright. I'll do us some pasta – is that alright for you?" He tipped the sauce into a pan, measured out some pasta and put some water on to boil.

She nodded. Her eyes looked swollen as if she'd been crying. She turned on the oven for the garlic bread.

"Are you OK?" Daniel asked.

"What do you mean?" She looked at him suspiciously.

He wasn't sure how to tackle it, but something had to be said. He tried to say it as gently as he could. "You… you seem different lately, Fay. Like you have a lot on your mind. Do you want to talk about it?"

"I'm fine."

"If you don't want to talk to me, would you have a chat with Shelly, perhaps?"

"Why? Do you think I'm batshit crazy or something? I don't need a shrink. I'm fine."

Daniel knew he had to try harder – stay with it. She needed treatment. "You just seem to be up and down with your mood. Like you're depressed one minute and excitable the next."

"You mean manic, don't you? You think I have bipolar disorder or something? I'm not stupid, you know."

"Absolutely, you're not stupid." He hesitated but decided to bite the bullet. "But I do think it would be good to talk to a professional and get some help. We all need a helping hand sometimes and you've been through such a lot over the past few years."

"Do you think a '*professional*'" – she hissed – "would be able to undo the murders I committed or bring Sophie back to us?"

"Of course not, but you seem to be having a hard time coming to terms with everything. I just thought it might help."

Suddenly, Fay turned and glared at him. "You want me sectioned, don't you? You want to be rid of me – have me put away where I won't be a bother to you anymore."

"Fay, no – no, that's not what I meant. I just want you to have a talk with Shelly and see if there is some treatment that might help."

"I'm a psychiatrist too, unless you've forgotten. They'll have me on antipsychotics, or I'll end up like a zombie with no feelings – just an empty vessel. I don't want that, thank you."

"I don't want that either, sweetheart."

"And don't '*sweetheart*' me. You don't care about me. You just want an easy life – someone to cook and clean for you – a good wife that will dote on you hand, foot and finger. Well, I'm not doing it. I've had enough."

Daniel didn't know what to say without this escalating into a full-blown row and that's not what Fay needed right now. He took a deep breath and tried again. "Fay, I love you more than life itself. I just want what's best for you. I want you to be happy, for things to be the way they used to be. Remember the fun we used to have? We were so in love, and I want that back. I want my beautiful, intelligent wife to be healthy and happy like you used to be. Please – just talk to Shelly. She can help you to feel better again – like your old self." He gave her a warm smile. "Please… just give it a try."

Fay looked at him with soulful eyes and for a moment, he thought she might relent and agree to see Shelly, but she blew up again.

"I don't want to talk to Shelly, and I don't want to talk to you. There's nothing wrong with me. Now bloody well leave me alone, for pity's sake." The tirade that was building was interrupted by a ping on her phone. She pulled it out from the pocket of her jeans and checked the screen before replacing it. "I'm going to bed." She grabbed her glass of wine along with a fresh bottle of Chardonnay from the fridge and disappeared upstairs.

Daniel switched off the oven and the hob. He'd lost his appetite.

SEVENTY-TWO

Daniel spent a second night on the sofa with the dogs and Maisie. He woke to a text message on his iPhone. It was from Mani Adebayo.

I can cover for your night shift tonight if you like – thanks for yesterday.

Daniel replied. *That would be great. Thanks Mani.* Not too bad a trade, he thought. He knew Mani preferred nights to fit in with the kids.

Daniel was grateful for being let off a night shift and it would give him some time to try to talk to Fay again. He got up, showered and decided to look in on her, plus he needed clean clothes from the wardrobe. He opened the bedroom door, but the bed was empty. She'd obviously slept in it but there was no sign of her. He looked out of the landing window – her car was gone. He dressed in jeans and a checked shirt and went downstairs. There was no note on the kitchen table – nothing to let him know where she was. Perhaps she'd decided to go into the hospital. It seemed too much to hope that she'd gone to talk to Shelly.

He grabbed the dogs' leads and walked them up the street, through the kissing gate, then let them off to run through the woodland. It was a crisp, November day, with a few ragged clouds against a blue sky. The mewing call of a lone buzzard echoed across the landscape as it rode the thermals and sheep dotted the fields like way markers to the horizon. Daniel threw a soggy tennis ball for Chester, but Ella bounded off after it and got there first. They ran off through the trees together.

Daniel's mind was churning with all that had happened. Fay's mental state and how he could get her to accept the help she needed. Then there was Isobel and the dodgy goings on at Regenex. There had to be a way to get inside the building. If he could just get some evidence, he could take it to the police and they would investigate but, as things stood, all he had was a gut feeling. Yet how the hell was he going to get in? He'd never get past reception. There was only one option – he would have to break in somehow.

Then he had an idea…

Eddie Bates. A seasoned burglar like him would know all the tricks of how to get past the security system and into the Regenex building. Maybe he would give him some tips – it was worth a try. Bates, for once, would be helping to stop rather than perpetrate crime.

Daniel's pace quickened as he thought it through. He had no way to contact Bates. He would have to get to the hospital and hope he was around. Now Mani was covering his night shift, tonight, under the cover of darkness would be the perfect opportunity to get into Regenex.

"Come on, you two," he called to the dogs. They turned and headed for home.

Fay was still out, so Daniel shut Chester and Ella into the Dog House and set their ball-thrower into action. He knew Rosie would collect them, as usual. He double-checked that he'd locked the back door and slid into the Defender. He drove through town to the hospital, parked and headed for the cleaners' room on the ground floor. There was nobody around.

He glanced down the corridor to see Oliver Davenport walking toward him in the distance. There was no way he wanted to bump into him after his behaviour toward Melissa, so he dodged down the back stairs to the basement and followed the concrete corridor to the room where Bates had his locker. The door was ajar, and he pushed it open to find Bates reclined in one of the chairs, a sandwich in his hand and the distinct smell of tuna in the air. The window he'd broken in order to escape from the other day had been boarded up.

"What the hell do *you* want?" Bates said around a mouthful of bread. He sat up straight.

Daniel held up a placating hand. "It's alright, Eddie – I just want a chat."

"Chat? About what?"

Daniel indicated the chair opposite Bates. "Do you mind if I sit?" It seemed surreal to be asking for advice from a career criminal.

"Go ahead." He chewed, swallowed and put the rest of his sandwich back in the packet.

Daniel sat. "I need your help."

Bates leaned forward, his forearms resting on his knees. "Help from me? Really?"

"Look, I'll just come out with it. I need your help to break into a building..."

Bates looked startled and spluttered. "Good God."

"I know we're not exactly prison buddies and it's a long story, but I need to break into a laboratory facility on the science park just outside town and I need some advice from someone who knows what they're doing."

Bates seemed to have regained his composure. "And what's the purpose of this break-in?"

"I believe there are some illegal activities taking place that could have serious consequences for people's health and I need evidence to take to the police."

“The police… and you want me to get involved? You know there’s no way I want to end up back behind bars. I have my mother to think of.”

“I know and you don’t have to get involved – it’s not a burglary – more a fact-finding mission. An investigation. All I need from you is some advice on how to get in there.”

He nodded slowly as if he was relieved to hear that. “Right… so tell me, what’s the security like around the building? You’ve already cased the place, I take it?”

Daniel explained that he’d done a quick drive-by and described the security fencing and the placement of various entrances around the building.

“Security dogs?”

“I didn’t see any, nor any warning notices.”

“Sounds like the side entrance would be your best bet for coverage, especially if there are a few trees there. Most burglars don’t force entry, so you might be able to get in through the door or a ground floor window. Any metal grilles?”

Daniel thought for a moment. “I don’t think so.”

“You’ll need to get in within about a minute, so grilles are a problem. What about CCTV?”

“Not sure – I didn’t notice.”

“As long as nobody is monitoring the building with CCTV or security guards, it should be simple to get in.”

“How will I get through the security fence?”

Bates shrugged as if it was a daft question. “Easy – just use a ladder and jump over.”

“And what about getting into the building?”

“Lock snapping – you break the cylinder and manipulate the lock to open the door – an Allen key will usually do it once you’ve snapped the cylinder. It’s dead easy if the lock is a Euro profile cylinder. Most cheap locks are a doddle to snap; all you need is a screwdriver and a pair of mole grips to break in through a PVC door.”

Daniel looked bewildered.

"Most burglaries happen in the daytime, believe it or not, but I think it's better to go in during the night if it's a business premises. The science park should be quiet then."

"What if there's a burglar alarm? Assuming I can get in."

"Simple – just cut the main wires to the power supply to disable it. You'll have to cut the telephone wires as well – most alarm systems send a signal through the phone lines when someone breaks in. Of course, if it's a wireless alarm system, you'd have to do a crash and smash."

"Eh?" Daniel was lost.

"Crash and smash – you crash in through a door or window and smash the security system before it sends a notification. You could also use a wireless alarm jammer if you've got money to burn but wire cutters are still the tool of choice." Bates looked at Daniel as if he was an eight-year-old.

Daniel wasn't sure if he was up to this. Too many things could go wrong and, really, he had no idea what he was doing.

"You say this is not a burglary – you just need information?"

"Yes, that's right. I've no intention of stealing anything. I just need to find out what's going on in there."

Bates thought for a moment. "OK, you've been nice to me, so I'll repay the favour. I'll come with you, get you in there and scarper. I was never there… do we have a deal?"

Daniel was relieved – he needed a professional on this job and Eddie Bates was just the man. "It's a deal."

"I'll need the address."

Daniel wrote it down on a scrap of paper and gave him directions.

Bates pocketed the note. "Wear dark clothing. I'll bring all the kit we'll need, including ladders. Meet me there tonight at 9pm sharp."

"Thanks Eddie – I appreciate this."

"No problem."

Daniel's stomach did a double flip – what the hell was he getting himself into?

SEVENTY-THREE

Daniel drove home, calling into the supermarket on the way for a few bits and pieces they needed as well as a couple of pre-prepared salads for their lunch. He picked out a huge bunch of peach-coloured roses with lilies and gypsophila for Fay. Part of him hoped she was still out – he wasn't sure if he was equipped to deal with her ups and downs. If only she would talk to Shelly…

There was no sign of Fay's Mercedes when he pulled into the driveway around 1pm. He let himself into the house. The dogs had been collected and Maisie was stretched out on the armchair. She opened one eye when he came in, lifted her head briefly, then went back to sleep.

Daniel put the groceries away and texted Fay.

Are you alright?

There was no reply.

He spent the rest of the afternoon and early evening catching up with jobs that needed doing around the house and he put the flowers in a vase on the kitchen table with a note that read *I love you xx*.

Rosie had brought the dogs home around 5pm. He texted Fay twice more but by 7.30pm there was still no sign of her and no reply to his messages. He checked with Shelly, but she hadn't seen her either. What the hell was she up to?

He had to get going if he was to meet Bates on time, so he changed into black chinos and a black sweater over his favourite grey T-shirt with a line of black pawprints across the front. He put on dark trainers and grabbed a torch from the kitchen drawer. He was beginning to feel like a burglar – all that was missing was a balaclava and a swag bag. The dogs were sleeping flat out in the living room, and he let them stay in the house, hoping he wouldn't be out too long.

Daniel locked up and drove the Defender back to the science park. He did a quick drive past the Regenex building and it seemed deserted. No cars in the car park and the lights were off inside. It was 8.45pm and completely dark but he parked up around the corner away from the street lighting and waited for Bates. He checked his phone – still nothing from Fay.

Eddie Bates turned up on the dot of 9pm and pulled up behind the Defender in a dark blue, unmarked Ford transit van. Daniel got out and spoke to Bates through the driver's window.

"The place looks deserted. No light on and I can't see any CCTV cameras."

"Good. Get in and we'll park around the side. No point in having two vehicles at the scene." Bates said. He was wearing black jeans, a black donkey jacket over a navy sweatshirt and a black knitted beanie hat.

Daniel grabbed his torch, locked the Defender and got into the passenger seat of the van. It smelled of cigarette smoke and sweaty feet. He glanced over his shoulder to see a set of ladders and a canvas tool bag. Like a night-time predator, stalking its prey, Bates drove slowly around the building, eyeing up the security fence and peering at the doors and windows. He stopped close to the side entrance.

"This is good, right here. See – there are some trees and shrubs for cover and no street lighting. We'll be in there in a jiffy." Bates surveyed the area for a few moments. "Coast is clear – let's do this." He put on thick black gloves.

They got out of the van and Bates opened the back doors and pulled out the ladders. He placed one ladder up against the metal security fence, grabbed another, climbed halfway up the first and eased it over to lean on the inner side of the fence. "We'll need to get out as well," he said.

Bates grabbed the tool bag from the back of the van, slung it over his shoulder, climbed the ladder, stepped over the top of the fence and jumped eight feet down onto the grass. He was inside the grounds. Daniel followed but climbed down the second ladder. There were no alarms, no baying dogs. It looked like they had a clear run.

Daniel followed closely behind Bates as he walked, bold as brass, up to the side door. Daniel kept a lookout as Bates unscrewed the plate and snapped the lock with a mole wrench. He fiddled in the lock for a moment with an Allen key and, as nifty as a Labrador pinching a sausage from a barbecue, they were in. Bates cut the wire to the alarm system, then the phone lines and that was it. No fuss – it was a textbook break-in.

"That was fast," Daniel said, surprisingly impressed. He flicked on the torch and shone it around the room.

"Piece of cake," Bates said, grinning. He propped the door closed behind them.

They found themselves in a large laboratory lined with dark wooden benches, on which stood various pieces of biochemistry equipment: microscope, centrifuge, Bunsen burner, spectrometer. Above, the walls were lined with shelves holding racks of test tubes and a selection of glass flasks and beakers. Below were cupboards crammed with bottles and jars of chemicals. There was a fume cupboard along one side, housing what looked like an experiment in progress.

Bates was picking things up with gloved hands, checking for valuables.

"We're not here to steal, don't forget." Daniel pointedly reminded him.

"Sorry, force of habit," Bates said.

"Weren't you going to scarper?" Daniel asked.

"Just being nosey."

Daniel walked through the laboratory and into a wide, white-painted corridor, with offices off to the right and smaller labs to the left. Bates followed. Then the corridor took a ninety-degree turn, and they walked through double fire doors into a huge, windowless room. The bare concrete walls were lined with around twenty large chest freezers and there was a refrigerator with a biohazard notice stuck to the door that read *No food or drink to be stored in this fridge*. In the centre of the room was a ten-foot-long, four-foot-wide, stainless-steel table. Daniel pointed the torch onto a line of glass jars that stood on one side of the table. They contained what looked like human tissue samples preserved in formalin, one Daniel recognised as a heart valve, another as the right hemisphere of a brain. The labels had serial numbers written on them and the handwriting looked remarkably like Isobel's scrawl.

"Hey, look at this," Bates said. He'd lifted the lid of one of the freezers and was gazing in, his torch illuminating binbags and clear plastic boxes. There were also clear plastic food bags containing slices of human brain and kidney tissue.

Daniel went over to Bates and opened one of the bin bags. It contained several clear plastic bags, the contents frozen solid. Daniel opened one of them. Inside was a frozen human heart and two kidneys. In another, two lobes of a liver and a chunk of lung tissue. Yet another contained a whole large intestine and deeper in the freezer was a man's lower leg. All had labels with serial numbers. He shone the torch around the room and on one wall was a whiteboard covered in Isobel's handwriting. The header read *Harvest* and beneath it was a list of organs with their serial numbers: *heart – 00242, liver – 00243, lungs – 00244, kidney – 00245…*

On a wall hung a headless spine and pelvis – like some macabre work of art. Daniel shone the torch around again. He saw the cool box that had been in Isobel's Bentley and made the sickening connection. She had paid the mortuary technician for human organs. Could they belong to some of the patients who had died in the department? He knew for sure that they hadn't donated their organs and, even if they had, what the hell were they doing here at Isobel's private firm?

"We need to find records – see if we can link the serial numbers to names of people," Daniel said.

"Over there." Bates pointed his torch at a desktop computer on a small table next to a grey metal filing cabinet.

Daniel fired up the PC, but the screen was demanding a password. "Shit, what do I do now?"

"Here, I've got that," Bates said.

Daniel moved aside and Bates typed in a sequence of keys, hit return and the screen cleared. "OK, you're in," he said.

"How the hell did you do that?" Daniel asked, astonished.

Bates grinned. "Easy: there's a sticky note on the side of the computer with the password written on it."

Daniel rolled his eyes and searched through the computer's files, while Bates rummaged through the filing cabinet. There was a list of surgical training institutions, educational establishments and researchers, along with an email to a training provider giving a price quote of £10,500 for six human hearts. Isobel was profiting from the sale of human organs and body parts like a modern-day grave robber.

"This is interesting," Bates said, pulling a record book out of the filing cabinet.

Daniel glanced at it. It was exactly what he was looking for – a record of the serial numbers on the organs that matched with the names of the people they had come from. Near the top were three names he recognised: Jean Wyatt, Don Hackman and Graeme Buckley. It must have been their organs that Isobel had taken from the mortuary. He felt sick with disgust at what she had done. To the right was a column headed *Institution* and, sure enough, next to his patients was written *Riverbeke General.* The names of other hospitals along with a couple of local funeral homes were also listed. Isobel was running a gruesome and illegal business; that much was certain.

"This is my evidence – along with that lot over there." Daniel twisted his head toward the chest freezers. "Regenex has been stealing and selling human organs and other body parts. She's a body broker."

Bates looked stunned. "And I thought I was a bad boy."

"Look, I'm calling in the police. I have enough evidence here for them to carry out an investigation. You'd better scarper if you don't want to be involved."

"Yes, time to go," Bates said. "I'll take my ladders, if that's alright – the police can easily break in through the security gate with bolt cutters."

"Thanks for your help, Eddie."

"Anytime." With that, he left.

Daniel flicked on the lights in the freezer room and pocketed the torch. There was no point in skulking around now. He pulled out his iPhone from his back pocket and found DS Harper's number, dialled and heard his familiar voice.

"Well, well, Doctor Kendrick. Now, what can I do for you?" It sounded as if he was being sarcastic, but Daniel ignored it.

"Detective, would you join me at Regenex Biologics? It's on the science park."

"I know it. Why?"

"I've uncovered some major criminal activity here – stolen human body parts that are being sold and I suspect people are being used as guinea pigs for drug trials without their consent. Isn't that actual bodily harm?"

There was a short delay before Harper spoke. "Doctor Kendrick, we need a search warrant and that could take some hours. I'll have to disturb the judge to sign it off and it's getting late. In fact, we can only search a premises before 10pm and it's getting on for that now."

"Please, detective, this can't wait." He knew Isobel could have the evidence cleared out before the police could get there.

"Alright, I'll do my best." There was another short silence. "Do I take it you broke in to get this information?"

"Yes, actually I did… and I almost forgot; could you bring some bolt cutters?"

SEVENTY-FOUR

Daniel decided to have a poke around while he waited for DS Harper. He wasn't going to let this drop now. Maybe there was more to Isobel's gruesome money-making schemes. He walked back along the wide corridor and opened a door marked *Anti-ageing Lab – no admittance for unauthorised personnel.* It was one of the smaller labs. He flicked the lights on to find a room lined with lab benches and, beneath them, boxes upon boxes of Flab Buster injections – there must have been hundreds of thousands of pounds' worth. There were also several boxes of injections marked either Regenebose or C5HL2, the anti-ageing cocktail Isobel had tried to get him involved with.

As he wandered around, he noticed a dank smell that seemed to be stronger near another doorway leading out from the lab. The door was ajar. He pushed it open, and it led into a larger laboratory – the walls lined with racks of shelving, five shelves high, crammed with plastic tanks containing lab rats, mice and guinea pigs, some with litters of young, their hairless pink bodies and tiny size suggesting they had been born just days before. Daniel peered into the tanks – there must have been more than a hundred white rats with red eyes, many of them with shaved patches of skin on their backs, covered in nasty red sores; some had turned black and necrotic. None of the animals seemed to have food or water, just a thin covering of sawdust that served as bedding. Several tanks had dead or dying rats in them and a putrid smell hung in the air. This was obviously where Isobel was testing her experimental anti-ageing drugs.

He wandered through another doorway into a huge room. He flicked on the light switch and two long fluorescent strip lights flickered into life. He felt the heat of raw anger at what he saw. The room was lined on one wall with shelving and rows of bare metal cages containing rabbits, some with shaved patches of sore, red skin, and eyes that were ulcerated and weeping thick pus. There were others with tumours growing on their backs that were almost as large as their bodies. The eye-watering stench of ammonia from urine-soaked bedding hung in the air and none of the cages had food or water. Daniel peered through the bars and the animals shrank away from him. They were so tortured and cruelly treated, they were obviously terrified of humans. Daniel's heart went out to the animals, forced to live in crowded, filthy cages with no protection from the abuse and torture they'd been put through beyond any ethical limit. They lived wretched, miserable lives, all due to vanity and the greed of people like Isobel and Oliver. The labels on the cages showed these animals were clearly being used for the illegal testing of cosmetics.

On the opposite wall of the room, at floor level, was a row of larger metal cages. Imprisoned in them were several dogs, mostly beagles and all watching him with pleading, soulful eyes. Some were drooling uncontrollably, others had weeping, ulcerated eyes and one looked almost blind – no doubt from the Draize test to assess eye irritation after having chemicals dripped into their eyes. There was not even a bowl of water in those hellish, barren cages. One beagle looked dreadfully unwell – weak and staggering, his head lowered in fear and despair. Daniel wanted to free them all and take the dogs home with him but, through his mounting anger and abhorrence, he knew he must wait for the police to investigate and go through the proper channels to put a stop to Isobel's barbaric and immoral actions.

Daniel walked along the cages. Two of them contained macaques. Miserable-looking and appallingly thin, with matted, threadbare fur, the monkeys were gripping one another's hands through the bars of adjoining cages, clinging desperately for any tiny shred of comfort they could get. They looked at Daniel with stark terror in their eyes. He couldn't begin to imagine the vicious abuse they had been put through.

Then he heard shouting and went out into the corridor to see Detective Sergeant Harper with a team of police officers.

"Thank God – you managed to get a warrant."

"Yes, but only just. Now, what is this all about?" DS Harper asked.

Daniel hardly knew where to begin but he led them into the labs first, showed them the plight of the animals and reminded them that animal testing for cosmetics had been banned in the UK in 1997. What Isobel was doing was illegal.

DS Harper looked appalled, gagging on the stench. One of the female officers tried to comfort the macaques through the bars of the cage; another shook his head in despair.

Daniel showed them the stocks of injections of Flab Buster and the two anti-ageing cocktails and told him about Isobel's proposition to him along with details of Oliver's clinic and the business arrangement they had. Then he walked them down the corridor to show them the freezers full of human body parts and the damning documents that he'd found.

"She's operating as a body broker," Daniel said. "There has to be a law against that."

"Alright, Doctor Kendrick. Leave this with us. We'll be in touch." He looked Daniel in the eye. "You know, I should arrest you for breaking and entering but since you seemed to have unearthed some important criminal activity, I'll let you go with a caution."

Being arrested for this would have been tame compared to what he'd gone through in prison, but he was grateful for the caution and relieved to have exposed Isobel and Oliver's despicable undercover operation.

Daniel was about to leave when he heard Isobel's shrill voice. She appeared in the doorway dressed in faded jeans and a fox fur gilet over an ivory sweater. Her hair was swept up into a pony tail.

"What the hell is going on?" Her eyes darted between the police, Daniel and the bags and boxes of body parts the police officers were pulling out of the freezers.

"Isobel Duncan?" Harper asked.

"Yes… what's going on here? I was tipped off that someone had broken in." Her eyes were wild and staring.

Harper casually walked up to her, a pair of handcuffs hanging from his belt. "Isobel Duncan, I'm arresting you for illegal activities at your business premises." He recited the police caution. "You do not have to say anything. But it may harm your defence if you do not mention when questioned something which you later rely on in court. Anything you do say may be given in evidence."

Isobel was visibly shocked and staggered backwards toward the door. Harper grabbed her arm.

"No… no, get your filthy hands off me." She tried to turn and run but Harper snapped the handcuffs on her wrists. "I haven't done anything wrong." She was squirming, desperately trying to get free. "It wasn't me that killed those people…"

"What do you mean – who has been killed?" DS Harper asked.

Isobel was pulling against the handcuffs, panic in her eyes. "I didn't kill them – it was Oliver…"

Daniel's mind was racing – so the deaths in the department – they were no accident. "Are you saying that Oliver murdered those patients on the ward?"

Isobel turned to Daniel; contempt etched into her face. "Yes, I am. Oliver killed them for the money. I had nothing to do with that."

Stunned by the revelation, Daniel walked over to the metal table in the middle of the room and picked up the record book that Bates had found earlier. He opened it and flicked through the pages. Four names were listed: Ava Hildegard, Louise Barlow, Sandy Lewis and Adrian Clifford. He ran a finger across the columns and Riverbeke General was listed as the source of their organs. An annotated note had been handwritten in the margin next to all four names – it was Isobel's scrawl but clearly read "Oliver Davenport".

Daniel looked at Isobel. "Wait a minute. You mean Oliver killed those people in order to profit from their organs?"

Isobel was desperate to exonerate herself of the murders. "Yes, it was Oliver. I didn't have anything to do with those killings." Her eyes were darting between Daniel and DS Harper.

"And yet you were business partners, and you were harvesting organs and body parts from the mortuary…" Daniel reminded her.

Isobel looked away, unable to answer.

DS Harper turned to two of the police officers. "Take her to the station."

Isobel glared at Daniel; any scrap of shame was overshadowed by self-righteous indignation. "You bastard," she hissed through gritted teeth before two WPCs marched her out to an unmarked police car.

SEVENTY-FIVE

Daniel looked around the room. The police team were searching through the freezers and two officers were going through the record book and other documents that Daniel had found along with Isobel's PC. "Is there anything I can do to help?"

Harper shook his head. "No – best you get off home and leave the investigation to us." He gave him a pointed look that said *please don't interfere in police business.* "Before you go, though, I'll want the details of her partner in crime – Oliver Davenport, wasn't it?"

Daniel told Harper all he knew about Oliver's clinic and wrote down the address in Park Road along with his home address. He was glad Melissa was away from there.

Harper made a call to Detective Inspector Emma Oaks, asking for her to arrange a team to raid Oliver's home and arrest him on suspicion of murder, asap.

Finally, Oliver would get the punishment he deserved.

"What will happen to the animals?" Daniel asked, his heart aching with pity for the poor creatures.

"We'll get the RSPCA in here first thing in the morning. They'll take care of them, and I expect they will carry out their own investigation into the abuse. Regenex won't get away with it."

"They'll need veterinary treatment," Daniel said.

"Yes, they will. But at least their ordeal in here is over."

"I'd be interested to know how the investigation goes," Daniel said before he turned and made for the side entrance where he and Bates had broken in.

As he walked toward the main security gate, which the police had opened, he checked his phone. Still nothing from Fay. Then he called Melissa to tell her what had happened and to warn her the police would be investigating Oliver. She seemed relieved that they would both be brought to justice and said she would postpone her trip to Barbados to help with the enquiry.

Once outside, Daniel looked back at the scene. Two Vauxhall Insignia incident response cars and a BMW X5, with strobing blue lights, were parked outside the premises. A police van, a white Mercedes Sprinter, was pulling up outside the gate. Daniel was still reeling from the revelation that Oliver had killed those patients on the ward. He was shocked and utterly disgusted at the cold callousness of the man. To think he'd worked with him, known him all those years and not seen the vile malevolence that seeped through his soul. Oliver would stop at nothing – even murder – to make money.

Daniel wondered how long Regenex had been operating as a body broker – or non-transplant tissue bank, as Isobel called it, according to the documents he'd seen. How long had she been getting away with this? She and Oliver must have made a small fortune and the thought of them profiting from the misery they'd caused was truly abhorrent.

The clinical trial at the hospital would have to stop – he was sure Colin Mathias would do that with immediate effect once he realised what was going on. He would speak to him in the morning. Now he had to get home and hope that Fay would listen to him. She needed professional treatment and soon.

Daniel walked around the corner to the Defender. He drove away from Regenex, trying to block the image of those tortured animals from his mind and the grisly freezers full of the stolen organs and body parts of people's loved ones. It was the stuff of nightmares. He sensed Harper would treat the investigation as an urgent matter and hoped a jury would throw the proverbial book at them.

SEVENTY-SIX

Detective Inspector Emma Oakes took the call from DS Harper and immediately began to scramble a team to raid the home of Oliver Davenport. They assembled in one of the meeting rooms of the Major Incident Team at Riverbeke Police Headquarters. Present were ten officers from the Armed Response Unit, including Detective Sergeant Laura Miller, Detective Sergeant Bill McKay, Detective Constable Jeff Blackburn and Detective Constable Alan Wright. The meeting was led by DI Oakes.

"OK, settle down." Emma Oakes waited for the police officers to stop chatting and pay attention. She sipped a coffee she'd just bought from the vending machine in the corridor.

Slowly the din abated and the officers took their seats.

"Now – DS Ian Harper has informed me that multiple murders have been committed by a doctor at Riverbeke General. A surgeon named Oliver Davenport. He also has a clinic in Park Road, Riverbeke, but we believe he is currently at his home address, and we are tasked with arresting him. I'm calling this Operation Anaconda." DI Oakes scanned the room.

DC Jeff Blackburn piped up. "Will we need a warrant? The magistrate won't be happy to be woken again tonight."

"No, Jeff, we won't need one. Serious offences have taken

place and we need to get him into custody before he murders someone else."

"Are we going in armed?" asked DC Alan Wright.

"Yes, we are. He could be a dangerous individual."

Emma Oakes gave the officers their final instructions for the raid on Oliver Davenport's home. "Alright – let's be careful out there," she said, as she closed the meeting.

The officers headed out to the car park after getting themselves kitted up with protective vests, helmets and shields. Authorised Firearms Officers DS Laura Miller and DC Alan Wright were armed with Glock 17 pistols and DS Bill McKay carried a Heckler & Koch G36C carbine assault rifle. DI Oakes drove the armed officers in a BMW X5, and the other seven officers travelled in two Volvo V90s.

The convoy followed the sat nav and drove through the town of Riverbeke before turning north toward the village of Catsash and on through the country lanes. They pulled into Oliver Davenport's driveway, gravel crunching beneath the tyres of the three vehicles, headlights illuminating a Georgian-style mansion complete with a fountain in the centre of a turning circle at the front of the house. They parked to the side of the front door. The house was in darkness, but a gleaming black Range Rover was parked in the driveway, indicating someone was home. DC Alan Wright quickly checked the police database and confirmed it was registered to Oliver Davenport.

DI Oakes gestured for three officers, including an armed DS Laura Miller, to cover the back door, while the others gathered around the front porch.

Emma Oakes went up to the door and knocked hard. "Police, open the door," she shouted and stepped aside. Without waiting for an answer, she shouted again, "Move away from the door."

A police officer with an enforcer – a 16 kg hardened-steel battering ram – stepped forward and bashed the door at the lock and it burst open. He stood aside and two armed police officers went into the house first, followed by two more officers and Emma Oakes. They were joined by the three officers that had broken in through the back door.

"No sign of him downstairs," DS Miller said.

They filed up the stairs and, once on the landing, checked bedrooms and bathrooms for signs of life; someone flicked on some lights.

"In here," shouted DS Bill McKay.

The officers, swathed in Kevlar, crowded into the main bedroom to see Oliver Davenport cowering in a supersized bed in his underpants. Someone flicked on the light switch and Oliver screwed his eyes against the bright light. DS McKay stood over Oliver; a red dot from the sights of a Heckler & Koch rifle played over his naked chest. DS Miller and DC Wright stood the other side of the bed, self-loading Glock pistols trained on their suspect.

"What the fuck..." Oliver said, a hand up, squinting against the light.

Emma Oakes stepped forward. "Oliver Davenport, I am arresting you for the murder of several patients at Riverbeke General Hospital." She repeated the police caution.

Oliver slowly lowered his arm and looked at the inspector for some seconds, shock etched into his face. "That fucking bitch, Isobel..." he muttered under his breath.

"Alright, cuff him and let's get him down to the station for questioning," DI Oakes said.

"Wait, I'll come quietly," Oliver said, "just let me put some clothes on." He grabbed a sweater and pulled on a pair of trousers and shoes.

Two officers stood over him while he dressed, then slapped handcuffs on him. They led him out to one of the Volvos and pushed him into the back seat.

He looked through the window of the police car at his £3.2 million house. His growing fortune would be totally useless behind bars.

SEVENTY-SEVEN

It was almost midnight as Daniel arrived home and pulled into the driveway next to Fay's car. Lights were blazing from inside the house. He let himself in and the dogs bounded into the hallway to greet him.

"Fay?" he called but there was no answer. "Fay?" he called again.

"In here." Her voice was coming from the living room.

He went in, the dogs following, to see her sitting on the edge of the sofa, stroking Maisie, an empty coffee mug on the table.

"Thank goodness you're alright. I was getting worried when you didn't answer my texts." Daniel was surprised she was drinking coffee and not her usual wine.

Fay just sat looking at him, an unreadable expression shadowing her face.

"You'll never guess what happened this evening..." He started to tell her what he'd found out about the body parts at Regenex and the animals in the lab. "These poor dogs in the cages – beagles – I just wanted to bring them home. They looked so miserable and dejected..."

Then he saw something in the corner of his eye and turned to see two holdalls packed and placed near the doorway. Sophie's big brown teddy bear from her cot had been placed on top of them.

"What's going on?"

"Daniel, I need to get away." Her expression had become sombre.

"What do you mean?"

"I'm leaving."

"Are you saying you're leaving me? Leaving our marriage?" He went into the room and sat on the edge of the adjacent armchair.

"Yes… I'm sorry."

He looked into her eyes and knew she meant it. "But why, Fay? I love you, sweetheart, and I thought you loved me." His hand reached out for hers, but she pulled away. He could feel himself trembling.

"I just don't think things are working out." She gazed absently at Maisie, running a hand along her back.

"But why? We have so much together – all those years of marriage, the memory of Sophie… you can't leave me now." He looked at her, waiting for a response. "Please, Fay…"

Fay's eyes snapped back at him. "The memory of her murder, you mean. It's been tearing us apart and we can never be the same again – never."

His voice was gentle, trying not to rouse her anger again. "But we have so many memories of her life too. Can't we focus on that? We must move past the bad things."

"How are we supposed to do that? Go on, you tell me: what are we supposed to do?"

"We have each other. We can talk, support one another. Get some professional help. It's worth a try, isn't it?"

Fay looked away again. "I need some space – to think. My head is all over the place. I just need to get away."

"Maybe if you had some professional help – some treatment – you'd be able to think straight."

She glared at him. "You just think I'm crazy, don't you? Mad as a box of frogs. Well, even if you're right, I'm still leaving, and you can't stop me." Her face was a picture of indignation.

"Fay… sweetheart, I don't think you're crazy, I just want what's best for you. To get you the help you need. We could all do with someone to lean on sometimes."

"I already have that…" Her eyes turned and she stared at Maisie again, her hand mechanically stroking her fur.

"You mean you've sought professional treatment?" He felt a small twinge of hope.

"No but I have someone…" her voice trailed off.

"What do you mean?" He looked baffled.

"Someone I trust. Someone that understands what I've been going through." She continued to stroke Maisie's fur.

"That's good, isn't it? Is it a self-help group? A counsellor?"

"No…" She seemed unwilling to say any more.

"But why do you need to leave? Can't we face this together?"

"I've told you I need to get away. You can't stop me, Daniel."

"So, where are you going to go? Are you staying with your mother? With Shelly?"

There was a long pause before she dropped the bombshell. "With Rick."

"Rick? What do you mean? Rick Estevez? Why would you want to stay with him?" He could barely believe what he was hearing.

She finally looked him in the eye. A sickening wave of recognition washed through him, and he knew. He knew that Fay had been seeing Rick. The bastard had taken his job from him – now he was taking his wife. It was too much.

"Oh God, Fay… how long has this been going on?"

"Not long."

He was stumped for words as a decidedly awkward tone hung in the air. He looked at her for several moments, hesitant to ask the question, not wanting to hear the inevitable answer. "Do you love him?"

She gave a slight nod that said all he needed to know. He wasn't sure if he should throw her out there and then or plead with her to stay. He put his head in his hands as if to block it all out – as if when he opened his eyes it would have been a mirage.

"I should go," she said, softly.

He sat up and rubbed his palms over his face. It *was* real; his wife was about to leave him for someone else and he'd had no idea. "Wait… please stay. After all we've been through, you can't leave me now."

She stood, giving Maisie one last stroke along her back.

Daniel's mind was racing. If they were so cosy together, what had she told him? He looked up at her. "Have you said anything about… you know, the past?"

"You mean about the four people I killed?"

Daniel nodded.

"Yes, Rick knows…"

Shit.

Daniel couldn't believe she'd spilled her deadly secret to someone she barely knew. What was it about Rick? Whatever had possessed her to tell *him* of all people? Bloody Rick Estevez – yet another sodding kick in the teeth.

"Why?" was all he could say.

"He knows what I went through, and he understands."

Daniel looked at her, incredulity etched into his face. He was completely lost for words.

She turned to leave, put Sophie's teddy bear under her arm and picked up a holdall in each hand. She twisted around and stood in the doorway. She looked at him with a sadness that was overshadowed by determination.

Then she left without even saying goodbye.

SEVENTY-EIGHT

Daniel heard the boot of Fay's car slam, then the revving of the engine as she pulled off the driveway. It felt as if the world had just flipped on its axis.

Would he ever see her again? Would he want to after what she had done? It was gone 1am but sleep was far, far away. He went into the kitchen and poured himself a stiff single malt whisky, downing it in one go, the alcohol searing his nostrils. He looked at the vase of flowers he'd lovingly bought for her and the note he'd written and felt the full force of bitter disappointment. Why? Was it his fault? Had he been such a rotten husband?

He poured himself another stiff whisky and wandered around the kitchen, then around the living room, too twitchy to sit. Chester and Ella had settled down to sleep, blissfully unaware of what had just transpired. Maisie was grooming herself, her spiked tongue catching in her long fur. He wandered into the hallway and then the kitchen, turning off some of the brighter lights, needing a gloom that matched his mood. Fay's colourful tiffany lamp glowed in the corner of the living room. He looked at a framed photograph of them both with the dogs, taken a few years ago; Chester was dressed in reindeer antlers and Ella in a flashing collar and silver tinsel. They were happy and in love – a poignant reminder of the lonely Christmas that lay ahead.

Was it really over? Had she gone for good? Was it an impossible hope that she could love him again? That she would come back, realising after all that she'd made a mistake? He couldn't bank on it. His mind raced ahead to divorce proceedings, the inevitable acrimony, the damaging financial settlement, the empty, aching loneliness. Life could be turned upside down in an instant and he could only guess at what the future might bring.

He paced around the living room, replaying their conversation over and over in his mind. Then he grabbed the whisky bottle and opened the kitchen door to the garden, needing to breathe fresh air, to try to make sense of the staggering revelation he'd just heard. To find the essence of himself amid the jumble of thoughts that were crowding his brain. He sat on their bench and tried to find peace in the stars. For a blissful moment, their domestic problems seemed insignificant in the vastness of time and space, and he let himself wonder at the universe – to know something bigger than himself – a fleeting escape from the prison of human existence and a feeling of being lifted out of time in a moment of pure being. He traced the constellations, the twinkling stars, and other worlds out there in the blackness of space. Orion, Cassiopeia, Ursa Major: the stars he and Fay had watched together so many times. But the empty space beside him echoed the void he felt in his heart. His wife was gone – just like that – and there was nothing he could do to stop her. In his mind he heard the excitement of her voice as she pointed to the night sky, the togetherness of her arm linked through his, the laughter and love they'd once shared. He sipped his whisky needing the fiery liquid to dull his senses – to ease the pain of betrayal.

Ella had come out into the garden and sat dutifully beside him, her body leaning into his leg. She seemed to have a sixth sense, a radar that told her when something was wrong. He smoothed her head, and she looked up at him with big nut-brown eyes that seemed to see into the very depths of his soul. A true friendship that traversed the arbitrary boundaries of species: pure consciousness locked in a compassionate embrace. He bent to kiss her head and lingered there, her soft warm fur on his lips. He knew the dogs and Maisie would always stay with him. Fay could take every last scrap of money and every single possession he had – but he would never let her take them.

He wondered when Fay's love had started eroding. Had her deadly secret really torn them apart or had he failed to notice her slipping inexorably away from him until it was too late to stop their marriage falling over a precipice? Since getting home from prison, he had been swept up with work, trying to make ends meet, the thing with Regenex and Oliver – even Bates – and he hadn't even noticed his own life disintegrating beyond repair. He remembered their conversation in the woods – maybe he should have agreed that they should try for another child. He should have realised her desperation and the fragile state of her mind when she tried to steal Megan Foley's baby. Was it then that she'd turned to Rick?

Rick.

What was it that she found so bloody alluring about him? What had enticed her to leave their marriage? And what would Rick do with Fay's secret? He couldn't bear to think about it. He had tried to protect her from a life in prison that would surely have destroyed her. Maybe he should have turned Fay in to the police when he realised that she'd killed those people. At least she would have been forced to get the psychiatric help she needed to cope with her grief after Sophie's murder. Ah, yes, hindsight… such a wonderful thing. But would that have been right for her? For society? And yet, perhaps the killing of more innocent lives has been prevented because Fay had managed to rid the world of those vile paedophiles and murderers.

Now he can't protect her or hold on to her.

She's gone…

He looked into Ella's brown eyes, then up at the stars. *Don't leave me, Fay. Don't lose your mind and leave me to face this alone.*

The crescent moon was rising over the ash tree in the garden, the stars were sparkling against the black void of space. In the vast stretch of cosmic time, newborn stars were beginning to glow and find their strength. Could he find his strength too?

Was it really over? Surely there was some small shred of hope. Was Fay leaving him because she'd stopped loving him or because she was drowning in a sea of fractured dreams, the aching isolation of despair and the torture of mental illness? Either way she was gone from his life – swept away by the promise of Rick.

But they had a bedrock of love to steady them through the storm. He couldn't imagine a life without her.

He had to hold on, to be strong, for Fay, for their marriage and the love they'd once shared. He decided to find her and bring her home to him and get her the help she needed to be whole again.

He was about to plunge headlong into the unknown.

SEVENTY-NINE

Fay drove with tears streaming down her face – she was heading for Rick's apartment. She had done it; she'd left Daniel but now she wasn't sure it was what she really wanted. When she went home to get her things and tell Daniel she was leaving, she was ecstatic – a new life lay ahead with Rick. It was the promise of happiness and an escape from the prison of the past that had wrapped itself around her like a boa constrictor – gripping tighter every time she tried to take a breath until she was gasping for air, for freedom.

Now her mood was sombre as the full realisation of what she'd done hit her like a tsunami. She hadn't stopped loving Daniel – she couldn't imagine she ever could – but her mind was a jumble, her thoughts colliding relentlessly in her brain, fragments of herself coalescing then breaking apart again. She thought of the flowers he'd left for her and the genuine concern in his eyes, the years of marriage and love they had shared. And the baby they had made together.

Sophie...

What on Earth had she done?

She tried to see the road ahead through a veil of tears and almost drove into a late-night dog walker but managed to swerve aside just in time to avoid an accident. She reached for a tissue and dried her eyes. She had to pull herself together. Had to, for her own sanity. She was driving away from their life together, from all the love, the home they shared and the wretched demons of the past.

She had to face reality and accept she'd made a choice. What was done was done and she had to move on into the future. It was too late to go back now. Daniel knew she'd been seeing Rick and she had betrayed the secret they had vowed never to tell. Would he be able to forgive her? To trust her ever again? To take her back with her secret out in the open? Things could never be the same.

She knew that she had just destroyed their lives.

She drove around the hilly outskirts of Riverbeke; she could see the scattered hospital buildings in the town and, in the distance, across a dark landscape littered with street lights, the monstrous black edifice of the prison. Constructions, solid and real – both parts of their lives for so long. Sophie had been born in that hospital and they had both spent a good part of their careers there. They were happy times. Now the shadow of the prison loomed over them with all the death, torment, grief and destruction it represented – Sophie's murder, Wixx, the killings she'd carried out. Could she ever really escape? Wherever she went in the solid world of matter, the flimsy wisps of her thoughts and memories would always be there, haunting her. There was no escape from them – or the demons that had reared up and stalked her for so long.

She left the ring road and headed toward the sea and Rick. A new life was beckoning and with each mile of road she left behind she forced herself to look forward. Now, it was all she could do.

She held the image of Rick in her mind: his smiling eyes, those rugged features, his soft Spanish lilt and strong, protective arms around her. He'd promised to take care of her, to shield her from the world, to be there for her. She had let herself be persuaded to leave Daniel and, she had to admit, she was starting to fall in love with Rick. They understood one another, knew the things that grief could do to a fragile mind. They shared something that Daniel could never understand – a way of healing the agony of grief, of easing the torment in their hearts. Rick had a hunger for saving lives, yet he understood why she had killed those people. They had a bond she had never known before – a special understanding that had the potential to heal them both.

Yet, somewhere in the murky depths of her mind, she knew she needed professional help. Sometimes her thoughts were lucid, and she knew she was seeing things, hearing things, tasting things that probably weren't there. Was she really hearing Sophie's cries or were they just an echo in her mind?

She would experience the amazing yet terrifying heights of ecstasy when the oiled cogs of her mind would spin faster and faster out of control, followed by the inevitable crash into the lonely, menacing abys of depression – plunged into an ominously dark world of shadows and paranoia. And somewhere in between these disparate worlds was the melancholy of impending doom and a mental trauma that will never truly go away.

Fay often knew she was going into psychosis but couldn't help being swept up in it. Sometimes it would sneak up on her when delusion blended with reality to hide itself in a magical, dreamlike detachment. Like living in some wraithlike, otherworldly movie. Other times it would steamroller its way into her psyche, with Sophie's haunting cries a frightening echo in her head, getting louder and louder with no way to shut them off. She should have let Daniel and Shelly help her but her pride, fear, shame, indignity, apprehension and a million conflicting emotions had been in the way. All she really wanted was to be a mother to Sophie and that had been brutally snatched away.

What would become of her?

Would she ever be herself again?

Was Rick a silent cry for help?

But this was her reality now and she had to make the best of it. To find some way to come to terms with what she had done. In her mind, Daniel was lost forever.

She rounded the corner to the full view of the old lighthouse and the cove. The tide was coming in and the pounding surf glowed briefly in the headlights. The apartment building was stark and white, seeming to shine with a light of its own against the blackness of the sky. She slowed the car, turned into the underground car park and manoeuvred the Mercedes next to Rick's Lamborghini. This was her future – for now at least.

She left Sophie's bear but grabbed her bags from the boot of the car and made her way up to Rick's apartment. She rang the doorbell, and he greeted her with a lingering kiss. He took her bags, and she followed him inside. There was wine and a warm welcome waiting for her.

She smiled – she had to. This was what she had chosen and there was no going back.

"How did it go?" Rick asked.

"Alright," she said, not wanting to relive the painful conversation she'd had with Daniel.

He took her hand and led her to the big soft sofa that faced the picture window overlooking the cove. Street lights lit up a distant headland and the sound of the crashing waves of the incoming tide was muffled behind the glass. She snuggled close to him and drank in his aura, her head resting on his shoulder. Now all she had was Rick and the secrets they shared. And yet there was something she wanted much, much more – something she desperately needed. Without it she couldn't see how she could go on.

"Rick..." she said softly. "I know from my research that many patients have a near-death experience when they are clinically dead." She paused for a moment and looked up into his eyes.

He smiled and stroked her hair.

"I want to die to be with Sophie, to see her and hold her again if I can. Will you help me?"

EIGHTY

Daniel finally fell into a fitful sleep around 4am, then woke at 8am in their bed, precariously on the edge with the dogs stretched out beside him. Maisie was nowhere to be seen. He lay there awhile going over the events of the day before. The gruesome discoveries at Regenex and then the bombshell from Fay. Last night, he'd been determined but now he was wavering on his decision to find Fay and try to persuade her to come home. Maybe he should wait a few days and see how things played out. A few weeks maybe? And yet she clearly wasn't thinking straight. What if she really was suffering with bipolar psychosis, as Shelly had suggested? She would need to get early and effective treatment. If she would be prepared to get a psychiatric assessment or at least have a chat with Shelly, they could seek the help she needed. Should he pursue this or leave it for now? He decided that, since he wasn't due in work for another two days, now was as good a time as any to sort things out.

He got up, showered and dressed in navy chinos and a checked pastel-coloured shirt over a white T-shirt. The dogs followed him downstairs, and he let them into the garden. They bounded across the lawn and into the shrubs, playing with Chester's squeaky toy. He put two slices of bread into the toaster and made a mug of strong instant coffee, buttered his toast, added a scraping of Marmite and sat in the kitchen surrounded by memories.

Where was Fay now? Had she gone into the hospital? Was she at Rick's place? He had no idea but would have to find out. He could call or text her, but it would be too easy for her to ignore him – it was better to see her face-to-face. He decided to call Matt. If she was going into work, she'd be there by now.

"Hey, Daniel, how are things?" He sounded upbeat over the constant sound of alarms bonging in the background.

"Been better, to be honest. I was just wondering if Fay was in the department today."

"Why? Has she gone missing again?"

"Sort of…" Daniel was reluctant to say more. "Have you seen her around?"

"Not this morning and I've only just come up to the HDU from the ward. I'm sure I would have seen her if she was in."

"Thanks, mate. By the way, there's been a development at Regenex with Isobel."

"Care to elaborate?"

Daniel gave him a brief rundown of what had happened and asked him to stop the Bravafloxacin clinical trial on the ward. "God knows what's going on with that, but we have to stop it."

"Of course. I'll tell Colin what's happened."

"One more thing before you go. Do you have Rick's address?"

"Sure – are you planning to send him a Christmas card?"

Daniel pretended to laugh.

Matt gave him the address and they hung up.

Daniel looked up the address on Google Maps. He'd been to the cove years ago and was sure he would find it, but he put the address into the sat nav on his iPhone anyway. He called the dogs to the Dog House and fed them just as Rosie arrived to collect them for the creche. He clipped on their leads and handed them over. "Have fun," he said.

"We will," Rosie said as she was pulled along the driveway to her van.

Daniel locked the back door, grabbed a jacket, his wallet, phone and car keys and went out to the Defender. He sat for several minutes, wondering if he was doing the right thing going after Fay. If it wasn't for her mental state and hearing what Shelly had told him about bipolar psychosis, he would have left it and tried to accept that she was gone but he felt that he needed to check she was alright and try to persuade her to get help. At the very least, he could ensure Rick was aware that she wasn't well. Perhaps she would listen to him. He felt a building resentment for Rick, but he would have to get over it if he wanted was what was best for her.

He started the engine, pulled out of the driveway and headed for the coast. Would she really listen to him? Could he persuade her to get help even though she'd left him? It seemed impossible but he had to try. He wondered if he would get past Rick, if he would even let him speak to her, but it was high time he stood up to him. He may have got away with his superior attitude at work, but this was about his wife, and it was getting personal.

He took the turning off the ring road and headed toward the coast. The sky was growing gloomy, with gathering storm clouds sweeping in from the sea, and there were flocks of gulls heading inland. He began to wonder if this was a good idea. The mood Fay was in last night, he doubted she'd listen to him but at the very least he had to try.

He stopped, checked the sat nav, then turned onto the lane that hugged the winding coastline. The wind was whipping up whitecaps on the water as he drove slowly past the lighthouse and then the cove. His stomach flipped as he saw the apartment building up ahead. He shouldn't have come. Maybe it was better to leave her to her new life with Rick. But he loved her – he couldn't just abandon her now after all they'd been through together. He had to get her to see sense.

Daniel parked on the road outside and wandered around the side of the building, looking for an entrance. There was an underground car park and he peered in and saw Fay's Mercedes parked next to Rick's Lamborghini. Evidently, they were both there. He began to feel nervous – not knowing what sort of reception he'd get, especially from Rick. But he had to see it through.

He found an entrance at the side of the building, but the door was locked and there was a security keypad that needed a pass number. He stood for a few minutes, wondering what to do, then the door flew open and a woman rushed past him. He managed to grab the door before it slammed shut. She was hurrying away and hadn't noticed him. This was his chance.

He went inside and took the stairs to the first floor. There was a wide landing with three doors to apartments. He checked the names above the doorbells – none of them was Rick's. He went up the next flight of stairs to a landing that mirrored the first. One of the front-facing apartments had a label that read *Rick Estevez*. He felt the crushing grip of apprehension twisting his gut but had to follow this through – for Fay's sake.

He pressed the doorbell and waited. There was a spyhole in the door, and he sensed someone watching him.

Then the door opened, and Rick stood in the doorway, dressed in faded jeans and a white open-neck shirt. "What the hell do you want?"

Daniel looked him in the eye and stood his ground. "I'd like to have a word with my wife."

Rick glared at him, stony-faced, for several uncomfortable moments, then Fay's voice came from inside.

"It's alright, let him come in."

Rick grudgingly stood aside, and Daniel went into the apartment. He could see Fay standing near the kitchen. She was wearing black trousers and a jersey wrap top in a jade green that matched her eyes. She looked hunched and bedraggled and hadn't even brushed her hair. Her eyes had dark circles beneath them as if she hadn't slept.

He walked toward her. "Fay... sweetheart. Are you sure you're doing the right thing? I wish you'd come home."

She looked at him like a lost puppy, her eyes vacant and staring. She glanced past him at Rick, then back to Daniel, her mouth moving as if she was trying to say something but couldn't get the words out.

"Fay?" He tried to prompt her but still she stood there in a daze.

Daniel turned to see Rick standing behind him. "What's happened? She wasn't like this last night. Has she taken drugs or something?" He'd seen that faraway look in some of the prison inmates.

"No – she hasn't taken drugs," Rick said defiantly.

"Well, why is she in this state? You don't give a damn about her, do you?" Daniel glared at him, waiting for an answer.

Rick's eyes narrowed and he suddenly lurched at Daniel, grabbing him around the throat and pushing him backwards. Daniel felt his back crunch as he was slammed against a wall. Rick's dark eyes were boring into his with pure contempt.

"Rick, no..." Fay pleaded.

"You're the one who doesn't care," Rick growled at him. "I took care of Fay when she tried to abduct Megan Foley's baby. Where the hell do you think she'd be now if I'd let her carry on? You've no idea what she's been going through."

Daniel's throat was closing up as Rick's grip tightened. He was rasping for breath. He brought his foot up, connected with Rick's stomach and pushed him away.

Rick reeled backward and Daniel went after him to get the upper hand. He remembered a self-defence move from his time in prison and grabbed Rick's wrist and twisted his arm behind his back.

Rick roared in pain and hunched forward. He twisted his

head to look up at Daniel. “She’ll never go back to you – you’re a fucking loser.”

“Daniel… please, stop,” Fay begged.

She was inching toward them, biting her lip, a look of shock etched on her face. Rick managed to twist his body around and break free, then thrust his fist into the side of Daniel’s head, knocking him sideways, colliding into Fay. She staggered and landed on the floor; Daniel tried to shake off the pain and help her up, but she managed to shuffle away from them with no more than a grazed arm.

“Stay back, Fay,” Daniel said firmly. He faltered, held onto his footing but Rick rushed at him, his forearm crashing down onto Daniel’s upper back.

Daniel sprawled forward and crashed headlong into the back of a sofa. He crumpled to the floor. Rick came at him with a kick to his flank and Daniel doubled over in agony.

“Fuck you, Kendrick.” Rick was seething with hatred.

Daniel rolled onto his knees, grabbed the top of the sofa and hauled himself to his feet. The two men stood, fists ready to punch.

“Please stop, both of you,” Fay was retreating to the kitchen.

Rick made the first move and walloped Daniel’s ribs, winding him. But Daniel managed to throw a punch himself, thumping Rick in the stomach.

Rick groaned but recovered and kicked out at Daniel, catching him painfully in the shins. Daniel backed away into the living room but Rick kept coming, kicking higher and higher until his foot slammed into the side of Daniel’s face. His head snapped sideways but he turned back to see the loathing in Rick’s eyes. Then he made the connection between Isobel and Rick.

“You were involved in the abomination that was at Regenex…”

Rick snarled. “What do you know about Regenex?”

"Everything and now Isobel has been arrested."

"Arrested? Because of your interference, no doubt." Rick stood transfixed for a moment before kicking out again with a whack to Daniel's stomach.

Daniel slumped to the ground and Rick was straight on him, grabbing his shirt and lifting his upper torso. He thumped him in the face three times before Daniel managed to twist his body and kick him away. His face was throbbing, his shirt was torn, and his body was aching from the pummelling he'd taken. Rick had a powerful punch.

"Isobel only has one use for me… I had nothing to do with what she was up to at the lab," Rick said breathlessly.

Daniel didn't believe a word of it and was about to tell him so when Rick came at him again and slammed his elbow into Daniel's chest. An agonising blast of pain seared through his ribs as Daniel fell to his knees, then Rick brought his knee up into his face, sending him sprawling across the floor. Daniel felt the crunch of another splinter of tooth snapping off and the tasted the coppery tang of blood. But, somehow, Daniel recovered, hauled himself wearily to his feet, wiped blood from his mouth with the back of his hand and kicked out, catching Rick in the thigh.

Rick rocked forward but within seconds was ready with his fists again. Both men were sweating and out of breath as they glared at one another, eyes dark with menace.

Fay sat on the floor in the corner of the kitchen, her back against the cupboards, her head in her hands. "Please stop…" she whimpered.

Rick threw a punch first, but Daniel caught his fist and twisted Rick away from him before forcing him to the floor with his foot. Rick caught the TV on his way down and it crashed from the wall and onto the floor; the huge screen cracked in several places.

Rick hauled himself up and barrel-rolled toward Daniel, sending him crashing into the bookcase – books thudded to the floor and ornaments crashed and broke from the top shelf; the tinkle of splintering glass echoed around the room.

Fay was rocking back and forth, her face still buried in her hands. "Stop… stop…"

Rick punched Daniel in the stomach, then again into his flank. He doubled over in agony and fell forward onto the coffee table. The legs of the table broke and it crashed to the floor with Daniel sprawled on top of it. One of the legs went skittering across the floor as he felt the hard thud of solid wood against his cheek bone.

Then Rick was on him again, thumping him in the kidneys once, twice, three times before he stood back.

Daniel groaned as searing pain tore into his flank. He wasn't sure if he could recover from the pummelling but, with a monumental effort, he managed to roll and push himself up onto his knees. He could hear Rick's laboured breathing above him.

"Please… stop." Fay was cowering, tears streaming down her face.

Daniel hauled himself to his feet but, as he stood there hunched in agony, Rick brought his knee up into his face, sending Daniel sprawling across the floor on his back; a huge Raku pottery vase smashed and went hurtling across the room. He was dazed for some moments as Rick disappeared, then came back with a syringe in his hand, poised to thrust it at Daniel.

Daniel tried to roll away from him but Rick held him to the floor with a foot on his chest and managed to stab the needle into his arm and depress the plunger.

"What the hell was that?" Daniel managed to say, his arm stinging, blood seeping from his injured mouth.

"It's just a sedative for now but make no mistake – I'll kill you like I killed the others – but this time I won't bother to resuscitate. You can die and go to hell for all I care." Rick stepped back.

"What do you mean – what others? Who have you killed?" He rubbed his arm.

Rick smirked then let out a sinister laugh. "Surely you remember Jean Wyatt, Don Hackman and Graeme Buckley… their deaths were no accident."

"*You* killed them? But why – why would you do something like that?" So, Oliver Davenport wasn't the only murderer at Riverbeke General.

Rick perched on the arm of the sofa, a smirk still playing over his lips. "For the thrill – the sheer and utter thrill. Haven't you ever had the adrenaline rush of bringing someone back to life?"

Daniel could feel himself detaching slightly as the drug started to bite. He had to fight it and stay alert.

Rick went on, smug with himself now that Daniel was incapacitated. "Aren't you fascinated by being around someone on the brink of death? Don't you wonder what lies beyond? Heaven, hell, purgatory – or a big, fat, black nothing?"

"You're sick," was all Daniel could say in the shock of what he was hearing.

"You see, I have a lot in common with your lovely wife – or, should I say, soon-to-be ex-wife. It's funny what grief will do to you, isn't it? Fay likes to kill people in her need to rid the world of evil. I kill to bring people back to life." He crossed his arms and gave Daniel a thin smile. "I understand her grief – I lost my child too, and my wife. It was my fault, you see – I was driving. It was me that crashed the car and couldn't save them. I tried and tried but despite my best efforts they died in my arms."

"And you deal with that by killing people and trying to resuscitate them? Dear God… what sort of deranged monster are you? How many people have died because of your self-serving, narcissistic and insanely arrogant actions?" He was feeling woozier and more detached by the minute.

Stay awake… for God's sake, stay awake…

"I've killed quite a few. Some survive, some don't, but that's the luck of the draw. I do try my best to save them." He uncrossed his arms and leaned forward, his hands on his knees, locking his eyes with Daniel's. "I need to do this, Kendrick, I can't live with what I did to my family. I need to save lives. You should understand that, seeing that your wife is a killer too."

Daniel blinked and shook his head, trying to regain his senses. "Are you asking for sympathy? You won't get it from me." Daniel was incredulous at Rick's astonishing revelation of self-delusion. It was beyond parody. "You're insanely dangerous – projecting your wife and son onto those patients – you can't bring your family back. You must accept that. You have to stop before anyone else dies. I *will* turn you in to the police and you'll never practise as a doctor again because you'll spend the rest of your life behind bars, where you belong."

Rick just smirked and started stepping around Daniel, his six-foot-three frame towering over him. "If I let you live – which, of course, I won't."

Daniel winced, his vision starting to blur as he tried to keep an eye on Rick, fearing he would kick him when he was down but needing to know more. "So, tell me, how did you actually kill these people? The police would be interested to know."

Rick shrugged as if he had nothing to lose by telling him the details. He walked menacingly around the top of Daniel's head. "Potassium chloride, usually – a quick and easy way to induce a cardiac arrest. The clinical trial was my perfect cover. All the patients had the Bravafloxacin. But the records showed that they had the placebo. If they lived, there was no further investigation. But if they died and there was a post-mortem with blood and tissue analysis, the Bravafloxacin would take the blame. A perfect alibi."

In his increasingly hazy mind, it all now made sense. "So, the clinical trial was all a cover, so you could carry out your contemptable killings." Even in his drugged state, he could see how Rick and Isobel had colluded to allow him to play God with his patients' lives for his own astonishing thrill-seeking.

Rick sighed. "Yes, my sweet little Isobel – she was only good for one thing and that was protecting me. She also gained by selling the organs of the patients that didn't make it. It was a good trade."

"But what about the potassium chloride – that would be found in the blood samples as well…"

"Yes, a synergistic effect between the two drugs could be blamed for the deaths. Isobel's metabolism group would confirm that."

Then the shocking realisation hit Daniel like a two-pound lump hammer. "Tell me something: you were going to frame me for those murders, weren't you? You were going to say that I had administered the potassium chloride and it would be your word as a consultant against mine." Daniel was starting to slur and felt decidedly woozy. His body was heavy and numb, and he couldn't move his arms or legs. What the hell had Rick given him?

"Of course. Everyone knows you're a murderer – you were the perfect choice. Nobody would question that – even Colin, once I'd told him a few things." He laughed. "And now I know Fay's little secret too. Who knows what we can achieve together; especially once you're permanently out of the way."

Daniel could almost smell the blackmail and had no doubt Rick would carry out his threat to kill him. But Rick's words were fading and echoing as the sedative took effect. He could barely hold his head up and the room was spinning around him. He battled to keep his eyes open as Rick sneered, then wandered off to the kitchen. He could just about see Rick and Fay through the woozy veil of the drug.

Fay was crying and upset. "Rick… please, I just want to die… let me go to Sophie. I know you can bring me back…"

"I don't know, Fay; what if I can't?"

"I don't care… I just want to be with my baby. I don't care if I live or die… please. Do this for me."

There was a long silence before Rick spoke. "You really want this, don't you?"

"Yes, I do. It's the only thing I want in the world… I need to be with Sophie. I know you can bring me back, Rick. I know you can… please…"

There was another long pause before Rick said, "Alright… I'll help you."

Daniel tried desperately to overcome the effects of the sedative. Rick was about to kill his wife and he couldn't do a damned thing to stop him – he was trapped in his own body, unable to move. He had to stay awake… try to move… lift his head up… keep his eyes open…

Then he heard the receding sound of Fay's voice before he was enveloped by the dark oblivion of unconsciousness.

EIGHTY-ONE

Daniel could hear the pounding of his own blood in his ears, then voices – they sounded distant at first, then became louder and closer as he gradually regained consciousness. His eyes flickered open, and he turned his head toward the sound to see Fay lying on the floor through the bedroom doorway. Rick, with his back to him, was hunched over her.

"Alright, the Venflon is in. Are you sure you want to go ahead with this, Fay?" Rick secured the canula in position with surgical tape.

"Please, Rick… just do it. I know you can bring me back. I must be with Sophie… I must…"

Daniel saw Rick reach for a syringe and begin to draw up clear fluid. "This will cause a lethal arrythmia and your heart will stop. Then I will resuscitate you."

Daniel had to stop him. He tried to lift his head, tried to roll onto his side to get up, but his muscles were weak and he could barely move. His body was wracked with pain and his vision was still blurred but he had to get to Rick and stop him.

"Give me some time with Sophie," Fay was saying.

"I'll give you as long as I can once your heart has stopped but we only have a few minutes. I can't risk you getting brain damage through lack of oxygen."

With an almighty effort, Daniel managed to roll onto his side and push himself into a sitting position. He shook his head, trying to regain his senses. The sedative still had a powerful hold over his body, making him feel punch drunk, but, overriding the stunned inertia in his brain, his instincts were urging him to move – he had to get to Rick.

Daniel could see Rick laying out his resuscitation equipment from his trauma team holdall; bag-valve mask, airway, small cylinder of oxygen, a portable defibrillator, syringes of adrenaline. He had to get to him before he delivered the drug that would send Fay into a cardiac arrest. He managed to crawl a few feet, gradually feeling the strength coming back into his trembling muscles. Then he hauled himself to his feet and tried to take a step forward. He staggered and managed to steady himself on the arm of the sofa.

Rick held up a syringe containing 5 ml of clear fluid. He pushed the nozzle of the syringe into the bung attached to the Venflon and slowly pushed the plunger.

Shit. Was he too late?

Daniel managed to take one step forward; his legs felt like lead. He had to get to get to Rick…

"That's just a saline flush to make sure the canula is patent," Rick said.

Fay looked up at him and smiled. "I'm ready," she said.

Daniel took another faltering step, grabbing onto the door frame. His legs were shaking with the effort, but his vision was clearing. He pushed himself forward, forcing his foot to move.

Rick picked up the syringe that contained the potassium chloride. "Are you sure? We don't have to do this…"

"Please, I want to – I need to be with my baby – if only for a while. I want this more than anything…"

Daniel knew he had to get there in seconds if he was to stop Rick. He forced himself on, battling against the effects of the sedative. Like a bear fighting a tranquiliser, he shook his head again, trying to clear the last of the wooziness, then saw a large piece of the base of the Raku vase that had smashed. He reached for it and almost toppled over but managed to grab the doorframe again.

Rick held the bung that was attached to the Venflon. "This will always be our secret."

"Yes, it will." Fay smiled again.

Rick kissed her lips. "I'll bring you back to me, I promise." He held the syringe, ready to insert it.

Terrified he wouldn't make it in time, Daniel lurched at Rick, his legs almost gave way under him, but he managed to stiffen his knees and put one foot in front of the other. He brought the pottery base down onto Rick's head, knocking him sprawling across Fay's prostrate body. The syringe fell from Rick's hand and rolled across the carpet.

Fay screamed and tried to get free, but Rick was pinning her to the floor. Daniel grabbed a handful of the back of Rick's shirt and pulled him off, hurling him to the ground beside Fay, scattering the resuscitation equipment across the floor. His limbs were shaking as the sedative began to wear off.

Fay screamed again and leaped to her feet. "No... Daniel... no..."

Rick had been stunned by the heavy blow of the vase, but his eyes fluttered open and he turned onto his side, pushing himself up with his elbow. "You bastard," he hissed. "I'll kill you."

Daniel stood over Rick, rocking on his feet, trying desperately to force his muscles to work. He looked across to see Fay grab the syringe of potassium chloride from the floor and run off into the kitchen.

"Fay, come back," Daniel shouted.

Rick was staggering to his feet.

Fay grabbed her bag and car keys and ran out of the apartment, the syringe of potassium chloride still in her hand.

Daniel had to stop Fay – God knows where she was going or what she was going to do.

But first he had to stop Rick.

He looked around and saw one of the legs of the coffee table lying on the floor. He staggered and bent to pick it up. Rick was lumbering toward him, but he swung the wooden table leg at Rick's shin and bashed him as hard as he could. Rick twisted away to the sickening sound of bone breaking and he crumpled to the floor, yowling in agony. Rick lifted his trouser leg to see a compound fracture of his tibia, the jagged end of the broken bone jutting through the skin, blood dripping down his leg and soaking into the carpet. His leg was twisted at an awkward angle.

"You fucking bastard… look what you've done." Rick looked at Daniel, his eyes dark with pain and hatred.

Daniel knew that would be enough to hold him there while he went after Fay. "I'll make sure you rot in prison for what you've done."

Daniel knew Fay was planning to kill herself – she'd taken the syringe and had seemed desperate to die. He gathered Rick's resuscitation equipment, pushed it into the holdall and took it with him as he staggered after Fay. His legs were still trembling, but his muscles were starting to regain strength. He grabbed furniture and door frames to steady himself as he staggered out of the apartment, slamming the door behind him.

Rick could stew in his own blood for now – he had more important things to deal with.

EIGHTY-TWO

Fay just had to get out of there – all she wanted was to die and be with her baby and Rick had been willing to help her – but that had all changed now that Daniel knew. Why had he come? Why couldn't he just leave her alone?

She grabbed her bag and car keys and ran down the stairs, the syringe of potassium chloride still gripped tightly in her hand. She knew that all she had to do was push the fluid into the Venflon Rick had put into the back of her hand and her life and all the pain it entailed would be over.

She ran to her car, a high-pitched beep echoing around the concrete walls of the garage as she unlocked the Mercedes. She threw her bag onto the passenger seat and carefully tucked the syringe underneath it. Then she slipped into the driver's seat, started the engine and revved away, tyres squealing on the concrete floor as she pulled out of the garage. She turned and drove past the cove and the lighthouse. The sea was grey and dismal under the gathering storm clouds and the surf was pounding onto the shoreline, driven by fierce onshore winds.

She accelerated hard along the winding lane, taking the corners way too fast, no longer caring if she lived or died. Her mind was a jumble of incoherent thoughts. A shattered hologram of memories and emotions. The only constant in all of it was Sophie. She heard her baby babbling all around her, her giggles and her cries. The ghostly image of her face was swirling in front of her.

Sophie…

Somehow, through a veil of colliding thoughts and images, she reached the turning to the main A road. She was headed toward the only place in the world she wanted to be. Rain was lashing onto the windscreen as she pulled out into the traffic.

She reached the ring road, swerved recklessly into the outside lane and accelerated past lorries spraying a thick mist that all but obscured her view. She could barely see up ahead as she sped toward the road that would take her back to Riverbeke.

She almost missed the turning but managed to cut in front of a lorry, tyres aquaplaning on the wet tarmac. She felt her mind begin to detach from reality. She knew she shouldn't be driving but she had to get home. She had to. Her mind was consumed with the desolation of her grief, Sophie, and how her heart ached to be with her baby.

Images paraded before her eyes: her psychic reading with Felicia Grainger, the darkened room, the crystal ball and the tarot cards – Felicia's promise that Sophie's soul had survived death. "Follow your heart," Sophie had said. She had tried to. She really had. She'd wanted another baby, but everything had conspired against her – none of her embryos had survived; her chance of getting pregnant was practically zero; Rick had stopped her from taking Megan Foley's little girl…

Now all she wanted was to be with Sophie. If only Daniel hadn't come looking for her – Rick would have helped her die.

Now she would have to face it alone, knowing she could never come back.

Rain lashed the windscreen as Fay retraced her route home along the hilly outskirts of town, past the dark, menacing edifice of the prison, the scattered buildings of the hospital and on past the town to their home. Neither the dreary grey weather nor the soothing, hypnotic metronome of the windscreen wipers failed to stop her mind racing out of control. As she drove closer to home, her thoughts began reeling faster and faster with euphoric anticipation of what she intended to do. There was no going back now.

She finally pulled into their street and turned sharply and impatiently into the driveway. She slammed on the brakes, the wheels locked, and the Mercedes skidded toward the garage doors; a sickening thud reverberated through the car as the front-end hit and buckled. Fay didn't care. Her mind was racing with exhilaration – all she wanted was to be with Sophie and nobody was going to stop her.

She grabbed her bag and the syringe of potassium chloride and headed for the house. She barely noticed as she was drenched in torrential rain. She fumbled with the key and let herself in, her eyes wide with excitement, darting around the hallway watching images that flashed before her like holograms – delusion blending with reality as her mind spiralled out of control.

She threw her bag on the floor and raced for the stairs, clutching the syringe. She reached Sophie's nursery and flung the door open. The room seemed to welcome her. This is where she was meant to be, and the last place on Earth she would ever see.

This room was where she had poured out her grief and those wretched secrets into her journal during the endless nights she'd spent alone with her memories of Sophie.

She saw the faces of the people she'd killed lurch before her – laughing at her, mocking her. She still hated them for the atrocities they had committed, the murders, the assaults on innocent children. She was glad they were dead, and she was glad she'd killed them. If she had a chance to do it all again, she would.

She looked around the nursery: Sophie's cot, her things still exactly as they were before she was brutally murdered. The room was seeped in memories that came alive before her eyes – images of Sophie started dancing wildly around the room; lights were flashing in her eyes as the terrifying, yet exhilarating hallucinations swirled all around her.

Fay knew she was slipping into a terrifying psychosis, but she couldn't fight it any more. She wanted this – wanted insanity to take her to her baby. She was tired of the world.

She found the rocking chair where she had nursed Sophie so many times and sat, rocking gently back and forth. Then she thought of Daniel; the tune of one of her favourite sad songs by Whitney Houston beginning to soothe her mind beneath the dancing images before her. She heard her own broken, disconnected voice whispering the words to "I Will Always Love You"...

She said a silent goodbye to Daniel and closed her eyes, and the hallucinations gradually coalesced into a single holographic image of Sophie's smiling face, her baby-blue eyes sparkling with joy.

She knew Sophie was waiting for her – all she wanted now was to end it all and be with her baby.

Nothing else mattered...

She felt the syringe in her hand and knew it was time. She inserted the nozzle of the syringe into the Venflon. Once she pushed the plunger, there was no going back – Rick wasn't there to save her. But she was ready for whatever lay on the other side of death, and she knew it would be forever.

She pushed the plunger, and the potassium chloride flooded her veins. She felt the cold, lethal fluid shoot up her arm and took a deep breath, knowing it would be her last. She felt her heart flutter and thud against her chest as its electrical activity faltered.

She felt the moment her heart stopped beating...

Then she was rising through the top of her head and a still, peaceful silence enveloped her. The terrifying hallucinations were swept away, the flashing lights had gone, and the relentless voices had ceased. A calmness washed over her as she found the true essence of herself. Her consciousness was draped in an ethereal form, and she was floating toward the ceiling of Sophie's nursery. She looked down to see a dead body slumped in the rocking chair with only an absent recognition that it was her own. Then she seemed to drift away and into a beautiful, comforting mist of light.

She sensed other beings in the distance and suddenly she was being drawn toward them as a wall of black cloud swirled and wrapped itself around her. She was speeding ever faster toward a pinpoint of light and, in an instant, she emerged into a bright white light that seemed to seep into her wispy form and become part of her. She realised she was made of light and the beings she sensed all around her, welcoming her, were also made of light. She felt an intense and unconditional love become part of her and realised that this was what her patients had described. She drank in a perfect peace that was unmatched in the dense world of matter she'd left behind.

Then she sensed a being she knew. A little girl with a wisdom far beyond her apparent age – an old soul that had joined her on her cosmic journey into life. A soul with boundless love to give and many lessons to teach.

Sophie…

Fay felt her draw closer and their souls connected like two bright stars entwined around one another. She sensed the eternal love they had always shared and finally, she felt at peace. She saw a gate ahead and beyond it a river and the most wonderfully captivating garden she had ever known, filled with lush greenery, graceful trees, bright colourful flowers and butterflies fluttering amongst them with vibrant, incandescent light. An exquisitely beautiful place of tranquillity and pure love.

She had found her way home…

The beings of light told her that death lay beyond the gate, that once she'd gone through to the other side there was no going back. More than anything, she wanted to go through the gate, to be with Sophie. To rest in peace and love…

But she sensed resistance and, in an instant, she experienced a vivid review of her life that made her relive every moment. Suddenly everything fell into place, and she understood the meaning of her life. Events from her childhood, her early adult life and then meeting Daniel and knowing once again the love they shared. Her memories of Sophie came alive before her as if she relived every precious moment all over again. But, most of all, she felt the love they shared and always would throughout eternity.

But then she felt a sense of urgency. Sophie was telling her that it was not time for her to die – that she still had things to do and achieve – that she must go back and complete her life.

But Fay looked beyond the gate and felt the love that emanated from Sophie and the beings of light and all she wanted was to stay…

EIGHTY-THREE

Daniel got away from Rick's apartment, staggered down the stairs and pushed open the side door. He headed for the underground garage. Fay's car was gone. Was he too late? He lumbered toward the road but there was no sign of her. Where the hell was she going? He made it to the Defender and got in, threw Rick's trauma bag onto the passenger seat, then fumbled to get the key in the ignition. It finally slipped in, and he turned the key, gunning the engine hard. An alarm was pinging for his seat belt to be fastened as he drove away, and he managed to slip the belt into position.

He scanned the road ahead for Fay's car, peered through the rain across the expanse of sand and the rocky headland of the cove but there was no sign of her. All he could see were gulls struggling to fly against the wind, the whitecaps on the water and dark storm clouds fast approaching. He pushed his foot to the floor and gathered speed. He had to find her and stop her from killing herself. The rain splattered the windscreen, and the wiper blades cleared an arc for him to see the road. Where the hell would she go in this state? To Shelly? The hospital? Then he knew – there was only one place she would go...

Sophie's nursery.

Daniel sped along the lane, taking hairpin bends way too fast, the tyres of the Defender churning up mud from the base of a hedge that lined the road. He turned onto the main A road with just a glance at the oncoming traffic. A horn blasted at him from the irate driver of a Vauxhall Astra and a transit van swerved as he pulled out just yards in front of it. He had to get home and prayed he wasn't too late.

He drove the Defender like a maniac, overtaking on sharp bends and straddling the white line in a death-defying dash to get home. He swerved back across the road, narrowly missing an oncoming lorry and clipping the kerb with his nearside wheel. A deluge of rain lashed at the windscreen as he turned onto the Riverbeke ring road, the spray from lorries blurring his vision. He ran a red light and a Ford Fiesta, coming from his right, spun 360 degrees as it swerved to avoid him. Car horns were blasting at him, but he couldn't stop – he was desperate to get home.

Finally, he took the turning for Riverbeke and dodged traffic that seemed to be coming at him from all directions. The windscreen wipers were barely coping with the deluge of rain, and he could feel the car shudder as gusts of wind blasted him from the side.

He finally arrived home and saw Fay's car in the driveway, the offside wing bashed in. He screamed to a halt and the Defender slid across the front lawn. He grabbed Rick's trauma bag and leaped out, the door of the Defender swinging on its hinges as he dashed through puddles into the house. His body was on high alert now, the sedative washed away with the adrenaline-drenched blood that was pounding through his arteries.

He fumbled with the key to the front door, let himself in and shouted, "Fay… Fay…" He desperately hoped he wasn't too late.

He ran up the stairs, two at a time, and burst into Sophie's nursery. Fay was slumped in the rocking chair, her legs outstretched, arms dangling over the arms of the chair, an empty syringe plugged into the Venflon.

Shit – was he too late?

He threw the holdall onto the floor next to Sophie's cot and shook Fay by her shoulders. "Wake up – Fay, for God's sake, wake up."

She was slumped and limp, her skin pale and clammy, her eyes half-closed and staring sightlessly into the nursery.

He lifted her head and pressed his fingers across her carotid artery. There was no pulse, and she wasn't breathing. He had no idea how long ago her heart had stopped.

He quickly lifted her from the rocking chair and placed her on her back on the floor. He reached for his phone to call an ambulance, but he must have dropped it in the car. There was no time to go looking for it – he had to start resuscitation. He knelt beside her lifeless body and began cardiac compressions. *One, two, three, four...*

"Fay... come back to me..."

Five, six, seven, eight, nine, ten...

Her lifeless body juddered as his hands pushed on her chest over and over again, trying desperately to get her heart started – to bring her back to life.

He stopped, felt for a pulse. Nothing. She was still in cardiac arrest.

He had to get air into her lungs. He reached into the trauma case and pulled out a plastic airway, twisting it into her mouth. With trembling fingers, he attached the oxygen, switched it on and applied the bag-valve mask over her mouth and nose before squeezing two breaths into her lungs.

He restarted cardiac compressions. *One, two, three, four, five, six, seven, eight...*

"Come on, Fay," he shouted breathlessly.

Daniel rummaged in the trauma bag for a syringe of adrenaline, checked the label, pulled out the empty syringe from the Venflon and pushed in a 1 mg dose. Then he completed another cycle of thirty compressions to two breaths and checked her carotid pulse. There was a faint flutter of a heartbeat. It wasn't a normal heart contraction but a chaotic sequence of useless quivers that wasn't pumping blood around her circulatory system. Her heart was in ventricular tachycardia – VT. The potassium chloride had deranged the electrics in her heart and stopped it from beating.

He would have to shock her.

He reached into the trauma bag and pulled out the portable defibrillator. He opened the bag, ripped open her top to expose her chest and applied the pads. He looked at the defib screen; the line was distorted, jagged and very erratic, confirming Daniel's diagnosis of VT. Her heart was weak but shockable. He pressed the "charge" button and gave a few more cardiac compressions until the defib had fully charged.

He sat back, pressed the button and a shock was delivered through Fay's chest and into her heart muscle. Her body jolted and convulsed. Daniel checked the defib screen – still in VT.

He started another cycle of chest compressions, then delivered two breaths via the bag. He checked her carotid pulse as he watched the defib screen. Still in VT. Fay's heart had failed to restart – it wasn't beating but quivering uselessly and now the rest of her body was shutting down.

Daniel delivered another shock to her ailing heart. Could he save her or was it already too late?

He felt for a pulse at her throat – as he pressed down, he felt a regular thump against his fingers. Elated, he checked her wrist and there it was again. Fay's heart was beating on its own again, but she still wasn't breathing.

He squeezed the bag-valve mask and ventilated her lungs several times before she coughed out the airway, spluttered and took a sharp breath… then another. Daniel checked her pulse again – it was fast but felt like a normal sinus rhythm. The defib screen confirmed it.

"Thank God…" He sighed with relief.

Fay moaned, then, gradually, a smile began to spread across her lips. Her eyes fluttered and opened, and she looked up at Daniel. Her voice croaked as she tried to speak. "I saw Sophie… Daniel. I saw her and she was beautiful."

Daniel pulled her into his arms. She lifted her head and looked at him, her eyes soft and dreamy.

"She's alright… she's happy and she loves us both."

Daniel rocked her in his arms. It had been a harrowing near miss, but Fay was alive.

"She's in a beautiful place, Daniel," she whispered. "I wanted to stay but she told me I must come back – that it was not time to die yet. She said I still had things to do here in this life."

Daniel pulled her close. Was this the end of it? Would Fay get the help she needed now?

"Fay, sweetheart. You need professional help. Will you let me call Shelly?"

Fay clutched at his arm. "Yes… yes, alright. It's what Sophie would want too. I'll try to get better. I promise."

Daniel held her close, his arms wrapped tightly around her, relishing the warmth of her living body. He had no idea what the future would bring and whether Fay would ever come back to him, but he knew he would always love her.

But now, as wrenching as it was, he realised he had to let her go – she had to get the help she needed to heal and find herself again.

EPILOGUE

Daniel sat alone in the kitchen with his coffee, surrounded by the ghosts of the past. Chester and Ella were in the sunlit garden, playing a game of tug with a new rope toy that Rosie had given them. Maisie was sitting on the bench watching them with her usual distain. He was glad of their company.

Fay had recovered at Riverbeke General from her cardiac arrest and was deemed fit to be discharged to the care of the psychiatric team. Today, Shelly was taking her to the psychiatric unit for treatment for bipolar psychosis and she had already begun a course of antipsychotics. She seemed a little more rational and the hallucinations were less troubling but there was still a very long way to go. He wasn't sure if her secret would come out during therapy or if Rick would say anything but now it was out of his hands. There was a very real chance that she could spend the rest of her life in a secure psychiatric prison. He'd done his best to protect his wife but now he had to let her deal with whatever she needed to do to face her own conscience and to get well. He'd agreed wholeheartedly to family therapy whenever she was ready.

Colin Mathias had ordered Daniel to take a break but, when he was ready to go back to work, he would have his old consultant's post back. He had his career, at least, and now he could focus on being a doctor. It was the core of his being and something that would never change.

Rick had been arrested for the deaths of his patients and his involvement in Regenex. He would never work as a doctor again and would probably be handed a whole-life sentence for murder. Oliver too was facing a lifetime in jail for the murders he had committed as well as his involvement at Regenex.

Isobel was on remand in a women's prison one hundred and fifty miles away and would face a crown court trial. The RSPCA had rescued all the animals at Regenex and the place had been cleared out and closed down.

Eddie Bates had found a new job with better pay at the nursing home where his mother lived and Miles Parker had launched an appeal on behalf of Jayden and had generously waived his fee.

Daniel had heard from Matt that Megan Foley was going to be discharged home to a brand-new purpose-built bungalow that she'd be sharing with her parents, brother and the twins. Social services were putting in the care package she needed to be independent.

Daniel sipped his coffee and wondered what the future would bring for them. He couldn't bring himself to clear out Sophie's nursery – not yet. Too much had happened and it was still too raw but one day he would have to lay down the ghosts of the past.

The doorbell rang and Daniel put down his mug and went to answer it.

Fay stood on the doorstep, her hair in loose waves around her shoulders. In her eyes, he could see a familiar melancholy but there was also acceptance and hope – the optimism of a new beginning.

Shelly was sitting in her car in the driveway and gave him a little wave.

"Shelly's just taking me to the psychiatric unit but I just wanted to see you for a minute." Sitting next to her was a waiflike beagle – it was one of the dogs that had been rescued from Regenex.

Fay smiled and stroked the dog's head. "Her name is Spirit."

She lifted Spirit and handed her to Daniel. He took her in his arms.

Fay looked at him and gave him a sad, regretful smile. "You'll be able to love her more than anyone I've ever known."

With tears in her eyes, she reached up and kissed his cheek, smiled and turned to finally get the help she needed.

ACKNOWLEDGEMENTS

I'd like to thank the amazing team at The Book Guild, Jeremy Thompson, Chloe May, Stephanie Carr, Sophie Morgan, Daniel Burchmore, Rosie Lowe, Megan Lockwood-Jones, Philippa Lliffe, Fern Bushnell and the sales and marketing team - plus all those I've not yet met but work tirelessly for their authors. Thank you all for your utmost professionalism, patience, guidance and expertise.

Also, thanks to Matt Taylor at Chepstow Bookshop and all at Chepstow Library for the amazing support they give to local writers.

Love and thanks to my wonderful husband, family and friends for believing in me.

www.ruthsearle.com